Author of:
Livvy
No Roses For Abby

# FOLLOW THE BUTTERFLY

Valerie S. Armstrong

Order this book online at www.trafford.com
or email orders@trafford.com

Most Trafford titles are also available at major online book retailers.

Printed in the United States of America.

ISBN: 978-1-4269-6273-8 (sc)
ISBN: 978-1-4269-6274-5 (e)

*Trafford rev. 04/05/2011*

 www.trafford.com

North America & international
toll-free: 1 888 232 4444 (USA & Canada)
phone: 250 383 6864 ♦ fax: 812 355 4082

In memory of my brother Henry Arthur Sinclair who had the ability to spin some yarns of his own.

# ACKNOWLEDGEMENTS

A special thank you to Nadia McKechnie and Eileen Usher for taking the time to read my manuscript and assist in the tedious process of editing.

# CHAPTER 1

I was nine years old when my mother killed my father, and I saw it happen. That was many years ago, but I remember every detail of that night. I had never liked Papa, he was a poor excuse for a human being. He treated Mama like a slave, and whenever she did anything to annoy him, even in the slightest way, he took great delight in punishing her. It always started out with verbal abuse, but usually ended up with him beating her with his fists. Mama was terrified of Papa and walked on egg shells most of the time. As for my sister, Lexie, and me, he never showed us one ounce of affection, but at least he didn't call Lexie names. Lexie was five years younger than me and very pretty. She had curly ash blonde hair, green eyes, rosebud lips and a sweet nose that turned up slightly at the end. She was the lucky one in the looks department. Meanwhile, yours truly, had a stick thin body, unruly mousy brown hair, blue eyes too big for my face, a wide mouth and a nose with a rather noticeable bump. Mama always told me that I was going to be beautiful when I grew up. "Cassie," she would say, "you just wait until you fill out, then your eyes and mouth will fit your face. You can always get your nose fixed, although I think it gives you character." If it wasn't for Mama, I would have felt like the ugliest kid in Millville, because Papa would look at me, shake his head, and remark, "That one can't be any child of mine. God knows who you were sleeping around with Ella."

Papa never raised his hand to Lexie or me but he was mean, never having a kind word for anyone. There were times when I hated Papa, and sometimes I wished he was dead but I didn't want it to happen the way it did.

It was a warm summer night in late August, and Lexie and I were already in bed when I heard the argument begin. It wasn't unusual to hear Papa yelling, but that night he seemed angrier than usual. I looked over at Lexie, who was sleeping soundly, and slipped quietly out of bed. Our room was right at the top of the stairs, and once I stepped out onto the landing, I could see Mama in the living room below. She was standing near the kitchen door and I could see she was crying. Papa was perched on the edge of our battered old sofa, red faced, and glaring at Mama. "Look at yourself, you stupid whore," he screamed, "what the hell happened to the woman I married? Your hair and clothes are a fucking mess, no wonder I can't stand the sight of you."

"I'm sorry Tom," Mama cried, "I'll try to do better, I promise."

Papa jumped up, eyes blazing, and strode across the room shaking his fist, "Did you look in the damn mirror? Did you?"

Mama cowered against the doorframe, "I'm sorry, I really am. I'll go and put on some clean clothes and comb my hair."

"Shut up," he yelled, "you're a rotten wife. I'm sick of you and those kids. Now get out of my way," and then he grabbed Mama by her hair and threw her clear across the room.

I held my breath, not daring to let Papa know I was there, even though I wanted, so badly, to help Mama. He was walking out to the kitchen when he stopped, looked back over his shoulder, and then licked his lips, "Just wait a few more years and then our little Lexie will be ripe for the picking"

I didn't know then why Mama snapped, but what happened next was like a nightmare, and I froze on the spot with my hands gripping the railings. Papa had already gone out through the kitchen door and Mama was crawling on her hands and knees towards the fireplace. She picked up the poker, and then still on her knees, hid it behind her back, and when Papa came back into the room, only a few seconds later, Mama didn't even give him a chance. She jumped up, running forward at full speed, then wielded the poker towards his head. He looked startled, for just an instant, and then the full force of the blow hit him squarely above his right ear and he went down like a ton of bricks. Mama didn't give him a moment to recover. She brought the poker down on his head, over and over again, until I was sure he wasn't ever going to get up again. There was blood everywhere. It covered the floor and the walls, and it was all over Mama. Everything happened so fast, but looking back, it's like watching a slow motion movie. My knuckles stood out, almost pure white, as I held onto the railings and watched Mama drop the poker, step back, and look down in disbelief at what she had done. Then she brushed the back of her hand across her forehead, leaving a red streak on her skin and that's when she looked up and saw me.

"Go to your room, Cassie," she screamed, but I couldn't move.

Suddenly she was racing up the stairs towards me, grabbing me by the shoulders and looking me straight in the eyes, "I want you to go to your room and wake up Lexie. Both of you are to get dressed and then I want you to get the old brown suitcase from the back of your closet and start putting some of your clothes in it. I'll be in to help you in a few minutes. Do you understand me?"

"Yes, Mama," I replied, thinking how calm she was, standing there with her dress all covered in blood.

"Go now, Cassie," she said pushing me towards my room.

A few minutes later, I had woken Lexie and I could hear Mama in the bathroom running the shower. Lexie looked puzzled when I told her she had to get dressed. "But it's dark outside, Cassie," she moaned.

"I know, but Mama wants us to get ready and I have to pack some clothes."

"What for? Where are we going?" Lexie persisted as she pulled her nightgown over her head.

"I don't know where we're going, it's supposed to be a surprise."

"Is Papa coming too?"

I hesitated, not sure what to tell her and then simply answered, "Papa had to go to work."

"This had better be good," Lexie responded standing on one leg while she tried to put on her underpants.

I tried to ignore my sister's mumblings while I finished dressing and started filling the suitcase. I had just taken some cotton tops and underwear from the old maple dresser, when Mama appeared in the doorway. She was wrapped in a bath towel and her hair was still wet, but even with her face scrubbed clean, and no makeup, Mama was still beautiful. She had the face of an angel, large green eyes the same color as Lexie's, full lips, a perfectly straight nose and a long neck that always reminded me of a swan. "I'm going to get dressed," she said calmly, "finish packing and I'll be back soon to get you."

"All right, Mama," I answered meekly.

She stared at me for a moment and then she was gone and that's when I got the idea to fool Lexie. I took a long scarf from the bottom drawer and told Lexie that she had to be blindfolded because of the surprise. At first she didn't like the idea, but after I told her she could take her favorite teddy bear, Pooh, with her, she agreed to let me tie the scarf around her head. I had just finished making sure she couldn't see, when Mama came back into the room. She had on a blue cotton dress and was carrying a small gray suitcase, that I hadn't seen before, and the large tan purse she used every day in the summer. When she saw Lexie, she dropped the suitcase, "What are you doing, Cassie?" she demanded.

I put a finger to my lips and shook my head from side to side, and that's when Mama knew that I was trying to protect my sister from the horror below, in the living room.

"Ah! You want to surprise Lexie," she said, "what a clever idea. Now let's hurry along, we need to get going."

Five minutes later, after guiding Lexie down the stairs and past the horrific sight of Papa lying in a pool of blood, we were backing out of the driveway in our old rattletrap of a car. I looked up at the house as we drove away and wondered if I would ever see it again, not that I cared. I had always hated that house. The paint was peeling off the doors and window frames. It had pokey little rooms and the furniture was like something from the Salvation Army store. I often wondered how Mama ever managed to cook a decent meal on the ancient stove in the kitchen, and every so often the refrigerator would go on the blink and Papa would curse because he had to pay to repair it. At night the pipes would make strange knocking noises and water came out of the taps at a snail's pace. As for the front yard, well it was just a patch of brown grass with one miserable half-dead maple tree and the back yard was non-existent because that's where Papa kept all kinds of junk that he'd collected over the years. No, I knew I wouldn't miss that house and I murmured "Good riddance," under my breath.

We drove a good few miles before Lexie fell asleep, clutching Pooh, in the back seat. She had been chattering away, still with her blindfold on, but Mama and I didn't speak. After I was sure she was asleep, I removed the scarf from her head and gently pushed her down so that she was lying comfortably on her side with her legs tucked up. I figured she wouldn't wake up for hours.

Mama looked back at me and suggested that I climb onto the front seat beside her. Once I got settled, she took one hand off the steering wheel and laid it on my thigh, "You're a good girl, Cassie," she said, "and we need to talk, but not now. I'm going to look for a side road off the highway so that we can stop. We'll have to sleep in the car tonight and tomorrow I'll figure out what we're going to do."

I looked up at Mama, with her golden blonde hair falling over her shoulders and her face even more beautiful in the moonlight, "Why did you do it, Mama?" I whispered.

Mama kept looking straight ahead, "I can't talk about it now, Cassie, but you have to know that I didn't mean to kill your Papa."

"You won't ever leave us will you Mama?" I pleaded, as I felt the tears begin to form.

Mama squeezed my thigh, "Always remember, I love you girls more than anything else in the world and that's why we have to get as far away from Millville as we can. I don't want us ever to be apart but I can't promise you anything, Cassie."

# CHAPTER 2

Sleeping in the car was no fun. We didn't want to disturb Lexie, so we left her in the back seat and Mama and I had to make do staying right where we were. Sometime in the middle of the night, I had to go to the bathroom but it was so dark that I had to wake Mama to take me outside. We both squatted down beside the car and I could hear all kinds of noises coming from the woods that seemed to surround us. I recognized an owl hooting close by and the chirping of crickets but when there was a sudden rustling in the bushes beside us, I couldn't move fast enough to get back inside the car.

When the sun came up, we turned back onto the main road and started traveling north. Lexie woke up, almost as soon as we started to move, and began to moan that she was hungry. I guess Mama knew that she would have to stop again to get some food and fifteen minutes later when we saw a sign that said "Rosie's Diner – Open 24 Hours – Turn Right at Next Exit" she turned onto the side road and drove through a heavily wooded area until we came to the diner. Mama didn't want to attract a lot of attention, especially as it was so early in the morning. She made Lexie and me duck down in the backseat, while she tied the scarf, from the blindfold, over her hair and put on her sunglasses in an effort to disguise herself.

I must admit, I didn't stay down; I just had to know what was going on. I could see Mama through the diner's front window. She was standing in front of the counter talking to a very large woman, wearing a bright floral dress and huge red hoop earrings. She looked like a jolly sort and had a constant smile on her face as she walked, back and forth, between the counter and the display case. Even Mama was smiling as she picked up two paper bags and handed over some dollar bills.

Mama drove a short distance, back towards the main road, and then stopped the car so that we could relieve ourselves in the bushes. I think that's when Lexie began to think that this was an adventure, especially when a beautiful golden butterfly settled on her shoulder. Lexie had always loved nature and animals. She had begged for a pet, not caring whether it was a dog, cat or anything else that she could lavish her affection on, but Papa hated all animals. He always claimed they were filthy creatures and there was no way he wanted them messing up the house. Lexie even suggested a fish, but Papa wouldn't allow it. Like I said, Papa was mean. Seeing Lexie with that butterfly reminded me of a song Mama would always sing to us.

*Stay the course when things go wrong; hold your head up high*
*Face your troubles with a smile; don't let them see you cry*
*For if you do the best you can but falter on the way*
*Remember there's another path; you do not have to stay*
*Just watch a new door open; don't even question why*
*Just walk on through, spread your wings and follow the butterfly*
*Follow the butterfly.*

We sat in the car munching on bran muffins and bananas and washed them down with Pepsi, while Mama only drank coffee. "Aren't you going to eat anything, Mama?" I asked.

She looked at me and smiled, "I'm just not hungry honey. Maybe in a couple of hours I'll have something to eat."

"But where are we going? How long are we going to keep driving?"

"I'm not sure but we have to get out of state and as soon as we cross the border into New York, I'm going to check into a motel so that we can have a proper rest."

I leaned my head against Mama's shoulder, "What happens if we get caught, Mama?"

Mama sighed, "I don't know. All the time we've been driving I've been thinking about that and what will happen to you both." Then she lowered her voice so that Lexie couldn't hear, "I do need to ask you something and it's very important that you tell me the truth, Cassie. Did your father ever touch you in a way that made you uncomfortable?"

I was puzzled by the question for the moment, after all I was only nine, but then I realized what she was really asking me. "No Mama, he never did."

"And is that the absolute truth, Cassie? You don't have to be afraid to tell me."

"That's the absolute truth, Mama."

Almost an hour later, back on the main road, Lexie began fidgeting, "I'm getting bored and I want to go home," she whined.

I looked at Mama helplessly, "Cassie, why don't you go and sit with Lexie and play a game," she suggested.

"What kind of game?" I asked, " I don't even have a pencil or paper."

Mama thought for a moment, "Well, you could play I Spy for a while. You remember how to play that, don't you?"

I nodded, "Yes, I remember, but that won't keep her quiet for too long."

Mama patted me on the back as I climbed over my seat and for the next half hour, I kept Lexie occupied. Then, thankfully, she fell asleep again.

We were about ten miles from the border when I heard the police siren and saw the red light flashing through the back window. "It's the police!" I cried.

Mama glanced in the rear view mirror, "Yes honey, but keep calm. We don't know if they're chasing us."

I got more and more agitated as the police cruiser got closer and suddenly they were right beside us. Then I saw the state trooper lean out of the window with a bullhorn and yell, "Pull over onto the shoulder and stop the car."

Mama kept driving and looking straight ahead with a panicked expression on her face. "Don't stop, please don't stop." I begged, clutching at her arm.

Mama let out a huge sigh and slowly pulled over to the side of the road. She was sitting, still staring straight ahead, with her hands in her lap when I heard those dreaded words through the bullhorn again, "Stop and get out of the car, real slow, and put your hands in the air."

Mama looked at me and shook her head, "I am so sorry, Cassie. Just always remember that I love you and your sister more than life itself."

That day was one of the worst in my life. With Mama in handcuffs, we were all taken back to the local police station and while Mama was being questioned, Lexie and I were forced to sit in a dismal hallway on hard wooden chairs.

"Is this the surprise?" Lexie asked, holding onto Pooh for dear life.

I had no idea how wrong I would be when I replied, "No Lexie, but don't worry everything will be all right."

# CHAPTER 3

Two days later we were back in Millville and Mama was charged with murder and in prison, awaiting trial. I found out later that when Papa didn't show up for work the next day and there was no reply to the phone messages left at our house, his boss decided to come by. That's when he ran into my teacher, who was also concerned about my absence, and they decided to call the police.

It didn't take a rocket scientist to figure out who killed Papa. Maybe if Mama hadn't left the poker lying on the floor with her fingerprints all over it and her bloody clothes in the hamper, they might have thought someone else had done it and we had all been kidnapped. As it was, the evidence was overwhelming. As for me, from the very beginning, when the police questioned me, I claimed I was asleep and didn't hear a thing and I stuck to that story. There was no way I was ever going to say anything bad about Mama.

Lexie and I were picked up by Child Services and were being turned over to my paternal grandparents, the weekend after the arrest. I had never liked my father's folks; Granny Taylor was like Papa, mean spirited and cold, while Grandpa Taylor had the personality of a block of wood. I knew they had no love for Mama and now any positive feelings they may have had for her, would have turned to hate. I wondered if that meant they would hate Lexie and me too, and how much our lives would change. Apart from that, missing my beautiful Mama would be the hardest thing to bear.

We spent the next two days in a group foster home. Lexie refused to speak unless spoken to and cried over and over again as though her little heart would break. I knew that she desperately wanted to go home and she couldn't understand why Mama had left us there.

The Child Service worker, a very sweet lady, nearly as old as Gran, with snow white hair and twinkling blue eyes, thought it might be best if Lexie was told the truth. I begged her to let me tell her my version of the truth and eventually she agreed. I had always been protective of my little sister and I couldn't bear seeing her so distraught. I made up a story that Papa had come home, after we had left on our surprise adventure, then he had tripped and fallen down the stairs.

"Did he hurt himself?" Lexie asked innocently

I put my arms around her, stroked her hair and whispered, "I'm afraid so. He hit his head so badly that they couldn't save him and he died, Lexie."

Lexie gasped, "Papa's dead?" she murmured in disbelief.

I hugged her even tighter, "Yes, and the policemen had to come and find us to tell us that Papa had died."

Lexie pulled away and looked up at me with tears in her eyes, "But what about Mama? Where is she now?"

I shook my head, "I'm not sure," I lied, "but the policemen need to talk to her and I don't know how long it will take."

My sweet Lexie stamped her foot, "I don't want to stay here, Cassie. Why doesn't Mama come?"

I tried to reassure her, "Mama will come, don't worry, but until she does, we're going to stay with Gran and Grandpa."

I was surprised when Lexie settled down after that and didn't ask any more questions. I often wondered what was going on in her little head, but was afraid to ask in case she got upset again. Meanwhile, I was sick to my stomach thinking about Mama and what she was going through.

That weekend, Gran and Grandpa came to get us. Lexie was her usual self and happy to see them but I wasn't so welcoming. I think Gran knew that Lexie was too young to even realize what was going on and fussed over her like a mother hen. Her attitude towards me was a different matter and she must have sensed my hostility, when she caught me scowling at her. Gran always reminded me of the wicked witch from the Wizard of Oz. She was tall and thin and had a pasty face with a pointed nose and grizzly gray hair, which she always wore in a bun. As for Grandpa, he looked more like the cowardly lion.

I was still scowling when Gran, eyeing me up and down as though I was something the cat dragged in, asked me abruptly, "And how are you young lady?"

"How do you think I am," I replied insolently.

"You see that, George?" she said turning to Grandpa. "Just like her mother."

Grandpa shrugged his shoulders and I felt like shaking him, "Don't you dare say anything bad about Mama," I said, aware that my voice had risen an octave. Gran ignored me and hand in hand with Lexie, stomped out to the parking lot, while Grandpa and I followed behind.

My grandparents lived on Coral Avenue in Bridgeton, about twenty miles from Millville, and all the way there nobody spoke. Their home was a ranch style house on the outskirts of town on a quiet street, where all the houses looked alike. Inside, the furniture was Danish modern, sort of flat and uninteresting, like Grandpa. At least it didn't look like the battered old furniture in our own house.

It was obvious, from the start that Gran was antagonistic towards me and I suppose I couldn't really blame her. Mama had killed her one and only child and I was going to defend Mama, no matter what, even to the point of lying.

By now it was September and Gran had enrolled us in the public school. I was never too enthusiastic about school. I had always been told that I was exceptionally bright for my age and had even skipped a grade but I got bored very quickly. At least, it got me out of the house and away from Gran. When we were at home, Lexie and I spent most of our time playing outside with the neighborhood kids and we made a lot of friends. There was one boy, Jimmy, who wasn't so friendly. He taunted me with nasty remarks about Mama being a murderer, but after I punched him as hard as I could in the stomach and he doubled over in agony, he never taunted me again.

Lexie and I had our own room with twin beds and I have to admit that Gran fed us well but she was as cold as ice to me. I asked her, over and over again, if I could visit Mama but she always turned her back on me and refused to discuss the matter.

Mama had no family and no money for her defense. I learned later, that our old house was repossessed and all of the furniture tossed out onto the front yard, to be picked over by the neighbors.

Mama was provided with legal counsel, a Mr. Douglas Hargraft. I first met Mr. Hargraft when my grandparents were requested to bring me in for a meeting with him. He planned to use me to defend Mama and I was ready for him. He was a soft-spoken, middle aged man, with thick dark hair and kind eyes, behind his tortoiseshell framed glasses. He made me feel comfortable right away and I felt I could trust him. He had two young children of his own and decided not to question Lexie. I was already nervous about what she might say, so his decision gave me a great sense of relief.

Mama had already told Mr. Hargraft her side of the story but I thought a little enhancement wouldn't hurt. The story I told him about the verbal abuse and the beatings was the absolute truth. I had heard Papa's vicious rantings at least three times a week for as long as I could remember and I had cowered in my room, or at the top of the stairs, countless times when the physical abuse was going on. Papa rarely hit Mama when Lexie or I were around, although one time, about a year before, he had burned her on the arm with the iron because she wasn't doing a good enough job of pressing his favorite shirt. I remember Mama screaming, Lexie looking up in surprise, and then crying when she saw Mama's arm. Of course, Papa claimed it was an accident and he was so sorry, but I knew better.

I told Mr. Hargraft about that incident and that's when I decided to make Papa look even more of a monster. I bowed my head when he asked me if there was anything else I wanted to talk about, "Cassie, it's okay," he said, "I'm here to help your mother and I need you to tell me anything you can remember."

I turned slightly away from him, trying to look very sad and at the same time avoiding his eyes, " Well, he tried to drown her once. I heard all this horrible splashing and gurgling coming from the bathroom and when I opened the door, there was Papa holding Mama's head down in the tub. She was thrashing about and I was so terrified that I pummeled Papa on his back until he let her go."

Mr. Hargraft shook his head, "Anything else, Cassie?" he asked.

Now I was on a roll, anything to help Mama, "He'd lock Mama in the closet, sometimes for an hour or more and one day when she didn't have time to comb her hair, because Lexie was sick, he took the scissors and cut a whole chunk off. He was always doing mean things."

"And on the night that your father died, did you hear or see anything at all?

I looked him straight in the eye and answered, "I didn't see or hear a thing."

"I see," commented Mr. Hargraft, "and do you think you could repeat all this in court, Cassie?"

It took me less than a second to reply, "Of course, I'm only telling the truth."

When our session ended, and before he turned me over to Gran, I begged Mr. Hargraft to let me see Mama. He leaned down and gently rested his hand on my shoulder, "I'll see what I can do, Cassie," he said, "but unless your grandparents agree, I'm not sure if you will be allowed to see her.

Naturally, Gran was furious that I was going to testify for Mama, while she was testifying for the prosecution. In her eyes, Mama and I were both liars and her precious son had been a pillar of the society. Never mind, that he had no education and could hardly even afford to support himself, let alone a family of four.

# CHAPTER 4

It was almost two weeks later when I ran away from Gran's for the first time. I just had to see Mama, even if I had to walk all the way to Millville. I crawled out of bed and slipped into a pair of gray flannel pants, a red woolly sweater and my comfortable old sneakers. I was scared to death creeping along the hallway, past Gran's room, and out the front door, and as soon as I got outside, I figured I was in trouble. I knew it had gotten a little cooler, especially at night, but I didn't expect it to be cold as it was. I debated whether to go back but I didn't have a key and I didn't dare wake Gran up. I even considered climbing back through our bedroom window but I might have scared Lexie, so I started off down the road.

By the time I reached the highway, I couldn't stop shivering. I didn't know how long it would take me to walk to Millville, and I hadn't even thought about how I would get to see Mama when I got there, but I was determined to make the effort.

Whenever I heard a car coming, in either direction, I darted off the road, and hid in the bushes. I figured that, being only nine-years-old I'd stick out like a sore thumb, all alone in the middle of the night. Sometimes it was downright scary, especially when I saw a large dark shape come hurtling through the bush beside me. I knew there were deer in the woods, but I'd never actually seen one, and I prayed that's what it was.

I had no idea how many miles I'd walked when I started to notice the sky getting lighter and there were a few more cars on the road. I do remember, that I was hungry, bone tired and very cold and just wanted to lie down for a while. It was only the thought of seeing Mama that kept me going.

I had only gone a short distance further, when I saw dark clouds on the horizon and I prayed that it wasn't going to rain. As it was, I was already in a lot of physical discomfort and now my feet were beginning to bother me too. I guess nobody heard my prayer, because a few minutes later black clouds were overhead and then the skies just opened up. Within seconds I was soaked through to the skin and shivering uncontrollably, and I knew I had to find shelter. I don't know whether it was fate or not but, at that time, I happened to be on a stretch of road with fields on either side and no trees or bushes to take cover under. Too late, I realized how easily I could be spotted by anyone driving by, because that's when I heard the roar of an engine. It sounded too loud for a car and when I turned around I saw a huge white truck racing towards me. I crouched down and tried to make myself as small as possible and could hardly believe my luck when the truck roared past me, but then with the squealing of brakes it suddenly stopped a few yards ahead of me. I didn't know whether to run, or what to do, so I just stayed where I was with the rain running down my face, and my arms wrapped around my body trying to stop myself from shaking. After a few moments, I heard the truck start up again. I willed it to keep going forward but whoever was driving decided to take a closer look and it backed right up to within a couple of feet of me.

I looked up as the door of the cab opened and a man jumped down onto the ground. He looked me up and down and then grinned, "Well, what do we have here?" he said.

For some reason, he didn't scare me. He looked very young, with jet-black hair, wearing jeans and a brown leather jacket and he had a red bandanna tied around his neck.

When I didn't answer him, he took a step forward and then got down to my eye level, "Running away are we?" he persisted.

I nodded very slowly but didn't speak.

"Well you sure picked a fine day for it, young lady. I suggest you get in the truck and you can tell me all about it"

I tried to resist when he took my hand and walked me around to the other side of the truck, then lifted me up into the passenger seat. To be honest though, I was glad to be out of the rain.

When the stranger got back in the driver's seat, he reached behind him and pulled out a towel, "Here," he said, "dry yourself off and then you'll feel better. We can just sit here while you tell me who you are running away from and where you think you're going to."

Before I knew it, I had told this strange man nearly every detail about Mama and my miserable life with Gran. When I had finished, he just looked at me sadly and said, "I'm sorry honey, but I have to take you back there."

I started to shake my head, "No," I protested, "I don't want to go back, I have to see Mama."

"You have to understand," he explained, "you won't be allowed to see your mother. Maybe if you go home and ask your Gran nicely, she'll take you to see her."

I slumped in my seat, "She'll never take me, she hates me."

"I'm sorry to hear that," the stranger remarked, "but I must take you back to Bridgeton," and he started the engine and made a u-turn in the road.

I had no choice but to tell him where Gran lived and I was amazed at how quickly we got there. I thought I had walked such a long way but I hadn't even gotten halfway to Millville.

While we were driving back, he told me his name was Lenny and that he had read all about my mother in the local papers. He was just returning from delivering a truckload of bakery goods to the supermarket in Bridgeton when he spotted me on the side of the road. He smiled when he suggested, that the next time I ran away, I should wear something less colorful.

When we arrived at the house, the police were there. Lexie had gone crying to Gran that I wasn't in my bed and after searching the house, Gran figured I had run away and called the police. They thanked Lenny for bringing me back and gave me a stern lecture about the dangers of running away and what could have happened to me. I sat there emotionless, while Gran stood frowning at me from the corner of the room. I knew that after the police left, I would be in a heap of trouble, and I wasn't wrong. Gran was mad as hell and sent me to my room for the rest of the day. As far as she was concerned, I was an ungrateful, badly behaved child and the longer I was out of her sight, the better.

# CHAPTER 5

I was surprised one day when Gran took Lexie and me to buy some new clothes. We had taken very little with us when we left home and most of what we had was suitable for fall, but not for the cold winters of the northeast. We weren't allowed to pick and choose, and typical of Gran, nearly everything she made us try on was dark, dowdy and old fashioned. I didn't understand why she insisted on us having, what she called, 'an outfit for best' and particularly hated the charcoal gray dresses and matching coats that ended up in her shopping basket. I couldn't help wondering what Mama would have said, if she had seen us. We may not have had much, but Mama always made sure we wore bright, cheerful colors and that we were happy with whatever she chose for us.

I realized, a week later, why we were subjected to wearing such somber clothes, when Gran announced that we were to attend Papa's funeral the very next day. I hadn't even thought about Papa being buried, or even what had happened to him. I suppose I just didn't want to think about Papa at all, my mind was too consumed with thoughts of Mama and how lonely she must be. I learned later, that, because of the autopsy required in criminal cases, Papa's body couldn't be released until weeks after he died.

I didn't want to go to the funeral. First of all, I had never been to one before and secondly, I had no desire to mourn the death of my father. When I immediately voiced my feelings out loud, Gran was incensed, while Grandpa just stood there like a lummox and shook his head.

"You are going to honor your father, whether you like it or not," Gran informed me in no uncertain terms.

I was so angry that I couldn't help myself, when I shouted back, "You can't make me go. I'm glad he's dead. He hurt Mama and now he can't hurt her any more."

Gran gasped and then, with eyes blazing, she slapped me hard across the face. I didn't even flinch but it made me even angrier and I bunched up my fists and yelled at the top of my voice, "Now I know why Papa always hit Mama, he learned it from you."

I watched then, as Gran seemed to grow smaller. She started to slump over with her hand to her heart and in a hoarse voice whispered, "George, get me some water."

I must admit I was a little scared that she was going to have a heart attack and die right there in front of me, but after Grandpa helped her into a chair and gave her some water, she quickly recovered. She looked up at me with hatred in her eyes and said, "You are going to your father's funeral, young lady, and that's the last word on the subject."

I knew I really had no choice, because I couldn't deny Lexie the opportunity to say goodbye to Papa. She still had no idea what had really taken place and there were times when I would catch her crying because she knew she would never see Papa again.

When we entered the First Presbyterian Church, I was surprised to see a number of people already seated in the pews. I held Lexie's hand as we made our way to the front and that's when I noticed the casket covered in white flowers and a framed photo of Papa when he was much younger. I looked around and recognized some of Gran's neighbors and Papa's boss from Millville, but I had no idea who the other people were.

We had been to church once or twice with Mama, but we had never been a religious family. I found the service long and dreary and Lexie was soon fidgeting in her seat. Gran gave her the evil eye, so I squeezed her hand and whispered in her ear, "Sit still Lexie, it will soon be over."

We were both relieved when the service came to an end, not realizing that we still had to bury Papa. At the cemetery, the cold north wind seemed to go right through me and when I looked up and saw the gray skies, I couldn't help thinking that it was just the kind of day that Papa should be put in that hole in the ground.

Lexie cowered against me as the minister rambled on and I could hear Gran, who was standing behind me, moaning and sniffling into her handkerchief. Maybe I was being heartless that day, but I felt no sadness or feeling of loss for the man who had brought me into this world. My whole being was focused on Mama and, as I buried my father, I vowed to do all I could to see that Mama was set free.

Back at Gran's house, I felt totally humiliated, when complete strangers stood around nibbling on dainty little sandwiches and drinking tea, while at the same time, patting me on the head and telling me to be a brave girl. I felt like screaming at all of them and telling them what a miserable person Papa had been, but I managed to hide my feelings and put on my saddest face.

# CHAPTER 6

The trial took place at the Cumberland County Court in Bridgeton during the last two weeks of March, just as spring started to break through. I knew I wouldn't be able to touch or talk to Mama but I was excited because I hadn't seen her since the day she was arrested, over six months earlier. Gran had stubbornly refused to allow me to visit, even though Mr. Hargraft had intervened and pleaded with her to change her position. Mama did manage to write me letters, which Mr. Hargraft would go out of his way to deliver to me, and I treasured those letters. They were filled with love and consideration for Lexie and me, and Mama never complained about her own situation. I would shut myself up in my room, away from Gran's prying eyes, and write letters back but I couldn't let Mama know how miserable I was without her. I mostly told her about how we were getting along at school and the friends we had made and I hardly ever mentioned Gran or Grandpa.

I was not allowed to be in the courtroom except for the time when I gave testimony. That happened on the second day of the trial and I was really nervous when Mr. Hargraft came to get me. I remember him taking both of my hands in his and saying, "Cassie, all you have to do is tell the truth. Remember what I told you, the prosecutor might try to trip you up, so don't let him confuse you. Now do you think you can handle this?"

I nodded, and he handed me over to a man in uniform, I had never seen before, who led me into the courtroom and into the witness box. Then, another man stood in front of me, blocking my view, and made me put my hand on the bible and swear to tell the truth.

When I was asked to state my name, I couldn't speak for a moment because my eyes were fixed on Mama. She was sitting next to Mr. Hargraft behind a large table, just a few short yards away. Even though her hair was pulled back in a pony tail and she was wearing a faded blue blouse, she was still my beautiful Mama, and as she looked back at me, she gave a hint of a smile and mouthed, "I love you."

I continued to stare until I was asked again to state my name, "Cassandra Mae Taylor," I said in a quavering voice. That's when the judge, who looked like a kindly Santa, leaned over and whispered, "Try to speak up, dear."

I faced forward and lifted my head proudly, then once again stated my name, but this time in a loud strong voice, "Cassandra Mae Taylor."

The judge leaned over again and smiled, "Well done," he said.

After that, Mr. Hargraft made me repeat everything I had told him about my life at home with my family. I tried not to look at the jury because I could feel all of their beady eyes on me as I told my story and I heard an audible gasp when I came to the part about Papa trying to drown Mama in the bathtub. When I looked across at Mama, knowing that only half of my testimony was true, while the rest was a figment of my imagination, she gave an almost imperceptible shake of her head. I stared back at her, willing her to let me continue, and not to expose me. She seemed to get my message, because she lowered her head and sat that way until I had finished. Mr. Hargraft then asked me what I had seen, or heard, on the day of Papa's death and, in a clear voice, I answered, "Absolutely nothing, Lexie and I were fast asleep."

I didn't feel quite as confident when the prosecutor cross-examined me. When he rose from the table, adjacent to where Mama sat, he seemed to dominate the courtroom. He was a tall, somewhat portly man, with thick white hair and heavy eyebrows that seemed to meet in the middle of his forehead. He had the most piercing brown eyes that seemed to stare right through me as he walked towards the witness box. I couldn't help noticing his clothes too. Unlike Mr. Hargraft, who wore a plain navy suit, white shirt and light blue tie, the prosecutor wore a black pin striped suit with a black shirt, and white tie. It seems odd now that I would notice the way he dressed but he reminded me of someone I had seen in a movie. He stood in front of me for a moment not speaking until the judge said, "We haven't got all day Mr. Phillips. Please proceed with your cross-examination."

Despite my nervousness and his booming voice asking me the same questions over and over, but in a different manner, just to try and trick me, the formidable Mr. Phillips never got me to change my story. Mr. Hargraft, repeatedly rose to interject and sighed as he said, "Asked and answered, your honor." I was so relieved when the prosecutor decided to finish with me and Mr. Hargraft declined the opportunity to re-cross, but at the same time I knew I would soon be taken out of the courtroom and away from Mama. As the bailiff escorted me down the center aisle towards the exit, I know I had tears running down my cheeks as I looked over at her and whispered, "I love you Mama."

The trial went on for days but the only way I got to hear about it was by watching the local news or reading the paper. Many people came forward as character witnesses for Papa, including Gran and Grandpa, who proclaimed him to be a kind and gentle man who wouldn't harm a fly. Others came forward to testify that they had never seen any evidence of physical abuse and Mama had never confided in them that she was a victim of any beatings. I felt like running out into the street and screaming, for the entire world to hear, that Papa was too clever to let anyone know what he was doing. He avoided hitting her where any bruises would be seen and usually punched her in the chest or stomach. Often she would double over in agony and drag herself into the bathroom, to vomit in the toilet.

If I couldn't tell the world, at least I could tell Gran and I didn't hesitate, but that got me in a whole heap of trouble. As usual, she called me a liar and sent me to my room without supper and imposed a weeklong curfew. Poor little Lexie had no idea what was going on, and I aimed to keep it that way.

On the second to last day of the trial, in the afternoon, Mr. Hargraft put Mama on the stand. I guess he felt it was the only way she might get her story across to the jury.

I was horrified that same night, to discover that Mama had lost a baby, a year before I was born. The miscarriage was a result of a beating, but at the hospital, Mama was too scared to tell any of the hospital staff what really happened, and claimed to have fallen down a short flight of stairs. When she was sure, just three weeks before Papa died, that she was pregnant again, she knew she had to make every effort to protect herself, just as she had with Lexie and me. She claimed that Papa's reaction to her that day, by throwing her across the room, threw her into a panic and she was terrified that she would lose another child. Then, when he made the remark about Lexie being ripe for the picking, she completely lost control and that's when she picked up the poker. The remark had triggered Mama's memory when, on two occasions, she had seen Papa fondling two of the neighbor's young daughters. He had been behind the house and she confronted him about it, but he had threatened to kill her if she mentioned it to anyone. This time, the idea of him molesting Lexie, was more than she could bear.

The next morning, Mr. Phillips cross-examined Mama and soon had her in tears. He questioned the truth of all of my testimony, and after being reminded that she was under oath, she admitted that I had made up the story about the near drowning and the hair-cutting incident. It was only natural, that he would then proceed to badger her into admitting that everything she had testified to had been a pack of lies and that there was no evidence to support her story. To make matters worse, Mama had to admit that she wasn't pregnant after all, even though she was sure that she was at the time she killed Papa. When I read this, I was mortified. Poor Mama, everything looked so bad for her and I hadn't helped her by lying on the stand.

Mr. Hargraft had attempted to get the two young girls, who had been the victim of Papa's advances to testify, but they denied that anything had ever happened. I knew both girls and remember thinking that the day would come when I would force them to tell the truth.

Mr. Hargraft gave a great summation, but the prosecutor was more eloquent. I learned much later, that he had only lost two cases in the whole of his career and was well known throughout the state of New Jersey. He stressed, over and over, that there was no evidence to support any of the testimony the defense had presented and there was no motive for such a brutal killing. His final words brought a shiver down my spine, "You must convict Ella Taylor for first degree murder and she should be punished to the full extent of the law." It took only eight hours for the jury to come back with a guilty verdict.

I actually saw all this played out on the news, which had extensive coverage of the trial each day. You can imagine my range of emotions, seeing Mama's face as they read the verdict and the reaction of Gran, who was seated two rows behind her. Mama didn't even blink, she just stood there stoically and I was so proud of her. Meanwhile, Gran let out a cry and then grasping Grandpa's shoulder, she turned to him smiling and nodding.

Sentencing was to take place the following week. I don't know how I managed to sleep a wink knowing that Mama was going to prison for a long time and on the day of the sentencing my worst fears were realized. Gran gave a victim's statement claiming that Mama had taken away her only child and abandoned her own children with her violent act. She said she wished she'd get the death penalty and burn in hell. I hated Gran with a passion that day.

The judge told the court that it had been a particularly brutal crime and that my father didn't deserve to die that way, then he sentenced Mama to twenty-five years to life in prison. He no longer appeared like Santa in my eyes.

# CHAPTER 7

I had no idea, how I was going to survive living with Gran and never seeing Mama. I was approaching my tenth birthday in April and couldn't face another eight years under Gran's roof. Even the thought of leaving Lexie behind didn't deter me from planning my escape. For some reason, Gran seemed to dote on her and she had even formed a bond with Grandpa. I knew she would be well looked after. This time, I was determined to see Mama and get away from under Gran's clutches altogether, but I wasn't quite sure how to go about it.

Two weeks after Mama had been moved to the Correctional Facility for Women in Clinton, I decided that I was going to make the break. I planned to leave the house the next day and take a bus to Clinton and then go and see Mama. It was pretty easy really. Before anyone was awake, I stuffed a few clothes into my backpack and then crept into the kitchen. I wanted to make sure that I didn't go hungry this time, so I took an apple, a bran muffin and a can of ginger ale, then raided Gran's cookie jar where she always kept a few dollars for emergencies. I figured I would take the bus from Bank Street, but hadn't a clue how much it would cost. To be on the safe side, I took all of the one-dollar bills and two ten-dollar bills, and hoped that would be enough for a one-way ticket.

By the time I had walked several blocks to the bus station, I was already tired, but I was excited too. I was on my way to see

Mama, and I could hardly wait. When I finally got to the station, I approached the ticket counter, head held high, trying to look very grown up. The lady behind the counter, who was extremely obese, and wore thick black-framed glasses, leaned forward on her elbows and asked, "What can I do for you, young lady?"

I pulled out the money I had, from my pocket, and offered it to her, "I want to buy a ticket to Clinton," I replied with as much confidence as I could muster.

She looked at me and shook her head, "How old are you dear? Do your parents know where you are?"

"Oh yes," I lied, "they gave me the money to buy my ticket. I'm going to visit my cousin."

I got the feeling she didn't believe me when she said, "I'll need your name and address before I can sell you a ticket, dear."

I was really suspicious and considered giving her a fake name but I couldn't think fast enough, so I replied, "Cassie Taylor and I live at 15 Coral Avenue."

She looked like she was writing the information down and when she finished, she told me she wasn't allowed to sell me a ticket until just before the bus was due to leave, at nine o'clock. Then she told me to go and sit in the waiting room and she would come and get me later. Something didn't sound quite right to me, but I did what I was told and sat on a hard wooden bench for the next half hour watching all the people coming and going. I was just looking up at the clock, for the umpteenth time, praying for the hands to move faster, when I heard Gran's voice right behind me. I whipped around and saw her stalking towards me with Grandpa following behind like a puppy dog. I tried to back up and run, but there was a wall about three feet behind me and I was trapped. I remember instinctively putting my arm up to shield my face. I was sure Gran was going to strike me but instead she grabbed me, by my left ear, and hauled me out of the waiting room. Once outside, she exploded, "Not only are you a liar, just like your mother, but you're a thief too. When we get home, you will be on a curfew for two weeks and don't think that's fun for me. I would rather you were out of my sight permanently."

I was defiant, when I pulled away from her and spat back, "That can easily be arranged."

"Why you insolent little hussy," Gran hissed through her little pointed teeth, get in the car and shut your mouth."

I knew that the next time I attempted to run away would have to be preceded by a great deal of planning. First of all, I needed to be patient and act like the perfect ten-year-old. Then, when the time came, Gran might not be quite so quick to think anything was amiss. It wasn't easy holding my tongue every time she snapped at me or made insulting comments about my appearance, but somehow I managed it. After a couple of weeks, she stopped being quite so mean, but I still hated her with a passion.

I planned to leave in mid June, just as school was breaking up for summer vacation, and I planned to do it on a school day. Lexie was to be an innocent collaborator in my deception, if I was to buy enough time and be far away before my absence was discovered.

One morning, when Gran was in the garden, totally absorbed in raking over her flowerbeds and Grandpa was napping, I raided the bureau where they kept their private papers. I found several notes in Gran's handwriting and quickly slipped two of them into my pocket. Later, in my room, I began the tedious task of copying the handwriting and after several days I was sure that, although not perfect, at least my forgery looked like that of an adult rather than a ten-year-old.

It was during this time that I raided the cookie jar, but I was very careful to only take a dollar at a time so that Gran wouldn't notice. By the end of three weeks I had twelve dollars stashed away in one of my socks in my dresser.

I was always tall for my age and already about five foot tall. I figured with some make up, and the right attitude, I could probably pass for a teenager. Gran didn't wear any make up, not that it would have helped her much anyway, but I knew where I could get some. They had a cosmetic section at the local pharmacy and it was a piece of cake swiping lipstick, eye shadow and some face powder and hiding them in my school bag.

My biggest problem was how was I going to travel the hundred miles to Clinton? Well, believe it or not, I had been thinking about that for weeks. I had considered attempting to take the bus again, but then I might run into the same ticket agent and I was sure she would recognize me. Hitchhiking was out of the question, because I had heard all about what could happen to people who got into strange cars, though I had trusted Lenny enough when he brought me back home in his truck but I just couldn't risk it again. I finally came up with, what I thought was, a brilliant idea. Many of the older students who went to my school walked, or took the school bus, but some of them rode their bikes and usually left them in a bike rack in a sheltered area of the playground. I knew that most of the bikes were chained and padlocked, but I observed a couple of students who never secured their bikes. I guess they were just lazy but I didn't hold that against them.

My friend Hannah, who lived two doors away, had a bike and let me ride it from time to time. One day, I rode it about five miles even venturing onto the highway and by the time I got back, Hannah's mother was waiting anxiously on the front steps of her house. Thank goodness, she hadn't told Gran I was missing and after a sharp reprimand for taking off for so long, without permission, she let me go. I felt really pumped up after my practice run, even though I knew it was only a fraction of the distance to Clinton. I had already figured out that it would take me at least nine hours to get there but I was convinced that I could make it all the way, no matter how hard it might be.

On the evening before I planned to leave, I prepared a note in Gran's handwriting excusing me from school because of a bad cough. The next morning, soon after Lexie and I left the house and turned the street corner out of sight, I pulled her over behind some bushes and put the note in her pocket. She looked at me with her astounding green eyes and said, "What are you doing Cassie, what's the paper for?"

I put my hands on her shoulders and replied, "I want you to give that note to Mrs. Barker, in the office, as soon as you get to school."

Lexie frowned, "Why can't you give it to her yourself?"

I squeezed her shoulders and drew her towards me, "I can't go to school today Lexie, so I have to send a note to say I'm sick."

Lexie pulled back and stared up at me, "But you're not sick. Gran's going to be mad if she finds out you weren't at school today."

I was getting a little impatient but tried to keep my voice steady, "Please don't ask me any more questions. There's something important I have to do and I just need your help, that's all"

Lexie just stood there uncertain what to do until I pushed her out of the bushes and onto the sidewalk, "I have to go now and so do you, otherwise you'll be late"

Lexie hesitated and I had to physically push her in the direction of the school, "Go," I said in a firm voice, "don't just stand there."

It broke my heart to see her little figure walking slowly away. Every few steps she turned to see if I was still there. I think she knew that she might not see me again for a long time.

I waited for nearly half an hour near the school until the playground was completely deserted, then I crept through the gate to the sheltered area where the bikes were stored. It didn't take long to find one that hadn't been chained up and I quickly wheeled it out, onto the street. My school bag was heavy with my text books, a pair of jeans, two cans of cola and a slab of banana bread stolen from Gran's refrigerator, but there was a basket on the front of the bike, so I dumped the bag in there and climbed onto the seat.

I knew exactly how to get to Clinton. I had studied the map of New Jersey in the school library but first I had to morph into a teenager. There was a park just a short distance from the school and I rode down the main path until I came to an area where there were several benches and nobody seemed to be around. It didn't take long to change into my jeans and make up my face. The powder compact had a small mirror and when I'd finished, I have to admit, I looked pretty good and couldn't help smiling at my reflection.

A few minutes later, I was back on the bike and excited to finally be on my way. I noticed that it was already quite warm, even though it was only just after nine o'clock, so I made up my mind to only ride for about two hours before stopping. By then, it would be close to noon and might be too hot to go very far so I might have to rest up for quite a while.   I hadn't really thought too much about how the weather might affect my journey and I began to berate myself for not planning carefully enough. Little did I know that the weather would be the least of my problems.

# CHAPTER 8

I had just gotten onto Highway 55 and was traveling north when I began to really feel the effects of the heat. I had made another mistake when planning my trip, I had forgotten to pack a hat and the sun was beating down on my head. I could feel the perspiration running down my forehead and my legs were beginning to get tired. I knew I had to stop and find some shelter. I remember taking my hand off the handlebars to push my hair back off my face and then suddenly hearing the screech of brakes. After that everything went black.

I don't know how long I lost consciousness, but when I woke up I was in an ambulance with the siren blaring. From the pain I was in, I knew something was seriously wrong with my right arm and I couldn't help moaning. The paramedic leaning over me was a young woman with a sweet face and a mass of curly brown hair. She took my hand and told me everything was going to be all right and that they were taking me to the hospital in Woodbury. When I asked her what had happened, she told me that I had swerved in front of a car and been hit head on, but I had been lucky to only have a broken arm and a few cuts and bruises. She explained that they had to be absolutely sure that I didn't have any other injuries and needed to put my arm in a cast. In the meantime, even though I protested, she gave me an injection to help with pain and I think I dozed off for a while.

*Valerie S. Armstrong*

We arrived at Underwood Memorial and I was prodded and x-rayed and declared perfectly fine, except for the arm. While the doctor was putting the cast on, an elderly man hovered in the doorway anxious to know if I was okay. Apparently, he was the man driving the car that hit me and he had called 911 immediately. I felt really sorry for him because it wasn't his fault and I felt sorry for myself because all of my plans had gone awry. Gran would be livid when she found out what had happened and I now had no idea how I would ever get to see Mama.

Two policemen came into my room and asked me all kinds of questions. I was feeling a little dopey by then and I can't remember everything they asked me but I do remember they talked very softly and wrote everything down in a yellow notebook. After they left, one of the nurses told me that I would be released in a few hours and it would be a good idea if she washed all the make-up off of my face before Gran saw me. I waited anxiously for Gran to show up. I expected her to ground me for at least a month and I was certain she would find other ways to punish me. By the time the sun went down, she still hadn't arrived and I was told that I was being kept overnight. Nobody would tell me why and I had trouble sleeping. All kinds of thoughts went through my head. I even thought that maybe Gran had died and I would never see her again, but that would have been too good to be true.

At nine o'clock the next morning the same Child Services worker, with the snow-white hair and twinkling blue eyes, who had picked Lexie and me up before, walked into my room. She smiled as she came towards me and then pulled up a chair beside my bed, " I'm Mrs. Jackson, Cassie, do you remember me?" she asked.

I nodded, "Yes, you're the lady that took Lexie and me to the group home."

Mrs, Jackson sighed, "That's right honey, and I'm afraid I have to take you back there. Your grandmother can't look after you any more and I hope you can understand that. She isn't a young woman and it's been very difficult for her. I know you haven't been happy there and I know how much you miss your mother but it's just too much for your grandmother to handle."

34

"But what about Lexie? Is she going to stay at Gran's?"

"Yes, apparently she's settled in really well and she seems content. I know she's your sister and nobody wants to see you split up but there's no sense in uprooting her again when she's fine where she is. Do you understand, Cassie?"

"Yes," I replied grudgingly, "but where will I go now?"

Mrs. Jackson leaned over and put her hand on my shoulder, "You'll come back to the group home until we can find a foster home for you. It may take a little time because most foster parents prefer to take younger children, but I know of one couple who might agree to take you in."

"What if I don't like these people?" I asked, anticipating the worst.

"The couple I'm thinking of are wonderful people and if they do take you and there's a problem Cassie, I can't imagine them being the cause of it. You can't keep running away and behaving badly. If you do your part and act like a sensible child you could become part of their family and they'll do everything they can to give you a good life."

I shook my head vehemently, "I don't want to be part of someone else's family, I have Mama and Lexie."

Mrs. Jackson sighed again, "I'm sorry honey, but your Mama isn't here and neither is Lexie," and then she rose from the chair and started to walk away, "I'll call for the nurse to get you discharged and then we can leave."

I went back to the group home and moped around a lot. There wasn't much I could do with my arm in a cast and I wasn't interested in making friends. Even though I realized it might be a long time before anybody took me into their home, I couldn't see the point of getting chummy with any of the other kids when, at some point, I would never see them again. I spent most of my time plotting how I was going to escape again. It all depended on where I would be living next. At the moment, I was back in Millville and no closer to Mama than before.

I was sitting in, what they called the reading room, browsing through an old copy of Seventeen magazine when Mrs. Jackson came through the door. There were two other girls, who I had never seen before, sitting on the other side of the room out of earshot, but Mrs. Jackson came right up to me and, in a hushed tone, said, "There's a telephone call for you, Cassie."

I looked up at her in surprise, "A telephone call, for me?"

I asked, "Is it Lexie?"

Mrs. Jackson shook her head and smiled, "No, it's your mother."

I was stunned for a moment and then slowly got up, afraid that I might be dreaming, and followed Mrs. Jackson to the hallway where the telephone was located. The receiver was dangling from its cord and I picked it up tentatively, put it to my ear and whispered, "Hello."

There was a pause while I listened and watched Mrs. Jackson give a small wave as she walked away, and then I heard Mama's voice, "Cassie, are you there? It's Mama."

I was so overcome with emotion that I couldn't speak until I heard Mama's voice again, "Cassie, are you there, honey?"

I felt the tears running down my face as I answered her, "Yes, I'm here Mama. Where are you? I miss you so much."

"I miss you too Cassie, it's so lovely to hear your voice but please don't cry. Listen honey, I don't have much time. We're only allowed to make calls at certain times and a lot of the other women want to use the phone. I'm sorry I couldn't call you before. I tried, but I'm afraid your Gran wouldn't let me speak to you. I wish you hadn't run away but now that you're not going back there, I'm going to see if you can come and visit me."

I remember gasping in surprise, " You really mean it, Mama. When can I come?"

Mama sighed, "I'm not sure. We may have to wait a little while but it will be soon, I promise."

"What about Lexie? Can she come too?" I asked, thinking how happy it would make my little sister.

"I don't think so, honey. She's so young and I don't want her to see me in this place."

"I'm going to get you out of there one day," I said, "You'll see, Mama, and then we'll be together forever and ever."

I remember Mama chuckling, and it was good to hear her laugh, "Oh, Cassie," she remarked, "my precious daughter, I know you really mean for that to happen but I did something bad and I have to pay for it."

"No, no," I protested, "Papa was the bad one. You shouldn't be locked up Mama and I'm going to get you out, I promise."

There was a moment of silence and I called out, "Mama, are you still there?"

I heard some voices in the background and then Mama came back on the line, "I'm sorry, honey, but I have to go. I love you, Cassie, and I'll write you and see you real soon. Bye, bye."

I started to say goodbye but I heard the click in my ear and knew Mama had gone. I stood there for a few seconds staring at the receiver in my hand and then slowly hung it back up. I only had a minute or two with Mama, but it made me happier than I had felt in a long, long time.

# CHAPTER 9

There were a lot of activities at the group home, all designed to occupy our minds and educate at the same time. There was a book club, which I particularly liked, a sewing circle, a woodworking shop and several fitness classes, including yoga. I joined the book club within the first week and I was one-third through 'Nicholas Nickleby' when I found it rather heavy going and thought I might try my hand at gardening.

It was a Sunday morning, right after a short non-denominational service, that we all had to attend. I was in the garden helping to water the rose bushes, when I saw Mrs. Jackson exit the back door and approach me.

"Hello, Cassie," she called out as she got closer, "you look like you're enjoying the sunshine."

I put down the watering can and looked up at her, "Good morning," I responded politely.

She fanned her face with the sheath of papers she was holding, "My goodness, it's getting a little warm, maybe we should go inside," she said and then turned and walked back up the pathway. Obviously she expected me to follow, and I did, all the time wondering what she wanted me for and hoping that Mama was on the telephone again.

When we got inside, she led me into the reading room and suggested that I sit down as she needed to talk to me. I did as I was told and watched, a little anxiously, while she fussed with her papers and then sat down opposite me.

"Cassie," she said. "You've been here for just about three weeks and I'm aware that you haven't been too happy. The director tells me that you keep to yourself most of the time and avoid the other girls."

I remained silent and there was quite a pause before she continued, "I mentioned to you, when you first came here, that I might know a couple who would be interested in opening up their home to you. Well, I expect you'll be surprised to learn that they want to see you. In fact, they're here now, waiting in the office."

I jumped up, my stomach lurching. I was scared, scared to meet these people, or anyone who might turn out to be even meaner than Gran. Mrs. Jackson, realizing that I wasn't prepared for her news, leapt out of her chair and reached for my arm, "It's okay, Cassie. They just want to meet you for now, nothing more. They have to be sure that you'll fit into their family. If they don't think it will work, they'll just go on home and you'll stay here until we find some other family. If, on the other hand, they feel that it might work, they'll come back again two or three times before making a final decision."

I could feel myself relaxing as she continued to talk, but I was still a little anxious and needed a little time to myself. "May I please go and wash up and change my clothes," I asked.

"Of course, dear," Mrs. Jackson replied, " and when you are ready, just come to the office."

I took my sweet time washing my hands and face and changing into the only decent dress I owned, blue and white cotton with a square neck and capped sleeves. After fifteen minutes, I figured whoever was waiting for me, would probably be getting impatient. Meanwhile, I had become perfectly calm, so I ventured downstairs and made my way to the office. I could hear the murmur of voices and the sound of a child giggling. That was rather a surprise, and I had no idea what to expect. When I opened the door, Mrs. Jackson turned towards me and announced, "This is Cassie Taylor. Cassie, I want you to meet Mr. & Mrs. Marsh and their son Billy."

I was aware of the Marshs' rising from their seats and moving towards me, but I was transfixed by the sight of Billy Marsh, who looked up at me with a huge smile on his strange face, the like of which I had never seen before. "Ullo," he said and then giggled and clapped his hands.

I'll never forget that first meeting. Frank and Jean Marsh were both about thirty years old and an attractive couple. While he was tall and slim with fair hair and blue eyes, his wife was the complete opposite. I was already five feet tall and she wasn't much taller than me, but her hair was almost jet black and she had amazing hazel eyes. They were both so kind to me that day. Instead of probing me about my past and asking me all sorts of questions, they told me all about their family, their house in Asbury Park, and how they wanted, so much, to foster an older child, preferably a girl. Their main concern was the relationship with their son. That's when I learned that four-year-old Billy was a Downs Syndrome child and had special needs. I had no idea what that meant, but later I looked it up in the library and sat fascinated for ages trying to understand Billy's condition.

The Marshs' wanted to come back the following weekend and take me out for a drive and possibly a picnic, weather permitting. I must admit, I was excited. The Marshs' were so far removed from Gran, it was laughable, and most exciting of all, they lived in Asbury Park, which was not only on the Jersey shore, but that much closer to Mama.

The day of the Marshs' second visit, it was sunny and warm without a cloud in the sky. They picked me up at noon and we drove to the park and had a picnic lunch near the lake. Billy made it all so easy because there were no awkward silences with him around and soon we were rolling over and over down a hill, roaring with laughter, while his parents stood at the bottom, grinning with delight.

When we got back to the group home and we all said goodbye, Billy threw his little arms around my neck and said, "I wuv you, Cassie." I know I had tears in my eyes when I hugged his little body and prayed that the Marshs' would take me home with them.

Thankfully, I only had to wait two days before I was told that it was official. Mrs. Jackson gave me the news, "You need to pack up your things tomorrow, Cassie. Mr. and Mrs. Marsh will be coming for you at noon. They are going to be your new foster parents."

# CHAPTER 10

When the Marshs' picked me up, I was feeling a little subdued and Billy wasn't with them, to help lift my spirits. Mrs. Marsh sat with me in the back seat and told me a lot more about the family. I learned that her husband was an attorney, a fact that got my heart racing and one that I tucked into the back of my mind, to take advantage of sometime in the future. Mrs. Marsh stayed at home to look after Billy, as he needed a lot of attention, but prior to his birth, she had been an actress starring in local theatre productions. Billy had a babysitter, Melanie, a nineteen-year-old college student who looked after Billy, on the odd occasion, when his mother had places to go. Apparently, they had intended to bring him with them when they picked me up, but he had gotten too excited, thrown up his breakfast and then had a minor temper tantrum.

I had always lived in New Jersey, just a stone's throw away from the Atlantic Ocean, but I had never been to the Jersey shore. When I finally saw the ocean, it took my breath away. It seemed to dance and sparkle in the sunlight and stretched as far as the eye could see. Mrs. Marsh rolled down the window so that I could get a better look and I felt the exhilaration of the wind blowing through my hair, and the wonderful salty smell of the sea. Mr. Marsh had deliberately chosen to take the long way round, so that I could experience my first sight of the Atlantic and I caught him glancing back at me and then smiling broadly at his wife. I remember thinking, what a handsome man he was and so different from Papa.

When we drove down the street where the Marshs' lived, I couldn't get over the size of the houses. They looked enormous; at least three times the size of Gran's house. Each one had a huge landscaped garden that sloped down to the road, with towering trees and rows and rows of colorful flowerbeds. The Marsh's house was just as impressive. It was three stories high with a wraparound porch and seven or eight steps that led up to the front door.

Mr. Marsh suggested we go ahead while he parked the car and I followed his wife up to the main entrance. I was feeling really nervous, when suddenly the front door was opened by a fresh faced, skinny girl with long auburn hair and frameless glasses perched on the end of her nose. I figured this had to be Melanie, and then I saw Billy peeking out from behind her skirt and another shadow moving in the hallway behind him. Melanie looked like she was just about to speak when the shadow bounded towards me. I stepped back, not knowing what to expect, when suddenly this very large golden retriever appeared at my side and began licking my hand. I was a little nervous until Mrs. Marsh laughed and said, "This is Sheba, she's as gentle as a lamb. There's no need to be afraid of her."

I stared down into a pair of deep brown eyes and I could see the gentleness there. I couldn't help myself, I bent down and threw my arms around her neck and felt the tears welling up. I suddenly felt surrounded by people that could give me the love and attention that had been taken away when Mama was arrested.

My first day, in my new home, was one that I will never forget. Melanie left soon after we arrived and then, with Billy tagging along behind, Mrs. Marsh took me on a tour of the house. There were four bedrooms, three bathrooms, a living, dining, and family room as well as a huge kitchen with granite countertops and a breakfast nook. It was a mansion, compared to anything I had ever seen before. My room was fit for a princess, but it wasn't all pink and frilly. It was decorated in soft shades of apricot and mint green with a cream rug I could sink my feet into. As for the closet, well after we unpacked my clothes, they looked so pitiful hanging there that Mrs. Marsh clucked her tongue and said, "I guess we're going to have to take you shopping, young lady."

When we came downstairs, I was surprised to see Mr. Marsh sitting at the kitchen table shelling peas, "Don't look so surprised, Cassie," he said smiling, "I like to cook sometimes. Mind you, no one's as good a cook as my wife, but I like to give her a run for her money."

"Can I help?" I asked, "I used to shell peas for Mama."

He patted the seat beside him, "Of course, come and sit down."

I looked over at Mrs. Marsh and she nodded, but then Billy grabbed my hand, "Me too, me too," he cried.

I led him around the table and sat down, perching him on my lap, and tried to show him how to pop the pods open and take the peas out. Soon we had peas rolling all over the place and all four of us were giggling like little children.

After supper, a delicious shepherd's pie with chocolate mousse for dessert, Mrs. Marsh took Billy up to bed and then suggested that we go to the family room to talk. I was feeling rather mellow by this time and with a contented sigh, sank down into a green velvet recliner. Mrs. Marsh sat down opposite me on a leather loveseat and looked at me rather intently, "We need to talk, Cassie," she said.

My brain instantly put me on alert, "Did I do something wrong? Are you sending me back to the group home?"

She shook her head and smiled, "No," she replied emphatically, "I just want us to talk so that we can get to know each other a little better. First of all, I'd like you to call us Uncle Frank and Aunt Jean and then I want you to know, that we have every intention of keeping you with us until you are old enough to step out into the world on your own. I know all about your mother's story, Cassie, and as much as you love her and miss her, you have to face the fact that she's going to be away for a long time."

I shook my head vehemently, when she said that, and started to get up but she leapt out of the chair and gathered me into her arms, "Come," she whispered, "sit next to me."

I reluctantly sat down with her and she stroked my hair and continued, "You can help your mother the most, Cassie, by letting her know that you are being well looked after. I know all about your attempts to visit her and I think you're a brave young lady, but you can't keep doing that. We can give you a good life, and at the same time, I can arrange for you to visit your mother on a regular basis."

"You mean that?" I cried, " I can go and see Mama?"

"Yes," she answered, "I've already made inquiries and I'm going to be put on a list of visitors that your mother has to approve, then I can take you inside the prison. You're a minor, Cassie, and you have to be accompanied by an adult."

My heart was pounding with excitement, "Can we go tomorrow?" I asked hopefully.

Mrs. Marsh, or Aunt Jean as I was to call her, chuckled, "Not tomorrow dear, there are only certain days for visiting and I still have to get all that information. I promise, as soon as I find out everything I need to know, we'll go on the next available visiting day."

I couldn't help myself, I leaned over and kissed her on the cheek and she smiled and said, "Now you promise you won't run away again?"

I nodded, but I was secretly keeping my options open.

I was so excited about seeing Mama, that I didn't think I could wait another moment, but Uncle Frank and Aunt Jean made sure they kept me well occupied while they waited to get the all clear from the prison authorities. Uncle Frank usually commuted every day to work in Lakewood but he took a week's holiday so that we could all get to know each other better.

The weather was glorious most of the time, and we spent half the week at the beach, swimming in the ocean, strolling the boardwalk or building sandcastles. Billy loved the ocean, he would totter out into the water on his little legs and giggle with delight. He had absolutely no fear and I had to grip his hand with all my might to stop him from getting away from me. Billy wasn't the only one obsessed with the ocean, Sheba kept us all in a state of anxiety as she raced out into the waves, paddled a few yards, and then came back, only to end up drenching us all when she decided she had had enough

The one day that it poured with rain, we left Billy at home with Melanie, lunched in town, and then went to a movie at the local theatre. They were playing 'Escape to Witch Mountain', a Disney movie about two orphans with psychic powers. I had never been to a movie theatre before and I loved it but I was wishing that Lexie could have been with me. Later, when Aunt Jean thought I was looking a little pensive and asked me if something was wrong, I told her how much I missed my little sister. Instead of trying to console me, she told me that she would call Gran and arrange for Lexie to come and stay with us for a day or two, even if she had to pick her up and drive all the way to Bridgeton and back. Sure enough she was good to her word and just two days later there she was, my sweet little Lexie getting out of Aunt Jean's car.

# CHAPTER 11

It was wonderful to see how Lexie took to the Marshs'. After spending a whole day and night with them, I knew that she didn't want to go back to Gran's. Lexie was enchanted with Billy, from the moment they first met, and she gave him a hug. They were only about a year apart in age, but Billy was so tiny and he had this adorable smile that melted everyone's heart. I believe, that on the drive up, Aunt Jean had prepared Lexie for his odd appearance and unusual behavior. Most of the time he was utterly endearing but sometimes he could be very difficult. Lexie seemed unfazed and I was proud of the way she greeted him.

Billy wasn't the only one who captured Lexie's heart. When she first saw Sheba, she couldn't stop stroking her. Animals were her passion and she had already decided, at the age of five, that she would grow up to be a safari guide in Africa, or work at a wild life center.

We took Lexie to the beach that day. Like me, she had never seen the ocean before, and we couldn't keep her out of the water. Aunt Jean was worried about her getting a sunburn, she had such fair skin, but all attempts to lure her back onto dry land were met with a coquettish grin and a dash back into the waves. Uncle Frank thought she was precious and in my naivety, I asked him, "Can Lexie stay with us until my Mama comes home?"

He looked at me sadly and shook his head, "I'm sorry Cassie, but that just isn't possible. Billy needs a lot of attention so we couldn't even consider taking another child into the family. Besides that, Cassie, you have to get used to the idea that your mother will be gone until long after you've grown into a young woman."

I knew this was my chance to try and help Mama. I sidled up closer to where he was sitting cross-legged on a blanket, "Uncle Frank, you're an attorney, can't you help Mama to get out of prison?"

He took my hand in his, "I'm in corporate law, Cassie," he explained, "That means, I deal with companies about all sorts of boring things, like patents and copyright issues."

I had no idea what that meant, "What are those?" I asked.

He chuckled, "Well, when someone invents something or writes something, like a book, no one else can just go ahead and steal the idea to make money for themselves. I do have an idea though," he continued," I could talk to one of my partners, who's in criminal law, and ask him to review the case. There's no way anyone can get your mother out of jail, but there maybe a way to get her sentence reduced. I'm not promising anything because this all takes time and I'm going to have to ask for it to be done pro bono, which means at no charge."

My heart started to race, "Really, Uncle Frank, you'll ask him?"

"Yes, I will, as soon as I go back to my office on Monday, but remember it takes time to review a case, so you 'll have to be patient."

I was so happy that night that I couldn't sleep and I was glad that Lexie was staying over in my room. She curled up beside me in bed and wrapped her arms around my waist, "When's Mama coming back?" she asked.

"Not for a while, Lexie," I answered, but, wanting to give her some hope, added, "but maybe sooner than we think."

"I miss her," she murmured as she started to get drowsy, "and I miss you too. Why do I have to go back to Gran's?"

I turned over and drew her head onto my shoulder, not sure how to answer her, "Go to sleep, Lexie, it's getting late," I whispered.

The next morning there were a lot of tears as Aunt Jean bundled Lexie into the car, to take her back to Bridgeton, but Uncle Frank assured her that she was welcome back any time and even suggested she spend Thanksgiving with us.

There was still no news about our visit to see Mama and the summer holidays were almost over. Aunt Jean enrolled me in the Asbury Park Middle School and took me shopping for a whole new wardrobe. We came home laden down with bags full of skirts, blouses, sweaters, shoes and a wonderful royal blue woolen coat. I felt like a princess and when I modeled everything for Uncle Frank, at Aunt Jean's insistence, he clapped his hands and called out, "Beautiful, beautiful," over and over again. For the first time in my life, I felt pretty. Papa had never said anything nice about me.

Just before school began, we got the approval to visit Mama. It was a Saturday and the night before, I had stayed awake nearly the whole time unable to wait for morning to come. By the time Aunt Jean and I left the house, Uncle Frank had already gone to his office to work for a few hours and Melanie had arrived to sit with Billy. The drive to Clinton took over an hour and when we finally arrived, all I could see were three huge gray buildings, all joined together and surrounded by fields. Once inside, there were a lot of metal gates with bars and a man in uniform who checked Aunt Jean's identification and looked in her purse, then asked us to wait with the other visitors in a large room with bare green walls. I kept looking around me and wanted to talk, but it was so quiet, you could almost hear a pin drop.

It seemed like forever before we were all ushered into an even larger room, where dozens of women sat, each at individual metal tables. They all looked the same to me, wearing identical white tee shirts, and although I knew Mama had to be there, I couldn't see her. I began to panic and gripped Aunt Jean's hand and then suddenly I heard, "Cassie, here honey," and there she was.

The next moment was a bit of a blur, as I ran full tilt into Mama's arms, then almost instantly felt a tap on my shoulder and heard a stern voice say, "No touching." Mama released me and sat down just as Aunt Jean reached us. She held out her hand, "Jean Marsh", she said, "It's nice to finally meet you Mrs. Taylor."

Mama shook Aunt Jean's hand, "I can't thank you enough for bringing Cassie to see me, and please call me Ella," she said.

Aunt Jean smiled and responded, "All right Ella, as long as you call me Jean."

It was a wonderful visit. Mama looked just as beautiful as I remembered even though she had lost a little weight and her lovely hair had lost its luster. She told us all about how she spent her days, working in the library and about her cell mate, Vicky who had a great sense of humor, and helped to keep her spirits up. Meanwhile, Aunt Jean told her about Uncle Frank and Billy, and Lexie's visit, and then she encouraged me to tell Mama about my new life in Asbury Park. I was very careful about what I said to Mama as Aunt Jean had warned me, on the drive up, to be sure and let Mama know how much I missed her.

By the time we were ready to leave, Mama had tears in her eyes. She was so grateful to Aunt Jean for taking her place in my life, but Aunt Jean assured her that no one could take her place and that I talked about her constantly. My last words to Mama that day were, "Remember, I'm going to get you out of here. I've got Uncle Frank working on it. I love you, Mama."

I was sad on the way home but Aunt Jean made me feel better when she remarked, "I can see why you love your mother so much, Cassie. She seems like a lovely person and I promise we'll go back and see her often."

That visit was the first of hundreds I would make in the following years and I always came away with mixed emotions. I felt devastated each time I had to leave Mama behind in that dreadful place, but happy to have been able to see and talk to her, if only for a couple of hours.

# CHAPTER 12

My first day at school was not particularly pleasant. I was the new girl, and while everyone else greeted each other like long lost cousins, I was totally ignored.

Mrs. Parenzo, our homeroom teacher, introduced me to the class, "This is Cassandra Taylor, she just moved here from Bridgeton. Please welcome her, everybody."

I heard a low murmur and then silence and that's when I decided that the only way to deal with my classmates was to show them how smart I was. In the past I had taken my aptitude for getting good grades in my stride. Now, I had a purpose in life, to make something of myself, and to get Mama out of jail.

One week later, after alienating myself from everyone else, a surprising thing happened, I made a life long friend. Jasmine Maboa came to Asbury Park from Selma, Alabama. Her parents were African American, having emigrated from Kenya just before she was born. Jasmine, or Jazz, as she liked to be called, had wonderful coffee colored skin and the largest brown eyes I'd ever seen on a ten-year-old. However, it was her hair that got the most attention, jet-black, finely braided and cascading like a waterfall onto her shoulders. It was her first day at my school and she was obviously uncomfortable, even though there were three or four other dark skinned children in class. Everybody ignored her, just as they had ignored me and so, at noon, when I found her sitting on a bench in the playground, I approached her, leaned down and said, "Hi there, my name's Cassie, I'm new here too. Do you mind if I sit down?"

She looked up at me and smiled, then shuffled over to make room for me and replied, "I'm Jazz, would you like half of my sandwich?"

I had already had lunch and wasn't really hungry but Mama had always told me that sharing food was a good way to make friends, so I responded, "I would like that very much, thank you."

She slowly opened the brown paper bag she had been clutching and pulled out a plastic box which, when opened, revealed a very large Kaiser bun, an apple, two Oreo cookies and a can of cherry coke. Jazz chuckled as she passed me half of the bun, "My mother always gives me way too much food, she thinks I'm too thin."

"I think you look just right," I remarked, "and I love your hair. I wish mine looked like that."

Jazz shook her head, "You wouldn't really want it, it takes hours to get it like this. I've always wanted fair hair like yours."

"Well, you could always dye it when you get older," I suggested.

We sat through the remainder of the lunch period just chatting like old friends but I didn't tell her about Mama, there was plenty of time for that. I just implied that Uncle Frank and Aunt Jean were my parents and that Billy was my little brother. I didn't even mention Lexie and that made me feel a bit guilty but I wasn't ready to open up. It was during our conversation that I learned about Jazz's parents and how they had come to America twelve years earlier and settled in Alabama. Her father was a doctor and had practiced in Kenya but it took a number of years before he was allowed to practice in the States. He had worked as an emergency room physician in a hospital in Selma and had only recently decided to move his family to New Jersey. Once settled in Asbury Park, he opened up his own practice and had become very successful.

Two weeks later when Jazz invited me to her home, I was astonished to discover that she lived in one of the most upscale areas in town and her house was twice as big as the Marshs'. It had taken some time for the neighbors to accept the Maboas', after all this was the seventies. Race was still very much an issue, but Dr. Maboa was in a profession that seemed to demand respect and they had already made a number of friends.

When I first met Dr. Maboa, I was immediately attracted to him. I guess you could say I had a schoolgirl crush. He was so tall and handsome, in fact looking back now, he resembled Sydney Poitier and he had a voice that I could have listened to all day. Mrs. Maboa was the perfect match for her husband, almost as tall, slim as a reed, and with the high cheekbones of a model. It was only later that I found out that she did, in fact, model in South Africa and was quite well known there. After arriving in America, she had become interested in fashion, taken a course in design, and was now producing one-of-a-kind outfits for a trendy boutique in town. Most of the clothes had the look of Africa. They were made of soft flowing materials and all the colors of the rainbow. With her love of fashion, she often dressed in her own designs, especially when out on a regular Friday night date with her husband. Even after fourteen years of marriage, they still seemed to have time for romance and I couldn't help comparing their relationship to the one my own mother had to endure with Papa. According to Jazz, they would like to have had more children but it just wasn't in the cards. They compensated by being doting parents and whatever extra love they had left over, they lavished on their two Siamese cats, Opal and Yum-yum. Mrs. Maboa, who had been known as Sisi in the modeling world, was very kind to me. From the first moment we met, she welcomed me into her home and encouraged my friendship with Jazz.

Over the next few months, I never once invited Jazz to the Marsh's house but I knew I couldn't hold out much longer. I was petrified that, when she found out I was just a foster child and had lied to her, she would cut me out of her life but I underestimated her true character. Parents Day at school forced me into telling Jazz all about myself. I couldn't risk the Maboas' talking to Uncle Frank and Aunt Jean when it was obvious that, not having the same last name, might raise a lot of questions. I had a feeling that Mrs.

Maboa would be empathetic when she heard my story, so I decided to confess to Jazz in the presence of her mother. It took all my courage to broach the subject, and I tried desperately not to show too much emotion, but when I saw tears start to form in both Mrs. Maboa's and Jazz's eyes, I just lost it. After that, my friendship with Jazz deepened and I was treated with even more kindness, if that were possible. Meanwhile, Uncle Frank and Aunt Jean finally met Jazz and her parents and I felt like a weight had been lifted from my shoulders.

# CHAPTER 13

Aunt Jean kept her promise, taking me to see Mama at least once a month and she was never far from my mind. I was so proud of the way she handled being confined in that miserable place day after day, never complaining and always encouraging me to talk about myself, rather than subjecting me to the details of her mundane existence. My attempt to get her case reopened, through Uncle Frank, was futile. An investigator had failed to persuade the two young victims of my father's sexual abuse to admit that anything inappropriate had taken place and there was no new evidence to support an appeal. I didn't talk to Mama about getting her out of prison any more but always, in the back of my mind, I was determined, at some point, to try again.

Jazz and I graduated from middle school at the top of our class and then continued our education at Asbury High School. There was never any rivalry between us, we always rooted for one another. I had long before decided that I wanted to study law so that I could help Mama, but my real passion was English and I loved to write. In my spare time I read a great deal, especially the classics, like Dickens, Jane Austen and the Bronte sisters. Their stories inspired me to write my own fanciful tales and I daydreamed about being a famous novelist one day. Jazz, on the other hand, had inherited her mother's love of clothes and although, brilliant in maths and physics, longed for the time when she could take a course in fashion design.

I have to admit that I was happy with my life. The Marshs' treated me like their own daughter, Billy adored me, and I felt the same way about him, and I had developed a special connection with Sheba who now slept at the foot of my bed every night. My one regret was, that I saw less and less of Lexie. She had never been allowed to see Mama and her visits to Asbury Park were few and far between. Aunt Jean did her best to persuade Gran to allow us to spend more time together but her pleas fell on deaf ears. I suspected that Gran was getting meaner as she got older.

The year that Jazz and I started high school was the year we finally reached puberty. We knew that some of the other girls were way ahead of us and we were beginning to wonder if we had some physical impairment. Aunt Jean had been a godsend in explaining all the pros and cons of entering womanhood and I never felt uncomfortable asking her questions. Sex education at school was very limited and most of what Jazz and I learned was from whispered remarks between the students, both male and female.

When Aunt Jean took me shopping for my first bra, I couldn't wait to show Mama my new shape. Even Jazz was a little envious because she was still as flat as a pancake, but I kept telling her what a great figure she had, and maybe she should forget fashion design and go for a modeling career instead. Anyway, her lack of curves, didn't keep the boys away.

Speaking of boys, that was when I first started to get really interested in Scott Cunningham. Scott towered over me by about four inches, which was a good thing, because I was the tallest girl in class. Not only that, he was movie star handsome with jet-black hair, deep brown eyes and lashes that most girls would die for. I certainly wasn't the prettiest girl in class, although my looks had improved somewhat, so I was surprised when he started paying attention to me.

Despite my attraction to Scott, I had mixed emotions about pursuing a friendship with him. I knew that eventually he would find out about my past and I wasn't prepared for that. If word got out, it was likely to make me even more unpopular with my classmates. With the exception of Jazz, I had kept my distance from everyone else, just to protect my privacy, and the idea of everyone discovering my secret was worrying. Don't get me wrong, I wasn't ashamed of Mama, but I knew how cruel kids could be. Jenny Barlow, for example, was what one could only call obese, and she suffered verbal abuse on a daily basis. I had no intention of becoming another target.

Regardless of my concerns, when Scott sought me out one day during lunch recess and offered to share his mother's homemade carrot cake with me, I just couldn't resist him. Over the next few weeks, our friendship grew and I came to know what a sweet person he was and just how much we had in common. He lived with his mother and younger brother, Kip, in the poorer part of town and he had no hesitation in telling me about his life. His father had abandoned the family right after Kip was born, and two years later, ended up in prison for armed robbery. In deference to his mother, Scott never mentioned his father in front of her, but he confided to me that he hoped to go and visit him one day and get to know him. When I discovered Scott's true nature, and the fact that we seemed to have so much in common, I decided to tell him the truth about myself. He reacted in the same manner as Jazz and her mother, with an expression of understanding and enormous empathy and he promised never to tell another soul.

I wasn't the only one that had snagged herself a boyfriend. Jazz claimed that she was madly in love with Damon Chandra and they were seeing each other on a regular basis. Damon was of Indian descent and his skin was almost as dark as Jazz's. They made a good-looking couple. Both Scott and I liked Damon a lot, so the four of us hung out together a great deal over the next year. Those days, when the weather was warm, we spent most of our time at the beach. Damon had a border collie named Skippy and on occasion he would bring him along and I would bring Sheba. We would have the best time of all, chasing the two dogs in and out of the water. Often, when we had just gotten our allowance, we would go to the Palace amusement park or ride the roller coaster. There were so many tourists in the summer on the beach and the boardwalk and we never wanted the school break to end. My only regret was, that Mama couldn't be with me. She would have loved it.

# CHAPTER 14

I remember the day I had my first real sexual experience as though it was yesterday. Scott and I had been dating for two years and we'd gotten into some pretty heavy petting in the last few months but we'd never crossed the line. Scott was always the perfect gentleman, never wanting to push me into doing anything that I might later regret. Deep down I was dying to find out what 'going all the way' really felt like, but I was scared.

It was Jazz who pushed me over the edge. I was having a sleepover at her house and we were already in our pajamas, sprawled on her bed, looking through the latest Photoplay magazine when, without raising her head, she said, "We did it, Cassie."

I had no idea what she meant, "What are you talking about?" I asked frowning.

That's when she turned on her side and looked me in the eye, "Damon and I, we did it last night."

I gasped and sat bolt upright, "Are you saying you had sex with him? Oh my God, where, when, what was it like?" I rattled on breathlessly.

Jazz grinned, "On the beach, right after you guys left. It was fabulous Cassie, and it didn't hurt one bit."

I couldn't wait to hear more, "Weren't you scared? What about getting pregnant, didn't you think about that?"

Jazz giggled, "I wasn't a bit scared, in fact, I made him do it. I just had to find out what it was like. I already warned him the day before that he'd better look out and I even told him to bring a condom."

I know I was shocked and that my eyes were as big as saucers, "You're kidding!" and then I giggled too, " Why you shameless hussy Miss Maboa."

Jazz rolled onto her back and stared at the ceiling, "Oh Cassie, if you only knew how I felt now. Damon really loves me. I know he does and we even talked about being together forever."

"But you're only sixteen, anything could happen. What will you do when you graduate? What if you go to different colleges?"

Jazz sighed, "I don't know, but I guess we'll have to see when the time comes."

We continued to talk well into the night, long after we had climbed under the covers and turned out the lights. I think that's when I decided that I was going to get Scott to make love to me and I wasn't going to wait.

My opportunity came earlier than expected when Scott told me about a beach party being held the following Saturday night. I planned to lure him away from the crowd and seduce him. I even bought a really skimpy red bikini, in the hope that he wouldn't be able to resist me, and it worked. The minute we hit the beach and I took off my jeans and top, he whistled, "Wow, you look terrific, Cassie. You're the best looking girl here."

I knew that wasn't true, I still had that bump on my nose and I was no beauty but I did have a good figure. Nevertheless, he made me feel really special and I could hardly wait until it got dark.

We had a great time at the party. Some of the boys brought beer and after I finished off almost two bottles, I was feeling really mellow. Jazz and Damon were all over each other and soon after the sun went down, I saw them sneak off with their arms around each other. That's when I asked Scott if he wanted to go for a walk, and he didn't hesitate.

We must have strolled for almost a mile, right at the water's edge, before I suggested that we stop and take a rest beside the sea wall. After that, it was only minutes before were kissing passionately and I could feel Scott's hands roaming all over my body. I heard his breathing getting heavier as I slipped off the top of my bikini, "What are you doing, Cassie?" he whispered.

I could barely see his face in the shadow of the sea wall, "I want you, Scott," I whispered back.

He took my face in his hands, "Are you sure? Is this what you really want?"

"Yes, I'm sure," I replied, "don't you want me too?"

He started to turn away, "Oh Cassie, I've wanted you for so long, you have no idea but I'm just not prepared. I didn't bring anything with me and we can't take any chances."

Chuckling, I said, "But I did," and I fished in my bikini bottoms for the condom that Jazz had gotten from Damon, after he was sworn to secrecy or suffer the consequences.

I still couldn't see Scott's face but I know he was shocked, "Where did you get that?" he asked.

"I'll never tell," I answered, "now how about we stop talking and get back to kissing."

I felt like I had suddenly changed from a naïve schoolgirl into a real woman and for a while I became the aggressor. I think I surprised myself and I know I surprised Scott. It seemed like the most natural thing in the world to lie naked beside another naked body and that night, Scott made me feel beautiful. I don't know how he knew exactly what to do and I didn't want to know, but even now after all these years, I can still look back on that night as one of the most memorable.

My foster parents had given me a lot of freedom, and I know they trusted me, but I was taking a lot of liberties. Two or three nights a week, I would stay out well after my curfew, until the time that Aunt Jean cornered me as I crept into the house over an hour late.

"Cassie, we need to talk," she said, "come and sit next to me on the sofa."

I followed her into the living room muttering, "Sorry, Aunt Jean, I didn't mean to be so late."

She waved her hand as if to cut me off, "That's not good enough, Cassie. We're worried about you, what's going on with you and Scott?"

I felt myself blush as I lowered my head and stammered, "What do you mean?"

"Cassie," she continued taking my hand, "I was your age once, believe it or not, and I know all about raging hormones. We've talked about intimacy and you know what can happen, so if you're being sexually active, it's best that you tell me and we can do something to protect you."

I looked up at her, hardly believing what I was hearing, "You mean you wouldn't be mad at me?"

"No, honey," she replied, "I wish you had waited, you are still so young, but what's done is done. I think you should see the doctor and get some form of birth control."

"Oh, Aunt Jean," I said trembling, "I'll be so embarrassed, isn't there something else I can do?"

"I'm afraid not. You can't rely on Scott to protect you. Of course you could always just stop, but I don't think that's going to happen. I'll call tomorrow and get an appointment, and one other thing, Cassie, I think your mother needs to know about this."

I wasn't sure that Mama would be quite as understanding as Aunt Jean, but she had as much right to know what was going on in my life as my foster mother. I nodded, as I got up from the sofa, "Thank you, Aunt Jean, and I'll try not to be late again."

She rose and gave me a hug, "Good girl, now off to bed, Sheba's already in your room, waiting for you. I peeked in and saw her just before you came in."

I crawled into bed that night, with Sheba beside me, and once again thanked my lucky stars for Aunt Jean. She had made me happier than I had ever been with Mama and Papa, although I never ever blamed Mama for that, and I never would.

# CHAPTER 15

Jazz and I had graduated from Asbury High with honors and were going to Monmouth University in West Long Branch, about twenty minutes north on the county road. We had fantasized about going much further away to more exotic sounding places, like Arizona State in Tempe or the University of Texas in El Paso but, when it came right down to it, we couldn't bear to be that far away from home.

My relationship with Scott had survived, which was unusual in an environment where temptation was always present, but it would take a huge commitment for us to stay together after we graduated. Scott had always been interested in engineering and had been accepted at Golden Gate University in San Francisco, clear across the country, directly west, but almost three thousand miles away. There was never any question about my moving to California, I had to be near Mama.

As for Jazz, her relationship with Damon had come to a rather bitter end almost six months earlier when she discovered he had been two timing her with Maya Jeeri, a stunning looking girl who, like Damon, was of Indian descent. It took Jazz about two months to get over the break up while Scott and I did our best to bolster her confidence re-assuring her, over and over again, that she was just as beautiful as Maya. After that she dated casually but seeing Damon every day was still painful. I was glad when he decided to take a year off and take a backpacking trip through Asia, leaving not only Jazz behind but also his latest conquest, the lovely Maya.

We decided to stay on campus during the week, even though we were so close to home. Several of our classmates from high school had transferred to Monmouth, so we soon settled into a comfortable routine. I majored in English, while Jazz majored in physics, although she still had her heart set on entering the world of fashion. I often teased her that she could be the next Einstein, but she would just laugh it off and say, she'd rather be the next Coco Chanel.

Scott and I talked on the phone at least once a week. Once or twice a year, usually at Thanksgiving and for part of the summer, he would come home to visit with his mother and Kip. During these times we saw a lot of each other and occasionally talked about having a future together. One year, at Easter, I flew out to San Francisco to spend a week with him and it was a magical time for us. We stayed in a first class hotel and visited all the tourist spots that I had only ever read about, or seen on television. We even took a drive up the coast and dined in quaint little restaurants, where they served delicious seafood that I had never ever seen on the Jersey shore. I remember that, towards the end of the week, I started to fantasize about moving to California but nothing could stop that small voice in my head that kept repeating, 'You can't leave Mama.'

When I got home I was a bit depressed but it was actually Mama who lifted my spirits. While Uncle Frank, Aunt Jean, and Jazz seemed enthused when I recounted my whole trip to them, it was Mama who wanted to hear every detail. I know she was living vicariously through me but, at the same time, I was reliving my own experience though her.

By the time I was nineteen, I hadn't seen Lexie for almost two years. We had talked on the phone occasionally but she was almost a stranger to me. Aunt Jean had given up trying to persuade Gran to let her stay with us and there was no question about me visiting Gran. She wanted nothing to do with me. Uncle Frank told me that Mama had a right to see Lexie, but Gran had poisoned her mind against us and, at the same time, put Papa on a pedestal. Mama decided that it was better to wait until Lexie was more mature and then maybe, just maybe, if she wanted to know more about what really happened, she might change her thinking.

While at Monmouth, I got a part-time job at the local paper, the Asbury Park Press. I was grateful for the generosity of Uncle Frank and Aunt Jean for giving me such a wonderful home and I was aware that the small government subsidy they received was a pittance, now that they were providing me with a college education. I insisted that they were to no longer give me another cent of allowance. I intended to earn a few dollars myself. At first, I believe they felt a little rejected by my offer, but when I explained to them that I needed to start looking towards the future and begin to do something constructive, they seemed more at peace with it. I only worked a few hours a week, mostly doing filing and odd jobs but it was enough to get me by. Jazz also got a job in a lady's dress shop, every Saturday, and she was in her element. It was only a few weeks before she was promoted from stock clerk to sales assistant and she loved it. One way or another, she was determined to break into the world of high fashion.

I wasn't doing too badly either. Some of the staff at the paper commented on my enthusiasm and my keen interest in what everyone else was working on. I would sometimes hover over the reporters while they typed up their stories and I know one or two of them found it rather disconcerting, but Jake Gardner enjoyed my fascination for what he was doing and even encouraged me to pursue my love of writing. Jake had been with the paper for over thirty years and worked mostly on human-interest stories. This suited him because he looked like everyone's favorite grandfather and people trusted him. It wasn't difficult for him to get people to open up to him and the public responded to his reports by sending him stacks of letters every day, commenting on his insightfulness and empathy for the common folk. He would often let me read over what he had written, even before approval by the editor and once, when I tentatively made a suggestion to change a sentence, rather than be insulted, he did as I suggested and thanked me. After a couple of years at the paper, I sensed, that with Jake's help, I might be able to get a full time job there and I could hardly wait to leave college but I didn't want to disappoint Uncle Frank and Aunt Jean and just drop out. I was still in a relationship with Scott and wondering if we might have a future together. I know he had fallen in love with San Francisco and would most likely want to stay in the area once he finished his education. I had no idea what I would do if he asked me to join him there permanently, especially now when I had two reasons not to leave Asbury Park. I might have a possible jump-start to my career at the paper and being away from Mama was not really an option.

About six months before graduation, I got a letter from Scott that resolved any issue I had about our future. He had met a girl on campus and they had been seeing each other for some time. He claimed he hadn't told me about it before because he didn't think it would become serious but now he realized he was truly in love and they had decided to move in together. Her name was Hilary, a native of California, and he was certain I would like her a lot because she had a sweet nature like me. He apologized if this news caused me any pain and hoped we would always remain friends. Finally, he let me know that he would be bringing Hilary home to meet his mother and Kip, as soon as school was out, and hoped to see me then.

I must have read that letter three times and at first I was angry and bitter, but the more I thought about it the more relieved I was that a decision had been made for me. By the time I showed the letter to Jazz that evening, I had already come to terms with it and she was surprised that I wasn't bawling my eyes out.

# CHAPTER 16

On May 20th, 1981 we graduated from Monmouth University and Lawrence Kudlow, host of CNBC's The Kudlow Report gave the commencement address. It was a wonderful time and my whole foster family was there including Billy, who was now thirteen years old. We were all on a high that day but our elation came to a screaming halt, two days later, when our beloved Sheba died. We knew she was nearing the end of her life, but we were all in denial, and when Aunt Jean found her early in the morning she knew immediately that she wasn't just asleep. Ironically, I cried more over the death of Sheba than my own father. In fact, when I think about it, I didn't shed a single tear for him.

Billy was devastated by the loss of Sheba. He kept running all over the house calling her name and it was pitiful to see. Uncle Frank finally decided that the only way to calm Billy down was to get another dog. When he brought a three-month-old puppy from the animal shelter, we hadn't anticipated a new problem; Billy wouldn't leave her side. The puppy was a Scottish Terrier/Poodle mix, with an almost apricot colored curly coat, and after much discussion, we decided to call her Pepper. Fortunately, she didn't seem to mind Billy's constant attention and he soon forgot all about Sheba.

I decided to take a break after college. I was waiting for word from the newspaper about a full-time position and I knew that Jake had put in a good word for me. During the break, I saw Mama every week and now that I was able to visit her without supervision, I learned a lot more about Mama's life with my father before I was born. I never thought of Papa as handsome but Mama claimed, when she first met him, he took her breath away. At the time they met, he was working at his Uncle Sam's garage as a mechanic and she was just out of high school. Mama, like me, had been in foster care but her foster parents couldn't afford to send her to college, so she ended up behind the counter of a bakery in Millville. She had always loved children and dreamed of becoming a pediatrician but, when she realized that could never happen, she settled for marrying Papa and having children of her own.

They had only been married a short time when Mama recognized that Papa had a drinking problem. Many nights, he would roll into their small, two-room rented apartment, after midnight, with liquor on his breath and clothes reeking of perfume. The first time Mama complained and accused him of cheating on her, she felt the back of Papa's hand and from then on the beatings began.

When Mama got pregnant, she was no longer able to work. The bakery didn't want a woman with a huge belly waiting on their customers, so they let her go. Being home all day alone in two small rooms with little to do was intolerable and when Papa didn't even show up for supper one night, Mama just couldn't take it anymore. She was almost four months pregnant on the night that she heard him staggering through the door, in the early hours of a Saturday morning, and she made the mistake of confronting him. He pushed her out of the way, but she couldn't stop ranting at him, while sobbing uncontrollably. Finally, in a rage he turned on her and kicked her savagely in the stomach, not just once, but several times. That was when she ended up in the hospital and lost the baby. She said that Papa was scared, but it didn't stop him from threatening her. He told her that if she opened her mouth, he would never be arrested because he would turn tail out of there and then come back later and finish her off when she least expected it. She had no choice but to claim that she had fallen down some stairs and although the doctor appeared to believe her, the nurse who attended her was suspicious and asked her, over and over again, to repeat her story.

Naturally, Papa played the distraught husband to the hilt and gained the sympathy of family, friends and his workmates. I practically had to pry the story out of Mama; she was reluctant to tell me just how diabolical my father had been.

After the recovery period, Mama got her job back at the bakery and tried to cope with the state of her marriage. She walked on eggshells most of the time, but even a minor slip on her part would result in another beating. She seriously thought about running away but she got pregnant again, with me, and had no source of income. During the pregnancy, she was more careful than ever not to upset Papa and when I was born she hoped we could be a proper family, but it wasn't to be. Papa had no use for another female and blamed Mama for not producing a son. When I cried, he complained. Other than that he paid no attention to me whatsoever. Mama doted on me and tried to keep the peace but the physical abuse continued.

Soon after my birth, Gran gave Papa enough money for the down payment on a house. It was the same house where Papa died and I always loathed that place. Papa was supposed to fix it up but he never did and, over the years, it became run down. Mama did her best to make it cheerful, sewing bright colored curtains and furniture covers, but it didn't help much. Papa had no interest in making a comfortable home for us.

When Lexie was born, things got even worse. Mama had less time to pay attention to Papa and he got more and more demanding. Supper had to be on the table at six o'clock precisely, no matter if he stayed out to the wee hours and often food was wasted. Fresh clothes had to be laid out for him every morning, which meant that Mama was forced to launder his grease stained jeans, shirts and socks on a daily basis. She was a slave to his demands and too frightened to do anything about it. That is until the night she snapped.

The more I learned about my father, the more grateful I was that he was dead and could no longer hurt anyone.

# CHAPTER 17

In between visits to Mama, I did a lot of reading and when Jazz was available, we'd spend time at the beach. One day, I got a phone call from Scott and learned that he was back in town and wanted to see me. When I asked about Hilary, he told me that she couldn't make the trip this time as her mother was in hospital in Sacramento with pneumonia, but she hoped to visit at Christmas.

I met Scott at the coffee shop where we used to hang out when we were dating. I got there first and I was nervous but when he walked through the door, it almost seemed like old times.

I rose from my chair as he approached and without hesitation, he threw his arms around me, "Cassie, it's great to see you," he said and then stood back and held me at arms length.

"Let me get a good look at you." he continued. "You're even prettier than when I left. What have you done to yourself?"

I punched him playfully on the shoulder, "Flatterer, I haven't done anything. I'm a little older and my hair's a little longer but that's about it. "

He beckoned to the waitress and ordered coffee then reached across the table and took my hands in his. "It really is good to see you, Cassie," he sighed. "I was worried that you would never speak to me again."

"Why would you think that?" I asked frowning.

"Well, I wasn't sure if you would answer my letter and when you didn't, I thought you were pretty angry."

"Actually, after the initial shock, I was quite relieved."

Scott looked taken aback, "Relieved? How come?"

"I had visions of you asking me to come and live in California and wasn't sure how I would handle it. Then you made the decision for me."

"But why didn't you write? You know I wanted us to remain friends."

I withdrew my hands and put them in my lap, "I'm not really sure. Maybe I thought your new girlfriend wouldn't appreciate it"

Scott grinned, "Hilary? No way. I told her all about you and she's anxious to meet you. You really will like her, Cassie, I guarantee it."

I couldn't help asking, "Is she pretty?"

Now Scott chuckled, "I think so, but in a different way from you. She's tiny, with short dark hair. I think she calls it an elfin cut. I actually have a photo of her, if you'd like to see it."

I nodded as he pulled his wallet from his jacket and then laid two or three photos on the table. "Here it is," he said, and slid one of the photos across to me.

I stared at a picture of an Audrey Hepburn look-a-like, in an emerald green bikini, lounging in a deck chair and mugging for the camera.

"She's lovely," I said, painfully aware of the green-eyed monster whispering spiteful thoughts in my ear.

I continued to stare at the photo, for a while, until Scott gently took it out of my hand, "I hope you're happy for me, Cassie," he said quietly.

"Of course," I responded even though I was secretly wishing he'd never met this person and that we could pick up where we left off.

"I'm glad. Now, tell me all about yourself. I understand you've applied for a full-time job at the paper. Are you sure that's what you really want?"

I was surprised at the question and felt somewhat defensive, "Yes, it's what I really want, " I replied a little too abruptly, "I love to write and this will give me the opportunity to do so."

"So you plan to stay in Asbury Park, and what about Jazz, what's she up to?"

"Jazz is in New York at the moment visiting with her cousin and looking for a job. She's been taking a fashion design course and she's desperate to get into the business but not having much luck at the moment. I have a feeling she may end up as a sales assistant in one of the big stores, like J. C. Penney or Macy's."

Scott nodded his head slowly and stared at me in a way that made me feel uncomfortable, "I see, well I hope she finds what she's looking for. You know, Cassie, New York is a great town and you might want to consider moving there yourself. You don't want to be stuck here all your life, there's so much more to see in this world."

"I like it here," I snapped, "I've been to New York, Jazz and I went there a few months ago for a weekend. It was exciting and a lot of fun, but it's not for me."

Scott hesitated, "Why, because it's just that much further away from your mother? What's it like being a martyr, Cassie, just waiting for the day your mother comes out of prison?"

I felt the blood rush to my head as I leapt up from the table, "How dare you," I said, aware that my voice was rising, "go back to your new girlfriend and leave me to run my own life," and with that I made a beeline for the door. Scott was immediately on his feet and grabbed my arm, but I shook him off and ran out onto the sidewalk. I don't know whether he tried to follow me or not and I didn't care. Looking back now, I know I reacted impulsively and that he only wanted what was best for me. In my heart, I knew he was right, I was sacrificing my future to be near Mama and hoped I didn't live to regret it.

I saw Scott again, briefly, the following Christmas when he came back into town with Hilary. I happened to be out to dinner with Jazz, who was home for the holidays, when he passed by the window of Marcello's Bistro. I recognized Hilary immediately, even though she was bundled up in a long suede coat with a fur collar and had a woolen hat, pulled down over her ears. There was no mistaking the face I had seen in the photograph and she was laughing as she hung onto Scott's arm and gazed up into his eyes. I no longer felt jealous, I genuinely wanted him to be happy and to move on with my own life.

A month earlier I had secured the position of Jake's assistant at the paper, and he had taken me on several assignments, even allowing me to contribute to some of the reporting. I was well aware that he was close to retiring and that if I proved myself, I would be able to take over his job.

# CHAPTER 18

It was the summer of the following year that I was called into the editor's office. Lester Graham had always treated me with respect but he had a gruff side to him and I was a little apprehensive about the meeting. His door was always open, so when I knocked gently on the doorframe, he glanced up briefly and ushered me in with a wave of his hand, "Sit down, Cassie, don't stand on ceremony", he said.

He then went back to shuffling papers on his desk while I just sat there staring at him. He wasn't a handsome man but he had an air of sophistication about him. In his early sixties, he still had a full head of dark hair, lightly sprinkled with gray, and a face that put me in mind of Abraham Lincoln. Finally he looked up and smiled, "Well young lady, how are you doing?" he asked, "I hear nothing but good things about you from Jake and I must say I've been quite impressed with your work."

"Thank you, sir," I responded shyly, "Jake has taught me so much and he's been very generous with his time."

Mr. Graham leaned back in his chair and nodded, "Well, I'm sure you're aware that Jake will be retiring in the fall and I think you might be the right person to take over his job. What do you think?"

This was exactly what I had been hoping for and I felt almost dizzy with excitement but I think I managed to appear calm, "I know I can do it, sir," I replied earnestly, "I love working here and I promise I'll make you proud of me if you give me this chance."

"That's what I was hoping to hear, but before Jake leaves I want you out on assignments on your own. You can start off with two or three assignments a week, turn in your reports to Jake and we'll go on from there. If you're as good as I think you are, you'll soon be our new junior reporter and I can guarantee you a substantial raise, but we can discuss that later."

I started to thank him, but I was a bit flustered and stumbling over my words, when he cut me off. "There's one more issue that we need to discuss and it's a little sensitive," he said lowering his gaze.

My heart started to beat a little faster, I couldn't imagine what the issue could be. My brain went into overdrive trying to remember if I had said, or done, something inappropriate but then he looked up and said, "It concerns your name, Cassie."

"My name, sir?" I stuttered, "What's wrong with my name?"'"

"Nothing's wrong with it, but there are a lot of folks out there who'll recognize the name Cassie Taylor, and it could put you in a difficult position. Obviously, I'm one of those folks, Cassie, I knew who you were the moment I saw your application. People have long-term memories around here and your mother's case was all over the papers, including ours, as well as on the TV news. I'm going to have to insist that you change your name if you're going to take the job I've just offered you."

My first reaction was one of indignation but I wanted the job so badly that I knew I had no alternative but to agree, "And what do you suggest I change it to?" I asked with an edge to my voice.

"Please don't be offended," Mr. Graham replied, "this is for your benefit as well as the paper's. What about taking the name of your foster parents, Marsh isn't it?"

"Well, you've certainly done your homework," I remarked insolently.

"Look, Cassie, no one means to make your life more difficult. I know you spend most of your weekends visiting your mother and you have my word that I'll never allow your job here to interfere with the time you need to spend with her, but this name issue needs to be resolved. Perhaps you'd like to take some time to think about it?"

I sat there for a moment and finally managed to speak up, "I just want you to know that I'm proud of my name, not because it was my father's, nothing of his means anything to me. It's still my mother's name, Ella Taylor. That's who she is and I'm her daughter. I don't care what anybody read or heard about the case, all I know is, my father deserved what he got and my mother shouldn't have to spend a single day in prison. I can't take the Marsh's name because that might hurt Mama, even though she thinks the world of Aunt Jean and will be forever grateful for all that the Marshs' have done for me. However, if you insist, then so be it, but I want to keep on using Cassandra because that's who I am."

Mr. Graham had been sitting quietly listening to me and when I finished, he got up and started pacing back and forth. I was wondering what he was thinking when he suddenly stopped and perched on the corner of his desk, "I appreciate everything you just told me, Cassie, and I understand why you feel the way you do, so let's keep Cassandra and come up with a new last name, something short and easy to remember. How about Cook, or Grey, or even King?"

I repeated all three names and then nodded, "I like them all," I said, " but I think I like the sound of Cassandra King. It will look really good in print."

Mr. Graham chuckled, "That's my girl. Well, that's settled and it wasn't so bad was it?"

And so I became Cassandra King and two days later I was on my first solo assignment, accompanied by Jamie Bruce, one of the best photographers employed by the paper. I was glad they had chosen him to go with me that day. He was just a couple of years older than me but already married with a two-year old son. He was a little overweight with a boyish face, always in an upbeat mood, and talked constantly about his wife, Gloria, and their little one, Justin, but he was dedicated to his job and wanted me to know, right from the outset, that he was there to support me.

My first assignment was to interview a one hundred and two-year-old woman in a senior's home just a few miles outside of Asbury

Park. Rosemary Wallace had outlived her four husbands and nine children, the last one having died a few months earlier. She was a tiny lady but with a round face and the brightest blue eyes framed by large wire-rimmed spectacles. Despite her age, she was amazingly well groomed without a single white hair out of place, a touch of rouge on her cheeks, and wearing a deep rose dress with a triple row of pearls. Her longevity was remarkable in itself, but the story of her life could have filled several books. One would have thought that bringing up nine children would have been enough but Rosemary had worked tirelessly for abused women until her ninety-ninth birthday and had even turned her former home into a safe house, which she named Rosemary's Retreat. No longer in good health, she had been forced to leave the running of the house to three of her grandchildren but she continued to donate funds from the substantial amount of life insurance left to her on the death of her third husband, and demanded daily reports about the women seeking sanctuary.

Because of my mother's situation, I was particularly interested in Rosemary's story. I found her to be exceptionally bright, speaking without hesitation and anxious to get the word out about the plight of abused women. When I asked her what prompted her to become interested in this cause, I saw her eyes tear up as she responded, "My youngest daughter, Helena, was married to a monster. He beat her so badly that he broke her back and she spent the rest of her life in a wheelchair. That bastard rotted in jail for two years and then he died a miserable death from colon cancer. I thanked the Lord when I heard that because he deserved every bit of pain and suffering and I hope he burned in hell."

I was shocked at the vehemence in Rosemary's voice but I completely understood how she felt and I wanted so badly to confide in her, but with Jamie there, it was impossible.

When I returned to the newsroom, I spent hours writing and rewriting a brief summary of Rosemary's life, until I was finally satisfied and turned it over to Jake. Later, Mr. Graham called me into his office and complimented me on my report. I could hardly wait for the next day to see the story in print, along with Jamie's photo of the remarkable Rosemary Wallace.

I went back to see Rosemary eight or nine times within the next year. She seemed to enjoy my visits and I would always take her a little gift of chocolate kisses, turtles or shortbread. It was on my second visit that I told her who I really was and why I had changed my name. It didn't surprise me to learn that she remembered nearly every detail of my mother's case and had prayed for her acquittal. She had seen too many other women fall prey to the violence of their husbands and knew in her heart that Mama had been telling the truth.

Rosemary died peacefully, in her sleep, fourteen months after I first interviewed her and I felt a profound sense of loss. I hadn't told Aunt Jean or Uncle Frank about our conversations. It was enough that they had to deal with my frequent visits to Mama, without listening to me raking up the past. So it was Mama herself who comforted me in my grief. I really missed Rosemary, she was such a wise old lady and I had cherished her friendship.

Over three hundred people attended the funeral at Trinity Church and I finally got to meet Rosemary's grandchildren. I needn't have worried about the future of the safe house. It had been well provided for in Rosemary's will and would continue to be a haven for abused women. I only wish Mama had had the courage to leave Papa and find refuge somewhere.

# CHAPTER 19

That fall, we had a retirement party for Jake and I felt like I was losing a good friend. I think it was a bittersweet time for him. He had worked for so long at the paper and took great pride in his job, but he also wanted to spend more time with his wife Betsy, who was in ill health. Thankfully, he liked to golf so at least he had a hobby and we all chipped in and bought him the finest set of golf clubs we could find.

I think I got a little tipsy that afternoon and eventually found myself in the passenger seat of a car belonging to one of the other reporters. Tim Stuart, was in his early thirties, single and attractive and had recently been hired to report on local sports events, but I had made it a rule not to date any of my colleagues so I surprised myself by agreeing to have dinner with him. We drove to a quaint Italian restaurant near the boardwalk and after settling down with two heaping plates of pasta, he began to tell me about himself. Tim had been born in Australia but moved with his parents and two younger sisters to New Hampshire, when he was eleven. Two years later, his mother died of leukemia and they moved in with an aunt and uncle. His father suffered a severe depression after his wife's death, and then feeling that he had to get away, he took a job in a mining camp in Alaska. He sent money back on a regular basis to support the children and still managed to save enough to buy a house in Portland, Maine just five years later. At the University of Maine,

Tim studied journalism and then landed a job with the Bangor Daily News. He worked there for several years and then decided he needed a change. He had a friend who lived in Belmar, New Jersey and the area appealed to him, so he applied for a job at the Asbury Park Press and was excited to get a call from Lester Graham just two days later offering him the position.

"How do you like it here, so far?" I asked.

"I love it," he replied with enthusiasm, "I caught the tail end of the summer so I managed to spend a lot of time at the beach. I've always enjoyed being near water, in fact I'm hoping to buy a small cabin cruiser next Spring."

I knew he was single but couldn't help asking. "Have you ever been married?"

He shook his head and toyed with the ravioli on his plate, "No, I haven't and I've never even come close. I guess I've never met the right girl."

"You're not gay, are you?" I blurted out and then blushed with embarrassment.

Tim roared with laughter, "No, I'm not gay, why do I look gay?"

I took a good look at his masculine jaw and unruly mop of light brown hair, "Hardly," I replied, "but one can never tell these days."

"Well, I'm not," he insisted, "Anyway, enough about me, let's talk about you. I don't know anything about you except that you just took over Jake's job and there's a buzz that Lester thinks you're pretty special."

I was hoping the conversation wouldn't get around to me but I soon lapsed back into my old tale of belonging to the Marshs' with no reference to my childhood and Mama.

"So you have a brother with Down's Syndrome." Tim commented. "That must be tough. My sister Julie is autistic and now she's in a special needs home. Dad couldn't deal with it any more, it was just too much to handle. He got married again about five years ago and my stepmother suggested that they bring her back to live with them but she had no idea what she would be letting herself in for. Naturally, Dad declined."

"I'm so sorry," I responded, "but Down's Syndrome is a little different, Billy actually functions very well. He's in his mid teens now, still lives at home and even has a girlfriend. He's got so much heart and I just love him. Most of the time he's a really happy soul and every time I see him he just makes me smile."

"And you? Do you still live at home, Cassie?"

"Yes," I replied sheepishly, "it's really convenient and I get along really well with my parents."

If the truth be known, Jazz had pressured me, time and time again, to move to New York but it would mean quitting my job or commuting for at least three hours each day. She had taken a position as a sales assistant at Bergdorf Goodman's and was living in a loft in Greenwich Village with three other girls. She came back home fairly often and I had visited her twice in the past year. I could understand her love affair with a city that had so much vitality and was the center of theatre, arts and, of course, shopping. I had considered the move carefully but I just couldn't do it.

Tim and I spent almost two hours over dinner and then he suggested that he drive me home. I had no objection, as he was well aware that I didn't live alone. We sat in the car outside the house for at least another ten minutes just idly chatting and then he leaned over, kissed me lightly on the cheek, and said, "We'll have to do this again, sometime soon, Cassie."

I went out with Tim occasionally after that although it was no great love affair. I did end up in his bed on our fourth date and found him to be a sweet and gentle lover, but the spark just wasn't there. I suppose I enjoyed his company because he didn't put any pressure on me. When I begged off of a date because, unknown to him, I was visiting Mama, he accepted it without question.

I'm not sure if anyone at the paper was aware of our relationship and I deliberately avoided making friends with any of the females on staff in order to discourage any interest in my personal life. Sometimes I felt rather lonely and just wanted to run away and then I would throw myself into my work, often putting in eleven or twelve hour days. Aunt Jean was concerned about me and tried to persuade me to get out more, make more friends and have some fun but my heart just wasn't in it. When I wasn't working, I seemed to be thinking about Mama.

The following Spring, Tim bought the cabin cruiser he had dreamed about and couldn't wait to take it out and cruise along the coast line. I loved being out on deck with the wind in my hair and the sense of freedom it gave me. We even made love in the tiny cabin and giggled when the rocking of the boat created some rather innovative positions. There was no doubt that we enjoyed each other's company but I don't think Tim was ready for any kind of commitment to me, or anyone else, and that suited me just fine.

# CHAPTER 20

I was twenty-three when my life took a dramatic turn and maybe it had something to do with Jazz's influence on me, although I prefer to think it had nothing to do with my looks.

Jazz had asked me to come to New York for a weekend visit as she had something special to tell me. I arrived believing that she had found the man of her dreams and was getting married but I was way off base. I took the bus into the city and she met me at the terminal bubbling with excitement, but wanted to keep me in suspense for a while. I couldn't help thinking how fabulous she looked. She had long ago dispensed with her braids and now wore her hair cascading in soft curls well below her shoulders. Her eyes were still her most striking feature and she knew how to play them up to their best advantage. I felt a little like a country cousin beside her.

We took a taxi over to the Village but just as we were getting close to our destination, she asked the driver to stop for a moment. When he pulled up at the curb, she asked me to look out of the window and look up. I had no idea what to expect but, when I did as she suggested, I gasped in surprise. Looming above a six story building was a giant billboard advertising a new brand of lipstick called Smooze, and there was Jazz looking like a million dollars in a leopard skin wrap-around dress and six inch gold stilettos.

"How, what, when?" I stuttered excitedly, while the driver looking back over his shoulder exclaimed in a heavy Brooklyn accent, "Pretty hot Miss, if I do say so myself."

Jazz grinned and patted my hand, "Isn't it great? One of the executives from the ad agency for Trend Cosmetics happened to be in Bergdorf's and noticed me. He thought I'd be perfect for their campaign, tested me out and then offered me the job."

"But why on earth didn't you tell me this was going on?"

"I just wanted to surprise you and didn't really want to say a word about it until it was a done deal. You know, I always wanted to be a designer and I never dreamed in a million years that I could be a model like Mom. I've already been asked to do some runway modeling and I get to keep my name and everything. This has opened the door to a better life, Cassie, and I want you to be a part of it."

"What do you mean?" I asked, frowning.

"I want to get a really nice place off of Central Park and I want you to come and share it with me. "

"Whoa." I said, "aren't you jumping the gun here, Jazz? That could be very expensive and are you sure you'll be able to afford it?

Jazz gave a curt nod towards the driver and said, "Let's go somewhere and get some lunch and then we can talk some more about it."

We stopped a short distance from the Village at a deli, where there were three or four tables and the best corned-beef-on-rye for blocks. I couldn't blame Jazz for being excited about her good fortune, but I tried to convince her not to make any rash moves and was relieved when she finally stopped pressuring me, admitting it could all be a flash in the pan.

We had an especially great weekend, visiting the Natural History Museum, The Guggenheim, the theatre and eating out on Saturday night at a fabulous French restaurant. It was Sunday, just before I was about to leave, that Jazz decided to open up to me about something that had been on her mind for some time. We were alone in the loft, having a last cup of coffee, when she looked across the table at me and said, "I've been meaning to tell you this for a long time, Cassie, but I just know you aren't going to like it."

"Well, that's a good way to start a conversation," I responded sarcastically.

Jazz sighed, "You know, I think you're lovely, you've got great skin and really pretty eyes."

"Do I hear a 'but' coming?" I interrupted, feeling more than a little apprehensive.

Jazz sighed again, "I just know you would look even lovelier, if you had you're nose fixed, Cassie."

"And what's wrong with my nose?" I demanded, knowing full well what was wrong with it.

"Well, it would look fine on somebody else," Jazz replied with a giggle.

I sat in silence gathering my thoughts, "Thank you for that vote of confidence, I will certainly consider it." I blurted out.

"Don't be mad, Cassie." Jazz pleaded.

"I'm not," I answered abruptly as I jumped up from the table, "now let's get going or I'll miss my bus."

Three weeks later, I made an appointment with a plastic surgeon and asked Mr. Graham for some time off. Figuring, I would look somewhat different after the operation, I thought it was best to tell him the reason for my request. He was actually very supportive, although he tried to assure me that I was already very attractive.

Aunt Jean and Uncle Frank were not so supportive. They couldn't understand why I thought there was a problem, while Billy was intrigued by the fact that I was getting a new nose and jokingly asked, "Will it be like Pinocchio's?"

I wiped out nearly all my savings paying for the surgery, but a few weeks later, I knew it had been worth it. The pain had been pretty horrendous and the recovery period seemed endless, but once all the swelling and bruising disappeared, I was left with a perfectly straight, refined nose that made a tremendous difference to my appearance. I must have looked at myself, in the mirror, a dozen times a day until everyone at home started singing, "Isn't she lovely!" every time they caught me at it.

I had dozens of compliments at the paper, especially from Tim who confided to me privately that I looked fabulous. It was then that I decided to go all out and make myself over. I lightened my hair to ash blonde, had it styled in soft, shoulder length waves, piled on the make-up and bought a whole new wardrobe, consisting of mainly formfitting clothes that showed off my figure. My figure was actually one of my best attributes. Tall, and very slim, but with curves in all the right places, I had never really shown my body off to its best advantage. Aunt Jean had often remarked on my clothes sense and tried to persuade me to discard my man-tailored shirts and sloppy sweaters, but I had never listened. Now I was getting wolf whistles when I walked down the street and I must admit, I loved every minute of it.

Jazz visited me right after my transformation and was blown away when she saw me but it was Mama, who hardly recognized me when I visited her, completely made over from head to toe. I had mixed emotions about going all out to impress her. I didn't want her to think that I was no longer her Cassie, but at the same time, I wanted her to be proud of me. When I walked into that dingy room, as I had many times before, I was wearing a pencil slim emerald skirt with a lighter green silk blouse and tan sandals with five-inch heels. I sensed several pairs of eyes staring at me, but Mama just glanced at me and then looked away. I stopped in my tracks for a moment, then suddenly she looked back and her eyes widened in shock. She started to rise as I came towards her and then she smiled, "Oh, my goodness," she said, "you're beautiful, Cassie. Here, sit down and let me get a good look at you."

I wanted to hug her so badly, just to let her know that I hadn't changed but any form of touching was forbidden, so I slipped into the chair opposite her as she slowly sat down again.

"What do you really think, Mama?" I whispered.

"I think you look like a movie star," she replied, "I didn't know what to expect but it's wonderful. Your hair reminds me of Lexie and your new nose is perfect. Are you happy with it, Cassie?"

"Yes, I really do like it. Honestly Mama, when I look in the mirror, I can hardly believe it's me. I have to be honest, I always felt I got short changed in the looks department. You were always so lovely, Mama and you still are and Lexie was such a pretty child."

Mama shook her head, "Looks aren't everything, Cassie. Mine didn't get me anywhere, that's for sure and I'm not feeling too attractive these days. As for your sister, I can't help wondering what she looks like now, I wish you would go and see her."

"I tried to see her, three or four times," I responded defensively, " but Gran didn't want to talk to me other than to tell me that Lexie wanted nothing to do with us. She's poisoned her mind against us, Mama."

"But she's not a child anymore," Mama insisted, "she's eighteen and able to think for herself. Perhaps if you went to her school and tried to talk to her alone, you could tell her how much we miss her. I heard she was attending Monmouth, so you know your way around the campus."

I felt cornered because I knew just how easy it would be for me to locate Lexie, but I wanted to keep Mama all to myself. I was the one who had stood by her for the past fourteen years and I didn't want to share her with anyone, even my own sister.

"Okay, Mama," I said half heartedly, "I'll see what I can do."


I found several excuses, in my own mind, why I didn't have time to go looking for Lexie and then a week later, Mr. Graham sent me on an assignment in Trenton. I was to attend a book signing and then interview the author, Jeremy Kent, who's current novel 'The Crimson Cord' was on the New York Times bestseller list. That was the day my life began its dramatic turn.

There were hundreds of people packing the bookstore waiting their turn to talk to Jeremy and get him to autograph his book. I stood over to one side, while Jamie snapped some photos, and studied the man sitting behind the table, piled high with copies of several of his earlier books. I had already done some research and learned that he was in his late thirties, divorced from a pretty socialite, and had no children. He lived in New York City, had a summer home in the Hamptons, and a private yacht named Dream Catcher.

The photos I had seen of him didn't do him justice. He had a thick head of almost coal black hair, deep brown eyes, a square masculine jaw and his skin was almost the color of copper. It was obvious that he spent a good deal of time outdoors. Dressed casually, in a beige cashmere jacket and caramel open-necked shirt, he still looked the picture of sophistication and I could see many of the women were practically gushing as they sidled up to the table.

It was almost two hours later, when I finally got to sit down with Jeremy for the interview. I expected him to be exhausted but when we were introduced he shook my hand with enthusiasm and, looking straight into my eyes, said, "Cassandra King, how delightful. Thank you for being so patient. I couldn't help noticing you and I've been looking forward to meeting you."

I don't know how I keep my composure after that but somehow I managed to get through the next hour.

# CHAPTER 21

It was close to six o'clock when we finished the interview and I turned off my recorder. I started to get up from my chair, when suddenly Jeremy was there helping me to my feet, "You must be tired," he said brushing a stray hair away from the side of my face.

I was a little startled by such an intimate gesture, "No, I'm just fine." I replied, "Thank you so much Mr. Kent. You've been very generous with your time."

Jeremy frowned, "Well, aren't we being formal, please call me Jeremy and as a matter of fact I have the evening free, so why don't you have dinner with me?"

The invitation was so sudden that I was momentarily flustered, "I have to get back to Asbury Park," I stuttered, "Jamie's driving me, and I need to get my report ready for the morning edition."

"I know exactly where Asbury Park is, I can take you home right after dinner and that will leave you plenty of time for your report."

I glanced over at Jamie, who was gathering up his camera equipment, "I'm not sure, I really don't think it's a good idea."

Jeremy took my arm, "It's a perfect idea, how can you possibly refuse? I know a wonderful restaurant, right here in Trenton that serves the best filet mignon you've ever eaten and I promise I won't keep you up past your bedtime."

I realized he was trying to intimidate me into joining him and I reluctantly agreed, "All right, I'll have dinner with you but I need to talk to Jamie."

I gently removed Jeremy's hand from my arm and left him standing there while I approached Jamie and led him to the far side of the room. I wasn't surprised when he tried to persuade me to leave with him, right there and then. He had always been very protective of me and I appreciated his concern, but I was a big girl and capable of making my own decisions. I called out to Jeremy that I would be back and walked Jamie out to the parking lot. After five more minutes, of what amounted to frustration for both of us, he got into his car with the parting words, "I'm calling your house at midnight and if you're not home, I'm calling the cops." I grinned and stuck out my tongue as he drove away.

Jeremy was right about the steak, it was heavenly and after three glasses of wine, I couldn't face dessert even though Jeremy insisted that the crème brulee was to die for. During the meal we got into a great discussion about books, movies and the theater. Jeremy, like me, enjoyed the classics and it didn't take long for me to realize that he was a man with many interests and a superior knowledge of the arts. He had traveled extensively, visiting every continent, with the exception of Australia, and could speak three languages fluently.

It wasn't until we were in his car, a sleek midnight blue Jaguar, on our way back to Asbury Park that he first mentioned his family. He had been born in Portland, Oregon and had one older brother, Ethan, who was married with three grown children. His father had dealt in antiques and once owned an upscale store in an affluent area of Portland, then two years ago he had sold the business and moved with Jeremy's mother to Laguna Beach.

Jeremy had always loved to express himself with his writing and attended Portland State University before working as a copywriter for an advertising agency. He started on his first novel, "Dreaming" when he was just twenty-three but was discouraged when his manuscript was rejected by several publishing houses. A year later he began writing his second novel, "Honor Roll" and decided to hire an agent to try and advance his career as an author. His determination paid off and, since then, he had turned out a book each year, becoming a well-known author of mystery novels by the time he was thirty-two. His success had bought him enormous rewards and he was living the lifestyle he had always dreamed of. His apartment, on the top floor of a high rise in Manhattan, overlooked Central Park and he was particularly proud of his Hampton House, where he spent most of the summer months. There was so much more I wanted to know about Jeremy, but when I asked him about his marriage he got really quiet. "I really don't want to talk about that," he said.

I was disappointed but didn't want to upset him so I gently touched his arm and whispered, "I'm sorry, I didn't mean to pry."

He looked down at my hand and then glanced over at me, "You haven't told me anything about your family, Cassie. Where were you born? Do you have any brothers or sisters?"

By now I had my story down pat and told Jeremy the same tale I told Tim when we first started dating. It had become almost second nature for me to fabricate the details of my life. I had almost come to believe it myself but there was always a part of me that felt guilty for denying Mama's very existence.

"You must get along with your family very well to still be living at home," Jeremy remarked when I had finished, "You seem like a very bright and articulate woman, not to mention beautiful. I'm surprised that you haven't made a move to New York, or somewhere with a lot more opportunities."

"I like Asbury Park." I snapped back, "And, yes, I love my family. As for opportunity, I'm doing what I always wanted to do."

Now it was Jeremy's turn to gently touch my arm, "Hold on there, Cassie, no need to get defensive."

I lowered my head because I could feel the tears starting to form, "Sorry, it's just that I get a little tired of other people telling me what I should be doing when I am quite happy the way I am."

Jeremy pulled over onto the shoulder of the road and then tipped my chin up so that he could see my face, " You don't look too happy," he said. "Is there something you're not telling me?"

I shook my head, "No nothing, I'm just tired and I'd like to go home now."

"Of course, but if you want to talk, I'm a good listener and I guarantee I can distract you from all of your problems."

I couldn't help smiling, "And what does that mean?"

"Well, we could fly off to Quebec City for a fabulous dinner at a quaint little French restaurant, or we could sail down to Atlantic City and gamble all night. I could think of a number of distractions, Cassie."

I was still laughing as he started up the engine and drove back onto the highway and when we reached my house, I didn't want to say goodnight. I was hoping that Jeremy would kiss me and I wasn't disappointed, in fact nobody had ever made me feel the way he did that night when he took me in his arms. He took my telephone number and promised to call as soon as his book tour was over in two weeks, but that seemed like an eternity. I stayed awake that night going over every detail of the last few hours I had spent with Jeremy and prayed that I would hear from him again.

In the morning, at the breakfast table, Uncle Frank remarked that I seemed to be in a really upbeat mood, "I gather your interview with Jeremy Kent went well," he said.

I had trouble looking him in the eyes, "Yes, it did," I replied, "he's an interesting man."

Aunt Jean looked sideways at me, "Any man that drives a car like that would be interesting."

Billy wandered into the kitchen at that moment, with Pepper at his heels. He looked really dapper in a smart pair of gray slacks and button down shirt, "What kind of car, Mom." He asked.

"Looked like some fancy foreign job to me," Aunt Jean shot back, "but it was so dark and I didn't get a good look."

"Okay, okay," I sighed, "so he drove me home and for your information it's a Jaguar."

Billy let out a whoop, "A Jaguar! That cost lots of money, he must be rich."

I proceeded to tell them all about Jeremy but I didn't mention the kiss or the fact that he had asked for my number. I should have known that they would want to know more, "So, I gather you're going to be seeing him again," Uncle Frank said. "Because you seem pretty happy today."

"Yes, I hope to," I answered, "he's not only smart but I think he'd be a lot of fun."

"Oh, Cassie's got a boyfriend, Cassie's got a boyfriend," Billy teased, grinning like a Cheshire cat.

"What about Tim?" Aunt Jean asked, ignoring Billy.

I got up from the table, taking my coffee mug with me, "Look, he may not even call me, so let's not jump the gun."

"Oh, he'll call," said Uncle Frank, "How could he not, after meeting someone like you. You're intelligent and beautiful and you've got a good heart."

I walked over and stood behind his chair and then leaned down and kissed the top of his head, "Thank you Uncle. If Jeremy is anything like you, then he's a keeper."

# CHAPTER 22

I was shocked the very next afternoon, when two dozen red roses arrived on my desk with a note, "Thank you for a wonderful evening, Jeremy."

I was just tucking the note into the pocket of my slacks, when Tim walked into my office, "My, my," he said, "nice flowers. Who's the secret admirer?"

I shrugged, as I answered, "No secret admirer. I interviewed Jeremy Kent yesterday and I guess he appreciated my style."

"I bet he did," Tim retorted, "Is that Jeremy Kent, the author?"

"Yes, have you read any of his books?"

"As a matter of fact I have, he's a good writer."

I've only read his latest novel, but I'm not a great fan of mysteries."

"I bet you like Danielle Steel, or those Harlequin romance novels."

I turned my back on Tim and walked around my desk, "Ha, shows just how much you know about me!"

Tim laughed, "Sorry, Cassie, just trying to rattle your cage. How about dinner tonight?"

I felt guilty as I looked over at him, "Sorry Tim, I'm still a little tired from yesterday. The interview was in Trenton and I didn't get home until late. How about a rain check?"

"Sure," he said as he turned to walk out the door, "let's get together sometime next week."

I watched him go out into the hallway and suddenly felt sad. I sensed in my heart that our relationship was about to end but I didn't want to lose Tim as a friend.

It was almost seven o'clock before I got through editing my interview with Jeremy but I had one more issue to deal with. Jamie had supplied me with five headshots to choose from and I still had to make a decision. I had just laid the photos out on my desk when the phone rang. I reluctantly picked it up, annoyed to be disturbed at that moment until I heard his voice, "Hello, Cassie. It's Jeremy Kent."

My heart started to pound as I shot back, " My aren't we formal."

"Touche," he said, "Just wanted to make sure you received the roses and it gave me a good excuse to call."

I glanced over at the arrangement, looking so beautiful in the glow of my desk lamp, "Yes, I got them and they are lovely. Thank you so much."

"You're very welcome. I was going to call you at home but I realized you only gave me your office number. I didn't expect you to still be there, but I thought I'd take a chance."

"Well, I've been cleaning up the interview from yesterday and now I'm trying to decide which of the headshots to use. Where are you Jeremy?"

"I'm in Princeton. I'm addressing the creative writing class at the university tomorrow. Actually, I'm in my hotel room feeling a little lonely and I wanted to talk to you. I have some spare time before the book tour finishes and I'd like you to come up to New York for the weekend. I can send a car for you."

I immediately thought of Mama. I had planned to visit her on Sunday and I didn't want to let her down. The only time I had ever missed a visit, was when I went to San Francisco to see Scott and the odd weekend when I stayed with Jazz. I didn't know what to do. Jeremy's voice broke into my thoughts, "Cassie, are you there?"

"Sorry, Jeremy" I answered, "I was just trying to remember what it was I had planned for the weekend."

"Well, if you can't remember, it couldn't have been very important. Please say you'll come."

I hesitated again before responding, "Would you mind very much calling me back tomorrow? I can't give you an answer right now."

"All right, but I expect you to say yes. I want to see you, Cassie, and I guarantee you'll have a great weekend."

"Call me tomorrow," I repeated, "Right now, I have to finish up what I'm doing. Forgive me for not being able to chat."

Jeremy sounded a little disappointed as he wished me goodnight and after that, I had trouble concentrating. I kept staring at the photos imagining myself spending a whole weekend with him, and the longer I looked at his face the more I managed to convince myself that Mama would understand.

I lied to Aunt Jean and told her that I was visiting Jazz and I lied to Jeremy when he called back, telling him I had a ride, feeling certain he would have been appalled had he known I was taking the bus and then a taxi from the terminal.

It was a crisp Saturday in early October when I arrived at Jeremy's address on Central Park West. It was obvious that only the most affluent individuals could afford to live there and as I stepped out of the cab, a doorman, immaculately dressed in a gray uniform, came towards me and took my suitcase, "Miss King?" he asked, extending a white gloved hand, "I'll show you to the elevator, Mr. Kent is expecting you."

Following him through the impressive lobby, with its marble floors and grouping of antique furniture, I was relieved that I had chosen my outfit carefully. I was wearing a black wool skirt, crimson silk blouse and short swing style gray jacket, with my favorite knee high black boots. Thanks to Jazz, my new appreciation for clothes had given me a lot more confidence and I really needed it at that moment.

The doorman put my suitcase in the elevator and told me he would inform Jeremy that I was on my way up, and then he pushed a button and the doors closed. It seemed like an eternity before the elevator finally stopped on the thirty-fourth floor and when the doors opened, there was Jeremy, looking even more handsome than I remembered in black slacks and a black polo neck sweater, "Well, hello there beautiful," he said, "you look absolutely stunning."

"Thank you kind sir," I replied batting my eyelashes and curtsying slightly as he picked up my case.

With his free hand, Jeremy took hold of my arm and steered me down a short hallway into a room that almost took my breath away. It was then that I realized the elevator had taken me directly to Jeremy's suite and I stood with my mouth open in astonishment as he said, "Welcome to my humble abode."

The room we were standing in was huge, with wall-to-wall mint green carpet that had to be at least an inch thick. Various sofas and wing chairs, in shades of ivory and caramel, were grouped in different areas of the room, all with their own tables in a dark, heavy wood. Three of the walls were covered in what appeared to be ivory silk, but the focal point was the expanse of windows overlooking Central Park, where the trees were just beginning to turn to various shades of russet or red.

I turned to Jeremy, shaking my head, "What a fabulous room, I'd love to see the rest of the apartment."

"Later," Jeremy replied, "I want you to sit and relax for a bit and right after lunch, I'll show you around. Here, I'll take your coat."

I let him help me off with my jacket and as I turned around, he caught me in his arms and kissed me. It was such a surprise that I started to pull away but he pulled me back and I felt my resistance start to fade. Before I even realized it, my arms were around his neck and I could feel my body responding. Suddenly Jeremy broke away, "Let's eat," he said grabbing my hand. He led me out of the living room into a magnificent dining room. A crystal chandelier was suspended above a gigantic oak table with at least a dozen chairs upholstered in champagne suede and the walls were adorned with dozens of paintings, mostly landscapes. I know my mouth dropped open in astonishment and I was about to speak when Jeremy chuckled and kept pulling me forward, "Don't worry," he announced. "We're not eating in here, this is for formal occasions, not that I entertain too often. It's a bit much for my taste but my decorator insists that it suits my personality."

I made no comment as we exited into a kitchen that was twice the size of Aunt Jean's. All of the cabinets looked like rosewood and the counters a wonderful copper colour, but the central focus was the island with its matching granite top. I was just about to speak when, through an open doorway, a woman appeared. She couldn't have been more than five feet tall, slight of stature with dark skin and jet-black hair drawn into a bun. She was wearing a floral apron and carrying a rather large bowl. When she saw us she smiled, dropping the bowl onto a counter, and scurried forward, "Ah, this must be Miss King," she said, offering her hand.

Jeremy put his arm around the woman's shoulders, "Yes, and Cassie, I would like you to meet Pilar. She's the best cook in New York City and she takes care of the apartment."

Pilar shook her head and leaned towards me, "Don't you listen to him Miss, he makes up stories."

I smiled down at her, "I'm pleased to meet you and I think I've already heard some of those stories."

"Never mind that," Jeremy interjected, "What's for lunch?"

Pilar nodded towards the open doorway, "You go see. It's all laid out for you."

"Come on," Jeremy said, dragging me into another room. I fell in love with it on sight. It looked like a solarium, with the same floor to ceiling windows as the living room but with greenery everywhere, including two towering fiscus trees. Lunch was set on a wicker table right beside the windows and the view was magnificent. "Oh, this is wonderful," I exclaimed gazing out over Central Park, "what a great place to eat."

"I know," Jeremy responded, "this is my favourite place in the apartment especially first thing in the morning. I usually get up early, eat breakfast, and while Pilar makes sure I don't run out of coffee, I just sit here and read the New York Times."

Jeremy pulled out my chair as I went to sit down, "When do you ever have time to write?" I asked.

"When I feel like it," he replied smirking.

"Seriously, you have to have some kind of discipline. I know I have to, writing for the paper."

Jeremy shook his head as he poured me a glass of wine, "It's not the same thing. You have a real tight deadline to meet whereas, in my case, although my publishers try to hold me to a date, I can sometimes be a bit of a rebel. No, Cassie, I have no set regimen for writing, sometimes I don't pick up a pen for days and at other times, I'll write for hours on end. Anyway, enough chatter about me, let's see what we have here," and he lifted the lid off a large platter sitting in the middle of the table.

"Ah, my favourite pizza," he said licking his lips, "it's got the works, including anchovies." He looked over at me frowning, "You do like anchovies, don't you?"

I grinned, "Love them."

Jeremy rubbed his hands together, "I can see we are going to get along. Fabulous, let's dig in."

The pizza, home made by Pilar, was wonderful, as was the Caesar salad. I didn't think I could eat another bite but then Pilar came in with a tray of miniature fruit tarts and freshly ground coffee. I was just about to thank her when I noticed a movement behind her. I was a little puzzled, when suddenly a small orange cat appeared and jumped onto Jeremy's lap. Pilar immediately dropped her tray onto the table and bent to pick up the cat, "You come off now, Teddy, you no sit on Mr. Jeremy."

"It's okay, Pilar, he can stay," Jeremy responded, then looking at me added, "He's a cute little fellow. I found him wandering around one day when I was at my place in the Hamptons. Nobody claimed him, so I brought him back here. Pilar is home all day so she looks after him. I trust you like animals?"

"Yes, I do, we have a dog at home named Pepper but I really miss Sheba, she was my favourite. She was the most gorgeous golden retriever and as gentle as a lamb. Actually it's my sister who's the biggest animal lover."

The minute I mentioned the word 'sister', I felt my stomach drop. I was hoping Jeremy hadn't noticed, but it was too late, "I didn't know you had a sister," he said, "You never mentioned her."

I had to think really fast, "Oh, I think of my best friend Jazz as a sister, we've known each other for so long."

I thought Jeremy looked at me rather suspiciously but then he said, "This is your friend that lives here in New York, right?"

"Yes, she lives in the Village."

"And does she have any pets?"

"Well no, not in the Village, but back home in Asbury Park she has two Siamese cats. They're pretty special and you'd never guess their names."

"Yin & Yang!"

I couldn't help laughing as I felt the tension lifting, "No Opal and Yum Yum."

Jeremy roared, "That's priceless, I'd like to meet this friend of yours. Why don't you call her and see if we can get together for lunch tomorrow?"

As soon as it had disappeared, the tension came flooding back, "Jazz isn't here this weekend," I lied, "she went home to see her folks,"

Somehow, I managed to keep my composure and by the time we'd finished coffee, I was feeling really comfortable. I had no idea what Jeremy had planned for the rest of the day but I was looking forward to spending more time with him. Just seeing how he treated Pilar and knowing that he had given a stray animal a home, gave me an insight as to the kind of person he really was and I wanted to learn even more about him.

An hour later, we were at Battery Park boarding the ferry. I had never been on the ferry before even though Jazz had suggested it once or twice. Soon we were heading for Liberty Park for a tour of the Statue of Liberty and I was excited but wishing the crossing itself would take a little longer. Jeremy and I were hanging over the railing and, although I had my jacket on, I was still shivering. Jeremy had his arm around me trying to keep me warm, "I forgot how cold it could get out here on the water," he said, "we could go inside if you'd like."

I smiled and snuggled closer, "I'm fine," I whispered, "just don't let me go."

"No chance of that," he replied, "too bad that we're almost there, I kind of like holding you like this."

"Well, you'll get another chance on our way back," I teased.

I didn't realize that after our tour of the Statue, Jeremy had another surprise for me. We were taking another ferry to Ellis Island and visiting the Immigration Museum. We spent almost an hour there and Jeremy was a wonderful tour guide. His knowledge of the millions of immigrants who had landed there since the late nineteenth century was impressive and I never got tired of listening to him. It was obvious why he had become a best selling author.

Before our afternoon adventure, Pilar had shown me into the guest room where she had deposited my small suitcase. At the time, I had been rather surprised because I believed that Jeremy had expectations of our sleeping together. I had actually been prepared to go through with it, after all I was no saint, and at that moment I felt a little disappointed. After our adventure, my growing attraction to Jeremy made me realize that there was no way I wanted to spend the night alone.

The guest room had it's own bathroom, all mint green marble, with a huge oval tub. Pilar insisted on running a bath for me and handed me the largest fluffy white towel I had ever seen, "Have a nice soak, Miss," she said, "You will feel better."

I thanked her, then stepped into the tub, sinking down into the steaming water with a sigh. The smell of jasmine permeated the room and I could hear soft music playing. This is what it must be like to be rich, I thought.

# CHAPTER 23

Jeremy had made a dinner reservation at Tavern on the Green and suggested that I took my time getting ready. After soaking in the tub, I took extra care with my hair and make up and slipped into my little black dress with its low-scooped neck and tight three-quarter sleeves. I loved the simplicity of it and it was the perfect backdrop for the silver and peridot pendant that Jazz had given me. When I put on my black sandals, with the five-inch stiletto heels, and twirled around in front of the mirror, I thought I looked pretty good and hoped Jeremy would think so too. I had packed a small beaded purse and with it in hand, I headed out into the hallway, only to feel somewhat lost. I had no idea how to go to get back to the living room then I noticed Teddy creeping along in front of me. I decided to follow him and when he turned into a doorway, I just kept on following. I was shocked to find myself in a massive bedroom, which was obviously Jeremy's. I was just about to turn and leave when Jeremy appeared in an open doorway on the far side of the room, "Well, hello there," he said as he walked towards me smiling.

I was a little flustered, "I'm so sorry, I got lost and then I saw Teddy and followed him. I didn't realize this was your bedroom."

Jeremy took both of my hands in his, "Didn't I tell you that Teddy lures all of my women in here?"

" So that's why you took him in, not to give him a good home but to entice poor unsuspecting women into your lair?"

Jeremy looked me up and down, "Yes, but he never lured anyone as beautiful as you."

I pushed him away playfully, "Flattery isn't going to help you get out of this one."

Jeremy sighed, "I wasn't trying to flatter you, Cassie. You look absolutely gorgeous, I can't wait to show you off tonight."

As we entered the restaurant less than half an hour later, I felt like the luckiest person in the world. Jeremy was the picture of elegance in a black cashmere jacket, gray slacks, black shirt and a muted silver tie. It was almost as though we had deliberately matched our outfits and even with my high heels, he was still a couple of inches taller than me.

It was obvious from the moment we walked through the door that Jeremy was well known to the hostess, and several of the people dining there that night. As we worked our way past the tables, Jeremy was obliged to stop several times to acknowledge friends or acquaintances and to introduce me, but when one old friend of Jeremy's insisted that we join him and his wife at their table, he politely refused. We eventually found ourselves in a secluded corner and that's when I finally took a breath and surveyed my surroundings. It was like being in a magnificent greenhouse, there were so many windows and there were flowers everywhere. Even the tablecloths were floral and there were gilt chairs and crystal chandeliers. "This is so lovely," I remarked, "I always wanted to come here."

"You probably don't know this, but they used to keep sheep here before it was a restaurant" Jeremy said, " Now they just serve them up as lamb chops."

I had to laugh, even though I thought it was a little maudlin, "Well, I'm definitely not ordering lamb tonight."

Just then the waiter appeared at our table and Jeremy ordered a bottle of champagne. "You didn't have to order champagne," I whispered in case anyone close by might hear me.

"I certainly did," Jeremy responded, "this is a special occasion. It's not often I get the chance to take a beautiful lady out on the town."

"Do you really expect me to believe that?"

"Actually, I do," he responded solemnly, "but let's not talk about that now. Why don't we just enjoy our evening and not get too serious."

I felt a little rejected but tried not to show it. I picked up the menu and then put it down again, "Why don't you order for me," I suggested.

We kept the conversation light all through dinner, which consisted of three courses, even though I had insisted beforehand that two was my limit. Jeremy ordered a delicious roast tomato and fennel soup, then an unusual potato crusted halibut with grilled peppers, zucchini and eggplant and for dessert, plum tart with cinnamon ice cream. I told him that I wouldn't be able to get up from my chair for at least another hour and that's when he signalled the waiter to bring coffee along with two glasses of Nocello, a wonderful walnut and hazelnut liqueur.

Jeremy reached across the table and took my hand, "How did you enjoy your meal?" he asked.

I felt so mellow and content that I let out a deep sigh, "It was fabulous, thank you so much. I don't know why Jazz and I have never been here."

"Tell me about Jazz, you said she was like a sister to you."

"Yes, she is, but since she moved here to New York, we don't see each other so much. She always wanted to be a fashion designer and was taking classes, but then she was discovered by a modeling agency and now her picture is all over town. Come to think of it, you've probably seen the billboards, she's promoting Trend cosmetics."

Jeremy grinned, "Well, I don't usually pay much attention to cosmetic ads, but I do notice a pretty girl."

"Then you must have seen her, she's African American and very striking."

"Actually I prefer blondes."

"Was your wife blonde?" I blurted out before I could stop myself.

Jeremy hesitated for a moment and then let go of my hand, "As a matter of fact, she was," he said.

"I'm sorry, I didn't mean to say that, it just came out. Just forget I even mentioned it."

Jeremy leaned towards me across the table, "No, it's okay, you have every right to be curious.  I don't usually like to talk about it because divorce, under any circumstances, is painful.  Courtney's a great girl but she couldn't deal with the way I wanted to live my life.  Her father is CEO of one of the most prestigious financial corporations in New York. She grew up watching her mother cope with the frustration of living with a man dedicated to his work and she thought she could handle a similar situation, should it happen. But she wasn't like her mother, Courtney was more independent, well educated, and used to being the center of attention. Despite her father's absences, she was still daddy's little girl and he spoiled her excessively.  When I met her, I'd just published my first novel and I was feeling pretty pleased with myself.  I had a lot more money to throw around and I did, eating in some of the best restaurants, drinking in some of the best bars and gradually infiltrating myself into the New York social scene.  Courtney was part of that scene and she knew all the right people.  I got on well with her father, I think he saw something of himself in me, not that I was interested in the corporate world, but I was ambitious and determined to make a success of myself.  We were married less than a year after we met and it was a huge society affair.  Even before the wedding I experienced some doubts about our future together.  Courtney's father just couldn't let go. We had talked about living in Manhattan, but about a month before we were married, he presented us with the keys to a house in Mount Vernon. Courtney was thrilled, it was the kind of house she'd always wanted, a place where she could entertain and impress her friends.  It was a generous gift, but it wasn't what I had planned for us.

We went to Europe on our honeymoon, courtesy of Daddy, and when we got back we spent almost three weeks shopping for furniture. At least, Courtney had insisted on furnishing the place herself.  After that, I tried to get back to my writing and Courtney went back to spending a few hours a week, playing at being an advertising executive for her father's company and socializing the rest of the time. There were endless parties at our house and at first I enjoyed them but, after a while, I got tired of seeing the same old crowd. That's when I started making excuses and staying away. Courtney accused me of being a bore and gradually the fights began. When I found out that she was having an affair with an old boyfriend, I knew it was over. No one in her family wanted to face the scandal of a divorce but I wanted out. Her father offered me a great deal of money to keep quiet about the reason for the split. That's the first time he ever saw me lose my temper. I never wanted anything from him before, and I sure wasn't going to accept any bribe from him then. I blame myself for what happened, I should never have married Courtney in the first place. We were two entirely different people and I should have realized that before I asked her to marry me."

I had been listening intently to everything that Jeremy had been telling me, trying to determine his true character, "Do you ever see Courtney now," I asked.

"I've seen her once or twice since the divorce and it was all very civil. I heard she got engaged again a couple of years ago, but it didn't work out. I just hope she finds the right guy, one of these days."

"And what about you? Hasn't there been anyone special in the last few years?"

"Believe it or not, there hasn't been. I've dated quite a bit, but nothing serious. What about you? Any deep dark secrets from your past?"

I immediately thought of Mama, "No." I snapped back, "I don't have any secrets."

Jeremy looked a little puzzled at my reaction, "Oh, oh I must have hit a nerve. Look you don't have to talk about it if it's too painful."

I felt a little ridiculous for imagining, even for a moment, that Jeremy had been referring to Mama, "There was someone a while back," I said thinking of Scott, "I guess you would call him my first love. We went steady for a few years and then he moved to San Francisco to continue his education. I visited him once and he came back home at holiday time but the long distance made it difficult to keep our relationship going. Eventually he met someone else."

"Did you ever consider moving to San Francisco? It's a great place."

I shook my head, "No, not really, I didn't want to leave Asbury Park."

Jeremy leaned back in his chair and looked like he was studying me, "Would you ever leave Asbury Park, under any circumstance?"

I stalled for a moment, not sure how to respond, "Why are you asking me that question?"

"Just curious, that's all. You seem to have quite an attachment for your home town."

I had had a moment to think about my answer, "I suppose I would be willing to move for a good enough reason, but I'd want to be close enough so that I could visit often. My family is important to me."

"How often is often?"

"Every week or every two weeks at the very least."

Jeremy slowly nodded, "I see. I don't think I've ever met anyone as devoted to his or her family as you are. I'd really like to meet your parents, and Billy, of course."

"Yes, well maybe one day you will," I responded rather abruptly as I rose from the table. Then, retrieving my purse, I excused myself and made my way to the powder room. There, I took a number of deep breaths and touched up my lipstick before returning to the table. Jeremy was in the process of taking care of the bill and looked up at me as I approached, "Don't sit down," he said, "they're bringing the car around."

On the way back to the apartment, I tried to keep the conversation light and asked about Pilar. I learned that she had her own separate suite of rooms that adjoined Jeremy's place and when he was out of town, she spent all her time there with Teddy. She was the sister of a housekeeper who had been employed by Jeremy's parents in California, and had moved to New York two years earlier, when Jeremy was looking for a housekeeper of his own. He claimed that he had never regretted it and that Pilar was like a surrogate mother to him.

Pilar was still up when we arrived and immediately ran out into the hallway to take our coats, "You have a nice dinner, Miss?" she asked.

"It was wonderful, thank you Pilar," I replied as I felt Teddy brushing up against my legs. I was just about to scoop him up when Pilar beat me to it.

"You no want hair all over your pretty dress," she said, "I go make coffee now."

I smiled at Jeremy as he took my hand and led me into the living room. He sat me down on one of the huge comfy sofas, put a Frank Sinatra record on the stereo and said, "How about a liqueur?"

After Pilar had served coffee and said goodnight, taking Teddy with her, Jeremy and I sat quietly talking. He wanted to know all about my job at the paper and I was pleased that he showed so much interest in my work. It was after I had thoroughly exhausted the subject, that he leaned across and kissed me gently on the lips and I found my hand creeping up to caress his cheek. When he broke away, he looked at me intently and said, "I'd like to spend the night with you, Cassie."

I just nodded, I didn't know how else to answer, and he took my hand and pulled me up from the sofa. We kissed again, this time with passion, and I could feel him become aroused as his body pressed against my own. I wanted him desperately but I didn't want to rush and just be another one night stand, "I'd like to change out of these clothes," I said meekly.

He looked me in the eyes and said, "I understand, why don't you change and I'll come to your room in fifteen minutes or so."

"Thank you, I'll be waiting," I whispered, touching his cheek again.

I know he was watching me as I walked away and I could feel my heart racing. It took all of my determination to leave him at that moment, but vanity and pride took over. I wanted to look pretty and I wanted the night to be special for both of us.

In my room, I stripped off my clothes, took a quick shower and slipped into a pale apricot lace nightgown. Almost fifteen minutes had passed and I was standing just inside the bathroom, ready to make my entrance, when I heard Jeremy open the door then call out in a sing song voice, "Oh, Cassie, where are you?"

I took one deep breath and then waltzed into the room, hoping I looked like a bride on her wedding night. Jeremy, still in his shirt and slacks, let out a wolf whistle, "Wow, I must be dreaming."

I ran over and threw my arms around his neck and murmured, "Just take me to bed."

He didn't need to be asked twice. I remember him picking me up and carrying me over to the bed and then gently depositing me on top of the comforter. Then he slowly peeled off his own clothes until he was standing naked in front of me and I couldn't take my eyes off him. He had a magnificent body, muscular, with wide shoulders, a broad smooth chest and flat stomach and it didn't take a rocket scientist to see that he was fully aroused. That's when I got a little nervous and suddenly had doubts about myself. Was I pretty enough? Was I experienced enough to satisfy him?

He didn't allow me much time to mull over my fears. He lowered himself onto the bed beside me, slipped the straps of my gown off my shoulders and began kissing my neck. Slowly he continued to work his way down my body, peeling away my gown a few inches at a time. It was a titillating experience and when I finally lay there, completely exposed, he sat back on his haunches and said, "You are a beautiful woman, Cassie."

"And you are a beautiful man," I responded, reaching out and stroking his chest.

I don't know how long, or how may times, we made love. I only know that it was wonderful. At times, gentle and sweet and at others wild and out of control. In the morning, we woke up in each other's arms and I didn't want to ever let go.

# CHAPTER 24

We spent Sunday morning in bed but I was nervous, at first, about what Pilar would think. Jeremy assured me that she wouldn't surface until late afternoon. I learned later that he had slipped a note under her door, to let her know that she could have most of the day off. I assumed she had the good sense to know that he didn't want to be disturbed, and discreetly stayed away.

Hunger finally forced us out of bed and I soon discovered that Jeremy was quite adept in the kitchen. By the time I had showered and dressed in casual navy jeans and a matching cowl necked sweater, he had set the table and prepared a wonderful Swiss cheese omelet with asparagus and home fries, "I didn't know you could cook too," I remarked as I sat down and poured myself a glass of orange juice.

"Ah well, I have lots of hidden talents you don't know about," he quipped. "Stick around and you might just find out what they are."

We bantered back and forth and I was feeling so completely at ease, that I didn't want to face the idea of going home. Then I remembered that I wasn't sure how I was going to get there. We were on our second cup of coffee when Jeremy suddenly asked me how I was getting back to Asbury Park. I avoided his eyes and said, "I'll take the bus back, they leave fairly frequently."

Jeremy looked taken aback, "No way you're taking the bus. I'll take you myself."

I held up my hand defensively, "No, I can't let you do that, it's much too far."

"Nonsense, I want to do it. Anyway, how did you get here yesterday? Didn't you say you had a ride?"

I began to feel pressured again, but managed to appear calm, "Yes, I got a ride from a friend," I lied.

"And isn't this friend driving back some time today?"

I knew I was getting deeper in the hole, but there was no way I could change my story, "Tim drove me. He works at the paper but he's not driving back until Tuesday."

Jeremy looked at me skeptically as I continued, "I really would prefer to take the bus, in fact I insist."

We argued back and forth, but my determination finally won out. I was certain that Jeremy didn't believe me and I couldn't face any more questions. When he drove me to the bus terminal, he held my hand and looked very solemn, "Are you sure this is what you want, Cassie?" he asked in a last desperate attempt to change my mind.

I didn't look at him as I replied, "Yes, it's what I want so let's not fight about it anymore and spoil a wonderful weekend."

Jeremy was silent until he walked me into the terminal, then he put his arms around me, "I'm going to miss you," he said," and I can't wait to see you again. I won't be back here in New York for ten days, so there's no chance of seeing you before then, but I'll call you tomorrow."

I leaned my head on his shoulder and whispered, "I'll miss you too."

As the bus pulled away, I could see Jeremy standing there but I still felt enormously sad, lonely, and full of self-doubt. What if he didn't call me?

When I got home, Aunt Jean greeted me at the door, "Hello dear," she said. "How was your weekend?"

I followed her into the family room and put down my suitcase, "It was very nice thank you. Where is everybody?"

Aunt Jean ignored my question and gestured at me to sit down, "Jazz called," she announced.

I hesitated, knowing I had been caught in a lie, "I'm sorry," I said, sinking down into a chair opposite her. "I don't know why I didn't tell you the truth."

"Well, Jazz didn't even know where you were, so I assume you went to see Jeremy Kent."

"You assume right. I spent the weekend with him but I didn't want to tell anyone in case it all turned out to be a big mistake."

"And was it a mistake?"

I couldn't help smiling at the memory, "No Auntie, it was wonderful. He has this fabulous apartment overlooking Central Park and he took me on a sightseeing tour of the Statue of Liberty and Ellis Island. Then we went to dinner at Tavern on the Green. We had such a great time."

Aunt Jean nodded, "So, I imagine you spent the night with him?"

I felt myself blushing, "Yes, I did. I didn't mean to, it just happened, but I'm not sorry. He's a wonderful man, unlike anyone I've ever met before. I know I've only seen him twice but I feel this connection and I can't wait to see him again."

Aunt Jean believed in coming right to the point, "Did you tell him about your mother, Cassie?"

I lowered my head in shame, "I couldn't, not yet. I don't know if I ever can. He may not want anything to do with me once he finds out about Mama."

"Then he wouldn't be such a wonderful man after all, would he? What your mother did is not your fault, Cassie."

"You don't understand Auntie, he's a famous author. He has to be careful about who he goes out with. He doesn't need any adverse publicity."

"I don't give a fig if he's the King of England," Aunt Jean declared indignantly. "You can't keep lying to him and if he can't handle it, then he's not worth thinking about."

I lay awake that night thinking about what Aunt Jean had told me but I couldn't convince myself to tell Jeremy the truth. I fantasized about him falling hopelessly in love with me, and not being able to give me up when I finally told him about Mama.

The very next morning I approached Mr. Graham about taking Thursday afternoons off. I assured him that I would make up the extra time at night and that he could count on me not to let him down. I explained to him that I wanted to be able to visit Mama during the week so that I could leave my weekends free and, being the great boss that he was, he readily agreed. I didn't tell him that I wanted my weekends free in case Jeremy wanted to see me.

That very next Thursday when I showed up at the jail, Mama was surprised to see me, "Cassie," she said beaming from ear to ear, "I didn't expect you."

Mama had always been the one person I could always pour my heart out to. I knew that she would never judge me, but I had lied to her about going to New York and I had to tell her the truth. We sat down at one of the gray metal tables and I told her all about Jeremy, asking her forgiveness for not confiding in her. She looked around furtively to make sure the guard wasn't watching, then she reached across the table and touched my hand, "It's okay honey," she said. "I understand. He sounds like a lovely man and a famous author too! You'll have to bring me one of his books to read."

I looked at Mama and noticed how tired she looked. Her skin was pale from spending so much time inside and her hair was showing visible strands of gray, "Oh Mama, I love you so much," I said. "Are you feeling all right, you look very tired?"

"I'm fine," she replied, "as long as I know that you're happy. It's not so bad in here, even though Vicky got released last week and I don't have a cellmate at the moment. I get a bit lonely but I don't suppose that will last very long. Now tell me, how are your foster parents and Billy and Jazz."

That was typical of Mama, never focusing on herself but always interested in other people. She was my role model, no matter that she killed my useless excuse for a father, and I yearned for the day when she would be released like Vicky. It had already been almost fifteen years since she had been incarcerated.

# CHAPTER 25

At noon, the very next day, I heard from Jeremy again. I had just arrived back in the newsroom, when Millie, the receptionist, handed me five pink message slips. Two were from Jeremy, telling me he'd keep trying until he managed to contact me. Millie gave me a sly smile, "Who's the secret admirer?" she asked.

"I'll never tell," I replied with a grin, as I waltzed away into my office.

Ten minutes later my phone rang, "Cassandra King, how may I help you?' I said, keeping my fingers crossed.

"Well now, I could think of a number of ways," Jeremy answered," but it might be difficult at this distance."

I couldn't help chuckling, "Hi there, I got your messages. Where are you?"

"I'm still in New York, just about to have lunch with my agent and then I'm off to Buffalo for another book signing."

I lowered my voice to almost a whisper, "I've really been missing you."

"I've been missing you too and I can hardly wait to see you again."

We continued to chat for a few more minutes and then out of the blue Jeremy asked for my home phone number. I didn't want him calling me at home, so I quickly made up a story that we were having a problem with the phone lines, but they should be fixed by the end of the week. I had already considered getting my own phone and I knew it was time. Jeremy appeared to accept my story and promised to call me the next day at noon. Later that afternoon, I arranged with the telephone company to install a phone in my room, but when I told Aunt Jean about it that evening, she questioned my motive, "Is this so that your Mr. Kent doesn't get to talk to any other member of the family?" she asked frowning.

"No," I lied, "it's just that he might call me late at night and I don't want to disturb anyone."

"Are you sure, Cassie, that's the real reason?"

"Yes, of course," I insisted and excused myself to take a bath. I couldn't wait to get away from being questioned. I felt so guilty but I didn't want Jeremy to know the truth, not yet, maybe not ever.

During the next few days Jeremy called three or four times and on Friday I received another huge bouquet of roses. Millie was beside herself with curiosity and Tim was quick to comment when he stepped into my office that afternoon. "Ah, I see you're very popular these days, Cassie, or is the notorious Mr. Kent still showing his gratitude?"

I was instantly on the defensive, "First of all, he's not notorious and also, it's none of your business."

Tim looked a little hurt, "Oops sorry, didn't mean to ruffle any feathers. How about a peace offering, let's have a drink after work."

I shook my head, "Can't tonight. Jazz is coming into town and we're going out to dinner."

Tim started to walk away, "Okay suit yourself, the offer's still open any time you're free."

I half rose from my chair and called after him, "Tim, please don't go."

He turned and took a few paces back, "Look Cassie," he said, "if you've got something serious going with this Jeremy chap, that's fine. There's no reason we can't remain friends."

"I'd like that, Tim," I responded, "No hard feelings?"

"None at all, I just hope it all works out the way you want it to. Enjoy your visit with Jazz and I'll see you on Monday."

I hadn't lied about having dinner with Jazz that night. She had called me unexpectedly on Thursday, announcing that she was coming back to see her Aunt Leoni who was arriving from Kenya on Saturday. Aunt Leoni was her mother's youngest sister and although Jazz had never met her, she had heard a great deal about her.

"You must come over to the house tomorrow," she said, just after we'd settled at a corner table in the Carousel, a popular family restaurant near the boardwalk.

"I'd love to," I answered. I hadn't seen Jazz's parents for a while and I was happy to have something to do, rather than sit at home and pine over Jeremy.

"So what have you been up to?" Jazz asked as she beckoned the waiter over.

"Actually, you're going to be annoyed when I tell you," I said.

Jazz gave me a puzzled look, then waited while we placed our orders, "Okay, why would I be annoyed with you?" she asked as soon as the waiter was out of earshot.

"I was in New York last weekend."

"And you didn't call me. Why on earth not?"

I hesitated and before I could answer Jazz smiled, "Wait a minute, you were with a man, weren't you? It's that guy you interviewed, isn't it? The one who drove you home and sent you the roses, right?"

"Yes," I whispered, "the author, Jeremy Kent."

"Oh my goodness," Jazz exclaimed leaning towards me across the table, "you spent the whole weekend with him, didn't you?"

When I realized that she wasn't annoyed with me, I dropped all my defenses and told her everything. She sat there staring at me intently and when I'd finished she asked, "And how was he in bed?"

I knew I was grinning from ear to ear, when I replied, "Wonderful! Gentle, wild, everything I ever dreamed of."

Jazz clasped her hands together, "Wow! Oh, Cassie, I'm so happy for you and you look absolutely fabulous."

I was wearing one of my favorite dresses, a scarlet jersey wrap, and I know it played up my fair coloring but compared to Jazz I still felt plain and uninteresting. She looked amazing with her jet black hair pulled back in a chignon, wearing a bright green silk blouse, tight leather pants and heavy gold bangles on each wrist. She had become the face of Trend Cosmetics and her career was blossoming, but she was still the same old Jazz, always humble, ever supportive, and I was proud to call her my friend. She even downplayed the fact that she was going on a photo shoot in Paris in mid December and moving into a new apartment soon after that. I know she didn't want to steal my thunder and my excitement over meeting Jeremy, but when I asked her about her own love life, I noticed a gleam in her eye.

"Okay. What's going on Jazz?" I demanded, "tell me all about it."

She sat back, took a sip of her wine and smiled, "There's not much to tell really, but there's this really hot photographer and I think he likes me. We kind of flirted a little and I was hoping he'd ask me out."

"Why don't you ask him out instead?"

Jazz shook her head, "Uh, uh, that's not my style, you should know that, Cassie. He's going on the shoot in Paris and we'll be there for a few days. Maybe I can work my magic spell on him there."

"And what's this hot photographer's name? What does he look like? Are you sure he's not married?"

Jazz laughed, "His name is Antonio, obviously Italian. He's not terribly tall, but he looks a lot like Armand Assante, all smoldering and sexy, and he's not wearing a wedding ring so I assume he's single."

"Well, I'm sure he won't be able to resist you, especially in a romantic setting like Paris."

"We'll see," Jazz sighed, "we'll see."

Earlier that day, Aunt Jean had called to tell me that my new phone had been installed, so when Jeremy called at noon, I was able to give him my number. That evening, after my dinner with Jazz, I excused myself to read a book in my room, anxiously waiting to hear from Jeremy. It was almost eleven o'clock when the phone rang and I heard him say, "How's the most beautiful woman in the whole of New Jersey?"

It was so wonderful to be able to speak to him without worrying about being interrupted and after chatting for almost an hour, I fell asleep almost immediately.

# CHAPTER 26

On Saturday, I visited Jazz's parents and met her Aunt Leoni. She was as striking as Mrs. Maboa but not quite as tall and she had some amazing stories to tell about her life in Kenya, where she worked with disabled children. There was something so maternal about her that even Opal and Yum Yum seemed to sense it and they cuddled up next to her, vying for her attention. It was a wonderful day and I felt, as always, like part of Jazz's family.

The next day, Sunday, it seemed strange to have the whole day to myself as that was the time I usually visited Mama. Thanks to Mr. Graham, I could now visit her on Thursdays. Not sure how to pass the time, I finally decided that I should begin to think about Christmas shopping, even though it was still November. I had always been very organized and sat down at the kitchen table to make a list. Suddenly I felt someone hovering over my shoulder and when I looked around, I saw it was Billy, "Watcha doing, Cassie?" he asked.

I covered the paper I was writing on, "Nothing you can see, Billy," I said.

"Cassie's writing a love letter," he sang out for the whole house to hear.

"Ssh," I whispered, holding my finger up to my lips, "It's not a love letter, it's a list."

"A list? What's it a list of?"

"People."

"What people?"

"Nice people," I couldn't help teasing, "so you're not on it."

His mouth turned down and he lowered his head, "Don't you like me any more, Cassie?" he muttered.

I got up and drew him into my arms, "I love you, Billy. I'm sorry I didn't mean that."

He looked up at me and started to grin, "I love you too," he said.

"Sit down," I said, motioning to a chair, "the truth is, it's a Christmas list. I'm writing down all the people I need to buy presents for."

Billy's eyes opened wide, "Am I on the list, " he asked. "Do I get a present?"

"Of course you get a present, and I'm getting one for Amanda too."

"Amanda loves me," he remarked, putting his hand over his heart, "we're getting married one day."

I looked at this wonderful young man, who saw the whole world through rose-colored glasses and smiled, "How could she not help but love you," I said.


That afternoon, I was no longer in the mood for shopping and decided to take in a movie. They were playing the 1976 remake of 'A Star is Born' at one of the local theatres and being a fan of Barbara Streisand, it was just what I needed to occupy me for an hour or two.

When I arrived home, just before suppertime, I was surprised to find Aunt Jean waiting at the front door.

"Is something wrong, Auntie?" I asked, feeling a little anxious.

"There's someone here to see you," she replied, motioning me to come in.

I looked at her and frowned, "Who is it?" I asked, half afraid and half excited that it might be Jeremy.

"Just go on through," Aunt Jean answered guiding me by my arm into the living room.

I stopped dead in my tracks when I noticed the slight figure with the long blonde hair and extraordinary face standing by the window. Then, I propelled myself forward, with my arms wide open, "Lexie, it's you," I cried.

Lexie looked at me as though I was a stranger but accepted my embrace. Then she pulled back, staring straight at me and said, "You look so different, Cassie. What have you done to yourself?"

I stroked her cheek as I replied, "I had my nose fixed and I colored my hair and now, it's almost the same color as yours. You look wonderful, Lexie. I'm so happy to see you."

I saw the tears start to well up in her beautiful green eyes as she whispered, "Gran died last night."

"Oh, honey," I said taking her by the hand and guiding her to sit beside me on the sofa, "I'm so sorry, what happened? Had she been sick?"

Lexie shook her head, "She was fine, just a little tired, but when Grandpa went up to bed, she was clutching her chest. He yelled at me to call 911 but by the time the paramedics arrived, it was too late. She'd had a heart attack"

I drew her into my arms and stroked her hair, "What's Grandpa going to do without her?"

"I don't know. He just seems lost."

"When's the funeral, Lexie?"

"It's on Thursday at the First Presbyterian Church. You will come won't you, Cassie? I know you didn't like Gran but you're my sister and I need you there."

"Of course, I'll be there," I said.

I tried to encourage Lexie to stay for a while but she was anxious to get back to Grandpa. I was hoping that we would find some time to really talk and catch up but it wasn't about to happen that day.

I never expected to find myself back in the same church where I had been forced to attend Papa's funeral. The service seemed to go on forever. It was a dreary overcast day and we shivered as we stood at the gravesite afterwards, in the old cemetery. Lexie held onto my hand and wept quietly and she only let go when she stepped forward and threw a handful of soil onto the casket. I heard her whisper, "Bye, bye Gran, I love you," and I felt her pain but I had no sorrow in my heart for my grandmother. She had hated Mama and I would never forgive her for that. Later, we went back to the house that I had attempted to escape from three times. It still looked the same and I didn't want to be there but I had to stay, for Lexie's sake. I helped serve the food, generously supplied by the neighbors, and tried to keep myself occupied. I had nothing to say to these people and I was glad when it was over. I suggested to Lexie that we meet somewhere for dinner on Thursday night but she felt it was too soon to leave Grandpa alone, and said she would call me. I hugged Grandpa as I left but he seemed to be in a daze. I felt sorry for him, his whole life had revolved around Gran and I didn't know how he was going to survive without her. I had borrowed Uncle Frank's car to get to Bridgeton and on the drive home, I prayed that Lexie would stay in touch. I longed to repair my relationship with my sister, but we still had to resolve the issue with Mama.

When Lexie came to visit me after all those years to tell me about Gran, I couldn't wait to tell Mama but I decided to wait until after the funeral. I was hoping that Lexie might show some remorse about her feelings for Mama and even want to visit her, but we hadn't even had time to talk. I knew that when the time came, I couldn't really push her. Ever since she was five years old, Gran had poisoned her mind and it would take a lot longer for her to realize the truth about Papa.

When I talked to Uncle Frank and Aunt Jean about it, they agreed that it might be better to give Lexie time to come around and suggested that I ask Mama what she thought. On Thursday afternoon, following the funeral, I walked into the visitor's area of the prison, somewhat excited to give Mama the news that I had seen Lexie, but totally indifferent to the fact that Gran was no longer with us.

Mama waved to me as I walked through the door and I couldn't help noticing that she looked happier than the last time I saw her. She had obviously just washed her hair and it fell in lovely waves to just below her chin and she was even wearing make-up. I sat down across from her and we touched fingertips across the table, "You look beautiful today, Mama," I said, "and happy. What's going on?"

Mama grinned, " I have a new cellmate, Ruby, and she's quite a character," she replied. "She looks a bit like Jayne Mansfield and she's even more comical than Vicky was. Every morning she puts on her make up and knowing that you were visiting today she insisted on making my face up too. I must admit I do feel a little more human."

"I'd like to meet this Ruby, isn't she here?"

"No, she has a daughter about your age but she lives in Oregon and she only sees her about twice a year."

"Why is she in prison, and how long has she been here?"

"She got mixed up with the wrong crowd and ended up being in the wrong place at the wrong time. There was an armed robbery and someone got killed. The police claimed she was an accessory and she was convicted and sent here. She's actually been here for almost a year and just got transferred from the east wing. Apparently her cellmate had some mental issues."

"Oh Mama, I'm so glad you're not all alone anymore. I've worried about you a lot since Vicky left."

Mama smiled, "You're such a devoted daughter, Cassie, but enough about me. What's going on in your life?"

I paused for a moment and then, watching for Mama's reaction, said simply, "Gran died."

Mama slowly shook her head, "Oh no, I'm sorry to hear that. What happened and how did you find out?"

"Heart attack. Lexie came to see me,"

I heard Mama gasp, "Lexie? She actually came to see you? How is she? What does she look like? What is she going to do now?"

"She's fine, Mama, and she looks like you, but then I always knew she would grow up to be a beauty. Even when she was little, she was so pretty. She's still living at Gran's house and she's going to stay there with Grandpa for now. He feels pretty lost and he needs her there. I didn't tell you about Gran when I first found out because

Lexie wanted me to be at the funeral. I thought I would wait and see what happened after that."

"What do you mean, Cassie, what did you expect to happen?"

"Well, I expected her to want to see you, but she didn't say anything. I even invited her out to supper but she used Grandpa as an excuse not to come. I thought that if we could just sit down quietly together, she might ask me what really happened to Papa and then I could set the record straight."

Mama reached across the table again and gently touched my hand, "No, Cassie, you mustn't do that. Lexie loved her father and you can't destroy her memory of him."

"How can she possibly have loved him after what he did to you?"

"She was very, very young and she doesn't remember those things. I know you want to have a relationship with your sister and I would give my right arm to see her, but I can't let you tell her the truth, Cassie."

I left the prison that day, still conflicted in my thoughts. Deep down, I knew that someday, somehow, I had to bring Mama and Lexie together.

# CHAPTER 27

I realized on reflection, that any effort to encourage my sister to reconcile with Mama and me would further complicate my relationship with Jeremy. I had no idea how I could continue to lie to him about my family. I briefly thought about not seeing him again but the attraction was too strong. Every night, we spoke on the phone, and twice during the next few weeks I traveled back to New York to stay with him for the weekend. Thanks to Uncle Frank, I no longer had to take the bus. He had generously given me his four-year-old Mustang after he had acquired a brand new Mercedes. I was always conscious of how lucky I was to have been selected by the Marshs' to be their foster child and I felt sorry for Lexie, left to be raised by Gran. My rebellious nature as a child had paid off, running away had been my salvation.

I had hoped to hear from my sister after the funeral but as the weeks passed without a word, I decided to take matters into my own hands. Christmas was only a few days away when I approached Aunt Jean about inviting Lexie and Grandpa to spend part of the holiday with us. At first, she was not sure that it was a good idea but when I assured her that I would not make an issue of the situation with Mama, she suggested that we invite them to spend Christmas Day with us if they had no other plans.

Jeremy was spending the holiday with his parents in Laguna Beach. His father had been under the weather, with a respiratory condition, and his mother had begged him to come. His older brother, Ethan, would also be visiting with his family and Jeremy felt obligated to go. We had fantasized on many occasions about spending Christmas together, walking the snow covered streets of New York, skating in Rockefeller Center, roasting chestnuts by the fire but it just wasn't to be. I think I wanted Lexie and Grandpa to visit, not only to repair our relationship, but also to take my mind off of Jeremy. I knew I would miss him terribly.

I was surprised when Lexie accepted my invitation and even more surprised when she told me that Grandpa was looking forward to seeing me again. She told me that after a period, when she wasn't sure if he would even survive the loss of Gran, he had suddenly come out of his shell and it was almost as though he had been liberated. It was with very little encouragement from Lexie that he decided to adopt a dog from the Humane Society. A two-year-old black & tan Welsh terrier who they decided to call Charlie, had captivated them both. Twice a day, regardless of the weather, Grandpa would take Charlie to the park and at night he slept at the foot of his bed. From what Lexie told me, it sounded like Grandpa had found a wonderful substitute for Gran.

The night before Christmas Eve, Mr. Graham hosted his usual party for the staff at the paper. He always held it at his home where his wife, Jill, was a gracious hostess. Everyone was in a festive mood and looking forward to the holidays. Tim had now become a good friend and we'd even been out for a drink on a couple of occasions after work. I still enjoyed his company but there was no longer any romance between us. At the party that night, I learned that he was involved with a young Canadian woman he met on a ski trip in Vermont and I smiled as he babbled on about her. It was obvious that he was falling in love and it made me think of Jeremy and how deep my feelings for him had become.

Later that night, Jazz called to say that she was arriving home in the morning and hoped we could find some time to get together. She had just returned from the photo shoot in Paris and couldn't wait to tell me all about it. When I asked what happened with the Italian photographer, she replied, "What photographer?"

"Come on, Jazz," I said. "You were all in a tizzy about him. Antonio wasn't it?"

Jazz laughed, "I was just being facetious," she said. "We didn't hit it off and in any case, he's married. Anyway, I soon forgot about him after I met one of the male models. Now, he's really hot, tall and slender and, believe it or not, looks a bit like my Dad. His name's Julius and he lives in Queens. We traveled back on the plane together and he invited me to go to a party with him on New Year's Eve."

"Well, it sounds like the start of something. When am I going to meet this Julius?"

There was a pause before Jazz replied, "Hopefully the next time you come to New York, but when am I going to meet the mysterious Jeremy Kent?"

I should have realized that Jazz would ask me that question and I couldn't keep stalling her, "Maybe the four of us can get together."

"That would be fabulous. We can discuss it some more when I see you. Would it be okay if I drop by tomorrow night for an hour or two? I'd love to see everyone and I have gifts for you and Billy."

"We'd love to see you too," I replied, "and I have other news to tell you."

Jazz was anxious to know what was going on but I decided to wait to tell her about Lexie. I knew it would open up a whole can of worms about Mama and my reluctance to tell Jeremy about her. I went to bed that night still conflicted about how I was going to handle the situation.

On Christmas Eve, because of the holiday, the prison had allowed special visiting hours and I joined a huge throng of people in the waiting room anxious to see their loved ones. We were allowed to bring small-unwrapped gifts but there were all kinds of restrictions. Every year, I had been forced to rack my brain trying to find something suitable that wouldn't be confiscated, and this year was no exception. I finally settled on a photograph that I had taken of myself with Pepper and Mama loved it. She thanked me over and over again and I saw the tears well up in her eyes when she told me she had no gift for me but I assured her that her love was all I needed. We had a wonderful visit but before I left, Mama made me promise that I wouldn't push Lexie to come and see her. I vowed that I wouldn't but Mama didn't see my fingers crossed under the table.

When I got home late in the afternoon, Billy announced that there was a parcel for me. I had to smile to myself as he followed me into the kitchen where the parcel sat on the counter, "What is it, Cassie?" he asked.

"I'm not sure," I answered, "but maybe I'll wait until tomorrow to open it."

"I wanna see, I wanna see!" he chanted jumping up and down.

"Oh all right," I said, turning the parcel over in my hands.

I could see it was from Jeremy and I was excited as I started tearing away the wrapping. Eventually I discovered the black velvet box and inside, a wonderful heart shaped diamond pendant with a note that read, "To my beautiful Cassie, the love of my life, Jeremy".

Billy was craning his neck to see what was in the box and his eyes grew as round as saucers when he saw the necklace, "Ooh, it's so pretty," he said, "did your boyfriend send it?"

"Yes, he did," I answered. "It's lovely isn't it?"

"Can I get Amanda one of those? Can I? Can I?"

"I don't think so, Billy. These are real diamonds, but you could get her something that looks just like this."

Billy looked downcast, "But I already got her some mittens."

I patted him on the back, "I'm sure she'll just love them, Billy. The important thing is that you were thinking of her."

That evening Jazz dropped by wearing a simple cowl neck, white angora sweater and black leather pants but she still looked like a million dollars. Billy couldn't take his eyes off her and when he opened the gift she gave him and found a Yahama Racer Swatch watch, I think Jazz established a life long admirer.

Uncle Frank and Aunt Jean were particularly happy to welcome Jazz. They hadn't seen her since she had started modeling and when some neighbors came by, the evening turned into a party. I managed to tell Jazz about Gran and Lexie but never really had the opportunity to go into details, and she didn't press me. I think we both knew that it wasn't the time or place to have a serious discussion.

# CHAPTER 28

On Christmas Day, Aunt Jean and I were up at the crack of dawn getting ready to prepare the turkey. We tried to be very quiet, hoping that Billy wouldn't wake up, but Pepper made our efforts almost impossible. Soon after we arrived in the kitchen, she was at the back door whining to be let out and when Pepper whined, she let everybody know that she wanted immediate attention. We breathed a sigh of relief once she was outside and then conveniently forgot about her, which was a huge mistake. Pepper didn't like to be ignored and within ten minutes she was back, scratching at the door and barking loud enough to wake the dead. Aunt Jean and I just looked at each other, shaking our heads and praying that Billy was still sleeping, but it was not to be. A moment later, a voice from the hallway called out, "Can I open my presents now, Mom?"

Aunt Jean sighed, "Billy, come and let Pepper in and have some breakfast and then you can open your presents."

Billy appeared in the doorway in his pajamas, rubbing his eyes, "But Mom, I don't want breakfast."

By that time I was afraid Pepper would wake up the whole neighborhood and let her in myself. Then I turned to Billy, "Don't you want us to see you open your gifts, Billy? Your Mom and I need to get the turkey in the oven and by then maybe your Dad will be up too. In the meantime, I'll whip you up a special breakfast. How about your favorite banana waffles with maple syrup?"

Billy cocked his head to one side as though he was thinking it over. I think the temptation of the waffles was too much and he finally agreed, "Okay, Cassie, I'll go and get dressed."

"Don't forget to wash your hands and face and clean your teeth," Aunt Jean called out as he wandered back into the hallway.

By the time breakfast was over, Uncle Frank had joined us and we all sat around the Christmas tree opening our gifts, while Pepper drove us mad tearing up the wrapping paper and chasing it around the room. I always treasured each Christmas I spent with my family, but every year I wished Mama could be with us and wondered what she was doing in that cold and lonely place she had called home for so long.

We decided to have dinner at four o'clock as it was at least a two hour drive from Bridgeton to Asbury Park and Grandpa and Lexie would have to leave by seven or eight to make it back home at a reasonable hour. I was feeling really anxious about their visit and tried to keep busy the rest of the morning helping Aunt Jean in the kitchen. Uncle Frank decided to take Billy and Pepper out for a drive just to keep out of our hair but the absence of activity elsewhere in the house, made me even more nervous.

Grandpa and Lexie arrived at three o'clock just as we were setting up the table. I heard Uncle Frank open the front door and introduce himself to Grandpa and then usher them inside. Wiping my hands on a dishcloth, ready to greet them, I was almost bowled over by Pepper and her newfound friend Charlie. It looked like it would be impossible to settle them down so I opened the back door and gently pushed them out onto the back lawn. By this time, snow had begun to fall and there was a fine layer on the grass. Pepper had always loved to play in the snow and it looked like Charlie was of the same mind. I couldn't have picked a better distraction.

The dogs taken care of, I turned back to Aunt Jean but she had already gone to greet our guests. I took off my apron and straightened my skirt then, taking a deep breath, I went out to the hallway where Grandpa and Lexie were taking off their coats. When Grandpa saw me, he extended his arms and I moved forward into them, "Hello Grandpa, how are you?" I managed to whisper.

He hugged me and murmured back, "I'm just fine for an old man, Cassie, thank you."

I leaned back and looked at his face and it was as though I was seeing him for the first time. He had tears in his eyes and I wasn't sure if he was thinking of Gran or just happy to see me. I patted him on the back and then turned to Lexie, who was waiting patiently. She looked amazing in a royal blue dress, which accentuated her slim figure, and with her hair swept back from her face. I could just picture Mama again all those years ago. I reached out for her hand, "Hi, Lexie," I said, "I'm so happy you came. Merry Christmas." She leaned forward and kissed me on the cheek, "Merry Christmas to you too, Cassie," she replied.

After that, I completely relaxed and we went into the family room, where Aunt Jean served up appetizers and eggnog. Billy had gone to fetch Amanda, who lived just a few houses away, and when the two of them arrived home and insisted on bringing Pepper and Charlie back inside, it got a little noisy. I was concerned that it would be too much for Grandpa, but he seemed to be really enjoying himself and very taken with Amanda, who like Billy, could be really charming, most of the time. I got a real kick out of seeing Billy and Amanda together. They were so affectionate with each other and looked like young children, sneaking kisses when they thought nobody was looking.

I learned that Lexie was now going to Cumberland County College but was still undecided what career path she wanted to follow. Her dream of working with animals had faded and I suspected that her current boyfriend might have affected her change of heart. Lexie, had been volunteering at the South Jersey Hospital along with three other students. One of them was Todd Willis, and he was passionate about improving the lives of unfortunate children in third world countries. Lexie told us that she was so moved by his dedication and compassionate nature that she fell in love with him and they had talked about a future together. I was actually very surprised that she was so open and honest about her feelings for Todd and it got me thinking about Jeremy again. I wanted so much, to be able to pour my heart out to anyone who would listen. I was feeling more and more committed to him, but unlike Lexie, I had no idea where our relationship was going.

Our dinner was proceeding without a hitch and I was amazed when Grandpa asked for a second helping of the mincemeat pie that Aunt Jean had baked that morning. I studied him across the table and noticed that even his appearance had improved. Other than at church, or at Gran's funeral, I had never seen him in a suit before. He usually wore faded corduroy pants or jeans with ill-fitting shirts, but here he was wearing a smart navy blue blazer with dark gray slacks and a matching gray polo neck sweater, and had obviously just had his hair trimmed. I couldn't help commenting, "You are looking really nice, Grandpa. I don't think I've ever seen you looking so well."

Grandpa looked across at Lexie, "You can thank your sister for that," he said. "She took me shopping and insisted I went to the barber."

"Well, it's wonderful to see how well you are coping now without Gran."

Grandpa hung his head and then looked up again at Aunt Jean, " I have to confess, Mrs. Marsh," he said in a low voice, "my dear departed wife wasn't the easiest woman to get along with. She was very harsh with Cassie, when she lived with us and she always seemed to favor Lexie. It was a sad thing what happened to our boy and I've never said this before, but if what Ella said was true about him, then he probably deserved it."

I sat there with my mouth open, unable to believe what I was hearing when suddenly Lexie jumped up from the table, "Stop it," she screamed, frightening Billy and Amanda, who cowered in their chairs. " I won't have you saying anything bad about Papa. It was Mama who was bad and she's right where she should be."

I stood up and reached for Lexie's arm but she pulled away, "Leave me alone," she yelled at me. "You lied about Papa, he didn't do the things you said he did and I'll never forgive you for that." Then she looked across at Grandpa, "We're leaving right now. Let's get Charlie and go."

Uncle Frank and Aunt Jean stood up while Grandpa sat there for a moment before saying, "I must apologize for my granddaughter. She's forgotten her manners but it's probably best that we leave now."

I hugged Grandpa as he left the room, stopping only to whisper in my ear, "I'll phone you, dear," but I couldn't bring myself to see them to the front door. I stayed with Billy and Amanda and tried to make light of what had happened while Uncle Frank and Aunt Jean helped Grandpa and Lexie with their coats and escorted them to their car.

It was hard to feel festive afterwards and after clearing away the dishes, I decided to take Pepper for a walk and try and clear my head. By then, the snow had formed a thick layer on the streets and large flakes were still falling. It was already quite dark and the Christmas lights decorating so many of our neighbors' trees made it look like a fairyland. I had pictured Lexie taking a walk with me and talking about Mama. I had even imagined her telling me that she had forgiven Mama and wanted to see her but that just hadn't happened. I wondered if I would ever get my sister back.

# CHAPTER 29

When I got back home, Uncle Frank and Aunt Jean were waiting for me. Billy had gone to Amanda's house and I was thankful for the peace and quiet. Uncle Frank wanted to assure me that what happened was not my fault. He suggested that I should accept the fact that Lexie might never change her attitude towards Mama, leaving a void between us that could never be bridged. I went up to my room that night with a heavy heart and even when the phone rang and I heard Jeremy's voice, he sensed immediately that something was wrong. I wanted desperately to tell him about my sister, and I almost did, but something held me back, "Everything's fine", I said, "I'm just tired. We were up at the crack of dawn cooking and I think I had one glass of wine too many."

"Well, that's what Christmas is all about, my love," Jeremy said cheerfully. "We even did some celebrating here because Dad was feeling so much better. I think having Ethan and the children here really bucked him up. He even took a walk along the beach with them and waded in the ocean."

"Oh, I'm sorry, Jeremy," I said feeling rather guilty, "I should have asked you how your father was. It's so odd thinking of you all in California at this time of the year and spending time at the beach."

"Well, I'm not spending much more time here, in fact I'm coming back in a couple of days. I can't wait to see you, Cassie, but

I have to meet with my agent first and I haven't set that up yet. I have some exciting news about my latest novel, there's some discussion about making it into a movie."

"You mean 'The Crimson Cord'? They're actually thinking of making a movie? That's wonderful Jeremy, I'm so happy for you. I want to hear all about it when I see you."

"I'll call you soon after I get to New York and take care of any business. I have to run now because mother's calling us all to the table. We're a few hours behind you, so I just wanted to catch you before you turned in for the night and wish you a Merry Christmas."

"Merry Christmas to you, Jeremy," I whispered. "I'll be waiting for your call, in fact I'll be counting the hours."

After we finally said goodbye I felt even more depressed than before. Lexie still weighed heavily on my mind and Jeremy's news made me realize that despite already being a well known author, he might become even more of a celebrity once his novel was made into a film. What kind of sensation would it cause for everyone to discover that he was associated with someone like me? What would happen when they uncovered my past and above all, what would it do to Mama to have everything raked up again?

The following day I went back to work and soon forgot all my troubles when Jamie and I were sent on assignment to Tom's River, about twenty seven miles south on the Garden State Parkway. A four-year-old girl, Hannah Devlin, had been abducted from her home in the middle of the night and the news had been aired on television stations across several northeastern states earlier that morning. When we arrived at the Devlin's house, it was chaos and there were police cars everywhere. We were hoping to get an interview with the parents but they were secluded inside the house, and while we waited for further developments, more and more media people showed up. A search party had already been organized and was searching the area but by late afternoon there was still no trace of Hannah. It was already dark and bitterly cold but nobody wanted to call off the search and I was chomping at the bit to join them. Jamie felt the same way but we needed to stay close to the police and see if there was any new information that we could pick up. We called in what we had to the paper and weren't surprised when Mr. Graham suggested we book into a motel and get back on the story early the next morning. Jamie wasn't too happy about that, but I was only too glad not to have to face the drive home that night. By now, it had turned so cold that the roads were icy and I had always been nervous driving in those conditions.

At ten o'clock, the search was called off for the night, and Jamie and I checked into our rooms exhausted but I couldn't sleep. I couldn't stop thinking about that small child somewhere out there in the clutches of some predator, or freezing to death. Finally, at around three o'clock I fell asleep for a couple of hours but was awakened by Jamie hammering on my door. When I opened it, he just looked at me and shook his head and I knew that whatever had happened wasn't good, "She's dead isn't she?" I said as I stepped aside to let Jamie in from the cold.

He brushed past me and then turned and put his hand gently on my shoulder, "They found her about a mile from here. She was naked and tied to a tree. It looks like she died from exposure."

I could feel the tears welling up, "Was she sexually assaulted?"

"They haven't released that information yet but it wouldn't surprise me if she was."

"And have they any idea who did this?"

"No clue at the moment, but I hope they catch the bastard and I hope he rots in hell. If anyone did that to my child, I'd hunt him down myself."

I knew Jamie was thinking about his son, Justin, "I don't think anyone would blame you either," I said quietly. "What do we do now?"

Jamie started for the door, "Well I guess we should stick around and see what else we can find out. Maybe the police chief will give a news conference sometime today. I'll let you get dressed and you can meet me in the coffee shop for breakfast in about half an hour, I hear it opens at six."

"Okay," I said as Jamie opened the door and a blast of icy wind made me shiver. The sheet that I'd wrapped around myself, in the absence of a robe, gave little protection against the cold air.

Jamie looked back at me as he walked away, "Nice outfit," he said grinning.

By the time we got back to Asbury Park later that day, I had gathered a lot more information about Hannah Devlin and her parents but the police still had no suspects. I spent the next few hours writing my story, mostly from a human-interest point of view. Our readers needed to know who Hannah was and what her family was like. I wasn't a crime reporter and had no ambition to be one. Murder was one thing I didn't like to think about.

# CHAPTER 30

Jazz and I spoke briefly on the telephone the next day but we didn't get a chance to see each other before she returned to New York. She suggested that, if Jeremy and I had no other plans, we meet up with her and Julius on New Year's Eve. Apparently the party they were going to was more of an open house where no formal invitation was necessary and it was being held at the Trend Cosmetics head office in Soho. I didn't make any promises. I was hoping that Jeremy might have something a little more private in mind, but when he called me later that night I learned that his agent was having a cocktail party at his new home and we were invited. Many of the other guests were also authors and Jeremy was anxious to introduce me to them. The whole idea made me very anxious but I didn't know how to refuse. I had gained a lot more confidence working for the paper, but I still wasn't comfortable around crowds of people. In the next day or two, I dreamed up several excuses for opting out of the party but my need to see Jeremy took precedence over any fear that I had. I had hoped to spend some time alone with him before the party, but Aunt Jean had planned a special luncheon for Amanda's parents and Billy begged me to stay. It was almost four o'clock before I managed to get away and the drive into New York was a nightmare. It had been snowing heavily for two days and the traffic was backed up after a minor accident just before the Holland Tunnel. By the time I got to Jeremy's apartment I was tired and feeling rather shaky. Jeremy took my coat and then put his arms around me, "What's the matter my love?" he asked. " I can feel you trembling."

I shook my head, "I'm okay," I answered kissing him lightly on the lips. "The drive up was a little nerve racking, that's all. I just need to sit down and relax for a few moments."

Jeremy took my hand and led me into the living room. "Take all the time you need. The party doesn't start for another hour and it doesn't matter if we're late. How about something to drink to calm your nerves?"

I had already started to sit down but got up again, "Let me get it, unless Pilar is here. I don't want to step on her toes."

Jeremy gently pushed me back down again, "I'll go. You just sit down. Pilar's taken Teddy to visit a friend. I gave her the time off so that we could be alone. Now how about some brandy, that should do the trick?"

For the next half hour we sat on the sofa, holding hands and sipping brandy while Jeremy told me about the movie deal that had been proposed. I was just starting to feel relaxed and reluctant to move when Jeremy glanced at his watch and announced that he had to take a quick shower. He had put my overnight bag in the guest room so that I could get ready undisturbed and after I had slipped into a midnight blue velvet dress which I had bought especially for the party, I took a good look at myself in the mirror. I loved the style, form fitting with long sleeves and a sweetheart neckline that showed off my figure and a little more cleavage than I was used to. I just hoped that Jeremy would be as happy with the way I looked as I was. He didn't disappoint me when I walked back into the living room. He looked amazing in a formal black suit, white shirt and gray silk tie and when he saw me he wiggled his eyebrows and said, "My oh my, you look fabulous and I can't wait to show you off to everyone."

I don't remember much about the party. I know I met a lot of people, many of whom congratulated Jeremy on his latest novel, but their names eluded me. I was nervous in case anyone asked me a lot of questions and I couldn't wait to get out of there. One guest in particular, mentioned that his family lived in Millville and I had to play dumb and pretend I'd never heard of it. I know I drank a lot of wine to give me courage and I was feeling a little tipsy when Jeremy suggested that we leave. I had no idea what his plans were for the rest of the evening and it wasn't until we got back to the apartment that I learned he had arranged for a specially catered supper just for the two of us. It was only moments after we had both changed into casual slacks and sweaters that the telephone rang announcing that the caterers had arrived. Jeremy had ordered all of my favorite foods, lobster thermidore, asparagus, brown rice and a wonderful chocolate mousse with real whipped cream.

The table was set up in the cozy dining area off the kitchen and we could see thousands of Christmas lights twinkling on the trees in Central Park. Jeremy had lit a beautiful rose-colored candle and I was thinking it was the most romantic meal I had ever had. I was gazing out of the window when Jeremy said, "I hope you didn't mind spending New Year's Eve alone with me."

I looked across at him as he passed me a cup of coffee, "I couldn't have wished for a better way to celebrate," I said.

He smiled and reached for my hand, "I'm glad, Cassie. You know I usually end up in Times Square with a bunch of rowdy friends, but I'd much rather be here with you."

"It's been wonderful," I whispered. "Jazz wanted us to meet Julius tonight but now I'm glad that I didn't commit to anything."

"I gather Julius is the new boyfriend?"

"Yes, she met him in Paris on the photo shoot."

"Well, Paris is a great place to start a romance. You'd love it there, Cassie and I plan to take you there real soon."

I pulled my hand away and frowned, "To Paris? That sounds so far away. I'm not sure I want to go."

Jeremy got up and came around the table, then taking my arm he pulled me up from my chair, "Look at me, Cassie," he said turning me towards him, "It's a long time since I've felt this way about anyone. After my divorce, I was determined not to get seriously involved with a woman again but lately I've come to realize that I'm falling in love with you and I think we could have a future together. I want to share my life with you and take you to all the places you've never been. Paris is only one of those places."

I tore myself away from his grasp and took a step backwards. I could feel my heart starting to pound, "Don't, Jeremy," I cried. "You don't know anything about me."

He pulled me back into his arms and chuckled, "What are you going to tell me, you're an axe murderer or something? I know how I feel about you and that's all that matters."

I was shaking as I pulled away again, "That's not even funny. I'm serious, Jeremy, I don't think I can do this, in fact I'd like to get out of here right now."

I could see the shocked expression on Jeremy's face as he stood there with his arms at his sides, "What's going on, Cassie? I thought we had something special."

I stared at him wringing my hands, "We do, but there can't be any future for the two of us. I can't explain it to you, don't even ask me to. You just have to trust me that I know what I'm doing and let me go."

"I can't do that, my love", he said walking towards me.

"I'm sorry but you must, I'm leaving now," I cried as I ran through the kitchen to the bedroom to gather my belongings.

Jeremy didn't follow me. I think he was too shocked and when I found him a few moments later in the living room, he was sitting with his head in his hands, "I am so sorry," I said, "but I have to go."

He looked up at me and I could see the tears in his eyes, "You just can't leave. I won't let you drive home at this time of night."

I threw back my shoulders, "I'm a big girl, I'll be all right," and with that I strode down the hall.

I heard Jeremy following quietly behind me and as I waited for the elevator, he murmured, "I think you owe me an explanation, Cassie."

Just then the doors opened and I stepped inside, "I can't give you one," I said.

# CHAPTER 31

I don't know how I managed to make it all the way home in one piece. I do know that my mind wasn't on the road and I was lucky, once I left the Manhattan area, that there was very little traffic. Tears were blurring my vision and I knew I had to pull myself together but I couldn't get the picture of Jeremy's shocked expression out of my head. I knew I was falling for him, but had no idea he felt the same way about me. I suppose I was in complete denial about where our relationship might be heading because I knew if it ever got serious, I would have to break it off. I just didn't expect it to happen so soon.

After I got to the house, I could see that the lights were still on so I parked in the driveway and stayed in the car for a while, trying to calm down. I knew Aunt Jean would be surprised to see me home before midnight and would be sure to give me the third degree. If I told her the truth, would she understand? I didn't think I could go through another confrontation that night.

When I let myself in through the front door, Pepper came bounding towards me. It's amazing how a beloved pet can stir one's emotions and as soon as I bent down to pat her head, I broke down and started to sob uncontrollably. Aunt Jean was there within seconds, taking me by the arm and leading me into the living room where Uncle Frank looked up from watching television with a look of alarm on his face, "What on earth is it, Cassie?" he asked as he got to his feet.

I just shook my head still unable to stop crying. Aunt Jean sat me down on the sofa and put her arm around me, "Turn the television off please, honey," she said quietly. "I think Cassie may need to talk."

I looked at the two most wonderful people I had ever come to know and who had cared for me for so many years and I just couldn't hold back. "I broke up with Jeremy," I whispered, wiping away my tears.

Aunt Jean stroked my hair, "Oh dear, Cassie," she said, "I figured it was something like that after seeing you in this state. What happened dear? Did you have a fight?"

"No, we didn't fight Auntie, but it was all getting too serious. There can't be any future for us, it just wouldn't work."

Uncle Frank walked over and sat on the arm of the sofa beside me, "Are you telling me that he just wanted a casual relationship with no strings attached?"

I looked up at him, "No, that's not what I'm saying. He's the one that started talking about a future together. It was me who walked away."

Aunt Jean sighed, "But I thought you were falling for Jeremy. Why would you break it off? It doesn't make any sense."

"It does to me. He's a well-known author and now they're going to make his latest novel into a movie, so he'll be even more famous. I couldn't risk exposing him to all the negative publicity if my secret came out."

Aunt Jean glanced up at Uncle Frank frowning, "Your secret. What secret?"

I shrugged her arm off of my shoulders then got up and turned to face them. I was feeling frustrated and spat out the words, "That my mother murdered my father, of course."

Uncle Frank stood up and stared at me. It was the first time I had ever seen him really angry. "You mean you haven't told him what happened when you were just a child? That your mother was abused and that now she's serving time in a state prison for ridding this world of a monster that didn't deserve to be born? That it was no fault of yours and you've been separated from your family all these years? My God, Cassie, if this man really loves you, it won't matter one iota what anyone says about you or your past."

Aunt Jean got up and placed her hand on Uncle Frank's arm, "Your uncle's right," she said. "You have to tell him. At least give him the opportunity to make up his own mind about what happened and whether he wants to expose himself to it. I can see now, why you never invited him here, he thinks we're your parents, doesn't he?"

I sank down into a chair by the window, "Yes, everything I've told him has been a lie. He thinks I'm Cassie King, not Cassie Taylor, that I live at home with my mother, father and brother and that I have no other siblings. How stupid I was to think that I could get away with it."

Uncle Frank came and stood in front of me, "Are you ashamed of your mother, Cassie?" he said.

I felt the blood rushing to my head as I looked up at him and snapped, "No, of course not. I love Mama more than anyone in the world. How could you even ask me that?"

"Well, it seems to me that you don't want anyone to know about her. How do you think she would feel about you sacrificing your future because of what she did? And how would she react knowing that you don't even acknowledge your own sister? It's about time you stopped being a martyr, Cassie, and gave some serious thought to what you're doing."

By then I had had enough and couldn't deal with it any more. I jumped up and ran into the hallway to pick up my overnight bag, "That's the way it has to be," I called out, "I'm going to bed. By the way, Happy New Year."

Aunt Jean called out, "Cassie, please don't go. Come back and we'll talk some more."

I was already climbing the stairs to my room. "There's nothing more to talk about," I whispered to myself.

I hardly slept at all that night and when I got up in the morning I had a headache and was feeling feverish. I went through the motions of getting washed and dressed knowing that I had the whole of New Year's Day ahead of me, and nowhere to go. Work had always been my salvation, but it was not an option. Mr. Graham had given me strict orders that he didn't want to see me until the holiday was over. When I went downstairs for breakfast, I was surprised to see that only Aunt Jean was in the kitchen. She was scrambling eggs and didn't hear me come in, "Where's everyone?" I asked.

She tipped the eggs onto a plate then turned around, "Billy's still at Amanda's house, he spent the night there and your Uncle's taken Pepper for a walk. How did you sleep?"

"Not very well," I sighed sitting down at the table.

"You look very pale, Cassie. Are you feeling all right?"

"Actually I'm feeling a bit feverish. I think I'm coming down with something."

"Well, eat these eggs and I'll make you some toast and fresh coffee. It's a good thing it's a holiday so you can stay home and rest."

I hesitated, "Thank you Auntie. Look, I don't want to talk about last night but I do want to apologize for flouncing off like that. I'm sorry I spoiled your New Year."

Aunt Jean put two slices of toast in the toaster and then came over and put her hand on my shoulder, "No need to apologize my dear. There will be lots of other New Years to celebrate."

After breakfast, I went back to my room and stayed there until lunchtime. Billy was back from Amanda's and sitting with Uncle Frank at the kitchen table. He glanced up at me when I walked through the door and I noticed Aunt Jean look over at Billy, then back at Uncle Frank and put her finger against her lips. It was obvious that she didn't want Billy to get in the middle of anything that might upset him.

Other than the fact that I was still feeling under the weather, lunchtime seemed perfectly normal. Billy was up to his usual antics, playing with his food and sneaking pieces of hamburger to Pepper, who was hiding under his chair. I was musing about what to do for the rest of the day when Aunt Jean informed me that they had been invited to a friend's house for dinner and she was sure they wouldn't mind if I tagged along. I declined, relieved to know that I had the house to myself and didn't have to keep up any pretense for Billy's sake. After they left, early in the afternoon, I tried to concentrate on the book I had been reading that morning but my mind kept playing out the scene with Jeremy and then the way Uncle Frank had reacted. I ended up in tears again and decided to get some fresh air despite the fact that it was bitterly cold and snowing heavily. I walked for about half a mile and then turned back when I realized I felt even worse than before. It was obvious that I was coming down with a nasty cold or the flu. Later that day, Aunt Jean found me shivering in bed with the covers up to my chin. Like a modern day Florence Nightingale, she fussed over me, bringing me lemon tea, cold medicine and a hot water bottle.

"I'll be all right, really Auntie," I croaked.

"Yes, you will young lady," she said, "but only if you stay in bed. I'm going to make you some soup and then you can get some sleep, and don't think you're going to work tomorrow."

"Yes, Auntie," I replied meekly.

I remained in bed or propped up on the living room sofa for the next two days. I was both physically and emotionally drained. Deep down, I had hoped that Jeremy would call and I was sad when I didn't hear from him. I wondered if he really loved me after all.

By the fourth day I was feeling like my old self. I persuaded Aunt Jean that I needed to go back to work and get on with my life and after her minor objection, she agreed that it would probably be for the best.

The first day back at the paper, Mr. Graham called me into his office and asked me if I felt well enough to go out on assignment with Jamie. He wanted me to interview a seventeen-year-old boy, Ben Wilkins. Ben, a cancer survivor, was running from his hometown in Lakehurst, across America to raise money for the Cancer Society. His family had begged him to wait until spring but he said he had to leave now, in case the cancer came back. There had already been a lot of publicity and Ben was a hero to his friends, family and the people in the neighborhood. It was an uplifting story and I welcomed the chance of getting out of Asbury Park for the day.

Meeting Ben made me feel that my problems were trivial compared to his. Here was a wonderful young man in the prime of his life, having just gone through a devastating illness. He had endured months of chemotherapy and radiation, unable to participate in all of the activities his friends took for granted but, instead of complaining, he turned his ordeal into something positive.

He was slight of stature with short flaxen hair, bright blue eyes and a ruddy boyish face. When I asked him what had possessed him to take up his cause, he smiled and said, "That's easy, because I can. So many people die but I survived. There has to be a cure for everyone and we need so much money for research."

I thought about Ben a lot on the way home and the courage he had shown. I was almost ashamed that I had spent so much time feeling sorry for myself.

# CHAPTER 32

It was after supper, and already dark, when I pulled onto our street and immediately noticed Jeremy's car parked in the driveway. My heart started to pound in my chest and my first reaction was to keep on driving. Instead, I stopped outside our neighbor's house and tried to compose myself while all sorts of thoughts raced through my head. What was he doing here? Was my secret out? Had Uncle Frank or Aunt Jean told him all about Mama? Suddenly I was angry, I felt he had no right to delve into my private life. I hadn't invited him to my home so I decided to just waltz right in and ask him to leave with no questions asked and no explanation.

I got out of the car, walked briskly up the driveway and opened the front door. I could hear voices in the kitchen and made straight for the entryway without hesitation. Aunt Jean was at the table cutting carrot cake and Jeremy was seated with a cup in one hand while reaching down with the other to pet Pepper. When I came through the door they both looked up at me but I didn't give either one of them a chance to speak, "I'm not going to ask you why you're here Jeremy," I spat out, " I just want you to leave."

Aunt Jean got up and started towards me, "Now wait a minute young lady, there's no need to be rude."

I held up my hand, "Stop right there. He wasn't invited and I don't want him here."

Jeremy got up and put his hand on Aunt Jean's shoulder, "It's all right Mrs. Marsh. I'll just go."

Aunt Jean shook her head vehemently, "No, I want you to stay. It's about time Cassie was honest with you." Then turning to me she said, "I invited Jeremy here. He knows we aren't your biological parents but that's all he knows. The rest is for you to disclose, Cassie."

I sagged against the doorframe, "How could you do this? You had no right to interfere with my life."

Aunt Jean looked angry now, " I had every right. We took you in. We looked after you and we love you, and whenever you're unhappy we try to do something about it. It's pretty obvious how you really feel about this young man, yet you're willing to throw it all away because of some stupid idea that he'll reject you if he finds out the truth. Well, let's see if you're right, Cassie. That's what you want, isn't it? To be right, even though you could be jeopardizing your future?"

I stared at her as she walked towards me and then placed her hands on my shoulders, "Talk to him," she said gently. "Tell him everything, Cassie," and then she walked past me into the hallway.

Jeremy came forward and took my hand, "Come and sit down and don't be angry with your aunt. It's obvious she loves you very much."

He pulled out a chair and I reluctantly sank down onto it, my thoughts still racing. Then I felt Pepper drape herself across my feet and I began to calm down.

"How about some coffee?" Jeremy asked, picking up the coffee pot.

I nodded and waited while he poured some coffee into a cup and handed it to me, "Well, Cassie," he said. "Do you want to talk?"

I nodded again slowly, "I don't know where to begin," I whispered.

Jeremy reached over and squeezed my hand, "Begin at the beginning."

An hour later he knew all about my life up until that moment and I didn't leave anything out. It was like a catharsis and I couldn't stop crying but Jeremy let me go on, never interrupting or comforting me, only allowing me the blessed relief of finally opening up to him.

When I had finished, I felt drained and I know I must have looked a mess but that's when he took me in his arms and said, "What a brave young woman you've been, Cassie. I'm so proud of you. Your devotion to your mother is remarkable and you have absolutely nothing to be ashamed of."

I looked up into his face and with tears still in my eyes said quietly, "But you can't be involved with someone like me, you have your reputation to think of."

Jeremy actually laughed, "To hell with my reputation. I don't give a rat's behind what anyone else thinks and you shouldn't care either. What your mother did was not your fault and I can understand why she snapped. It's too bad your sister can't see it that way. Maybe one day she'll come around but, in the meantime, you have a great family here. I actually met Billy earlier and he was a delight. He was fascinated with my car and talked me into giving him a ride around the block."

I was a little startled, "What? How long have you been here?"

Jeremy chuckled, "Oh about four hours. Your aunt even invited me to dinner, she's a great cook."

I shook my head in disbelief, "So she invited you here knowing that I wouldn't be back until late."

"Yes, I guess she wanted to get a good look at me."

"But how did she find you in the first place?"

"Simple. She just called information. My number's listed, so it wasn't a problem."

"But what did she say to you when she called?"

"She said she was your aunt and invited me to dinner. She said she wanted to meet me and thought I might be interested in what she had to say. I didn't know until I got here that she was your foster mother. I assumed she was your mother's sister and lived here too but, I did think it was a bit strange."

"What about Uncle Frank, did you meet him too?"

"Yes, he seems like a really nice guy. We had quite a chat about books and the law but then he had to leave. I understand he's on the local bowling team."

"So you met the whole family. I still can't believe all this has happened."

Jeremy smiled, "See, everything worked out just fine. I think your family is great and I think you're a very special woman. Now I can't wait to meet your mother."

I was shocked when Jeremy said that, "You mean you'd actually go to the prison with me?"

"Why not? It wouldn't be the first time. I've been inside a few state prisons when researching for a book."

I shook my head as I looked at this man who had come into my life and now accepted me for whom I was. I knew then, without a doubt, that I was madly in love with him.

# CHAPTER 33

The next few months were a whirlwind of activity. Jeremy visited me in Asbury Park on many occasions and I spent several weekends in New York. I still hadn't allowed Jeremy to accompany me on any of my visits to Mama, even though he had mentioned it a number of times. I told Mama what had happened the day Jeremy had turned up at the Marshs' and she was relieved that I had finally managed to tell the truth. She confessed that she prayed every night that I had found my soul mate. She had even found several of Jeremy's books in the library and, although not usually a lover of mysteries, she enjoyed his writing style and the imaginative story lines. I think she got great pleasure in showing the other inmates Jeremy's picture on the back cover and telling them that he was her daughter's young man.

The negotiations on the film rights for 'The Crimson Cord' had fallen through but Jeremy just shrugged it off. He had already started on a new novel with the working title Code Indigo but was struggling with writer's block and in May he decided to take a long break and spend some time at his Hampton house. I had never been there but, two weeks after depositing himself, Pilar and Teddy in his summer home, I found myself driving along Dune Road in the Village of Westhampton Beach. Jeremy had shown me photographs of the house but I wasn't really prepared for its location, almost at the edge of the ocean.

Jeremy greeted me at the door wearing chinos and a white tee shirt, with Teddy in his arms, "Where's Pilar?" I asked kissing him on the cheek while stroking Teddy's head.

"She's just gone to pick up some groceries. Come on in sweetheart. I'll get your suitcase out of your car in a minute."

I walked into the house and looked around in wonder but Jeremy stopped me in my tracks. He dropped Teddy, rather abruptly, onto the floor and gathered me into his arms, "I can't believe you're really here, Cassie."

"Well, I am and you're stuck with me," I responded playfully.

"Come," he said dragging me by the hand, "I want to show you the place."

The house was wonderful, with four bedrooms, four bathrooms a huge kitchen and a solarium with unobstructed views of the ocean and the bay. Outside was a guest cottage with a huge deck and pool and a walkway to a private beach. It was pretty obvious that Jeremy took great pride in showing me around and if he wanted to impress me, he succeeded. After much persuasion from Jeremy and Aunt Jean, I had decided to spend my whole two-week vacation in Westhampton. I needed the rest and being with Jeremy night and day was ideal but I couldn't help feeling guilty. While we walked the beach, able to gaze out on miles of ocean, Mama was locked behind prison walls. While Pilar waited on us hand and foot, or we ate in one of the upscale restaurants, Mama was forced to endure unsavory food every single day. One morning, I was particularly pensive and Jeremy, picking up on my mood, decided to confront me, "Cassie, what's bothering you? Every now and then I see such sadness in your eyes. Don't you want to be here with me?"

I took his hand and pulled him towards me, "I love being here with you," I sighed, "but I can't help thinking about Mama. I have so much and she has so little. Here we are in this beautiful place and we can go anywhere we like, but she's in that dreadful prison. She doesn't deserve to be there and I wish I could help her."

"I understand, Cassie, I really do but you can't go on living your life feeling guilty about your mother. She wouldn't want that now would she?"

I shook my head, "No, she wants me to be happy and I am when I'm with you but I can't help thinking about her. When I was younger, I vowed I'd get her out of there, but there's nothing I can do."

Jeremy hesitated, "That's what I love so much about you. You have this wonderful compassionate nature and perhaps there's something I can do to help."

I held my breath, "What do you mean, what can you do?"

Jeremy chuckled, "Well, I'm sure you've noticed that I'm not exactly destitute and, let's face it, money talks. Not only that, I have contacts."

"What contacts?"

"My lawyer is a senior partner with Adams, Bernhardt and Greenberg. You may have heard of them, they are one of the most prestigious law firms in New York State and they have connections in other states, including New Jersey. I'm not promising anything, Cassie, but maybe they can file an appeal to the governor requesting commutation of your mother's sentence."

I started to shake, "Are you really serious? You mean they can really do that?"

"Now hold on, Cassie," Jeremy said grabbing both my arms. "This is a long shot and I'm not even sure it can be done, remember I'm not a lawyer. When I get back to the city, I'll contact Ben Greenberg and see what he has to say. He'll probably need to do a lot of research into your mother's case but it will all be on public record. Maybe there's something that can be done but I don't want you to get your hopes up. Even if there is a chance, sometimes these things take years."

I could feel the tears starting to flow, "But she's already served so many years, it just isn't fair."

Jeremy pulled me into his arms, "Life isn't always fair," he whispered.

I returned home, after my vacation, on a Sunday afternoon, feeling rested but sad to leave Jeremy in Westhampton. I knew that he needed more time to be alone in an attempt to break through his writer's block but I was anxious for him to get back to New York and contact his lawyer. Despite his words of advice, not to place too much faith in a positive outcome, all I could envision was Mama walking out through those prison gates.

I was surprised, when arriving at the house that nobody was home. There was a note from Aunt Jean propped up on the hallway table, telling me that they had been invited to Amanda's for dinner and taken Pepper with them. It also told me that there was a letter in my room and it looked like it was from Lexie. I left my suitcase by the front door and raced up the stairs to find an envelope on my night table with Grandpa's address on the back flap. I have to admit, I was both excited and anxious when I opened it up. I was praying that Lexie had finally reached out to me but at the same time I had an ominous feeling. The letter was written on a single page and dated just over a week before.

> *Dear Cassie,*
>
> *Just thought I should let you know that Grandpa died two weeks ago. He had a stroke and was gone four days later. We buried him beside Grandma last Friday.*
>
> *He left the house to me but I am selling it and leaving New Jersey. I have left it in the hands of a real estate agent because I will be leaving for Somalia with Todd next week and not sure if we will be coming back.*
>
> *You won't be able to get in touch with me but once we get settled I'll send you a postcard with my address. I'm sorry that you continue to support our mother after what she did. I can never come to terms with that.*
>
> *Keep well. Your sister, Lexie.*

I let the letter flutter to the floor then, after a few seconds, slowly picked it up again and read it through twice more. It was like reading a letter from a complete stranger and I was both angry and sad. I couldn't believe that Lexie hadn't given me the opportunity to attend Grandpa's funeral. I know that I hadn't been close to him but he was my flesh and blood and I was sure, in my heart that he felt badly for Mama. As for Lexie leaving the country without even giving me the chance to say goodbye, well that was unforgivable. I had intended to visit Mama that afternoon but how could I tell her that Lexie was thousands of miles away and might never return. I had always believed that Lexie and I would reconcile one day but now it looked hopeless. Suddenly I felt a deep sense of despair and dropped down onto my bed with the letter clutched to my chest. That's when the tears started to fall.

An hour later, I was on my way to Clinton determined to keep my composure when I told Mama about the letter but I forgot just how strong Mama was. She smiled when I told her that Lexie might never come back and said, "I always knew your sister had a good heart. Think of all the wonderful things she can do for those poor people. You have to let your anger go, Cassie, or it will eat you up. You have to forgive your sister and maybe one day you can work it out between you."

I shook my head, "How can you be so forgiving, Mama? She's never once been to see you. It's almost as though you don't exist and now she's gone, maybe forever."

Mama reached across the table and grasped my fingers, "Stop it, Cassie. Lexie was much younger than you were when she lost her father. She's been brainwashed ever since into thinking that her father was some kind of hero and that I, her mother, was at fault. Any doubts that she may have had were pushed aside by your grandmother. Lexie is a victim. Think about it, Cassie, she has no family. Her grandparents are all dead and she has no contact with her mother or sister. You, on the other hand, have your wonderful foster family and me. You should feel sorry for her and hope that she finds happiness with this Todd, whoever he is, and that she finds some purpose in her life."

I immediately felt a little ashamed and by the time I left the prison that day, I felt so much more at peace with myself.

When I told Aunt Jean and Uncle Frank about Lexie's letter, Uncle Frank immediately went into lawyer mode. "This is all a little strange. How do you know that your grandfather really left the house to your sister? In today's market, it's probably worth quite a bit of money."

"I don't want any money, Uncle," I replied.

"Well, I think you're making a mistake at just accepting this at face value. If I were you I'd demand to see a copy of the will."

"No," I said forcefully, "I won't do it so please, let's not discuss this any further."

Uncle Frank threw up his hands and rolled his eyes at Aunt Jean, "Okay, if you insist on being stubborn, so be it."

"I do insist," I said. "Now, how did you enjoy your dinner at Amanda's?"

# CHAPTER 34

I had only been home for two weeks when I began to feel very restless. I had spoken to Jeremy every day but he had made little progress with his writing. When I asked him when he was going back home, he seemed a little evasive and couldn't give me a straight answer and that made me even more restless. I considered surprising him by showing up on his doorstep unannounced but on second thought, decided against it. I wasn't sure how he would react, even though he claimed he missed me more and more each day.

When Jazz called and invited me for the weekend, I jumped at the chance to leave Asbury Park for a few days. With Mr. Graham's blessing, I left the paper at noon on Thursday and drove to Clinton to see Mama, with the intention of continuing my journey onto New York later that day.

Mama looked particularly lovely that afternoon. She had put on a little weight and I believe it added to her beauty. Somehow it made her face a little softer even though I could see tiny lines starting to form around her eyes and mouth. Unable to embrace me, she reached across the table and lightly touched my fingertips, "You look like you're going somewhere special, Cassie. Are you going to meet your young man?"

I smiled, "No Mama, I'm going to visit Jazz for the weekend. Jeremy is still in Westhampton."

"Ah, I see, and when are you bringing him to visit me? You know I would like to meet him."

"I don't know Mama, he's very busy with his new novel."

Mama looked me straight in the eyes and shocked me when she said, "Are you ashamed of me, Cassie?"

I started to reach for her hand but caught the guard staring at me, "Oh no, Mama," I replied, "I could never be ashamed of you. I am more proud of you than you can ever imagine."

"Then why haven't you brought him for a visit?"

I hesitated trying to think of the right words, "I'm not really sure. I think it might be this place. It's so depressing and I don't like the idea of him seeing you here."

Mama persisted, "But I'm going to be here for a long time. What if the two of you decide to get married? Am I never going to meet my son-in-law?"

I pondered telling Mama that Jeremy had agreed to consult with his lawyer about her, when he got back, but I didn't want to get her hopes up, "I don't know what's going to happen with Jeremy but I promise I will bring him for a visit soon. Just give me a little more time."

Mama leaned across the tale and whispered, "Do you love him, honey?"

I lowered my head, unable to look into those knowing green eyes, "Yes, I love him and I know he loves me but I'm not sure I fit into his world."

When I left the prison that day, I kept thinking about our conversation. It wasn't the first time I had imagined being married to Jeremy, but it was the first time I had vocalized my fears about fulfilling the role of Mrs. Jeremy Kent. As I entered Manhattan, I tried to shake off my thoughts and concentrate on the weekend ahead. I was anxious to see Jazz especially now that she and Julius had bought a brownstone on Lennox Avenue and moved in together. For the past two months they had been decorating the house and, on the telephone, she had seemed deliriously happy. I couldn't wait to see her and when I rang the doorbell and she opened the door, we couldn't stop hugging each other. Finally she pushed me away, holding me at arm's length, "My oh my, looking pretty good, baby," she said looking me up and down and admiring my new outfit, a multi-colored loose fitting dress reminiscent of something her mother might wear.

Jazz was casual, in jeans and a peasant blouse, holding a spatula in her right hand. "You look very domesticated, don't tell me you're actually cooking?" I teased.

"Ha!" she chuckled, grabbing my hand and pulling me down a hallway, "You know I don't cook. This is a pooper-scooper."

I wrinkled my nose as I was dragged through a doorway into a kitchen, "And what are you doing with it?" I asked, frowning.

"Well, I was about to run after Julius. He just left, before you arrived, with Badger."

"Who's Badger? Don't tell me you have a dog now as well?"

"He's actually Julius's dog. He's had him for almost ten years. He's a beagle and a real sweetheart. I got two for the price of one, Cassie, and I'm so happy."

I felt genuinely pleased for Jazz, but after she showed me around the house, I was even a little envious. It was obvious that she and Julius had poured a lot of love into decorating. Everywhere I looked there were reminders of their heritage, bright bold colors, and huge comfy chairs with enormous pillows in animal prints, framed pictures of jungle scenes and all kinds of wooden artifacts.

"It's a wonderful house, Jazz, you and Julius have done a remarkable job," I said, once we were back in the enormous modern kitchen sipping on Amarula.

"Thanks, Cassie. We fell in love with it right away and it's been so much fun shopping for everything."

"And Julius, how is that going? Is there going to be a wedding coming up or are you just going to live in sin," I said teasingly.

Jazz got up from the table to refill our glasses and then slowly sat down again, " No wedding I'm afraid. I didn't want to tell you this before because I wasn't sure you would approve but Julius is still married."

I know I must have looked a little surprised but Jazz continued, "His wife won't give him a divorce. I'm not really sure why she's hanging on to him. They were only married for just over three years and Julius claims it was like hell on earth."

"Surely there has to be another side to the story," I suggested.

Jazz shook her head, "I can only repeat what Julius has told me. About six months into the marriage, his wife had a miscarriage and it sent her over the edge, She went into a deep depression and her whole personality changed. Despite intensive therapy and medication, she was never the same again. Apparently she went from being this vibrant beautiful woman into a miserable shrew and eventually Julius had to get out."

"How sad," I said, "but why won't she let him go? Are they fighting over support?""

"I told you, I'm not sure but I think she just can't bear to see him happy. She blames him for not standing by her, but he spent over two years putting up with her behavior until he couldn't take it any more."

Jazz put her finger to her lips as she heard the front door open and the scrabble of paws running down the hallway. Badger stopped in his tracks when he saw me until Jazz called out, "It's okay Badger, this is my friend, Cassie. Come and say hello."

I stayed seated so as not to startle the dog and then suddenly, there he was sitting at my feet, head cocked to one side surveying me with curiosity. I reached out a hand at a level with his chest and said, "Hi Badger," and to my surprise, he lifted his paw and placed it inside my palm.

"Watch it," came a voice from the doorway, "he'll have you eating out of that paw soon if you're not careful."

I stood up, patted Badger on the head and made my way over to Julius, who looked as handsome as ever, "He's adorable," I said giving him a hug.

On Friday, Julius was at a photo shoot for most of the day so Jazz and I took Badger to Central Park for a run and then spent the rest of the day shopping on Fifth Avenue. By evening, I was feeling much more relaxed and perfectly comfortable in Jazz's new home. So relaxed, in fact, that after a wonderful supper cooked by Julius, consisting of an arugola and nectarine salad and a seafood pasta, along with an abundant amount of white wine, I dozed off on one of the huge comfy sofas.

On Saturday, we took a drive into Stamford, Connecticut, had dinner at a quaint restaurant on the way back and then took in a movie. All in all, it was a wonderful day and I had managed to put thoughts of Jeremy to the back of my mind, but on Sunday morning I got a disturbing surprise.

Julius was out walking Badger and Jazz and I were lounging in our robes, already on our third cup of coffee, and leafing through the New York Times. I had just turned to the society section when a photo caught my eye. It was a picture of Jeremy, in a tuxedo, embracing a very attractive blonde wearing a beaded strapless dress that showed off a rather voluptuous figure. I was stunned for a moment and then I read the caption 'Author, Jeremy Kent and his ex-wife, socialite Courtney Locke in attendance at the Ellen Addison-James Benefit for the Blind in Westhampton on Saturday night.'

My hand started to shake as I attempted to put my coffee mug back on the table and Jazz immediately looked up, "What is it, Cassie, you look like you've seen a ghost?"

I silently handed her the paper and waited for her reaction. Finally, she shrugged and handed the paper back, "So?" she asked. "What's the problem?"

I stood up and walked over to the window, "It's pretty obvious isn't it?" I snapped, "He's supposed to be working on his novel but apparently he's fooling around with his ex."

Jazz came over and placed her hand on my shoulder, "Now hang on, that's absurd. You can't make that kind of judgment from a photograph. He was probably there alone and she happened to be there too. I gather from what you told me before that there was no ill will between them, so it's only natural that they might hug if they run into each other."

I turned and looked Jazz in the eye," I want to go home," I said.

Jazz took a step back and then threw her hands in the air, "Now you are being ridiculous. What is that going to achieve?"

"I don't know," I replied walking out of the room, "I just know I can't stay here. I'm going up to change and pack."

Jazz didn't follow me and was in the kitchen when I came back down, "I'm sorry, " I said, "thank you for a really lovely weekend. Say goodbye to Julius for me."

Jazz looked angry, "You really are serious aren't you?" What do you intend to do now, sabotage your relationship because of some insane jealous reaction to a photograph which probably means absolutely nothing?"

"Goodbye, Jazz", I said firmly and quickly walked away and out of the front door,

# CHAPTER 35

When I arrived home, earlier than expected, Aunt Jean greeted me at the door, "How come you're here so early?" she asked.

"I wasn't feeling very well," I lied, " I think I'll just go on upstairs and lie down for a while."

Aunt Jean looked at me suspiciously, "Well all right, but if you need anything just call downstairs. Your uncle and Billy are at the beach with Pepper but I'll be in the kitchen."

"Okay, thanks," I mumbled and took off for my bedroom.

It was almost suppertime when there was a tap on my door, "Cassie, are you all right? Mom said you weren't feeling well."

It was Billy. "Come in," I called out then watched while he poked his head around the door.

I was lying fully clothed on my bed with a pen and writing pad in my hand, "Come in, come in," I called out again.

Billy walked over and sat down gingerly on the side of the bed, "Watcha writing?" he asked.

"Oh nothing much, just a letter," I answered putting the pad face down, on the night table.

"Are you coming down for supper? Mom made spaghetti and meat balls and I saw this yummy chocolate cake in the fridge."

I smiled and took his hand, "No, I won't be coming down now, Billy. I may come down later for something to eat though."

"But you should eat if you're sick, Cassie."

I squeezed his hand, "I'll be all right, Billy, really. You go on down now."

Slowly he got up to leave but paused before he closed the door, " I hope you feel better, Cassie. I love you," he murmured.

I couldn't help myself after that. I just managed to wait long enough for Billy to leave the room and then I burst into tears.

I tried to write a letter to Jeremy but finally gave up and eventually drifted off. It was nine o'clock when my phone rang and I realized I'd been asleep for two hours. I knew immediately that it had to be Jeremy but I still had no idea what I was going to say to him. I picked up the receiver on the third ring and whispered, "Hello."

For a moment there was silence and then I heard his voice, "Cassie, are your there?"

"Yes, I'm here." I said in a hushed tone.

"Oh, I thought I had the wrong number. How are you doing, sweetheart? Tell me, how was your trip? I want to hear all about the new house."

"My trip was just fine," I replied abruptly, "and the house is very nice."

"That's it?" Jeremy said, "How's Jazz and how's the relationship working out? What did you do all weekend?"

"I should be asking you that question," I snapped back.

Jeremy paused, "Hey, wait a minute, what's the problem here? Have I done something to upset you?"

"You could say that. I would suspect that cavorting with one's ex wife would fill the bill."

"What?" Jeremy sounded incredulous, "What on earth are you taking about, Cassie?"

"Your picture is in the New York Times. Don't tell me you didn't see it. Looks like you were having a lovely time."

Jeremy started to chuckle, "Ha! You're jealous and I didn't think you had a jealous bone in your body."

"What were you doing with her?" I demanded.

"If you saw the picture, you already know," Jeremy answered, starting to sound a little annoyed. "There was a benefit for the Ellen

Addison-James Foundation. In case you've never heard of the woman, she was a rather well-known writer of historical novels who lost her sight at the age of fifty-two. Both Courtney's family and I have long been a supporter of the foundation. Her grandmother, on her father's side, was blind and I became involved for that reason, and the fact that Ellen Addison-James was an author. So, that's how Courtney and I happened to be in the same place at the same time."

"And you weren't her escort?" I asked rather sheepishly.

"Hell, no. I told you, she's a great girl and we have a history. For God's sake, Cassie, I was married to the woman, so I gave her a hug. What's the big deal?"

"I just felt sick when I saw it, that's all."

"Look, I love you and maybe that's why I'm having so much trouble writing. I just keep thinking about you and I have this complete mental block every time I sit down at the computer. If that doesn't convince you, I don't know what will. Anyway, I'll be back in New York tomorrow and then I have quite a bit of business to attend to but I'll be in Asbury Park early on Saturday evening, so don't make any dates."

My heart suddenly leapt into my chest, "Oh, Jeremy, I'm so sorry. Jazz told me the photo probably meant absolutely nothing but when I saw you with Courtney I really did feel sick. How can you ever forgive me, I've been so stupid?"

"Forgiven and forgotten," Jeremy replied.

I was surprised when I saw Jeremy pull up in a cab at seven o'clock on the following Saturday. I watched him step out onto the driveway and couldn't believe had taken a cab all the way from New York. He looked so handsome in white slacks and a black polo shirt and I felt that familiar flutter in my chest. I waited while he paid the driver and then raced out of the front door, straight into his arms. In the next moment he was kissing me tenderly on the lips and then looking into my eyes, "And how's my lovely lady?" he asked.

I brushed a stray lock of hair from his forehead and replied, "I'm wonderful now that you're here." Then taking his hand I took him into the house, "Let's go inside, everyone wants to say hello."

Once a few steps down the hallway, I stopped for a moment, "Surely you didn't come all the way here by cab?"

Jeremy grinned, "No, that would have been a little extravagant even for me. I took the yacht and moored it at the Belmar marina. We'll go there after I've seen your folks but you might want to change."

I looked down at the lilac silk dress I had put on especially for the occasion, "Don't you like my dress? I thought we were going out to dinner."

Jeremy took me by the shoulders, "It's lovely, you're lovely, but it's not quite suitable for where we're going. I'm sorry I should have warned you earlier but I'm whisking you away for the night and not letting you out of my sight until tomorrow afternoon so you might want to put on something comfortable and throw a couple of things in a bag."

Just as Jeremy finished speaking, Pepper came running along the hallway and then proceeded to run around his legs barking like crazy with excitement. Jeremy just chuckled and tried to catch him but it just made things worse. Then Uncle Frank appeared at the living room door and walked towards us, calling out in a stern voice, "Pepper, settle down."

"It's okay," said Jeremy extending his hand towards my uncle, "she's just having some fun. How are you doing, Frank?"

Pepper had already stopped barking and flopped down at Jeremy's feet, "I'm doing just fine thanks," Uncle Frank replied. "Come on in and say hello to Jean and Billy. They're in the kitchen making a cake for Amanda. It's her birthday tomorrow and Billy promised to bring the cake. Of course, Jean had no alternative but to help out."

"I see," Jeremy remarked then looking at me said, "Does that mean you have to be back in time for the party tomorrow, Cassie?"

I shook my head and smiled, "No, it's okay. I'm sure Billy won't mind if I beg off. Now, why don't you go in and chat with my folks while I go up and change."

Forty-five minutes later we were driving towards the marina in my car. It hadn't taken me long to pack an overnight bag and change into a navy and white striped top, white jeans and a pair of Keds.

I figured we would be doing quite a bit of sailing and I was bound and determined to look like a seasoned yachtsman.

Once on board the Dream Catcher, I took my belongings down to the cabin and then went back up to the deck where the sun was just beginning to go down. Jeremy was talking to two men in uniforms, that I couldn't identify, and they were placing three metal containers on a table covered with a white linen tablecloth. I held back, not wanting to interrupt, but as soon as the men left I stepped onto the deck and asked, "What's going on, who were those men?"

Jeremy smiled, "Well my love, you see these containers, they hold something special."

On closer inspection I could see that they were food containers and I could already detect a rather tantalizing scent wafting towards me in the breeze. "Yes, I bet they do," I said reaching out and touching the metal and then leaping back when I encountered the hot surface.

Jeremy quickly stepped forward, "Careful darling," he said and lifting the lid off of the largest container cried out, "Voila, Madame!"

The array of steaming hot seafood assaulted my senses. There was lobster, king crab, huge bay scallops and even jumbo shrimp. "Oh, my goodness," I exclaimed, "it looks wonderful."

"But that's not all," Jeremy said laughing, as he opened the other containers. One was filled with tiny new potatoes, baby carrots and asparagus while the other, smaller one, displayed chocolate mousse, macaroons and sugarcoated almonds.

I clapped my hands together, "I can't believe you arranged all this. It all looks so amazing."

"Ah, but you have to work for your supper, " Jeremy teased. "Bring me plates and silverware from the galley wench, and I will open the champagne."

"Are you serious," I asked. "Champagne? What's the occasion."

"Just being together," Jeremy replied picking me up and whirling me around, " and if you're really nice to me there might be another surprise."

"In that case, " I said, "I will do as you bid," and with that I disappeared below deck.

Just over an hour later, we had eaten as much of the delicious food as we could possibly eat and were feeling wonderfully mellow from the effects of the champagne. It was dark by then and with the lights along the deck and those of the other yachts beside us, it was so romantic that I didn't want the night to end. Suddenly I remembered what Jeremy had said earlier and asked coyly, "Well, have I been nice to you?"

"You've been very nice," Jeremy answered nonchalantly.

I hesitated expecting him to say more and when he didn't I said, "So, where's my other surprise?"

Jeremy grinned, "Oh that, I almost forgot all about it. It's under your chair."

"What?" I said, "What's under my chair?"

"Why don't you look and see?"

I leaned right over, nearly falling on my head and peered under the chair but couldn't see anything, "Nothing's there."

Jeremy just sat there with his arms crossed, smiling and shaking his head.

"Oh rats!" I muttered then stood up and went down on my knees. I still couldn't see anything on the deck but when I stuck my head under the chair and looked up I saw a square shaped box covered in gold paper taped to the bottom of the seat. Slowly I pulled it away then got up and sat gingerly back down.

"Open it," Jeremy said.

I looked across at him, then down at the box in my hand and after hesitating I began to peel away the wrapping revealing a black velvet box that I knew could only mean one thing. My heart started to race as I opened the box and then gasped when I saw the ring inside. It was the largest emerald cut diamond that I had ever seen and breathtaking. My hand started to shake and Jeremy reached over, took the box from me and removed the ring. Looking very serious he got up and came around to my side of the table then, to my astonishment, got down on one knee, "Marry me, Cassie," he whispered.

I started to cry and he put his arms around me, "I didn't expect that kind of reaction," he said.

I slipped out of his arms, "Oh Jeremy, I'm only crying because I'm so happy. Of course I'll marry you."

He gently wiped the tears away from my eyes and said, "I was hoping you would say that but I do have one condition."

"What is it," I asked imagining that he was just about to tease me all over again.

"I want to do the right thing, Cassie. That means asking your mother's permission to marry you. I know she can't be at our wedding but, at least, she will feel as though she has played some part in it."

I was stunned by Jeremy's thoughtfulness, "It's a wonderful idea and I love you even more for thinking about Mama. I know I haven't been fair to you, not letting you visit her but that's all going to change. She already had you added to the visitor's list in the hope that I would bring you with me one day. She's going to be so happy and right now you've made me feel like the luckiest woman in the world."

# CHAPTER 36

Jeremy's visit with Mama caused quite a stir. An elderly man approached him in the waiting area and proceeded to reel off all of Jeremy's novels that he had read and how much he enjoyed them. This encounter, witnessed by several others, suddenly alerted everyone as to who the celebrity was in their midst and Jeremy was soon surrounded by a small mob of fans. I wasn't used to seeing him in this type of situation. In New York, people were pretty blasé and Jeremy always kept a low profile when we went out. Meanwhile, in Westhampton Beach, everybody knew who he was and there were several other well-known people in the area. I thought the excitement was over when we entered the room where Mama was waiting, but there was a buzz when Jeremy walked in behind me and I could see a lot of women craning their necks to get a good look at him. Of course, Mama was the epitome of serenity and sat quietly, with her hands clasped together on the table, as we approached.

When we reached the table, she smiled up at me and said "Hello honey, I see you've brought your young man with you," and before I had a chance to respond she turned to Jeremy and said, "I am so happy to meet you, Cassie has told me so much about you."

I could see that Jeremy felt a little awkward, not being able to shake hands, but he gave a little nod and replied, "It's my pleasure Mrs. Taylor and I must apologize for not coming sooner."

Mama grinned and remarked graciously, "Oh I think I know who's responsible for that." Then glancing in my direction she said, "Cassie, why don't you pull over another chair and then Jeremy can sit down with us."

Jeremy turned and gazed around the room but I placed my hand on his arm, "It's okay, I'll find one."

It took me a few moments to find an available chair and I was wondering what Mama and Jeremy could be talking about. When I returned I found them engrossed in a conversation about Jeremy's latest novel, but then the topic quickly turned to our engagement and Mama was anxious to hear if we had set a date for our wedding. I had imagined the visit being uncomfortable for both Mama and Jeremy but I couldn't have been more wrong. By the time we left, one would have thought they were old friends just catching up.

I didn't have to ask Jeremy what he was thinking. Before we were out of the prison gates, he remarked, "What a lovely lady, Cassie. I know now where you get your good looks and even some of your mannerisms."

"Really, so you liked Mama?" I asked anxiously.

"Yes, very much. She's an intelligent woman and it's obvious she thinks the world of you. It's too bad that your sister is estranged from her."

At the mention of Lexie, I felt sad and then a little annoyed, "Well Lexie had every opportunity to visit but she just can't forgive Mama. As far as I'm concerned it's her loss."

Jeremy put his arm around my shoulders as he led me to the car, "I understand, Cassie but don't forget your sister was brainwashed by your grandmother, so maybe you should try and let that anger go."

We decided to have the wedding in the middle of December and Jeremy said I could make whatever arrangements I wanted with money being no object. The only condition was that he didn't want to be involved with any of the details. I was a little hurt by his attitude at first but when he explained that Courtney had driven him almost mad arranging their wedding, I began to understand why he felt the way he did. We would be living in the New York apartment and, even though it was almost a ninety-minute commute to Asbury Park, I was going to keep on working for the time being and if the weather was too bad for driving, I could always stay over with Aunt Jean and Uncle Frank.

I wanted a traditional wedding in a church and Jazz suggested that we get married at St. Bartholomews on Park Avenue and have our reception at the St. Regis. It sounded all very grand to me but Jeremy reminded me that I had carte blanche to do whatever I wished and by September, with a lot of help from Jazz and Aunt Jean, most of the arrangements were made.

The guest list numbered well over a hundred with most of the names put forth by Jeremy. As well as his immediate family, there were several aunts, uncles and cousins, friends from New York and Westhampton Beach as well as several business associates. My guest list looked pathetic by comparison, numbering only twenty people, most of whom were colleagues from the paper. Uncle Frank had agreed to give me away and Jazz was my one and only bridesmaid. She was adamant that she did not want to be referred to as a matron of honor. She said it made her sound old.

Shopping for a dress had been the most difficult and nerve racking. I must have tried on at least fifteen gowns with Jazz shaking her head every time I stepped out of the dressing room. Then, when I was beginning to give up in despair, her face lit up and she dashed over from her seat in the elegant salon and danced around me clapping her hands. "Oh, Cassie, it's beautiful and it fits perfectly, I don't even think it will need altering."

I surveyed myself in the large three-way mirror and had to admit I loved what I saw. The dress was strapless with a simple bodice made of chiffon but the skirt was organza and resembled thousands of soft swans' feathers. I felt like a princess and I knew that Jazz was right. Now all we had to do was focus on her outfit but, unbeknown to me, she had already picked out a dress and couldn't wait to show it to me. Later that day, back at her home with Julius looking on in amusement, she modeled a marvelous lavender gown that set off her dark skin and she looked fabulous.

# CHAPTER 37

It seemed strange that I had never met Jeremy's family and yet in a few months I would be part of their lives. Jeremy suggested that we spend Thanksgiving in Laguna Beach and, although anxious, I was glad that he was astute enough to realize that I needed to make a connection with his parents before we got married.

Both October and November were very mild that year and the leaves had only just begun to change color, but I was looking forward to getting away and spending a few days in the sun. I had lived near the ocean most of my life but there was no comparison between Laguna Beach and Asbury Park. As we drove along the ocean road I couldn't help noticing the palm trees, which towered above us, and there were surfers everywhere riding the waves. It was no wonder that Jeremy's parents decided to move into such a lovely area.

When we parked the rental car outside of the Kent's home, I was struck by the beauty and yet, the simplicity of the house. It resembled a Spanish villa with a red tile roof and the surrounding gardens were full of shrubs and colorful flowers. I could hardly wait to see the inside.

As we stepped onto the driveway, the front door opened and Jeremy's mother came running towards us. Vivienne Kent was my height and slim with coal black hair and large deep brown eyes. It was obvious whom Jeremy took after. "Hi darling," she said as she threw her arms around his neck, "I'm so glad you're here."

Jeremy returned his mother's embrace and then looked over her shoulder at his father, "Hi Dad," he said cheerfully, "you're looking good."

I only had a moment to check out his father, who was even taller than Jeremy but fair skinned with light brown hair, before his mother turned to me and held out both arms, "Come here, Cassie," she said, "let me look at you."

I felt a bit awkward being given the once over as she took my hands and then slowly looked me up and down, "Why you are even lovelier than your pictures," she remarked.

"Thank you so much, Mrs. Kent," I replied, "That's very kind of you. I'm so happy to finally meet you."

Jeremy watched with a smile on his face while his mother waved her husband over, "Come Mark, say hello to your future daughter-in-law."

Once inside the house, I was shown to my room so that I could empty my suitcase and change out of my traveling clothes. At the sight of the lonely single bed, I realized that I would be sleeping alone for the next three nights. I didn't really mind because I treasured my alone time and suspected that I would have had my fill of socializing by the time we flew back to New York. The room itself was as far from Spanish as one could imagine, all pink and blue chintz and fluffy rugs, but I loved it, it was so cozy.

I changed into a pair of lightweight cream slacks and a coffee colored top and when I eventually joined the Kents' in the living room, I felt a lot more comfortable. Jeremy was nowhere to be seen but I was told that he had already changed and was just out in the back garden catching up with a neighbor. I was offered a glass of wine and informed that from that moment on, it was no longer Mr. and Mrs. Kent but Mark and Vivienne, "We won't ask you to call us Mom or Dad," Vivienne said, "that would be far too presumptuous of us."

At that, I lowered my head and it was almost as though she picked up on what I was thinking. "I want you to know that Jeremy had told us all about what happened with your parents and we don't want you to feel that our relationship will be affected by that in any way".

I lifted my head and looked her straight in the eyes, "I have nothing to be ashamed or embarrassed about," I said rather forcefully. "My father deserved what was coming to him and my mother means more to me than anyone else in this world".

Vivienne Kent hesitated for a moment and then whispered, "Even Jeremy?"

I shook my head, "I don't know," I muttered, "I just can't compare the two. I love Jeremy but my mother is my flesh and blood and I'll always stand by her no matter what anyone else thinks."

Mark Kent walked over and sat down beside me taking my hand, "My dear girl," he said, "we completely understand and I hope we haven't offended you. It's obvious that Jeremy is in love with you and I can see why. It's admirable the way you support your mother and I, for one, are happy that you will soon become part of the family."

"Me too," Vivienne added perching on the arm of the chair and putting her arm around me.

Just then Jeremy entered the room and seeing the little tableau asked, "What's going on?"

"Just getting to know each other, that's all," his father replied releasing my hand and getting up. "Now how about something to nibble on?"

That night we all went out to dinner at a local seafood restaurant and then Jeremy and I took a walk on the beach. It was so romantic and later we had trouble tearing ourselves away from each other but there was no chance of us sharing a bed in that house. All the rooms were on one level and apparently Vivienne was a very light sleeper.

The next day was Thanksgiving and, despite her protestations, I decided to help Vivienne prepare dinner for later that afternoon. I admitted to being a poor cook but was useful at menial tasks like peeling potatoes and scrubbing carrots and I was actually enjoying myself as we chatted about the upcoming wedding and our plans for the future.

Because the family would all be together at the wedding, Jeremy's brother Ethan decided not to join his parents for Thanksgiving. I thought there would only be four of us at the table and wondered why we were preparing so much food but Vivienne informed me that there would be four more guests. The Kents' belonged to a dinner club that was comprised of six couples. They rotated to each other's houses once a month and occasionally dined out. One of the couples had no children while one of the other couples had a son but he had moved to Australia and they rarely saw him. These were the four other guests and the whole evening turned out to be a lot of fun.

I actually enjoyed my three days at the Kents', especially the time we spent at the beach and my pitiful attempt at surfing. On the day that we left to return home, I even felt a little sad to be leaving.

# CHAPTER 38

I spent the night at Jeremy's before returning home the next day. I really needed that time with him. Being in the same house and not being able to share the same bed had been a strain on both of us. By the following morning, despite little sleep, we felt all the tension drain away and even though we knew we would not see each other for almost a week, we felt closer than ever.

Uncle Frank was at work when I got home and Billy was at the community center with several other mentally challenged youngsters, including Amanda, taking a simple woodworking class. It was pleasant having time alone with Aunt Jean and she wanted to know every detail of my visit to the Kents'. I felt a little disloyal when I told her how comfortable they had made me but I should have known better because she responded, " I am so glad to hear that. It's so important that you have a good relationship with your in-laws. I can't wait to meet them at the wedding."

"What about Uncle Frank's parents? You never talk about them. I remember a long time ago, I asked him where they were and he said he didn't know and when I asked him to explain, he walked out of the room. He seemed upset so I didn't want to ask him again."

Aunt Jean sighed, "Your uncle was an orphan. He was moved around from one foster family to another and he never knew his parents. As far as he knows they simply abandoned him at birth and it still hurts him to this day even thinking about it. He's an amazing man, Cassie. He became a lawyer through sheer hard work and determination and I've never ceased to admire him for that."

"I had no idea. And what about you Auntie, why don't you ever see your parents? I know they live in Ireland but you never ever talk about them."

I noticed my aunt's eyes tear up when she answered me, "I came here on holiday because I had heard so much about America and I wanted to see it for myself. I was only in New York for a week when I met your uncle and quite honestly, it was love at first sight. We were married two weeks later."

I gasped in surprise, "Oh, my goodness, that's amazing. So you stayed and you've never been home again?"

"That's right and just over eight months after we got married, Billy was born a little prematurely. My parents are Catholic and have strong family values. They accused me of sleeping with your uncle before the wedding and even worse, and something I couldn't forgive, when they found out that Billy had Down's Syndrome, they told me that was God's way of punishing me for my sins."

I slipped my arm around my aunt's shoulders, "I'm so sorry but I feel even sorrier for them missing out on so much. Have you never thought about just going there and taking Billy with you. Maybe they would change their minds if they met him and saw what a wonderful young man he is."

Aunt Jean shook her head, "No, we wouldn't be welcome. I never had a close relationship with my parents even as a child, so there's no hope for that now. I have to be honest, Cassie, I don't know if my mother and father are still alive and you may not like what I am going to say but, I don't really care. My one regret is that I never had any siblings. It's all rather sad, neither your uncle or I have any other family except you and Billy."

I kissed my aunt on the cheek, "You'll always have me Auntie. I can never ever repay you for what you've done for me. Right now, I feel terribly guilty that I am just learning about you and Uncle Frank. Maybe I've been too wrapped up in myself."

Aunt Jean patted my hand and then got up, "Nonsense. Now enough of this, let's put on our coats and take Pepper for a walk. It's starting to snow and you know how she loves that."

During the weeks leading up to the wedding, my life fell back into its normal pattern. All of the arrangements had been made and I could relax although there was an underlying anxiety just thinking about walking down the aisle and being the center of attention. We had decided to forgo a rehearsal dinner and I made Jazz and Aunt Jean promise me that there would be no bridal shower. I just couldn't cope with a lot of socializing.

On the eve of the wedding, as much as I wanted to see Jeremy, I stayed over at Jazz's house. Julius was the perfect host, cooking up a special dish of tarragon chicken and risotto and breaking open a bottle of Dom Perignon. By bedtime, I was feeling so mellow that I had no problem sleeping through the night only to be awakened by Jazz at seven o'clock singing, 'It's a Lovely Day Today'.

Preparing for the wedding was actually a lot of fun. Jazz had arranged for two experts from Trend Cosmetics to come to the house to do our hair and makeup. It took some persuasion, on my part, to ensure that I looked like me, and not some fancy model with a sophisticated hairdo and false eyelashes. By the time I was ready and standing in front of the mirror in my dress and veil, Jazz had to admit that I was right, "You look just gorgeous," she said, "still you, but even more beautiful."

It was a clear and sunny December day with very little snow on the ground when we arrived at St. Bartholomew's. Uncle Frank, looking absolutely dapper in a black tuxedo and silky lilac tie, was waiting for me and took my arm, "You look stunning," he said. "I feel so proud today, Cassie."

I gave him a peck on the cheek and then with the thought of Mama on my mind and a silent prayer for her forgiveness, I lied, "Thank you Uncle, there's nobody else in the world I would rather have by my side right now."

Jazz, looking amazing in her lavender gown, joined us while we waited but I could feel myself getting more and more nervous. Suddenly I heard the strains of the wedding march and Uncle Frank was guiding me down the aisle. I can hardly remember that long walk. I was aware of a blur of faces on either side of me but I kept facing forward with my eyes on Jeremy, who was smiling at me from the steps of the altar. I hardly even noticed his brother, Ethan, who was his best man and I know when I said my vows, my voice was shaking.

When the minister finally said, "You may kiss the bride," I was so relieved that I felt all the tension drain from my body. Jeremy took me in his arms and kissed me rather passionately causing a wolf whistle from the front pew on my left. I broke away from Jeremy only to see that it was Billy grinning from ear to ear and I couldn't help myself. I ran down the steps and planted a kiss on his cheek and that's when the applause broke out.

It was at the reception at the St. Regis that I eventually got to meet Ethan, his wife Jan, and their three grown children Noah, Christopher and Beth. Ethan looked more like his father while Jane was a tiny woman, rather plain, but witty and a lot of fun. I could tell that I was going to get along with the whole family. I think Jeremy's parents were especially happy to see so many of his family reunited at one time. There were so many aunts, uncles and cousins that it was a little overwhelming. My own family seemed so small in comparison and the most important member was missing, Mama. I tried not to think too much about Lexie but I did wonder what she would think of her big sister getting married in such a grand place. Aunt Jean looked amazing in a rose silk suit and when she caught me looking a little pensive at the reception she was her usual perceptive self, "Try not to dwell on your mother not being here, Cassie," she said, "I'm sure she is with you in spirit."

I gave her a hug, "Thank you Auntie," I responded, "today has been wonderful and I am so grateful to have you and Uncle Frank and Billy here with me but if Mama had been here it would have been perfect."

When Jeremy and I left to spend the night in the Astoria Suite, the party was still in full swing. We were leaving on our honeymoon early in the morning and didn't expect to see any of Jeremy's family again for quite some time. It was sad saying goodnight to everyone but especially to my own family because I had finally moved out of my home in Asbury Park. Billy seemed particularly upset and I had trouble prying his arms from around my neck, "It's okay Billy," I whispered in his ear, "I'll be back so often you'll get sick of seeing me and you can come visit me in New York whenever you like."

That seemed to settle him down and I had to laugh when he said, "Can I come on the boat too in the summer?"

"Of course," I answered, "and you can bring Amanda."

I could hardly believe that I was really Jeremy's wife but after a memorable night when he assured me over and over that I wasn't dreaming, we flew out of La Guardia for our honeymoon in Venice. I had never been out of the country before and didn't really know what to expect even though I had poured over dozens of travel brochures and even read a book on Italian history.

When we arrived at the Marco Polo airport after a long flight, we took a water-taxi to the Gritti Palace Hotel, situated right on the Grand Canal. I began to think I was in a completely different world and Jeremy was amused by my excitement especially when we were shown to our room. I gasped as I looked around at the furnishings. The bedspread, draperies and inch thick carpet were all gold and the paintings in matching gold frames looked like the masters had painted them. I felt like Cinderella.

We spent eight days exploring Venice. We visited art galleries, museums and churches. We sat in St. Mark's Square and ate at some wonderful restaurants including Harry's Bar, which Ernest Hemingway made famous. And every night we made love in the gigantic bed.

I didn't want our honeymoon to end but I had deliberately planned our time away so that I would be home in time for Christmas. Despite my state of sheer bliss, knowing that Jeremy and I would be spending the rest of our lives together, there was still a corner of my mind that I reserved for Mama. I just couldn't abandon her during the holiday season.

We arrived back in New York on a Wednesday night and the very next day I drove to Clinton. Mama was so excited to see me and wanted to hear every single detail about the wedding and the honeymoon. She couldn't wait to see the photographs of me in my bridal gown and all of Jeremy's relatives. I promised her that I would have them by Christmas and hoped to bring Jeremy with me again.

# CHAPTER 39

Jeremy wanted to spend a quiet Christmas after all the excitement of the wedding. He was having a problem getting back to his writing and having a new wife to distract him wasn't helping. I was anxious to ask him about any progress his lawyer might be making with Mama's case but I decided to wait two or three months until things had really settled down. He did agree to a Christmas day celebration at the apartment with my family and Pilar and I spent hours coming up with the menu for dinner. I was a little reticent, at first, about stepping on Pilar's toes but she treated me with the utmost respect and I enjoyed her company. I had never been a good cook but with her guidance, I learned to bake and when I presented Jeremy with my first attempt at blueberry muffins, he was impressed. Teddy was getting used to me too. After hours of laboring in the kitchen, while Pilar seemed to have boundless energy, I just slumped into the nearest chair with Teddy purring contentedly on my lap.

My family had never been to Jeremy's apartment before and they were overwhelmed by the sheer size of it and the glorious view overlooking the park. There had been a heavy snowfall overnight and everything looked pristine, just a blanket of white with all of the trees glistening in the sunlight. Billy raced from room to room wanting to see everything and when he discovered Jeremy's study, which looked more like a library, we had trouble enticing him back to the living room, "But there are so many books," he moaned, "I want to see them all."

Jeremy grinned, "Some other time, Billy. You can come back one day real soon and I'll let you spend the whole day in there."

"Okay," Billy responded rather grudgingly as he turned his attention to Teddy. I had insisted that Uncle Frank bring Pepper with them even though Jeremy was concerned that she might go after Teddy, but he needn't have worried. It was an extraordinary sight to see Teddy creep up slowly, circle Pepper and then gently lie down with her back against Pepper's belly. They were almost the same color and they looked like they belonged together.

Dinner was wonderful. Pilar had done most of the cooking but I had helped with all the chopping and mixing and I managed to bake a rather non-traditional dessert, a caramel flavored sponge cake covered in chocolate icing and whipped cream. Even Aunt Jean was surprised how much my culinary skills had improved.

The next day, I visited Mama and took her a gift that I knew she would love. It was a wedding photo of Jeremy and me in a walnut frame. I wanted to give it to her all wrapped up in tissue in a beautiful gift box but prison regulations didn't allow that and I watched in horror when the guard, inspecting everyone's packages, even took the backing out of the frame to make sure nothing was hidden inside. I begged him to let me put it back together and he relented and even allowed me to wrap it back up in some colored tissue. I had wanted Jeremy to come with me but he was insistent that he needed to work and so I sat alone in the anteroom anxiously waiting to see Mama.

When I finally entered the visitor's room, Mama wasn't sitting in her usual place. I hesitated not sure what to do and then a moment later I saw a door open and Mama was led in by a guard. She smiled when she saw me and waved me over to an empty table, "What happened, Mama?" I asked when I reached her and sat down.

"Nothing honey," she replied, "Ruby was feeling sick and I had to call for the nurse to come and see her. I didn't want to leave her until the nurse got there."

"Oh, I'm relieved. When I didn't see you, I thought something had happened to you."

"You worry too much, Cassie. You have a husband now and you should be concentrating on him."

"I can't help it, Mama. I've heard so many stories about what goes on in these places."

Mama shook her head, "How long have I been here, Cassie? We've talked about this before. Yes, some of the women are difficult to get along with but I've managed to keep my head down and so far I've been lucky. Now, I want you to stop worrying because nothing is going to happen to me and I'd much rather talk about you. How did your day go yesterday?"

I told Mama all about dinner and her eyes lit up when I mentioned the cake. Then after a nod from the guard, who was circling the room, I gave her the photograph. At first she just stared at it and then I saw the tears start to form in her eyes, "Oh, Cassie, you look so beautiful. I just wish I could have been there with you."

That was the first time in all the years that I had been visiting Mama that she had ever wished anything for herself and even then it was because she wanted to be with me. If it was possible, I think I loved her more than ever at that moment.

# CHAPTER 40

By the end of February, I was finding the commute back and forth to Asbury Park demanding and each evening, when I arrived home, I was tired and sometimes a little irritable. It was Pilar who suggested that maybe I should see a doctor, "Maybe you pregnant," she said one night when she was drying dishes and I was resting with Teddy in my lap.

I looked up in surprise, No, I can't be," I said, "I'm just tired. Maybe I should quit the paper and find a job closer to home."

"Maybe," she remarked without turning around, "but maybe you quit altogether."

I got up and laid Teddy gently on the chair, "I'm going to bed, Pilar. This conversation is making me nervous."

Jeremy was out doing some research for his book and was surprised to find me in bed when he got home at just after eight, "Are you sick, Cassie?" he asked.

"No honey just tired. Pilar thinks I might be pregnant."

Jeremy sat down on the side of the bed and took my hand, "Oh my goodness, is that possible?"

I had been thinking about nothing else since leaving the kitchen, "I suppose it could be possible but I hope not. We just got married and we need to spend some time together before we even consider children."

Jeremy looked pensive, "It's strange that we've never talked about this before but I'm almost forty and maybe this is the right time to have a child. My Dad was only twenty-two when Ethan was born and it was fun growing up because he enjoyed being with us. He was always out in the back yard shooting hoops with us or playing hockey in the winter. If we wait much longer I'll be too old to do any of that."

I felt so conflicted at that moment. I understood what Jeremy was trying to tell me but I wasn't prepared for motherhood and I was scared. When I didn't respond, Jeremy squeezed my hand and said, "Why don't you make an appointment with the doctor and if you are pregnant, we'll deal with it. If you aren't we can talk about having a family a little later."

After that, I decided to visit my own doctor in Asbury Park and two days later, the phone rang to tell me the tests were positive. I was having a baby. Jeremy was overjoyed when I told him he was going to be a father and couldn't wait to call his parents and his brother, Ethan. I was not as eager to tell my own family. I thought it would be better to wait in case something happened and I lost the baby and no amount of assurance from Jeremy could dissuade me. I kept waiting for signs of my body changing and studied myself in the mirror daily. The only other person who knew about the pregnancy was Pilar and she found it all very amusing. Every now and again she would tease me, "Missy getting fat," she would say as she patted my stomach but after three months I was still as flat as a pancake and hadn't had a moment of morning sickness. I was beginning to wonder if it was all a mistake and then two weeks later I started to notice some changes. I had gained three pounds and looked thicker around the waist and my breasts were beginning to feel a little tender. That was when I was finally convinced that a baby was really on the way and it was time to tell the family. Aunt Jean and Uncle Frank were ecstatic at the news and when they told Billy he jumped up and down yelling, "I'm going to be an uncle. I'll be Uncle Billy!"

Now I had to tell Mama and I couldn't wait to see her face when she heard she was going to be a grandmother. I drove to the prison on Thursday afternoon and sat quietly in the waiting room trying to gather my thoughts. I knew that this would be bittersweet for

Mama. She would be so happy for me but sad that she could not be with me while I experienced this major event in my life and not be able to hold her grandchild in her arms.

As soon as I approached the table where Mama was sitting, she seemed to sense that I had something to tell her. She looked up at me frowning, "Hello, honey. Is something wrong?"

I sat down and reached across the table to grasp her fingertips, "Nothing is wrong, Mama, but I do have some news to tell you."

Mama continued to frown as she asked, "You're not ill are you, Cassie? You're looking a little thinner in the face."

At that, I had to laugh, "Oh, Mama, no I'm not ill and as for being thinner, you should see my tummy."

There was a moments hesitation and then I saw Mama's eyes open wide as she guessed what I was about to tell her, "Oh, my goodness, you're pregnant aren't you? I've been waiting for this day but didn't expect it quite so soon. How far along are you? How are you feeling?"

"I'm about fourteen weeks and I'm feeling fabulous. Jeremy is over the moon and Pilar is treating me like an invalid. I hope you're really happy for me, Mama."

"Oh, Cassie, how could you think otherwise, I'm overjoyed. I know I can't be with you but just knowing that you're happy and well gives me so much peace of mind and I can't wait to be a grandmother."

We continued to talk and once again the conversation seemed to be all about me. Mama was the most selfless person I had ever known.

Jeremy encouraged me to quit my job but I decided to wait until the end of the second trimester. At sixteen weeks, I told Lester Graham that I would be leaving in three months and would probably not be coming back. He told me he had suspected that I was pregnant and was pleased for me but sorry to see me go. He suggested that I should cut down on any assignments and stay closer to home. He also praised me for the dedication I had shown to my job and hoped that, one day, I would return to journalism. I felt teary-eyed listening to him and wasn't really sure if I was doing the right thing. Was I really ready to become a full time wife and mother? In late August, when the time came for me to finally say goodbye to all of my colleagues, I was a wreck. They threw a shower for me and everybody came and I couldn't stop crying. In the end, Tim called Jeremy to come and get me because he didn't think I would make it home all in one piece.

The next couple of months were difficult for me, I felt so lonely. Jeremy was holed up in his study most of the day writing and I was left to my own devices. Pilar would encourage me to go for a walk and sometimes she would go with me but I felt fat and lazy and just wanted to sleep most of the time. When I looked in the mirror, the sight of myself disgusted me. I looked like a beached whale and even though Jeremy claimed I was more beautiful than ever, that just made me feel even more miserable. It was obvious that I wasn't cut out to just stay at home and I prayed that this baby would give me the sense of self worth that I needed.

The day before my baby was born, I had this sudden surge of energy and Pilar remarked, "Baby coming soon, mark my words, Missy." Later, that same night, I woke up with a sharp pain in my lower belly. I sat for a while on the edge of the bed and then I experienced it again. That's when I decided to wake up Jeremy. Seeing me sitting there bent over in obvious discomfort, he immediately jumped up, ran around to sit beside me and put his arm around me, "What is it, Cassie? Do you think it's time?"

I groaned and nodded my head, "I think so, but I'm not sure. I'd like to get up, please help me."

He helped me to my feet and suddenly I felt my water break and my nightgown was drenched in the process. Jeremy didn't waste any time, he called the hospital to say that we were on our way, threw a robe around me, grabbed my already packed overnight bag and practically carried me to the elevator. I can hardly remember the ride to the hospital, I was in so much pain and terrified that we wouldn't get there in time. I needn't have worried; I was in labor for the next fourteen hours. Jeremy was there with me in the delivery room and helped me through those last agonizing moments. It turned out to be a breech birth and there was talk of giving me a cesarean but I finally managed to push the baby out. I was exhausted but not too exhausted to hear the doctor say, "It's a girl, congratulations."

Every woman thinks her child is the most beautiful, but mine really was. She looked just like Mama and Lexie, with a fuzz of pale blonde hair and blue eyes, which I swore, had a greenish tint. Jeremy couldn't take his eyes off of her and we decided to call her Miranda.

Aunt Jean, Uncle Frank, Billy and Jazz all arrived at the hospital the next day and agreed that Miranda was the prettiest baby in the nursery. Billy wanted to hold her but I told him she was too small and fragile. I know he was disappointed but I promised that the next time he came to visit he could push her in her carriage. Aunt Jean offered to stay and help me when I got home but I had Pilar and she turned out to be a godsend. She had never had any children of her own but had several nieces and nephews she had helped to raise.

I took dozens of photos to show Mama and when she saw what a beautiful grandchild she had, she cried, "She looks just like Lexie."

Having my own baby now, I began to understand how she felt about my sister. It didn't matter that she had never forgiven Mama or that she had never come to visit her, she was still her child and she would always love her. "You miss her a lot don't you?" I asked.

"Yes, I do but having you and now Miranda, it makes it so much easier to bear."

I slowly nodded my head, "I understand Mama, I really do."

# CHAPTER 41

Jeremy gave me an exquisite diamond bracelet to celebrate the birth of our daughter and then just two weeks later I felt like I had won the jackpot when he told me that Ben Greenberg had called requesting that I set up an appointment. I was so excited I could hardly breathe and questioned Jeremy over and over again as to what Ben had discussed with him but Jeremy insisted that there had been no discussion.

The following Monday I arrived at the offices of Adams, Bernhardt and Greenberg on Wall Street and was shown into Ben Greenberg's office. "Good Morning, Mrs. Kent," he said rising from his desk and extending his hand, "I'm pleased to finally meet you." It seemed all rather strange as he was exactly what I expected, middle aged, medium height and dark with heavy horn rimmed glasses. He reminded me of Mr. Hargraft, Mama's attorney, from all those years ago. I shook hands and then sat down opposite him in one of the green velvet chairs lined up in front of the desk. "I'm surprised we haven't met before. I got the impression you were a friend of Jeremy's as well as his lawyer."

"Well, Cassie, I trust that I may call you Cassie, that's true but we both seem to have been very busy lately. I did get the invitation to your wedding but unfortunately I was out of town that weekend."

I gave him a weak smile, thinking it would be nice to chat at any other time but I was getting impatient, "I assume you have news about my mother's case?"

He shuffled some papers and then clasped his hands together, "I'm afraid it isn't good news but I felt I should talk to you in person."

I felt my heart start to sink in my chest, "So there's nothing you can do? Is that what you're going to tell me?"

He nodded, "Basically, that's correct. We have gone over the transcript of the trial and contacted the two women who your father allegedly abused."

"Not allegedly," I said abruptly, "if my mother testified to that, then she was telling the truth."

Ben held up his hand, "As I said, we contacted both women but they deny that your father had any interaction with them whatsoever and we have no way of proving otherwise. I am reluctant to say this, but by enhancing your own testimony you gave doubt to the credibility of your mother's testimony."

"Yes, and I've lived with that knowledge every day, but I was only ten years old," I protested.

"No one's blaming you. What you tried to do is admirable and what you're trying to do now shows just how much you believe in your mother but we have no new evidence, Cassie."

I got up feeling frustrated and angry, "So you're not prepared to do anything more?" I snapped.

Ben rose and came around the desk, "I'm sorry," he said quietly.

"Not half as sorry as I am." I replied as I headed for the door.

I was sitting in the nursery with Miranda later, when I heard Jeremy out in the hall. I had been alone for over an hour with my beautiful baby in my arms but felt totally alone. I looked around at the wonderful room that Jeremy had transformed into a little girl's dream. Months before Miranda was born, we had purchased all the nursery furniture; everything was white. Jeremy insisted that the room itself would be completed while I was in the hospital and not until we discovered whether we had a son or a daughter. It was all to be finished in record time and when I came home I was amazed. The walls were painted in blush pink with tiny gray elephants dotted here and there, the ceiling was white with pink clouds and all of the soft furnishings were pink and white and very frilly and feminine. I just loved it, and now as I sat there and thought about how lucky I should be feeling to have such a wonderful, thoughtful husband and such a precious child, all I really felt was despair. I could hear Pilar whispering to Jeremy and I knew she was warning him that I was upset and had hardly said two words to her since I arrived home. A few minutes later, I heard footsteps and looked up to see Jeremy smiling at me from the doorway, "Hi honey," he said. "Now there's a pretty picture."

I frowned up at him, "Why didn't you tell me that Ben couldn't help? I went over there full of optimism only to hear that nothing else can be done. How could you do that to me?"

Jeremy came over and pulled up a chair to sit beside me then he slowly reached out to stroke Miranda's head and replied, "I'm sorry, Cassie, I just felt it was better that you heard the truth from Ben. If there was anything he could have done, he would have."

I shook my head and looked down at my beautiful daughter, "Miranda will be a teenager by the time Mama gets out of prison. It just isn't fair."

"Life isn't always fair. Honey, and I know you've had more than your share of hardship but you have Miranda and me now and we can have a good life together. I know you miss your mother and nothing would make me happier than to see her here with you, but you can still visit every week while Pilar looks after the baby."

"I know," I said taking Jeremy's hand, "I just miss her so much, that's all."

By the following March, Jeremy had finished his latest book and it was at the publishers ready to go into its first printing. He had struggled so much with the writing that he decided to stop for a while and take up painting as a hobby. This was a surprise to me, as I had no idea that he had any talent in that area, although when I thought back, I remembered that he showed an inordinate interest and knowledge of art when we were in Venice.

Two weeks later, we were on our way to the Westhampton house with Pilar and Teddy and a load of luggage, mostly baby paraphernalia.

Jeremy had purchased a station wagon to accommodate all of us and when we got to the house I discovered, to my surprise, that he had taken one of the spare rooms and duplicated Miranda's room in New York. His thoughtfulness and generosity never ceased to amaze me.

It was chilly in March by the ocean but I enjoyed strolling near the beach with Miranda in her carriage and decided to invite my family down for a weekend. Billy finally got to push his little niece along and I was so proud of him. During this time, Jeremy turned the guesthouse into a studio and I was astonished when I saw his first attempt at painting. He had captured the seascape perfectly and it almost looked like a photograph. After I commented that I couldn't believe he was so talented, he admitted that he had majored in art as well as writing in university and had excelled at both.

"Is there anything else I don't know about you?" I teased.

"Mmm, let me think," he answered, looking rather endearing with paint smudges on his nose and both cheeks. "Well, I did get suspended once for putting a mouse in my teacher's desk."

"Oh, really." I said with my hands on my hips.

Jeremy smiled, obviously recalling the scene, "She screamed like a bloody banshee. It was pretty hilarious."

"And that's it?" I asked. "No other great revelations that might humiliate your daughter when she finds out?"

Jeremy put his hand on his heart, "That's it, I promise. Now out of here woman, I need to work."

# CHAPTER 42

In April when I was just beginning to really appreciate how fortunate I was, despite missing Mama so much, I began to notice something about Miranda that disturbed me. She was almost six months old but didn't seem to be responding to the sounds around her. One day I remembered the lovely lullaby Mama used to sing to Lexie and me. When I put Miranda down for the night, I would sing the same song but she always just stared at me or at the light that played on the ceiling from the rotating lamp by her crib. One night, Jeremy, stood by the doorway listening and seemed intrigued by what he heard, "That's a pretty lullaby, Cassie. Where did you hear it?"

"Mama used to sing it to us. It is pretty isn't it?"

"It is, but why the title, Follow the Butterfly?"

"Mama explained it to us once. I can remember her telling us that butterflies aren't born that way. They start out as an egg, then a caterpillar and after a while the caterpillar hides in a shell and eventually changes into a butterfly. They have to struggle and go through so much to become so beautiful. Some butterflies can fly thousands of miles and nobody can understand how they do it. I think Mama was trying to tell us that we can't give up when things get tough because there's always a light at the end of the tunnel."

"Sounds like a great way to teach one's children how to face life's challenges."

I covered Miranda with her blanket and then turned to Jeremy with tears in my eyes, "I think there's something wrong with our baby," I whispered.

Jeremy strode towards me and took me in his arms, "What on earth are you talking about? She's beautiful and she doesn't give us any trouble. Look how she sleeps through the night already."

I buried my head on his shoulder, "She's not responding to any noise, haven't you noticed? I've been watching her for the past two weeks and I've even tried to startle her but she doesn't react. I've not wanted to believe that she has something wrong with her hearing but I can't deny it any longer. We have to take her to the pediatrician."

Jeremy pushed me away and went to stand a foot behind Miranda's crib, where she couldn't see him, then clapped his hands loudly several times but she didn't even blink. He looked at me hopelessly and then came back to embrace me once again, "We'll call first thing in the morning and get a referral to a specialist. Don't worry, honey, if you're right we'll move heaven and earth to do whatever needs to be done."

The following week in New York, Miranda was being subjected to an audiological evaluation and later we got the devastating news. Our baby had sensorineural hearing loss caused by faulty development of the inner ear. We were told that this condition could have several degrees of severity and in extreme cases; the loss of hearing is total. Miranda was one of the unlucky ones. She was profoundly deaf.

I don't know how I got through the rest of that day but I knew that I needed to talk to the one person who would have some understanding of how I really felt. That was Aunt Jean. When I called her, sobbing on the telephone, she immediately drove to our apartment and arrived just after I had settled Miranda for her nap. I heard Jeremy talking to her in the hall and then suddenly she was there in the nursery and taking me in her arms, "Oh, my darling," she whispered. "It's going to be all right. You have to believe that."

I hugged her for a moment, then took her hand and led her into the living room, "I really needed to talk to you, Auntie. I have so many questions"

Aunt Jean sat down on the sofa and patted the seat beside her, "Come, sit down, Cassie, you can ask me anything you want."

I sank down beside her but couldn't look her in the eye, "How did you really feel when Billy was born?"

She hesitated for a moment and then replied, "I have to be absolutely honest with you, I was shocked. I expected my baby to be perfect. The chances of me having a Downs Syndrome child at such a young age were rare. I knew the moment he was born that something was wrong, I only had to look at the faces around me, hear the whispering and the sideways glances. When they finally put Billy in my arms and I saw his facial features, I was horrified, but when he opened his eyes and looked up at me I felt such compassion that I knew I could never let him go."

"If you had known before he was born, what would you have done?"

"I probably would have aborted him. God forgive me for saying that because today I can't imagine our lives without him. Yes, it's been a challenge, but he's a lot better off than a lot of other children with his condition. Many of them have heart problems or other serious medical conditions. We have had some difficult times with Billy when his behavior has been out of control but on the other hand he brings so much joy to our lives."

"I feel so guilty, Auntie. When I'm not crying my eyes out, I just feel like running away."

Aunt Jean took my hand, "That's only natural, Cassie. You need time to come to terms with Miranda's condition and maybe there's something that can be done. If not, you will have to cope just like we did with Billy. Your daughter is no less beautiful because she can't hear and I'm sure she'll be just as intelligent as her mother. With sign language, lip reading and the right education she can lead a productive life. I think what you're really feeling is shame, Cassie. Like me, you expected your baby to be perfect and you wanted to show her off to the world, but none of us are perfect. I promise you, you will love her even more because she needs you and if she turns out the way I think she will, then one day she'll make you very proud."

After Aunt Jean left, I put Miranda in her crib and just stood staring at her. For the longest time, she stared back and made the odd gurgling sound but the doctors had assured me that because she made noises, it didn't mean she could hear. She looked like a little doll lying there with her eyes wide open and I wondered what on earth she could be thinking. I didn't hear Jeremy come up behind me and was a little startled when he touched me on the shoulder, "You must be exhausted, Cassie. Let her sleep and come and sit down. I'll get Pilar to make you something to eat."

I shook my head, " I couldn't eat anything, I just want my baby to be normal. Look at her, Jeremy, we can't even tell her how much we love her."

Jeremy gathered me into his arms, "I'm going to do everything I can to see if anything can be done. There's a clinic just outside of the city that specializes in hearing, maybe they know of a procedure that will restore her hearing. Maybe they can refer us to someone who's an expert in this field. I'll leave no stone unturned, but if it turns out to be absolutely hopeless, then we'll get all the help she needs so that she's able to communicate with other people."

"Why can't I help her, I'm her mother?"

"You can, honey. You can even start tomorrow if it makes you feel better. Show her some objects, like her rattle or her teddy bear and just keep mouthing the words to her. I know she's just a baby but it couldn't hurt and if you keep at it, she'll be able to lip read by the time she's ready for a special school."

"What about sign language, I could learn that too," I said eagerly.

Jeremy smiled, "I think it might be a little too soon for that. Now come on, honey, I insist you let her sleep and try to get some rest."

I didn't sleep much that night and the very next morning, I phoned Jazz to tell her the news. Half an hour later, she was stepping out of the elevator and crushing me in her arms. We talked for hours and I agonized about telling Mama. I knew it would be difficult and I didn't want to break down in front of a room full of people.

"Well, you have to tell her in person, there's no doubt about that," Jazz said. "You'll just have to put on a brave face. I know you don't want to get your mother upset, so try to be optimistic about everything."

I kept thinking about what Jazz had said as I drove to the prison the following Thursday and when I finally sat down with Mama, I managed to smile.

"You look pretty happy today, Cassie. Tell me all about your week and that wonderful grandchild of mine."

"Well, Mama. We decided to come back to New York for a while."

"Oh, I thought you were staying in Westhampton until the fall. What brought you back?"

I hesitated before replying, "Jeremy has some business to wrap up and he didn't want to leave us behind. We'll be going back again soon."

Mama proceeded to ask me questions but I couldn't bring myself to tell her the truth. When I eventually walked out through the prison gates, I was terribly conflicted. I hadn't wanted to upset Mama but at the same time I felt so guilty because somewhere deep down, I didn't want to admit that my beautiful daughter was less than perfect.

Jeremy was true to his word and we visited three other specialists, only to confirm that Miranda's ability to hear was almost non-existent. The FDA had approved the use of cochlear implants for adults just two years earlier and was about to approve the procedure for children of two years old and over but the very idea of my baby having such a device horrified me and there was no guarantee that it would work in her case. Knowing that it looked pretty hopeless, I spent at least an hour each day with Miranda in my arms showing her one object after another in an effort to help her read lips. The kitchen was my favorite place because there were so many things I could show her, a spoon, a cup, a cookie and so on. Pilar would watch me and smile and Teddy would lie at my feet with yellow eyes narrowed to slits and purring with delight. In fact, when Jeremy suggested we return to Westhampton, I really didn't want to go but the weather was getting warmer and I knew it would be better for Miranda by the ocean, in the fresh air.

The summer was wonderful in Westhampton, but by the time Miranda was a year old it was already getting very cold and it was a lot easier getting around in the city, so we moved back to New York. We decided to have a party and invited Jeremy's folks including Ethan and his wife and, of course, my own family. Billy was still seeing Amanda and as she had never been out of New Jersey before, I thought it would be a wonderful opportunity to take her sightseeing.

Miranda looked adorable in a pink silk dress, all ruffles and bows, and Pilar prepared a superb birthday supper of veal marsala and new baby potatoes. The cake, which we ordered from one of the best pastry chefs in the city, was amazing with two layers covered in pink icing and topped with a menagerie of zoo animals in every color of the rainbow. Miranda's eyes grew as big as saucers when Pilar brought the cake to the table and Billy finally coached her into blowing out the single candle.

It was wonderful having both families around for the whole weekend and we enjoyed many happy hours together. The Kents' got along so well with Aunt Jean and Uncle Frank that, before they left, Vivienne invited them to come for a vacation in Laguna Beach. When I looked around and saw all the smiling faces, I began to convince myself that I could have a really good life, despite the fact that our child was unable to hear and the fact that Mama was still shut up in that dreadful place. However, after everyone had returned home, I became concerned about Jeremy being back in the city and not having a studio to paint in and suggested that he convert one of the guest rooms but he seemed a little reluctant and claimed that he was thinking about writing another novel. On several occasions I would go into his study to see how he was progressing but he just seemed to be staring at the computer. He claimed he was doing research and I assumed this was true, having been a reporter myself and familiar with having to substantiate many of the facts associated with the pieces I had written. I offered to help, but he brushed me off and I went back to my rather mundane existence of being a wife and mother. Don't get me wrong, I loved Jeremy and I adored Miranda, but my days were no longer fulfilling. I didn't even have to cook or clean, Pilar did all of that, except for the odd time that I helped out in the kitchen. Even the hours I spent coaching my precious child were beginning to wear on me and I didn't seem to be making any headway. Frustrated, I contacted the St. Francis De Sales School for the Deaf in Brooklyn. They specialized in auditory-oral education and even provided in-home therapy for infants and pre-kindergarten children. One week later, Natasha Ozerov arrived to evaluate Miranda and it didn't take her very long to confirm that early intervention was necessary. Jeremy and I spent an hour with Miss Ozerov while she explained the various programs that the school offered but that was for future consideration. In the meantime, she guaranteed twice-weekly home visits specializing in speech, auditory-verbal, occupational and physical therapy. I was expected to attend all visits in order to educate myself in the various therapies and be able to help Miranda between visits. At first, I was a little skeptical as I considered Miss Ozerov to be very young but she assured me that she was well qualified in her profession and had almost seven years experience with infants and young children.

After the first actual in-home therapy session, I felt a lot more comfortable about the situation. Tasha, as she insisted I call her, bonded with Miranda immediately. She was an extremely attractive young woman, slight of stature with a cloud of blonde hair and light blue eyes but her most charming feature was her smile. I think that's what captivated Miranda. I was a bit concerned, at first, about Tasha's obviously strong Russian accent but she satisfied me that it would make no difference as she had extensive training in sounding out words. By the time Tasha had completed her fourth visit, I was convinced that she was an accomplished therapist and I was relieved to have found someone I could open up to and express my fears to about Miranda's future. It was after I had literally bared my soul and even cried on her shoulder that she convinced me to come to the school and observe the older children.

Going to the school was a revelation and I was encouraged by what I saw. Children as young as three-years-old were in full-day preschool programs and I knew immediately that as soon as Miranda was old enough, I would be enrolling her in classes. I wished Jeremy had come with me but he seemed preoccupied with his writing and had begged off at the last minute. I was irritated by his attitude and lack of interest at the time but when I got home he wanted to hear every detail and spent that evening sitting beside Miranda's crib and reading her a story. Obviously she couldn't hear a word but he made such faces that every now and then she would just smile or look a little alarmed. I always wondered what was going through that little head of hers.

# CHAPTER 43

Miranda was three-years-old when she became eligible to attend the full-day preschool program. She had already made some progress, thanks to Tasha, and appeared to understand much of what we were trying to communicate but she still hadn't uttered a sound. When she wanted something she would just point and, although we would mouth the name of the object over and over again, in the hope that she would make some effort to respond, nothing seemed to work. Tasha and I both felt that being with other children her own age, might be the best thing for her and so it was with mixed feelings that I left her at school on that first day, but she never made a fuss. In fact, when I picked her up in the early afternoon, I discovered that she had already made friends with one of the other children. Poppy was an adorable looking child with huge brown eyes, cornrows and skin the color of café au lait. I couldn't help thinking of the first time I met Jazz and it seemed ironic that my own little girl had taken a liking to a child of African American descent. I couldn't wait to tell Jazz. The very next day, Miranda seemed anxious to go back to school and practically dragged me towards the elevator. I knelt down in front of her and slowly mouthed the words, "What is it, honey? Do you want to see Poppy?" She nodded her head and grinned and when I looked at her sweet face I felt such pride. How could I ever have thought, even for one moment, that my daughter was less than perfect.

As for Jeremy, over the past two years, he had begun to show more and more signs of disturbing behavior. He had completely lost his interest in writing and even when we spent the summer in Westhampton, he avoided the studio where he had loved to paint. While there, he would walk along the beach for hours and in New York, he would either hole up in his office staring at the computer and claiming to be doing research or take long walks in the park. I tried to talk to him about the change in him on several occasions, but he insisted he was fine and when I mentioned that we hadn't been intimate for weeks at a time, he would just get angry and leave the room. There were also other noticeable changes in his behavior. He had always been concerned about hygiene but now he had become obsessive and would wash his hands dozens of times a day. On top of that, he was driving Pilar mad with his criticism when any dishes were left in the sink for more than a moment or two. When things started to get really out of hand, I begged him to see his doctor but he refused and demanded that I leave him alone.

The most alarming incident happened right after Miranda started preschool when Jeremy was telling me about a friend he had met on one of his walks in Central Park that morning. Suddenly he just stopped talking in mid sentence and I could see that he was struggling to find a word and then he started to tell the story all over again right from the very beginning. I was horrified at what was happening and knew that I had to force him to get help. The one person that seemed to have some influence over him was Vivienne so, as reluctant as I was to tell them about Jeremy's condition, I called his parents later that night. Vivienne was a no nonsense type of woman and was on the next available flight to New York and when I picked her up at the airport, I finally broke down sobbing in her arms.

I had decided not to tell Jeremy his mother was coming and when we walked into the apartment, he looked shocked, "What are you doing here, Mom?" he asked. "Is Dad okay?"

"Your Dad's fine," Vivienne replied. "Now how about giving your old Mom a hug?"

Jeremy came forward, put his arms around his mother and glanced at me over her shoulder with a frown, "Sorry, Mom, I'm just surprised to see you here. Cassie didn't tell me you were coming."

"Well there's a reason why I'm here son. Just let me unload my suitcase and then we can have a nice chat."

I took Vivienne to one of the guest rooms, left her to get settled, then asked Pilar if she would make some coffee and serve up some of her wonderful scones with fresh raspberry jam. Jeremy stood in the kitchen doorway watching me and the minute I came towards him, he began to walk backwards motioning me into the living room, "What's going on, Cassie?" he asked.

I knew I had to stall for time, "Your mother needs to talk to you. Why don't you just sit down and relax, she'll be here in a moment or two."

"What does she want to talk to me about?" he said, his voice rising. "She could have just phoned. What's so important that she had to come all the way here?"

I was just about to answer when Vivienne came through the door, "It's okay, Cassie," she said, "I'll take it from here. Why don't we sit down son?"

"I'd rather stand," Jeremy replied defiantly.

"Sit down," Vivienne responded in a commanding voice and much to my surprise Jeremy reacted by sinking into the closest chair and folded his arms defensively across his chest.

I decided to leave them alone while I went back to the kitchen to help Pilar and I was only gone a few minutes when I heard Jeremy's raised voice, "There's nothing wrong with me. You're all crazy," he yelled.

Pilar looked alarmed but I assured her it would be all right and waited with the tray of coffee and scones until I could only hear a low murmur from the living room. When I eventually decided to go back to see what was going on, Vivienne was perched on the arm of Jeremy's chair with her arm around his shoulder. His head was down and I couldn't see his face but Vivienne looked up at me and shook her head solemnly. I slowly put the tray down on the table and then Jeremy looked up at me, "You win," he said. "I'll make an appointment with Paul. I know I haven't been myself and I really can't explain how I feel but maybe Paul can find out what the problem is."

I went over and knelt down in front of him, taking his hands in mine, "Oh, honey, I'm so glad you listened to your mother."

He looked up at Vivienne and grinned, "Well, she does have a rather commanding attitude at times."

Vivienne ruffled his hair, "Children are supposed to listen to their mothers," she remarked, "no matter how old they are. Now how about we have some of those delicious looking scones?"

Vivienne stayed for two days and only returned home when she was absolutely certain that Jeremy had committed to keeping an appointment with his doctor on the following Monday. She was reluctant to leave but wanted to get back to Mark and assured us she would be back if we needed her. We arrived at the medical center soon after we dropped Miranda off at preschool and I could see that Jeremy was anxious as we sat in the waiting room. Paul Radcliffe had been his doctor for a number of years and they were good friends, having originally met at a fund raising benefit when Jeremy was married to Courtney. We had dined out with him and his wife, Sherry, on a number of occasions and I know that Jeremy trusted him. We didn't have long to wait before Penny, the receptionist, told us we could go into Paul's office and as soon as we stepped through the door, he came forward to shake hands with Jeremy and give me a hug, "Sit down, sit down," he said motioning us towards the two suede chairs facing his desk, "It's great to see you both but I know this isn't a social visit, so what seems to be the problem?"

Jeremy looked at me and I nodded. I really needed him to talk to Paul himself and describe the symptoms he had been experiencing. Paul listened intently, occasionally scribbling on a notepad, while Jeremy explained his lack of drive to write or paint, his compulsion for cleanliness and problems expressing himself. When Paul asked what he meant by that, I intervened and elaborated on Jeremy's failure to conjure up a word in the middle of a sentence and the times when he even repeated whole sentences all over again. Jeremy looked a little alarmed when I said that and I knew that he hadn't even realized what had been happening. I leaned over and gently took his hand in mine, "It's going to be okay, honey," I whispered even though I knew deep in my heart that something was dreadfully wrong.

Paul pondered over his notes for a moment and then asked, "How have relations been between the two of you?"

I sighed, "If you are talking about sex, it's almost non-existent. Jeremy seems to have lost all interest."

Paul hesitated for a moment then said, "I can't tell you anything until we run some tests. You're still a young man Jeremy so I'm hopeful that it may just be some kind of chemical imbalance but we can't rule out something more serious. I'd like to do a complete physical checkup early next week and I'm going to arrange for you to have and EEG and a brain scan. The results should tell us what's going on and, in the meantime, I suggest you get a lot of rest and Cassie, try not to worry."

"How can I not worry?" I said helplessly, getting up from my chair.

Paul came around the desk and took both of my hands in his, "I know it's difficult but I'll try and get Jeremy booked in for the tests as quickly as possible."

"Hey, I'm still here people," Jeremy said.

"Sorry, my friend," Paul responded, "just trying to assure Cassie that I'll do all I can to move things along. Get Penny to book you in for the check up and she'll arrange for the tests. Should be within the next couple of weeks and if it's any longer I may have to pull some strings."

"I appreciate it, Paul," Jeremy answered shaking Paul's hand, then steering me towards the door with his arm around my shoulder he said, "Come on, Cassie, let's go home."

# CHAPTER 44

It was almost a month later when Paul called to ask us to come back to his office for the results of the series of tests. I will never forget that morning drive as long as I live. I knew, without a doubt, that whatever was to come would change our lives and we were both silent as Jeremy drove through the late afternoon traffic and we rode in the elevator to Paul's office on the fifth floor. So many things were going through my mind, not the least of which, how Jeremy's behavior had become even more alarming during the few short weeks since our first appointment. He had become more distant, no longer paying any attention to Miranda and any amount of encouragement on my part to write or paint or even to engage in simple conversation, just seemed to fall on deaf ears.

The reception area was empty when we arrived and it felt like an omen. My imagination went into overdrive, asking myself if Jeremy was the last patient and if it had been planned so that Paul could allow us as much time as it took to explain his condition. Penny even looked a little grim as she ushered us into Paul's office and offered us both a cup of coffee. We declined and I followed Jeremy through the door only to discover that Paul was not at his desk. We both sat down, still not speaking, and only moments later Paul came in through a side door, which I hadn't noticed before, and immediately shook both of our hands. When he sat down at his desk and opened the file in front of him, my heart was beating like a jackhammer and I felt sick to my stomach. Then, looking over at Jeremy, he said, "I'm not going to beat around the bush, Jeremy, the news isn't good."

Jeremy stared ahead with a blank expression, "It's Alzheimer's isn't it?"

Paul shook his head, "No, actually it isn't, although it's similar. What you have is Pick's disease."

"I've never heard of Pick's disease, what is it? What does it mean?" I asked feeling a little calmer although I had no idea why at that moment.

"It's a disease that can affect the temporal or frontal lobes of the brain, or even both. In your case, Jeremy, it appears that the frontal lobes have been affected. All of the personality and behavioral problems that you have been experiencing are typical symptoms and I have to be honest with you, these symptoms will increase as the disease progresses."

"But what caused this? What's the treatment?" I asked, anxiously.

"It could be genetic but in most cases the cause can't be determined. As for treatment, I have to be honest with you; there is no effective treatment. There are some medications that can help to reduce some of the behavior and there are even some counseling services that can help with coping with the disease."

I looked over at Jeremy but he was stone faced, "How much time does Jeremy have?" I asked turning back to Paul and holding my breath.

"Well, it can vary. The cause of death is usually an infection. From the onset it could be anywhere from two to fifteen years, but the average life expectancy is probably around nine years."

Jeremy started to get up and I reacted by reaching over and grabbing his hand, "Where are you going, honey?"

He stared back at me with the same blank look on his face, "I'm going home, I've heard all I want to hear."

Paul came around his desk and took Jeremy's arm, "Sit down old chap," he said, "you need to understand what's going to happen. If you don't care about yourself, think about how this will affect Cassie and Miranda."

Jeremy pulled his arm away, "What am I supposed to do? Am I supposed to sit here and listen while you tell me that I'm going to turn into some blithering idiot? Maybe I should just shoot myself and then it will save everyone a lot of trouble."

I could hardly believe what I was hearing. I jumped up taking both of Jeremy's hands in mine, "Don't you dare talk like that. I love you and I'll take care of you. We'll find the best medication to help you and we'll get the counseling that Paul mentioned."

I had just finished speaking when Jeremy laid his head on my shoulder and started to sob. I put my arms around him and felt his whole body shudder as all the emotion started to pour out of him. At that moment I felt a strength that I had never experienced before and I was determined to do whatever I could to help him. We stayed with Paul for a long time after that while he took us through all of the stages of Pick's disease. I was forced to face the fact that the Jeremy I had known and loved would eventually change into a completely different person but I was determined to stand by his side, come what may.

That evening, I telephoned Mark and Vivienne. It was a difficult conversation and I could hear Mark's voice breaking when he asked me how long Jeremy had left. Vivienne was much more stoic and suggested that she fly back to New York the following week but I dissuaded her. I knew that Jeremy wouldn't appreciate his mother being around, he would just interpret it as pity and I knew he couldn't tolerate that. Later that night, I finally found the courage to call Aunt Jean. I needed courage, because I knew that I wouldn't be able to hold it together when I told my family about Jeremy's condition. The phone call turned out just the way I expected. I ended up in tears and Aunt Jean did her best to comfort me. More than anything, I wanted to feel her arms around me. I wanted to be with my family but at the same time I felt like running away and somehow all the strength I had felt in Paul's office, gradually began to leave my body. When I eventually put down the phone, I realized that I wasn't sure if I could cope. My life seemed out of control again, just like when I was a child. Eventually I would lose Jeremy; my sweet daughter would never hear the sound of birds singing and Mama was still in that horrible place.

# CHAPTER 45

A year later, Jeremy's behavior had become even more bizarre and harder to manage. I am not sure what I would have done without Pilar, she had the patience of a saint. She was always there for Jeremy while I took Miranda back and forth to school and she was there for both of them when I went to visit Mama every week. It had been no longer possible to hide the reason for my absence on Thursday afternoons. One day, almost a year earlier, I had gathered up my courage and told Pilar the truth about Mama. She listened with tears in her eyes and then told me about her own mother who had been the victim of abuse and how, when she was only eight-years-old, her father had walked out leaving behind six small children. She understood why Mama had done what she did and why I hated Papa so much, "I also hated my father," she said. "If he hadn't gone, I think my mother might have killed him too, so I no judge your Mama. My Papa was a very cruel man and we were terrified of him. When he left, we kids were so happy but it was hard for Mama because she had no means of support. We lived in one of the poorest areas of Mexico City and she started taking in the neighbor's washing. She worked like a slave, day and night, just to put food on the table. She was only forty when she died. We never knew she had a heart condition until after she was gone. My poor Mama was worn out and I have never forgiven Papa for what happened to her. So, I understand, Miss Cassie, and I will take care of things here whenever you want to see your mother. No worry, no worry."

I could hardly believe that this woman had been part of our household for so long and yet I knew nothing about her, "I am so sorry," I whispered, "I had no idea you had been through so much. What did you do after your mother passed away?"

"Well, I was eighteen and the oldest of all of my brothers and sisters so I became the head of the family. I got a job in one of the best hotels as a maid and took care of everyone. Then when the youngest one was old enough to be out on his own, I applied for a job as a housekeeper in California.

My sister and I worked together for a long time and she's still there but all the rest of the family are still in Mexico."

"Wouldn't you like to visit with them, Pilar?"

"Yes, I would like that, Miss Cassie, and I will do that one day but right now you need me and I'll be here for as long as you do."

After that, we seemed to have a connection that wasn't there before and I came to rely on Pilar more than ever. She was especially helpful with Jeremy who had become obsessed with eating green vegetables, it didn't matter what kind of vegetable as long as it was green. It was a blessing that he had picked a healthy food group to be obsessed about but at the same time he needed protein and food with other nutrients to keep him physically healthy. Pilar would often sit at the table with him and coax him to eat some chicken, or fish or cereal and he would take a bite or two and then shake his head. Often Pilar and I would sit with both Jeremy and Miranda and it was like having two children at the table, one that couldn't speak and one that had no interest in talking. Sometimes, I felt like screaming and Pilar, sensing my frustration, would touch me gently on the hand to calm me down.

I really wondered how I could go on living this way. I had no social life and my visits to my family or to Jazz were few and far between. Pilar seemed to be my only salvation. She was the one person who was there for me all the time. I still hadn't told Mama about Miranda and I had hidden Jeremy's condition from her too. I just couldn't let her sit in prison worrying about me; she had enough to contend with. When I visited her, I always put on my bravest smile and I lied. I lied about how smart Miranda was and I lied about Jeremy, claiming that he was writing, what would probably be his best work, and that he was up to his neck in research. Uncle Frank, Aunt Jean, Pilar and Jazz all thought I was making a big mistake not telling Mama the truth and tried to convince me otherwise, but I was adamant. I wanted her to be happy and I knew that if she thought I was living this fabulous life with my famous husband and my bright beautiful daughter, she would sleep well at night.

By the following summer, I hardly knew the man I had married. Most of the time he was totally withdrawn and the only person who seemed able to get through to him was Pilar. It was only when we went to our summerhouse in Westhampton that he took any interest in his surroundings and when Mark and Vivienne came to visit he would spend hours out sailing with his father. Vivienne loved spending time with Miranda and she even made an effort to learn sign language. It was wonderful watching them building sandcastles on the beach but I couldn't help wishing that the grandmother my daughter had come to know and love had been my own mother. Things seemed so much more relaxed during those summer months and I took the time to do as much research as I could about Jeremy's illness. Some of the potential symptoms, like promiscuity and violence really frightened me and I prayed it would never come to that. I dreaded going back to New York, Jeremy seemed so much happier near the ocean, but Miranda was due to go back to school in September and I couldn't allow her to miss even a week of the new term. Pilar suggested that I let Jeremy stay in Westhampton and she would remain behind with him but I was reluctant. It took Aunt Jean to persuade me that this might be the best solution for everyone and so we returned to New York alone.

I kept in touch with Pilar every day by telephone and she assured me that Jeremy was doing well. On good weather days, he spent most of the time sitting on the beach staring out to the sea, or leafing through a magazine. At other times, she would find him back in his studio where he had taken up painting again but now he painted pictures of all kinds of bizarre creatures like goblins and gremlins. I just couldn't imagine what was going on in his head.

Back in New York, I had very little to do so I spent more time with Jazz and drove to Asbury Park often to see my family. Billy was now living in a community home with Amanda and thriving so Aunt Jean was always pleased to see me, as she was feeling a little lonely herself. I still visited Mama every week and continued to fabricate the story of my life. I had become exceptionally adept at hiding the truth.

In mid November I got a call from Aunt Jean with some surprising news. Scott was back from San Francisco visiting his mother and he wanted to see me. "What about Hilary?" I asked.

"What about her?" Aunt Jean replied.

"Well, did he mention her? Did she come back with him?"

Aunt Jean sighed, "I didn't speak to him, your Uncle did but I gather he just said he was in town and had some business in New York and then asked for your telephone number."

I felt my heart do a little pitter pat before I answered, "Oh, so he's coming to New York. Well I'd like to see him. Did Uncle give him my number?"

"No, he wasn't sure if it was appropriate. He got Scott's number so that you can call him if you want to talk to him."

When I got off the phone I stared at the number Aunt Jean had given me for several minutes before I picked up the receiver again. I assumed that it was his mother's number and sure enough, Mrs. Cunningham picked up the phone after the third ring. After a few pleasantries, suddenly there was Scott on the line and a whole lot of memories came flooding back. Whatever I had to reveal about my family life wasn't something I wanted to do on the telephone and I had the feeling that he felt the same way. We only spoke for a few moments before he suggested that we meet for dinner in New York, providing that my husband wouldn't mind, "That would be absolutely lovely," I remarked without hesitation.

Two days later I was combing through my walk-in closet looking for the perfect outfit. I felt like I was going on my first date and I was as excited as a schoolgirl but feeling guilty at the same time. I had been confined to the apartment for days and without Pilar I had nobody to care for Miranda at night but on this particular night, Jazz had come to my rescue. I was still sorting through my closet when she arrived and it only took her a moment to settle on a teal blue, form-fitting dress with a neckline that plunged almost to my waist.

"I can't wear that!" I cried.

"Of course you can, you're going to dinner with a man. A very handsome man if I remember correctly," she said smirking.

"But I'm married, Jazz," I protested.

"Yes, but you're not dead and it's about time you felt like a desirable woman again, Cassie. I know you still love Jeremy but what you had between you doesn't exist anymore. It's nobody's fault, just a horrible twist of fate. I know you'll stick by Jeremy to the bitter end but you need a break. Go out with Scott and have a little fun, it's only dinner. You need to enjoy yourself for a change."

I sighed and took the dress from her, "I know you're right. I feel like I've just been marking time lately. Actually I'm glad that Jeremy stayed in Westhampton. You have no idea how hard it is watching him deteriorate and knowing that it will only get worse. He pays no attention to me or to Miranda, it's as though we don't exist. I think he cares more for Teddy than anyone else. The last month, before I came back here, he moved into one of the guest rooms and Teddy slept on the bed with him. In the mornings I would creep in and find them together. Can you believe it, Jazz, I'm jealous of a cat."

Jazz slipped her arm around my shoulder, "I'm so sorry, I had no idea things were that bad but all the more reason why you need to put a little spice in your life."

Jazz looked at her watch, " Oh, oh, it's getting late. You'd better get dressed and I'll go check on Miranda."

# CHAPTER 46

An hour later I was walking through the door of the Sea Grill and feeling extremely nervous. Even before the hostess had taken my coat, I saw Scott rising from a table at the side of the room. He looked even more handsome than I remembered and my heart seemed to leap in my chest as he approached. He took both of my hands in his and said, "Cassie, I can't believe you're here and you look absolutely beautiful."

I suddenly became aware that several people at nearby tables were watching and I felt very self-conscious, "Hi Scott," I said nervously, "why don't we sit down."

I felt his hand in the small of my back as he directed me to our table, "I hope this is fine near the window," he said, "you can see them skating at Rockefeller Center."

As I sat down I looked around me and noticed that the restaurant was packed with people and I wondered if there was anyone there that knew me. What would they think if they saw me there wearing an outrageously sexy dress and with a man that wasn't my husband. Scott reached across the table and touched my hand, "Penny for your thoughts," he said.

I smiled, "I was just thinking that it's been such a long time since I've been out to dinner. This place looks really interesting."

"So you've never been here before?"

"No, I haven't. Obviously they specialize in seafood, what do you recommend?" I asked as I picked up the menu.

Scott slowly shook his head, "There's no hurry, Cassie. Let's have a drink first, how about a glass of wine?"

I put down the menu, feeling a little foolish, "That would be nice, I'd like a glass of Chardonnay please."

"Good choice," Scott remarked as he beckoned the waiter over.

Waiting for our wine to be served felt like an eternity, even though it was only a few minutes. I was fiddling with the napkin on my lap and staring out of the window when Scott leaned forward, "Cassie," he said. "Why are you so nervous, I thought you'd be pleased to see me? I'm going to be in New York for quite a while working on some engineering problems at the new Four Season's Hotel. I was hoping that we could get together from time to time. I heard all about what you've been going through with your husband and I was hoping I could be of some help."

"There's nothing you can do, there's nothing anyone can do. Jeremy stayed behind at our summer home in Westhampton and I'm here with our daughter. I don't really have a husband anymore."

"I'm sorry, Cassie. Your husband is well known so when a story showed up in the New York Times about his illness, it wasn't long before the Ashbury Park Press picked up on it. You can't really blame them for printing the article; after all you were a local girl who worked for them and then married a famous author. Mom always kept me up to date on what was going on. She even knew all about Jazz and her modeling career."

"Did your Mom also tell you that our daughter is deaf?" I snapped back.

"Yes, she did, and I'm sorry about that too. I can't begin to put myself in your place, Cassie, and I meant what I said, if there's anything I can do to help, you only have to ask."

Suddenly I felt ashamed, Scott didn't deserve the treatment he was getting, "Please forgive me, my nerves are strung up so tight lately that I've been snapping at everyone. I really am pleased to see you and I apologize for spoiling our evening."

"No need for an apology, Cassie. Why don't we try and lighten it up a bit, have some more wine and take a look at the menu."

Over a wonderful dinner of jumbo crab cakes, sea scallops with asparagus and calorie laden raspberry soufflé, we reminisced about the past and all the wild and crazy times we spent during the summers on the beach back home. It was only when we were finished and relaxing with coffee and Cointreau that I finally got up the courage to ask about Hilary. Scott shrugged his shoulders and sighed, "Big mistake, she wasn't what she appeared to be. Two years after we met I found out she was cheating with one of my closest friends. I just walked out of her life and never looked back."

"Surely there have been others since then?"

"No, there hasn't been anyone. That's not to say I haven't been out on dates, in fact I've seen a lot of women, but there hasn't been anyone I wanted to spend the rest of my life with."

I was feeling rather mellow by then and reached over to grasp Scott's hand, "I'm sorry to hear that, really I am. Hopefully you'll meet someone soon."

It was then that he looked at me with an expression that I couldn't quite interpret and said, "Maybe I've already met her."

I pulled my hand away sharply and excused myself to go to the powder room. I needed a moment to pull myself together. By the time I had repaired my makeup, my mind was still in turmoil. I had heard, all of my life, that one never forgot one's first love but I never expected to feel the way I did after seeing Scott again. I knew I had to calm my nerves before I returned to the table so I engaged in conversation with an elderly woman who was gazing in the mirror and fussing with her hair. It seemed to do the trick and when I finally made it out of the powder room and approached Scott, I managed to put a big grin on my face. He immediately jumped to his feet and pulled out my chair, "Are you okay, Cassie?" he asked looking genuinely concerned, "I was beginning to worry that you weren't feeling well."

I sat down and looked up at him, still smiling, "I'm just fine thanks. I got talking to a lady from New Orleans. It was her first time in New York and she was loving every minute of it."

"Well who can blame her? I remember asking you why you didn't want to move here and you were pretty adamant about staying in Ashbury Park. It's strange the way life turns out sometimes. A few years later you married Jeremy Kent and ended up living here anyway."

I took a sip of Cointreau and hesitated before answering, "I suppose I have to be honest and tell you that I didn't want to be that much further away from Mama. It seems rather silly now because the difference in miles is pretty insignificant and almost nothing stops me from visiting her every week."

"How's she doing, Cassie? I've often thought about her and wondered how you were coping"

I felt myself tearing up and tried to put on a brave face, "It's been nineteen years, Scott. I don't know how she stands it. Every time I see her, she only ever wants to talk about me, never herself. She's the most unselfish person I've ever known and you know something else? She's still beautiful even though she's fifty-three now. Sometimes, I can't help staring at her and thinking she looks almost the same as she did when they put her in that miserable place."

"Has she ever seen your daughter? Miranda isn't it?"

I felt my spine stiffen, "No," I replied abruptly, "and I don't want her to."

"Why? Don't they allow young children to visit?"

I suddenly decided to tell Scott the truth, "She doesn't know Miranda is deaf."

Scott looked shocked, "Why on earth not, are you ashamed of the fact?"

"Of course not," I snapped back, "I just don't want Mama to worry, that's all."

"I see, and does she know about your husband's condition?"

I started to gather my napkin from my lap and threw it on the table, "Why are you asking me all these questions?"

Scott reached across and grabbed my hand, "It's okay, Cassie. I understand why you wouldn't want your mother to know. You're concerned that she would worry about you."

I felt myself relax as I removed my hand, "You really do understand. Thank God, because nobody else does. I just can't put an extra burden on Mama's shoulders. She thinks I'm living this wonderful life and it makes her happy. I'm not going to shatter that illusion."

"Like I said, Cassie, I know why you're doing this but have you thought about what you will do when your mother is released?"

"Not really, that's still six years away. All I can think about is seeing her walk through those gates and being able to hug her and take care of her. As for me, I have no idea what my own situation will be when that day comes."

Scott nodded, "You're a good daughter and you always have been, but what about Lexie? Where does she fit into the picture?"

"She doesn't fit into my life at all now. After both of my grandparents died she married someone she met at university, a boy named Todd Willis, and the last thing I heard, they were living in Somalia doing humanitarian work."

"Somalia? I hear things are pretty tense there."

"Really? I haven't been paying much attention to the news lately."

"Apparently people are starving to death every day and it looks like an intervention by the UN involving thousands of American troops is imminent."

I felt a sense of alarm. Lexie was still my sister and the thought of her being in the middle of any conflict sent my heart racing. "Do you think Lexie might be in danger?"

Scott pursed his lips, "There's no way to tell but I can do some research, if you'd like, and try and track her down."

"I would like that. I just need to know she's safe, that's all. I don't think I can ask for more than that. As long as she feels the way she does about Mama, I can't see any way that we can mend our relationship."

"Well, one never knows. Her life must have changed profoundly and I'm sure she's matured to a point where perhaps things aren't quite as black and white as they were. Never give up hope, Cassie."

"Hope is all I have these days."

Scott reached across the table again and took my hand, "You have me now, at least for a while and I'll help in any way I can. No strings attached."

# CHAPTER 47

The following week, Scott invited me to dinner again at a small Italian restaurant, Bella Luna. I was reluctant to go at first but I wanted to see him and, after dropping Miranda off at Jazz's, I took a taxi to the Upper West Side.

We kept the conversation light and had a truly wonderful evening. He mentioned briefly that he hadn't had any success locating Lexie and was still working on it but that was the only reference to my immediate family. Scott had suggested that we make the evening a casual one and I was pleased to see that, like me, he had thrown on a pair of jeans and a sweater. I think he looked even more handsome than in the suit and tie I had seen him in earlier and I couldn't take my eyes off him. It was obvious that I found him physically attractive, but then I always had.

After dinner, we decided to walk for a while. We donned our heavy coats and took a stroll along Broadway to the Lincoln Center, finally ending up at Columbus Circle. By this time we were both shivering so we took refuge in the Stone Rose Lounge and ordered brandy toddy's to warm us up. I could see the lights in Central Park and it all seemed so romantic but I couldn't let myself be swept away by the moment. I was a married woman with a very sick husband and a child that needed me. I had no business even thinking about another man but I couldn't help wishing that Scott was staying in New York. It was almost as though he read my mind when he said,

"I have to fly back to San Francisco next Monday to clear up some loose ends but I'll be back again in a week or two."

"And how long will you be here after that," I asked, crossing my fingers under the table.

"Could be as long as six months. As a matter of fact I've been thinking of renting an apartment. It would be a lot cheaper than staying in a hotel and I wouldn't have to eat out all the time."

"But surely you're on an expense account?"

"That's true, I am, but I'd be a lot more comfortable in an apartment and I like to cook."

I know I looked a little shocked, "You do? I don't remember you ever cooking."

"Ah well, I'm full of surprises. Maybe one evening you'll let me cook dinner for you."

I immediately imagined the two of us alone together and got very nervous, "Maybe, I'm just not sure that's a good idea."

"No strings attached, remember?"

"Yes, I remember," I replied, but I wasn't totally convinced.

After Scott left to go back to San Francisco, I felt a sense of loss. In the days following our dinner at Bella Luna we had seen each other briefly, on only one occasion, but we had spoken several times by telephone. We talked about every topic under the sun and tried to stay away from the issues that were troubling me. It was so refreshing having him back in my life and I was looking forward to his return to New York but it was not to be. Just over a week after we had parted ways over a couple of martinis, I got the call from Scott telling me that something important had come up with one of their clients, in the Los Angeles area, and he was liable to be stuck there for a at least a couple of months. As it was only a few weeks before Christmas, I was surprised to learn that he was not coming back to see his family for the holidays but then remembered that he hadn't been back for a number of years, so it wasn't really unusual. I was terribly disappointed and wondered how I would get through the holidays. I kept telling myself that nothing had really changed, I still had my folks back in Asbury Park, Jazz and Jules and, of course,

Mama, Miranda and Jeremy but somehow that didn't seem enough anymore.

I made plans to go to Westhampton on Christmas Eve after visiting Mama. Jazz had come to my rescue again and had taken Miranda to the Central Park Zoo, along with Badger, and I had arranged to pick her up on the way back from the prison. Every year, coming up with an acceptable gift for Mama had always been an ordeal but when I gave her a framed seascape that Jeremy had painted over three years earlier, she was thrilled. "This is beautiful," she said, misty eyed, "the colors are so vibrant. When did he paint this?"

"He painted it a few weeks ago, especially for you," I lied.

"How generous of him," Mama remarked. "I'll write a little thank you card to him although I would rather thank him in person. Why haven't I seen him in such a long time, Cassie? Is everything okay with him?"

I looked Mama straight in the eyes and replied, "Everything is fine Mama, but he's just been so busy with his writing and then painting in his spare time. He's already gone ahead to Westhampton with Pilar and Teddy so that everything is ready for tomorrow. Aunt Jean and Uncle Frank are arriving early in the morning and staying over for three or four days."

"And what about Billy? Isn't he going too?"

"No, as a matter of fact, at the community house where he and Amanda are living, they are having their first big Christmas party and no parents are allowed. We think it's all very amusing because they think they are being so grown up and independent but they still have a chaperone in the house."

"And Miranda, where is my beautiful granddaughter right now?"

"She's with Jazz at the Central Park Zoo." I answered as I dug into my purse and fished out Miranda's latest photo. As I handed it over to Mama I was feeling so proud, "Here's her latest picture, taken on her fourth birthday. Doesn't she look pretty in that blue dress."

I saw the tears in Mama's eyes as she stared at the photo, "She is absolutely adorable and I still can't get over how much she looks like Lexie when she was that age."

I immediately felt a little jealous and reached to take the photo back, "I'm afraid I can't stay too long today," I said. "I need to pick Miranda up and then drive straight to Westhampton."

Mama grasped my hand even though one of the guards was standing less than six feet away, "Have a wonderful Christmas, honey. Give my love to everyone and a big hug for Miranda."

"I will, Mama," I said rising from my chair. "I hope you get a really special dinner tomorrow and I'll be back to see you on New Year's Day."

Five minutes later I was walking out of the prison gate, for the umpteenth time, feeling relief but so much guilt. How could I keep on lying to Mama and what would happen when she found out the truth?

# CHAPTER 48

When I got to Westhampton, Jeremy was in his studio. Pilar suggested that I leave him alone for a while, as he had been particularly withdrawn. I was torn between following her advice and Miranda's constant tugging at my skirt, indicating that she wanted to see her father. This surprised me because he had paid so little attention to her for the past year. Soon however, she forgot all about Jeremy when Uncle Frank and Aunt Jean arrived with Pepper. This immediately caused a commotion when Teddy started to hiss in protest and Pepper scrambled out of the back door heading right for the beach. Uncle Frank had no choice but to chase after him and bring him back, but not until Pepper had run into the water and then quickly raced out again. I imagine that she wasn't prepared for the icy cold of the ocean, at that time of the year, but fortunately she only got her paws soaked. In the meantime, Miranda watched the whole game play out from the back porch and giggled hysterically.

Once everyone was settled, I decided it was time for Jeremy to play the host and greet our guests so I took Miranda's hand and headed for the studio. I opened the door very quietly and looked around expecting to find Jeremy splashing color onto a canvas but he was sitting quietly at a table and looked like he was sketching. He obviously heard us come in and slowly looked around. When he saw Miranda, he turned in his chair, throwing his arms wide open, and Miranda ran full tilt towards him. I couldn't help noticing right then, how much grayer his hair had become and how much weight he had lost. This was not the handsome man I had married but just a shell of his former self.

"Hello, my darling. How's my pretty girl?" he said hauling Miranda onto his lap and stroking her hair.

She just smiled back at him and laid her head against his chest then he looked up at me and said, "How are you, Cassie? Has your family arrived yet?"

I walked over and kissed him on the top of his head, "Yes, honey," I replied, "and Teddy scared the life out of Pepper. It's a riot to watch those two."

At that, Miranda started to giggle again and Jeremy started laughing too. At that moment I saw a glimmer of the old Jeremy.

"How are you feeling?" I asked. "Do you feel up to coming into the main house and having a bite to eat with my folks?"

Jeremy gave Miranda a hug then picked her up from his lap, set her on her feet, and stood up. "If you'll just give me a few moments, I'll be right in," he responded.

Aunt Jean was anxious to know how Jeremy was, "Actually he seems really with it today," I told her. "He hasn't been paying any attention to Miranda lately but today, he was very affectionate. The doctors have warned us there would be some good days and some bad days. I'm just thankful that today is a good one."

"Will he be joining us soon?" Uncle Frank asked.

At that moment, Pilar came through the doorway, "I think he may be a while. I just peeped through the studio window and he was back painting again."

I sighed, "Well, I guess we'll just have to carry on without him. Pilar, would you please bring us coffee and some of that delicious carrot cake you made. If Jeremy doesn't show up in a half hour or so, you can take something to the studio for him."

Pilar stared at me, started to walk away, and then turned back, "I can look after Mr. Jeremy," she said abruptly.

I suddenly felt a little affronted at her tone of voice and was ready to respond but Aunt Jean laid a hand on my arm and whispered, "Leave it."

After Pilar was safely out of earshot, I turned to Aunt Jean, "Thanks, I'm glad I didn't say anything. I sometimes forget that Pilar took care of Jeremy long before I came on the scene. She's been more of a wife or mother to him than I could ever be. Quite frankly I don't know how I would have coped without her."

Aunt Jean nodded, "We understand how difficult this must be and we'll always be here to support you. If you need a complete break, you can even leave Miranda with us for a few days."

I looked over at my sweet daughter sitting on the floor and smiled. Pepper was at her side, having been placated after the banishment of Teddy behind closed doors. They looked so content together that I couldn't help remarking, "I think Miranda is a true animal lover, just like Lexie."

At that, Aunt Jean got up and reached for her purse. Retrieving, what looked like, a section of newspaper from inside, she held it against her chest and looked at me rather intently, "Speaking of Lexie," she said gently, "I think you should read this. It's an article from the New Jersey Times."

My heart started to race a little as she handed over the paper and then sat down beside me. I stared at a grainy black and white photo of a young woman with long braided hair, dressed in a tee shirt and jeans, standing behind a podium. By her side was a tall man, with a beard, in what looked like army fatigues. I couldn't tell if it was Lexie or not but above the photo in bold letters it read, 'Bridgeton Girl Returns Home From Somalia.'

I glanced up at Uncle Frank who was hovering nearby and he just nodded, then I turned back to read the article.

Alexa Willis, 25 and her husband Todd, 26 returned home last Friday after spending a number of years providing humanitarian aid to the people of Somalia where a drought, over several years, has taken the lives of thousands of people. Earlier this month, they became aware of the imminent invasion of U.S. troops in a covert operation with the United Nations Under Cover in

225

Somalia, who were determined to put an end to the civil war. Because of the possible danger to themselves and their unborn child, they fled to Ethiopia. From there, they flew directly home to New Jersey and are expected to appear at a number of speaking engagements in the near future. Mrs. Willis, nee Taylor is the daughter of Ella Taylor, who is currently serving a twenty-five-year sentence for the murder of her husband Thomas Edward Taylor, of Millville, in 1973. Her sister, Cassandra, lives in New York City and is married to well known mystery writer, Jeremy Kent.

I looked up at Uncle Frank with tears in my eyes, "Why did they have to mention Mama?"

Uncle Frank sat down on the side of my chair and put his arm around my shoulder, "It's news, Cassie, and people are interested in reading every little sordid detail. The important thing is, Lexie's back here and it looks like you're going to be an aunt. Maybe now you'll be able to repair your relationship."

I shrugged my shoulders, "This article is a few days old, Lexie must have read it. If she wanted to see me, she could have easily found me."

"Maybe she didn't see it. They've only been here for about a week. You have no idea where they are staying, if they are looking for a place, or what their situation is. You have to give her some time, Cassie. On the other hand, you could try and contact her."

"But I wouldn't know where to start looking."

Aunt Jean spoke up, "Why don't we just all wait until the holidays are over then I can make some inquiries in the Bridgeton area. At the same time we'll watch out for announcements of any speaking engagements but, then again, maybe Lexie's too far along in her pregnancy and may not be up for it at the moment."

I stared at the photo again and then slowly folding the paper, laid it on the table. "I think I'll go and see what's holding Pilar up," I said.

I found Pilar in the kitchen busily cutting up carrot cake but she didn't turn around when asked if she needed any help. I walked over and touched her gently on the shoulder and when she faced me, I could see tears in her eyes. "Oh Pilar, what is it?" I asked, wrapping my arms around her. She started to sob on my shoulder and I could feel her body trembling, "It's Mr. Jeremy," she said, her voice shaking and barely audible, "he's getting worse every day and I can't bear to see him like this."

I kept on holding her as she continued to cry, "This is too much for you. When the holidays are over, you have to come back to New York and then I can help"

She pulled away from me, "I don't think he'll go, Miss Cassie. I think he gets confused with all the noise and bustle. He likes it here because it's so peaceful and he has his studio to paint in. Nearly every day he walks along the beach, even though it's freezing but he doesn't always tell me when he's leaving the house and I worry because he's not dressed for the weather. Sometimes, he's gone so long I feel like I should go and look for him, but then he might come home and I won't be here."

"Maybe Miranda and I should stay here. I can start looking for a school for her in the area. You shouldn't have to take all the responsibility, Pilar. I know you've looked after Jeremy for a long time but things are different now. Let me take some of the weight off your shoulders."

Pilar turned back to cutting the cake, "If you think it would be best, Miss Cassie, but I don't want that poor child to suffer."

"I'll make sure that Miranda has the best education and that all her needs are met. I don't want you worrying about her too. Let me see what I can find out right after the holidays and then we'll go from there."

# CHAPTER 49

Four days after they had arrived, my family returned to Ashbury Park. Our Christmas celebrations had been very low key but both Aunt Jean and Uncle Frank had welcomed a change of scenery. My uncle had spent quite a bit of time with Jeremy and had accompanied him on a couple of his walks along the beach, followed by an excited Pepper who still hadn't quite remembered that the Atlantic was icy cold. I was curious, after one of their walks, as to what had transpired between them but apparently Jeremy was either silent most of the way or spoke only about his paintings or his surroundings. The fact that he never mentioned Miranda or myself was upsetting but I knew it was the disease that had taken over his brain. I tried to get through to him myself, on several occasions. I reminded him of the wonderful times we had shared and told him how much I loved and cared for him, but he was always non responsive. Westhampton at that time of the year, was almost deserted and only two of our neighbors had decided to spend the holidays there. Greg and Sally Hayes were an older couple and preferred the quiet life and so, although it was difficult entertaining considering Jeremy's condition, I decided to invite them over for New Year's Eve. Pilar cooked up an elegant rack of lamb with a honey, lemon, and garlic sauce, along with tender glazed carrots and crisp garlic bread and a maple mousse cake for dessert. Even Jeremy, who had become even fussier about his food, seemed to enjoy every bite. Thankfully, Greg was well informed about Pick's disease, having been a neurologist at St. Luke's Roosevelt Hospital Center for many years before his retirement. It was a relief not to have to explain Jeremy's strange behavior and I enjoyed the company.

Miranda was not due back at school for another week, so right after New Year, I began to look for a facility, in or near Westhampton, that provided education for special needs children, especially those with hearing loss. It didn't take me long before I discovered the Cleary School for the Deaf in Nesconset, a forty-five minute drive away. After making a call to the admission office, I realized that it was not a simple matter to transfer Miranda from one school to another, particularly if it might only be a temporary arrangement. I needed to obtain all of her records from St. Francis De Sales and even then she still needed to be evaluated to determine the appropriate program for her. I decided to take a drive with Miranda just to take a look at the area and I was impressed. The school was housed in a long single storey, white building surrounded by trees and I could just imagine how wonderful it would be when the weather turned warmer. We stopped at a nearby drive-through and munched on cheeseburgers and French fries and I got a kick out of seeing Miranda with ketchup all over her face. She looked so adorable and when she saw herself in the mirror she started to giggle. Actually, she always seemed to be giggling at something and I couldn't help wishing, for the umpteenth time, that she could talk.

I realized that we would have to return to New York before I could even think about transferring Miranda to Cleary so, a few days later, we packed up and drove back to the city. There had been very little snow in Westhampton but by the time we reached Manhattan, the streets were covered in a white blanket. It looked like fairyland with all of the Christmas lights still lit up and Miranda clapped her hands in delight, but I knew it wouldn't be long before the snow turned to slush and it wouldn't look quite so pretty. As we rode the elevator to our apartment I wondered if Jeremy even noticed we were missing. I had told him the night before that we would be leaving early in the morning but when I went to say good-bye, I found him still asleep in the spare room with Teddy snuggled up beside him. I didn't have the heart to wake him up so I kissed him lightly on his forehead and then left a little note with Pilar to tell him that I would call him that night. Later, when I did call, he seemed to be excited about some shells he had found on the beach and our conversation made little sense. I went to bed that night feeling alone and depressed and then found myself thinking about Scott.

I had planned to visit Mama, as it had been almost two weeks since I had seen her, but I was conflicted about showing her the newspaper article about Lexie. On reflection I realized that, unlike me, she might have paid more attention to what was going on in the world and knew about the situation in Somalia from CNN, which aired on the TV in the common room every evening. If that was the case, I suspect that she was keeping any concern for Lexie's safety to herself and didn't want to worry me. I decided then that, I had no choice; I had to put her mind at rest.

Because of the lengthy process involved in transferring Miranda to Cleary, she was continuing her education at her old school for at least another term. This meant that we could not return to Westhampton, except on weekends, and so we were to remain in New York during the week for two or three months. On Thursday morning, I dropped Miranda off at school, as usual, and early that afternoon I drove out to Clinton to see Mama. When I walked through the door of the visitor's room I picked her out immediately. She was wearing a bright red vest over her white sweatshirt and she was grinning from ear to ear. I ran over to where she sat, glanced around to check if any guard was nearby, then quickly grasped her hand and whispered, "Happy New Year, Mama."

Mama nodded, "You too, honey. Now sit down and tell me all about your holiday. I bet your aunt and uncle had a lovely time and how about Miranda, how did she enjoy all her presents?"

I spent the next twenty minutes making up wonderfully exaggerated stories about those days in Westhampton. Some had a lot of basis in truth but others were sheer fabrication. I think she got the greatest pleasure when I told her about Pepper's antics and thankfully those stories were not a figment of my imagination.

When I finished, Mama just slowly shook her head and said, "Oh, I wish I could have been there it sounds all so lovely."

I leaned towards her across the table, "Tell me about your Christmas, Mama. Where did you get that vest, it looks hand knitted?"

Mama got this proud look on her face, "I knitted it myself. One of the women started a knitting club and, at first, there was a lot of concern about us all having knitting needles, so we are very strictly supervised but it's nice being able to make things."

We talked a little more about how Mama had spent Christmas Day and the special meal they had been served at noon and then, when the conversation lulled for a moment I excused myself and approached one of the guards. He stepped back abruptly when I started to pull the newspaper article out of my purse, but when he saw what it was, he visibly relaxed, "What is it, ma'am?" he asked.

"I just want permission to allow my mother to have this. It's about my sister and she hasn't had any contact with her for a long time. It's very important that she sees this."

He took the paper out of my hand then after glancing at it, passed it back, "Go ahead."

I walked back to the table and sat down while Mama looked at me with a frown, "What's going on, Cassie?" she asked.

I slid the paper across to her, "It's Lexie, she's back home."

Mama gasped as she looked down at the photo and then started to read the article. When she had finished she looked back at the photo again and then across at me, "She looks different but I can see it's her. I'm so relieved that she's here and away from all that trouble."

"So you did know that she could have been in danger?"

Mama nodded slowly and I could see tears starting to form, "I have to confess, I've been watching the news, day after day, wondering what she was doing over there and whether we would ever see her again. Now, here she is and she's pregnant. I wonder how far along she is."

"Oh, Mama, why didn't you tell me you were worrying about her? I've been a little preoccupied lately and I haven't been watching the news. I had no idea how serious things were."

"I wasn't sure if you knew and I didn't want you worrying too."

"I'm going to try and find her, Mama. Maybe she'll change her mind about coming to see you."

Mama wiped away her tears, "Thank you, honey, but if you do find her, please don't put too much pressure on her. I'm just thankful that she's alive and well."

Every weekend after that, we drove to Westhampton. I knew that Jeremy's condition was deteriorating and we needed to spend as much time with him as we could. This was difficult because, he was even more withdrawn and usually wanted to be alone. Sometimes, I dreaded making the trip and would have preferred to stay in New York. There was so much more to do in the city, especially in the winter months. I felt lethargic most of the time and had made no effort to locate Lexie. Thankfully, Scott called me on several occasions and I was relieved to hear his voice. Even though we kept the conversation light, I always felt better after speaking to him and whether it was just in my own mind, I sensed an undercurrent between us. Then, in March, just as I was beginning to make final arrangements for Miranda's transfer to Cleary, he called to tell me he would be coming to New York the following week. I spent the next few days in a state of confusion. My heart told me I wanted to stay in the city but I knew I had no choice; for Jeremy's sake, we had to go back to Westhampton whether it be for months or even years. That's where Jeremy was most comfortable and where he deserved to live out the rest of his life, however long that might be.

Two days later, at Jazz's house, while Jules took Miranda for a walk with Badger, I poured out my heart to her and ended up in tears. It was good to have someone to talk to who never passed judgment on me. I was so grateful to have such a good friend. That Friday, Scott called to tell me that he had arrived and was at the Royal Park Hotel on the Upper West Side. He was going to be in New York for at least four months and was making arrangements to rent an apartment. He wanted to see me that same night but I had already packed up our belongings to go to Westhampton. When I heard the disappointment in his voice, I just couldn't help myself, moments later I was calling Pilar to tell her that we had been delayed until the next morning. Then, with Jazz being out of town on a photo shoot and nobody to take Miranda, I had no alternative but to invite Scott to the apartment. I wondered what my daughter would think of Mommy's new friend.

When I explained to Scott that he would have to come to my home for dinner, he graciously offered to pick up some steaks, if I could manage to throw together a salad. He obviously knew that cooking was not my forte and I couldn't help laughing, "I think I can do that, but don't be surprised if I chop off a finger."

"Don't you cook supper for Miranda?" he asked.

I sighed, "Well, I try my best and she doesn't complain but I could have used a lot more lessons from Pilar. She taught me how to bake cakes and cookies, but when it comes to everyday meals, I am not so good."

"Not to worry," Scott assured me, steak is my specialty."

# CHAPTER 50

That evening with Scott was wonderful and when he left just after midnight, after kissing me gently on the lips, I fell into bed feeling more content than I had felt in a long time.

When I met him at the elevator he had been carrying a rather large bag, which I discovered later contained, not only steaks, but also two bottles of wine, fresh asparagus and mushrooms. 'You shouldn't have gone to so much trouble," I said.

"No trouble is too much for such a beautiful lady, " he replied then, putting the bag down on the floor, he gave me a hug and stood back to look at me. "You look wonderful; that color really suits you, it makes your eyes look even bluer."

I was wearing a lilac top with a cowl neck and a pair of dove gray slacks. The whole outfit was new, having been bought only a few days earlier in anticipation of my first meeting with Scott after so many months. "Thank you." I responded. "Let's go to the kitchen and drop off whatever you have in that bag. Then I want you to meet Miranda but you'll have to talk very slowly and enunciate every word and make sure you're facing her."

"Who did you tell her I was?" Scott asked as he followed me down the hallway.

"I just told her you were someone I went to school with, that's all."

When we reached the kitchen, Scott looked around in amazement, "Wow, this is some kitchen. I can't wait to see the rest of the place."

"In that case, follow me," I said grinning, knowing exactly how he would react when he walked into the living room.

He didn't surprise me. He just walked towards the windows, stared out over Central Park for a moment or two and then turned and opened his arms wide, "This is fantastic, Cassie. What a view and what a beautiful room."

"Yes, it is lovely and I promise to show you the rest of the apartment later."

"What about your summer home, is it just as spectacular?"

"It's lovely too but totally different. Not only is there a main house but also a guesthouse and we're right on the beach. Jeremy likes spending all his time there now."

"Do you have any other property? I would imagine you could afford it."

"Actually no, the only other asset we have is the yacht. Jeremy has always been generous but at the same time he's been careful with his money. We've been fortunate not to have any financial worries. Jeremy's books are still very popular and they've been published in several languages."

"So you'll be well looked after?"

I looked at Scott and felt a lump in my chest when I realized what he was asking, "If you mean, will we be okay when Jeremy dies, the answer is yes."

Scott reached out his hand, "Sorry, I didn't mean to........."

Just then I heard a noise behind me and turned to see Miranda in the doorway smiling. She was wearing a pink organdy dress with white ribbons in her hair and looked adorable.

Scott followed my gaze and then immediately walked forward and crouched down directly in front of her, "Hello Miranda," he said extending his hand, "my name's Scott. I'm very pleased to meet you."

Miranda looked down at Scott's hand, and then, after reaching out and gently grasping his fingers, she looked back up again and nodded.

"Will you come and help Mommy and me make dinner?' he asked.

Miranda looked at me and I could see she wasn't sure what to do so I went over and signed to her, "Scott is going to broil some steaks and you can help me with the salad."

She nodded again and then took my hand and the three of us headed for the kitchen.

Scott looked perfectly at home in the kitchen after Miranda handed him an apron. He had looked a little surprised and then laughed and graciously put it on mouthing, "Thank you."

The steaks turned out to be perfectly cooked and Scott carefully cut up Miranda's into bite size pieces. I couldn't help commenting, "One would think you had children of your own, you look like you've had some practice."

He turned and winked at me, "My mother used to cut up my meat for me when I was little. By the time I reached my teens, she finally stopped. She used to embarrass me in front of my friends."

"My mother used to do that for me too," I said, getting up from the table.

"Where are you going?" Scott asked.

"Just getting some water," I replied, walking quickly over to pick up a glass from the counter.

I heard Scott get up and the next moment he had his hand on my shoulder and turned me to face him. I had tears in my eyes and he gently wiped them away with the tips of his fingers, "It's okay, Cassie," he whispered. "Memories can bring out all kinds of emotions."

I reached up and touched his cheek, "Thanks for understanding, even though I try and see her every week, I really miss her."

After we had finished eating, I insisted on cleaning up the dishes while Scott entertained Miranda. I knew I was putting him on the spot and wondered how he would handle dealing with a child who was profoundly deaf. You can imaging my surprise when I walked into the living room only to find them playing tic tac toe and it was pretty obvious, after a while, that Scott was letting Miranda win. I sat quietly watching the two of them and thinking of Jeremy and I wondered just how much Miranda missed her father. After a few more games, I could see that she was getting tired and decided it was time she went to bed. I excused myself while I helped her brush her teeth and change into her pajamas, then sat and read to her from her favorite book, 'The Wind in The Willows'.

It didn't take long for her to fall asleep and when I got back to the living room Scott was standing near the fireplace and holding a photograph in his hand. When I got closer, Scott turned around and I could see that it was my wedding picture, "You made a beautiful bride," he said.

I took the photo out of his hand and stared at the image of the man at my side. It was hard to believe that Jeremy had changed so much, "Yes, that was one of the happiest days of my life," I said.

"Your husband is very handsome, but then I already knew that because I'd already read a couple of his books and seen his picture on the cover."

I sighed, "I'm afraid he doesn't look like that any more. He used to be so full of life and now he's totally withdrawn."

"What are the doctors saying?"

"Well, that's another thing, he refuses to see anyone other than Paul Radcliffe. Paul's his doctor in New York and an old friend. Jeremy wants to stay in Westhampton all the time now and we've only managed to persuade him back into the city for an appointment twice in the last year. Even getting him to take his medication is a problem. He's on antidepressants but they don't seem to be helping too much and Pilar has to stand over him to be sure he takes them."

"Isn't there anything they can do?"

"No, there is no cure. Eventually he'll be in a vegetative state and will need constant care."

"How long will he survive in that condition?"

I placed the photograph back on the mantel, "I'm not sure but the body eventually starts to shut down and death often occurs because of an infection, like pneumonia."

Scott put his hand on my shoulder, " I am so sorry, Cassie, I can't imagine how difficult this must be for you. How on earth do you cope?"

I shrugged my shoulders, "Not very well I'm afraid. I'm dreading going back to Westhampton tomorrow but I can't let Pilar take all the responsibility for Jeremy. I can see the toll it's taking on her lately. She worries about him all the time, especially when he wanders outside and she doesn't know where he is. Thankfully, it will start to get warmer soon and it's a wonderful place to be in the summer. Miranda loves the ocean and I think she's going to like her new school. It's a lot different than the one here in the city."

"She's an amazing little girl and pretty too, like her Mom."

I punched him on the arm, "Flatterer. Now, enough about us, what about you? Tell me all about the kind of work you'll be doing while you're here and where you're hoping to find a place to stay."

After drinking almost all of the wine that Scott had brought with him and hours of good conversation, I suddenly realized that it was very late. I was reluctant for him to leave but with an early drive ahead of us in the morning I needed to get some sleep. Scott made no effort to delay his departure and I felt relieved that no more than that gentle kiss had passed between us as he said goodnight. I gave him my phone number in Westhampton without any concern about how Jeremy would react. My husband was now almost incapable of caring about those of us that loved him and there was nothing we could do to change that.

When I saw Jeremy the next day, he was quite lucid and wanted to walk on the beach with Miranda and me. We dressed up in some warm clothes, as there was still quite a chill in the air, and wandered along, hand in hand, close to the water. Every now and again, Miranda would break away and stoop to pick up a shell or a pebble and then slip it into the pocket of her father's jacket. If anyone had been observing us, they would have thought we were a normal family but if they had been close enough they would have been aware of the silence. I tried to talk to Jeremy now and again but he only answered me in monosyllables, or not at all. He seemed to be captivated by the waves and constantly gazed out across the ocean as though he was in a completely different world. I knew that the man I had married had ceased to exist and I felt more alone than ever that day.

Back at the house, Pilar made us a wonderful lunch of roasted tomato and fennel soup and grilled cheese sandwiches but Jeremy refused to eat and retired to his studio. I was going to go after him and try and coax him back but Pilar stopped me, "No use, Miss Cassie," she said. "He no like to eat lunch. He had an egg and two slices of toast for breakfast and now, he no eat until dinner time."

I sighed, "I seem to have completely lost touch with just how bad things have been getting, Pilar. Now that I'm here, I want to help as much as I can."

"He no trouble really, it's me that's the problem."

"What do you mean?"

"Well, it's just so hard to see him this way. I feel sad all the time and I'm not sleeping."

I got up from the table and walked over to where she was pouring coffee at the kitchen counter, "I think you need a vacation, Pilar."

She put down the coffee pot and shook her head, "I can't leave now, he needs me here."

I took her hand and drew her over to sit down, "I'm here now and I can look after him. Why don't you go and visit your sister in California or your family in Mexico?"

"But who will watch Mr. Jeremy when you have to take Miranda to school and then pick her up again later?"

"It's two weeks before Miranda has to be at Cleary so that isn't a problem. I promise, I won't leave the house unless Jeremy is with me and if he goes out I'll find out where he is going and when he's coming back. You haven't been back home for so long and I'm sure your family would be thrilled to see you. We can call the airlines today and probably get you on a flight by tomorrow."

Pilar shook her head, "But what about Teddy? Who will look after him?"

I chuckled, "I think I can manage to look after a cat. Don't worry, Miranda and I will feed him, give him fresh water and even change his kitty litter."

"Now you laughing at me, Miss Cassie."

I reached over and rubbed her shoulder, "Yes, I am and I've finished with listening to excuses. The next thing you'll tell me is, you can't afford to go."

Pilar look up at me with a wry grin on her face and shrugged her shoulders.

"Right," I said decisively, "that's it. I'll pay for your ticket."

Pilar waved her hand in front of my face, "No, no, I pay my own ticket."

"You'll go then?" I asked.

She bowed her head and muttered, "Okay, I go. I'll call my sister and tell her I'm coming."

# CHAPTER 51

I didn't realize how difficult it would be after Pilar left the next day. Even before that, I had completely neglected to think about how I was going to get her to the airport. I tried to persuade Jeremy to drive into New York with us but he absolutely refused and I couldn't leave him alone. I considered allowing Pilar to take one of the cars but that would mean leaving it parked for two weeks. Then, when I was almost out of ideas, other than hiring a limousine to make the trip, which was well over an hour away, our neighbors, Greg and Sally, came to my rescue. After breakfast, while Pilar was packing, I was taking a walk along the beach, with Jeremy and Miranda, when I saw Greg walking towards me with, what looked like, a golden retriever puppy running along beside him. Miranda let go of my hand and darted forward, sinking onto the sand and gathering the startled animal in her arms. Greg just looked down and smiled then took a step forward, "Good morning," he said. "I'd like you to meet the new addition to our family. Her name's Lacey."

I bent down to stroke the puppy's soft fur while Jeremy stood muttering under his breath, "She's adorable, Greg. How old is she?"

"She's almost nine weeks and a bit of a handful at the moment. Sally sent me off for our walk this morning because she has trouble running after her. I like to let her run free on the beach. Can't see any sense in keeping her on a leash out here."

"She looks like a golden retriever. Is she?"

"Yes, but I think she's got something else in her somewhere because she sure is a frisky one."

I smiled remembering our beloved Sheba, "She'll settle down as she gets a bit older. My family in Asbury Park used to have a golden retriever and she was the gentlest creature. Now they have a terrier-poodle mix, Pepper, and she's a bit of a handful. She was here at Christmas but you missed seeing her then. Anyway, what are you doing here at this time of the year?"

"Well Sally thought it would be a good place for Lacey to be, especially while we are still training her and fortunately for us, the rain has stayed away. It's looking a little cloudy though at the moment, probably time to head in soon. How would you folks like to come back to our place for coffee?"

I bent down and gently released Miranda's arms from around the puppy's neck and she immediately ran to the edge of the water and then back again, "That's really kind of you, Greg, but we can't be out here too long because Pilar is leaving this afternoon to visit her sister in Los Angeles. I need to spend a little time with her before she leaves."

"Oh, how nice for her, she's a wonderful lady. How's she getting to the airport?'

I sighed heavily, "Well, that's a bit of a problem. I would drive her but I can't leave Jeremy here alone and he refuses to come with us. I'm just about to phone a limousine company."

Greg shook his head, "Nonsense, we'll keep an eye on Jeremy and Miranda. They can come over to our place or we could come to yours if you prefer."

"I can't ask you to do that, it's way too much trouble."

"You're not asking, I'm offering, that's what neighbors are for. I know Sally would be happy to have some company, besides me, anyway."

I leaned towards Greg and whispered, "I'm afraid Jeremy and Miranda aren't very good company."

Greg patted my hand, "That's all right, Cassie, dear. I didn't mention this before but my oldest son is autistic and unable to cope at all in society so he's locked away in an institution. We spent a lot of years trying to take care of him ourselves, so we have some idea of what you're going through."

I could feel the tears start to well up in my eyes, "I am so sorry, I had no idea."

Greg's eyes started to light up, "Well, we are just grateful that we have two other healthy children and three great grandkids. Wait till they see Lacey here, they'll be crazy about her."

I smiled, "How could they not be, she's adorable."

"Yes, she's quite something. Anyway, what about it, Cassie, will you allow us to look after your family while you drive Pilar to the airport?"

I nodded my head feeling relieved but a little reluctant, "Thank you so much. Greg. It would probably be better if you came to our place. May I call you just before we are ready to leave at about two o'clock?"

"Perfect," Greg replied, then, tipping his hat, started to walk away. "See you later folks."

When we got back to the house, Pilar was waiting for us. I told her about Greg's offer to stay with Jeremy and Miranda and although she said little, I knew she was concerned as to whether this had been a good idea. She was a little abrupt when she announced, out of Jeremy's earshot, "Some man called you, Miss Cassie, he no leave his name but he left a number for you to call him."

I knew it had to be Scott so I excused myself and went to the bedroom to use the telephone there. There was only one ring before a rather breathless Scott picked up the phone, " Hi, is that you, Cassie?" he asked.

I chuckled, "Yes it's me, but what if it had been someone else?"

I could hear the teasing in his voice as he answered me, "I have several exclusive numbers, one for each of my ladies."

"And since when was I one of your ladies? I asked.

He hesitated for a moment and then sounded a little serious, "Sorry, Cassie, I didn't mean anything by that. I just wanted to know how you were. How are Jeremy and Miranda?"

"Well, Jeremy seems about the same and Miranda is fine. I just hope I can cope while Pilar is away, she's going on vacation to visit her sister for two weeks."

"When is she leaving?"

"This afternoon, in fact I'm driving her to the airport."

"Are Jeremy and Miranda coming with you?"

"No, my neighbors have offered to watch them while I'm gone, so I'm coming alone."

There was a pause and then Scott asked, "Is it possible to see you while you're here?"

I wanted to tell him it was possible but replied, "I can't stay. I have to get back here as quickly as I can."

"I'll come to the airport. Surely you can stay for a half-hour or so?"

I hesitated but I knew I wanted to see him so I agreed, "Okay, but I can only stay for a short while. Pilar is catching the American Airlines four-thirty flight to LA so you could meet me in the departure lounge but don't come up to me until she's gone through the gate."

"I understand, I'll be there just after four. Drive carefully."

"I will," I said softly, "bye Scott."

I was sitting with Pilar waiting for the boarding call when I saw him. It wasn't hard to pick out the tall handsome man in the black leather jacket walking past the departure lounge. Scott walked straight on by and quickly scanned the crowd, then caught my eye and grinned. I didn't dare to acknowledge him because I thought Pilar had noticed him too, but she merely sighed and said, "I hope Mr. Jeremy will be all right. I feel so bad leaving like this."

I put my arm around her, "We've been over this already, Pilar and it will be fine. I have the list of instructions you gave me, which incidentally is a mile long, so how can anything go wrong."

Pilar looked at me a little sheepishly, "I know, Miss Cassie, I just wanted to try and make it easier for you"

"And you have, and I'm grateful for it. Now, I just want you to go away and relax for two weeks. Spend some time with your sister and have a little fun too. No one deserves it more than you do."

Pilar was just about to respond when the boarding call was announced. I could see how nervous she was as she gathered up her belongings and we approached the gate. "It's going to be okay," I said trying to reassure her.

"Oh, I'm not worried about that now, Miss Cassie," she said fidgeting with the cross she wore on a chain around her neck, "I no like flying."

I couldn't help laughing, "Now you tell me. Well it's a bit too late to start having a panic attack. Millions of people fly every day and I don't think it's your time yet."

Pilar gave a weak grin, "I call you when I get to Rosita's."

I gave her a hug and pushed her towards the gate where she glanced back at me briefly then disappeared into the jetway. I then turned slowly around and saw Scott waiting for me, only a few feet away, and beaming from ear to ear. I was smiling as I walked towards him and he embraced me, kissing me lightly on the lips, "I thought that boarding call would never come," he said.

I took his arm and we started to walk away from the departure lounge, "I know, the plane was a little late and now I have even less time to spend with you."

"Let's find a place and have a drink," he suggested.

We found a bar in the terminal and I ordered a glass of chardonnay while Scott ordered a beer. He looked pensive as he took off his jacket and hung it over the back of the chair.

"Is something the matter?" I asked.

"No, of course not. I'm just happy to see you, that's all."

I took off my own jacket and Scott looked me up and down and grinned. I couldn't help following his gaze, "Do I look odd, or something?"

"No," he replied continuing to grin, "You look terrific as always, just a little more casual today. I like it, you should wear jeans more often and that red sweater really looks good on you"

"You're not looking too bad yourself," I countered. "Did you catch a glimpse of Pilar, by the way?"

"Yes, just briefly. She reminded me of Mrs. Romano who used to live around the corner to us in Asbury Park, such a motherly type. Is that the way Pilar is with you and your family?"

"Yes, she's been wonderful and I don't know how I would manage if she left us permanently. As it is, I'm not sure how I'll cope for the next two weeks."

"What about your Aunt Jean, can't she help?"

"I have actually been thinking about that because I didn't realize just how trapped I would be for so long"

Scott frowned, "Trapped? That's a pretty strong word."

"I didn't really mean that," I said, shaking my head. "Maybe restricted would have been a better word. I won't even be able to get up to see Mama until Pilar gets back and I hate to miss a visit."

Scott reached across the table and took my hand, "I'd like to see you too, Cassie."

I quickly withdrew my hand, "I don't know, Scott. I would feel so guilty asking Aunt Jean to watch over Jeremy and Miranda while I'm here with you."

"But if you went to see your mother, surely you could spend an hour or two with me. I'll be settled in my apartment by the end of the week and I'd love you to see it."

"Oh really? I didn't know you had rented a place already. Where is it?"

"On West 60th, near Amsterdam. It's a one bedroom and fully furnished. I think the decorator must have had me in mind because it's got a lot of leather and several bookcases filled with some rather intriguing titles."

"What sort of intriguing titles?"

Scott threw his head back and laughed, "You'll just have to come and see for yourself," he said.

# CHAPTER 52

When I arrived back at Westhampton, I found Sally in the kitchen and Greg with Miranda, in the dining room, playing snakes and ladders. Jeremy was nowhere to be seen. Sally turned when she heard me come in and, seeing the anxious look on my face, said, "Don't worry, Jeremy's in the studio, I checked on him about ten minutes ago. He was painting but when I went towards him I got the impression he didn't want me to see what he was doing so I just told him that I was fixing something to eat and would let him know when it was ready."

"How did he react to that?"

"He didn't react at all, other than to turn his back on me. I thought he'd be hungry and so I thought I'd just make some hamburgers and fries. He'll eat that won't he?"

I sighed as I sat down at the kitchen table, "Who knows, Sally. At one time, he would only eat food that was green. You can imagine what a problem that caused. Both Pilar and I spent ages coaxing him to eat some meat or fish just to get some protein into him. I think we're through that stage now but he's still very fussy, in fact, he's worse than a child to deal with."

"Well how about Miranda? Does she like hamburgers?"

I couldn't help smiling, "She loves them especially if they come from Macdonalds."

Sally chuckled, "Well, I can't promise mine will taste as good as theirs."

Of course, Sally's were a whole lot better and I was grateful that she had taken over the kitchen that evening. I was emotionally and physically exhausted and not in the mood for dealing with Jeremy and his eccentric eating habits. Sally even offered to take Jeremy's supper out to him while I sat with Greg and Miranda and although I felt guilty, I let her make up a plate and take it to the studio.

It was a little after eight o'clock when Greg and Sally left to go home and I got Miranda ready for bed. She pointed out of the window in the direction of the studio indicating that she wanted to say goodnight to her father but I dissuaded her. After settling her in bed, I laid down beside her until she fell asleep and by that time I was almost asleep myself. Suddenly I heard the back door open and knew that Jeremy had come back to the main house, so I got up and went looking for him. He was in the kitchen emptying most of his supper into the garbage can, "Jeremy, you have to eat something," I said.

He swung around looking a little annoyed and shook his head, "No, I don't."

I walked over and gently took the empty plate from him, "Let me get you something. What would you like? How about some fresh strawberries and vanilla ice cream."

He grabbed me by my arm and pulled me towards him, "I said no!"

I tried to pull away but he looked at me angrily and then took the plate out of my hand and threw it into the sink. Right then I felt fear but I looked straight into his eyes and said in a quiet voice, "Let me go, Jeremy."

I was relieved when he released my arm and without another word headed for the guest bedroom, where he had been sleeping for the last few months. That was the first time I felt afraid of my own husband and a few moments later I found that I was shaking. I had read extensively about the behavioral changes in someone with Jeremy's disease but this was the first time I had seen him react that way. I was wishing Pilar had been there, I felt so alone, and then I saw a movement out of the corner of my eye and there was Teddy rolling onto his back and begging for attention. I picked him up and held him against my shoulder, nuzzling my face into his thick fur, "Oh, Teddy, what am I going to do?" I murmured.

I went to bed early that night and was reading John Grisham's 'The Pelican Brief' in an attempt to get my mind away from all that was going on in my life. I always left my bedroom door a little ajar, in case Miranda or Jeremy needed me, but I was a little startled when it was flung wide open and banged loudly against the wall. Jeremy was standing in the doorway wearing nothing but a pair of boxer shorts. I dropped my book and instinctively drew the covers up to my chest, "What is it, Jeremy?" I demanded.

He stood there for a moment then strode towards the bed, stopping just about a foot away. "I think you know what I want, Cassie," he replied with a menacing look on his face.

I moved quickly to the other side of the bed and jumped up, grabbing for my robe at the same time.

Jeremy backed up and rounded the foot of the bed blocking my path to the door, "You don't need your robe," he said looking me up and down.

I was acutely aware of the gown I was wearing, which was satin and showed every curve of my body, "Stay away from me," I cried.

The next moment I was thrown back onto the bed and Jeremy was on top of me tearing at the straps to my gown, "You're my wife and I'm going to have you," he hollered.

I was panicked and lashed out hitting him in the face, "Get off me," I yelled.

He grabbed both of my hands with one of his and started to pull down his shorts with the other, "You know you want me, or are you getting it somewhere else these days?"

I struggled to get free, "Stop it, please, I'm asking you to stop. You'll wake Miranda."

Jeremy threw back his head and roared with laughter, "Ha, good one, Cassie. She's as deaf as a door post, she won't hear a thing."

With that he tried to pull my gown up with his other hand and then crudely thrust his fingers into me. All fear left me at that point and I felt angrier than I had ever remembered feeling before. I found the strength to get my hands free and struggle out from under him. He tried to pull me back again but I was too quick for him and raced towards the door. I didn't turn back to see if he was following me but I heard him yell, "You bitch, come back here."

I ran to Miranda's room, locked the door from the inside, and then sat in the chair beside her bed. I fully expected Jeremy to come pounding on the door but he never came and an hour later when I ventured out to the hallway and peeked into his bedroom I could see that he was sound asleep with Teddy curled up at his feet. In that hour, waiting for him to come, I sat thinking about Mama. Now I understood, more than ever, why she had killed my father.

The next morning I got up early, having had a restless night, and found Jeremy sitting in the kitchen eating cornflakes out of a bowl but without any milk. He looked up at me as I came through the door, "Where's Pilar?" he asked as though nothing had happened the night before.

"You know where she is," I replied rather abruptly, "she needed a vacation, so she's visiting her sister in California."

"When is she coming back then?" he asked looking rather like a sullen little boy.

I realized that I just had to be patient with him but it wasn't easy, "She won't be back for almost two weeks but if there's anything you need, you only have to ask. I'll get you some milk for your cereal, it's not very appetizing like that."

"Don't want milk," he said rising from the table and heading for the door.

"Please don't leave the house without telling me where you are going," I pleaded.

He completely ignored me and kept right on going, but as I raced quickly after him I saw that he was heading for the studio. Feeling somewhat relieved that I didn't have to deal with him, I returned to the kitchen to prepare breakfast for Miranda and myself and mulled over how I was going to handle this drastic change in Jeremy's behavior.

Later that morning, I noticed Greg walking along the beach with Lacey and I walked out to the patio to wave to him. He immediately changed direction then came up the steps and after a brief conversation, where we exchanged pleasantries, he suggested taking Miranda for a walk. I was so grateful to have some time alone because I was finding it difficult keeping Miranda occupied and I needed to call Paul to fill him in on Jeremy's latest change in behavior. Paul was with a patient when I telephoned but Penny assured me that she would have Paul call me as soon as he was free. I paced the living room, glancing out of the window occasionally in the direction of the studio, and as the time went on I got more and more anxious. Finally, after what seemed like an hour, the phone rang and I ran to answer it. Paul didn't even wait for me to speak, "Cassie, what's the problem," he asked. "Is Jeremy okay?"

I was reluctant to tell Paul every detail of what had happened the night before but he quickly understood exactly what had taken place, "I don't know what to do, Paul." I cried, "I don't think I can handle this."

Paul sighed, "I'm afraid it could get worse, Cassie. Unfortunately one of the symptoms of Pick's is sometimes aggressive sexual behavior."

"But why now?" I moaned, "What's happening to him?"

"Unfortunately we don't have all the answers. The only thing I can recommend is to increase his anti-depressant medication. He's been on a very low dose, so it might help to some degree."

I felt thoroughly frustrated and I know I sounded it, "That's all you can do? What if he gets really violent? What if he hurts Miranda?"

Paul sighed, "I doubt that will happen, Cassie, but if you become really concerned, then we may have to consider putting him in an institution. In the meantime let's try more medication. I'll fax a prescription through to the pharmacist there."

After I got off the phone, I called the pharmacist to ask him to have Jeremy's medication delivered as soon as he could fill the prescription, then I paced the floor again trying to figure out what to do. I finally decided to ask for Aunt Jean's help. She was upset and astonished when I explained to her what had happened and announced that she was leaving that very afternoon and would stay until Pilar's return. After I got off the phone, I just sat down and cried from utter relief.

By the time Aunt Jean arrived in mid afternoon, Jeremy was still in the studio, ignoring the lunch I had prepared for him and left on a table just inside the door. I had gone over and peeked through the window several times but he was still engrossed in his painting. Miranda had arrived back from her walk with Greg, delighted with the amount of seashells she had gathered and was happily gluing them to a wooden picture frame. When Aunt Jean drove up, I ran out to greet her and startled her when I threw my arms around her and started to cry, "I'm so happy you're here," I muttered into her shoulder. "I knew I could count on you."

Aunt Jean returned my embrace and then wiped away my tears, "I'm always here for you, Cassie, and Miranda too. Where is she and where's Jeremy?"

I led her into the house and pointed to the studio, "He's in there. He's always in there and I wish he would stay there."

Aunt Jean stopped me and turned me to face her, "It's going to be all right. If you're worried about what happened last night happening again, then I suggest you lock your bedroom door and I'll sleep in Miranda's room."

"But what if he comes in there anyway," I asked wringing my hands.

"I'll lock that door too. "

"But what if he gets violent and starts trying to force his way in."

Aunt Jean chuckled, "Don't worry, I'll hit him with a baseball bat." Suddenly her face grew serious, "Let's face it, Cassie, if the medication doesn't help you may have to move him out of the house, just as Dr. Radcliffe suggested. In the meantime you need to get some rest, you look worn out."

"Well, I didn't sleep much last night, that's for sure," I said taking my aunt's hand and leading her through the front door. "Come, let's have some coffee and you can take a look at what Miranda's doing."

# CHAPTER 53

In the next few days, things seemed to settle down. Jeremy had always liked Aunt Jean and with her presence, and the increase in medication, he fell back into his introverted behavior, spending nearly all of his time in the studio. My aunt tried, on several occasions, to draw him into a conversation after she had coaxed him from the studio to eat with us, but he was monosyllabic as always. Miranda would just sit and stare at him and I know she was wondering where her daddy had gone. I had tried to explain her father's illness to her but it was difficult, with her struggle to read my lips and my limited use of sign language. I tried to keep it as simple as possible but I'm not sure she fully understood. The odd time when he was close by, I would see her slip her little hand into his as though she was telling him everything was going to be all right. It broke my heart to see this precious little girl being deprived of the love of the man who once held her in his arms with such pride.

Aunt Jean, Miranda and I spent most of our time close to the house, leaving only for an hour or so to walk the beach or take a short drive to pick up groceries. Jeremy was so preoccupied with his painting that I felt secure about leaving him alone for short periods and the break from being confined inside for so many hours was a welcome relief. At the end of the week I felt comfortable enough to ask Aunt Jean if she would be able to hold the fort while I went to see Mama and she was more than happy to let me go. As I drove away, just after lunch, I felt the weight of the world lifting off my shoulders and then I realized the irony of it all. I was visiting a prison, just a different kind of confinement.

Mama was so happy to see me. She was eager to know what we had been up to in Westhampton, how we were coping without Pilar and if Aunt Jean was enjoying her visit. As always, I painted her a portrait of a wonderful family having a marvelous time, involved in all sorts of activities. I often wondered why she couldn't see through the façade but that was Mama, the eternal optimist. After I left the prison, I couldn't face the idea of returning home so I decided to call Scott. He had actually called me at the house the night after Jeremy had burst into my room. I didn't tell him what had happened, as I was very much aware that Aunt Jean was close by. I discreetly let him know she was there and he understood why I kept the call brief, and rather formal, and asked me to call him back when I had a chance. I had no idea if he would be available to answer the phone later in the afternoon and was surprised when I heard him pick up after two rings, "Well, you're home already," I said, not even thinking to say who was calling.

"Hi, Cassie," he responded immediately. "Where are you?"

I had stopped at a gas station to use the telephone and looked around me, "I just came from visiting Mama and I'm about to pull onto I-78 to go back to the house."

There was a pause before Scott responded, "Do you have to go back right away?"

I hesitated before I answered because I wanted to see him so badly but I knew I needed to get home, "I really should," I said, "I told Aunt Jean I'd be home early this evening."

"Why don't you meet me somewhere just for an hour or so. You could tell her you were delayed by traffic."

"I'm not sure, Scott. I'd love to see you but….."

Scott cut in, "There's a Holiday Inn near the Queens Midtown Tunnel. It's on your way back and I could meet you there. It should take you about an hour from where you are. I can meet you in the coffee shop there. Please say yes, Cassie."

I sighed heavily. My head was saying no but my heart was saying yes, "Okay, I'll be there waiting for you."

Scott chuckled, "No, I'll be waiting for you," he said.

When I got to the Holiday Inn, Scott was already there. He was standing leaning against a wall, in the parking lot, looking very casual in a tan suede jacket and jeans and I couldn't help grinning as I got out of the car. "Hi handsome," I said. "Are you waiting for somebody?"

He came towards me and gave me a peck on the cheek, "Just the most attractive lady I know" he replied.

I was dressed pretty casually myself in a heavy cable knit sweater and black tights tucked into calf high black boots and didn't feel very attractive but I was comfortable. We headed for the coffee shop and waited for the waitress to bring our espresso before we got into any deep conversation and that's when Scott asked me what was going on at home. As I told him about the night that Jeremy came to my room, I could see his expression change. It was obvious that he was not only concerned but also angry. I reached across and touched his hand, "It's okay, we think we have him settled down now. Aunt Jean seems to have a calming effect on him and we believe the change in medication is helping."

"But how can you be sure?" Scott asked covering my hand with his own.

"We can't be sure of anything but we've taken precautions and if there are any more incidents, we may have to put him in an institution."

"And how do you feel about that?"

I bowed my head and withdrew my hand, placing it in my lap, "Sad, terribly sad. I loved this man with all my heart and to see him like this is unbearable. He was so vibrant and he had so much to live for, not only for Miranda and for me, but also his writing. It's so hard to comprehend how someone so intelligent and so in touch with life can get this disease. It's all so unfair and I have to admit I haven't been much help."

Scott leaned over and tipped my chin up so that he could see my eyes, "What do you mean by that?"

I shook my head, "I just don't think I've been supportive enough but it's so hard being around him. He hardly ever speaks and when he isn't in the studio painting, he just stares off into space"

"You can't blame yourself, Cassie. You have Miranda to think of and that must be stressful. Maybe you would be better off if you didn't wait. Maybe now is the time to put Jeremy in some type of facility, where he can get the care that he needs."

I started to get up from the table, "No. I can't do that, not yet. Sorry, Scott, but I have to go. I don't know why I agreed to meet you, I just have to get home."

Scott rose from his chair and grabbed my arm, "Cassie, sit down. At least finish your coffee and then you can go. I promise I won't try and stop you but I do want to see you again, and soon."

I sat down rather reluctantly but I felt edgy and anxious to leave. I know Scott sensed this and as soon as I drained the last drop of coffee, he got up and said, "Okay, let's get you on your way."

He embraced me just before I got into my car and kissed me lightly on the lips, "You promise you'll call me, no matter what time it is? If you have to leave a message, I'll get back to you as soon as I can."

"I promise and as soon as Pilar gets back, I'll try and get away again to see Mama and spend some time with you. I just don't want to take advantage of Aunt Jean right now."

"I understand, I really I do but I need to talk to you long before that, so call me."

I climbed into the drivers seat and started to close the window but Scott stopped me, leaning in and kissing me again, a little more forcibly this time. He waved when I pulled away and, as I turned onto the highway, I felt reluctant to leave but I had to get back to my family.

When I arrived at the house, the dinner dishes had already been cleared away but Aunt Jean had kept some homemade lasagna warm for me. She was anxious to know how my visit with Mama had gone but I never mentioned seeing Scott. While I had been away, she had coaxed Jeremy into taking a walk along the beach with her and Miranda and they had collected even more shells. Now, Miranda was busy with a very large jig-saw-puzzle depicting Snow White and three of the dwarfs while Jeremy was back in the studio again.

After dinner, while I was enjoying one of my aunt's specialties, a cappuccino laced with Kahlua, she announced that she had a surprise for me and laid a copy of the Asbury Times beside me on the table. I glanced up at her and she just nodded and said, "Page 10."

I tentatively turned the pages and came to the heading on Page 10, 'Notice of Births' – then below that, an area circled in red ink.

It's a Girl !!

WILLIS – Alexa and Todd are thrilled to announce the birth of their daughter Caroline Ruth. Born at Community Memorial Hospital in Tom's River, NJ on Thursday, April 29, 1993 weighing 7 lbs 2 oz.
The proud grandparents are Robert and Hannah Willis of Camden, NJ.

I had known my sister was pregnant from the article I had seen in the newspaper months before but I had put it out of my mind. Even Scott, had not brought up the subject of Lexie again, even though he had agreed to try and locate her. Now, as I read the announcement again, I found it hard to believe she had a daughter, just like me and at that moment I desperately wanted to see her.

"How did you get the Asbury Times?" I asked looking across at Aunt Jean who had sat down opposite me.

"When I was leaving home, I asked your uncle to send me the Saturday newspaper. He knew it was the one day I enjoyed having it to read after lunch. It arrived this morning in the mail."

"And did he know about the announcement?"

Aunt Jean looked a little sheepish, "Well actually he did. When he called on Sunday he told me that he'd highlighted something we would be interested in but when I pushed him to tell me what it was, he said it was a surprise."

I got up and searched for a pair of scissors in one of the kitchen drawers and then carefully cut the announcement from the page. "I'm going to try and find her," I said resolutely.

Aunt Jean nodded, "That shouldn't be too difficult. I would assume that she lives in Tom's River or somewhere close by. If not, maybe you can trace her through Todd's parents in Camden."

"It makes me sad that they mentioned his parents but there's not a word about Mama. She'll be so happy to know that she has another grandchild."

"You know how Lexie feels about your mother, Cassie. You shouldn't be surprised that she made no reference to her in the announcement."

I took the scrap of paper and put it in my wallet, "No, I'm not surprised, I'm just disappointed."

# CHAPTER 54

Five days later, I called Scott and arranged to meet him again at the Holiday Inn, after my visit with Mama. I was relieved that I had something else to talk to her about, other than my own family, and when I pulled the scrap of paper from my wallet and passed it to her, I watched her face intently. At first she looked across at me with apprehension, and then began to read. Slowly I saw a smile that began in her eyes and spread throughout her face, "Oh, how wonderful," she cried. "Your sister's had her baby and it's a little girl. I've wanted to ask if you'd heard any more about her but I didn't want to upset you. I know how you feel, Cassie, but I wish you would put all that behind you and forgive Lexie, after all you are both mothers now."

"I'm not sure if I can, Mama, but I've made a serious commitment to try and find her and then we'll see what happens."

"Perhaps Jeremy can help you locate her, he must know so many prominent people."

I paused trying to think up a plausible response, "I'll ask him but he's very busy with his book right now."

"I wish he'd hurry up and finish it, I'm looking forward to reading his next best seller. It seems like such a long time since he published anything."

"He had a dry spell," I lied. "It happens to a lot of authors and even when he's finished, the manuscript has to be edited so it could be a year away or more."

Mama sighed, "Well, I guess I'll just have to go on reading the classics. They have several of them in the library and I think I'm one of the few women here that bothers with them. Ruby, my cellmate, only reads the tabloids and then she fills me in on all the gossip."

I laughed, "Well, at least she keeps you up to date with what's going on in the world."

Mama laughed too, "It's hardly earth shattering news. I've never heard of most of the celebrities she talks about. What happened to the real stars like Joan Crawford and Bette Davis?"

I shook my head, "You really are out of touch, Mama, but then even I can't keep up with all the new faces today."

Mama looked pensive, "I think I'll be like a fish out water when I get out of this place. It's only five more years, Cassie"

I reached across and took her hand, not caring if the guard saw me, "Don't worry, Mama, I'll take care of you," I whispered.

When I left the prison and drove towards the Queen's Midtown Tunnel, I kept thinking about what my life would be like when Mama was released. There was no question in my mind that Jeremy would no longer be with us and by then Miranda would be ten years old. Long before that, Mama would learn the truth but I hoped she would understand why I kept everything from her. Maybe Lexie would be in the picture too and we could be a family again. Then my thoughts turned to Scott. Where would he fit into my life? Would we just be friends or something more?

I was still thinking about Scott as I pulled into the Holiday Inn lot but he wasn't waiting outside as before. I found him in the coffee shop munching on a bagel slathered in cream cheese and flirting with the waitress, who was a rather buxom redhead but old enough to be his mother. As I approached the table, she sidled away, and I wagged my finger at him, "So this is what you're up to when I'm not around."

He got up and gave me a hug, "Always get better service that way," he said rolling his eyes.

I stayed with him for almost an hour and we talked about all kinds of things including Lexie. He promised to make more of an effort to help me locate her especially as we now knew where she was likely to be living. Before I left, I reminded him that Pilar would be back that weekend and I would try and come into the city the following weekend to check on the apartment and do some shopping. "Why don't we have dinner when you're here?" he suggested.

"Absolutely," I replied, "I can hardly wait."

That weekend I picked Pilar up from the airport while Aunt Jean watched over Jeremy and Miranda. It was obvious that Pilar was happy to be back on firm ground. As she walked towards me and gave me a hug, "Oh, Miss Cassie," she cried, "so good to see you. I thought I was going to die up there."

I chuckled, "What happened, did you have a little turbulence?"

She nodded her head vigorously, "There was a lot of bumping and swaying and we had to keep our seat belts on. I was so scared, I no think I fly again."

I rubbed her shoulder, "It happens all the time and it's nothing to worry about. You'll soon forget about it. Now let's get your luggage and find the car and then you can tell me all about your trip."

As we headed for the baggage claim area, Pilar insisted on knowing how Jeremy and Miranda were and if Teddy had been behaving himself.

"Everyone's fine," I assured her. "My aunt has been here and helping out but don't worry she's going home this afternoon so she won't get in your way. As for Teddy, well we did have a couple of incidents after you left when he decided to use the kitchen floor instead of the litter box, but I think he was upset because you weren't there."

Pilar looked alarmed, "Oh, I'm sorry, I thought he would be all right"

"He is all right. It only happened twice, right after you first left, and then it stopped. I think he was suffering from separation anxiety."

"But he seems to spend more time with Mr. Jeremy than me," she said sadly.

"You're still his Mom and he missed you."

That caused a big grin to break out on Pilar's face and she quickened her pace, anxious to find her luggage and head on home.

On the drive back, Pilar was anxious to tell me every detail of her vacation at her sister Rosita's home in Ingelwood, a short distance southwest of Los Angeles. Two of her brothers and their wives had also been visiting from Mexico and I could see her becoming tearful as she remembered leaving for the airport, just a few hours earlier, and the anguish of having to say goodbye to her family. A short time later, when we walked through the front door of the house and she saw Teddy, her whole demeanor changed. Scooping him up in her arms and burying her face in his fur, she murmured gently in Spanish just as Aunt Jean emerged from the kitchen to greet us, "Hello there and welcome back Pilar, it's so nice to see you again but you must be tired after that long flight. I've just brewed some coffee and there are some blueberry muffins, although they aren't home made like yours, I'm sorry to say".

Pilar put Teddy down gently on the floor, "Thank you Mrs. Marsh. I am happy you were here to help Miss Cassie."

"Well, I don't know how much help I've been. I just hope I haven't mixed up your kitchen too much. I wasn't sure where you kept everything."

"No worry, Mrs. Marsh, I soon put everything straight."

Aunt Jean smiled then touched me on the shoulder, "Well now you're in more capable hands, honey, I'm going to pack my bag and take off for home."

It was sad seeing my aunt leave, she had been a godsend while Pilar was away and the only other person I could trust to look after Miranda and Jeremy. There had been occasions when I had allowed Jazz to care for Miranda but there was no way she would have been able to take on the responsibility of Jeremy. Thinking about Jazz, I realized I hadn't seen her for some time. We had talked on the phone nearly every week, when she wasn't out of town somewhere on some exotic shoot, but our lives were so different now. She lived an exciting life with Jules, traveling a great deal and enjoying all that the city had to offer. I had to admit I was envious.

Pilar's return seemed to delight Jeremy; in fact I was surprised to see a huge smile on his face when he first saw her. Miranda wasn't quite as welcoming. She was used to my aunt taking her for walks, playing board games or watching her favorite movies with her. Pilar didn't do any of these things and while she took care of her in so many other ways, like cooking her special foods, these weren't as important to a child of her age.

I let a few days go by before I suggested that it was time to visit Mama, check out the apartment and pick up any mail that might have been accumulating. Pilar readily agreed that it would be a good idea and so, with a little hesitation, I then asked if she would mind very much if I stayed over for one night so that I could do some shopping the next day. Again, she was perfectly happy to be left alone with Miranda and Jeremy and assured me that she would have everything under control. I couldn't wait to call Scott. I had to leave him a message that I was coming into the city and if his offer of dinner was still open, I would love to see him. Fifteen minutes later, when the phone rang, I raced to answer it and in a rather awkward conversation, because Pilar was hovering nearby, I agreed to meet him at The Boathouse Restaurant in Central Park.

The next couple of days seemed to drag by and I couldn't wait to get away. I knew once this weekend was over, my time would be limited as Miranda was due to start the new term at Cleary. I would have to take her there each morning and pick her up at night and the only time I would get to see Mama and make any attempt to see Scott would be on a weekend. Too many weekends away from home, and I was certain that Pilar would become suspicious. I tried not to think about that too much as I packed an overnight case and immediately after lunch on Friday, I was on my way to Clinton. Mama was nursing a rather nasty cold when I got there and had been tempted to call me and dissuade me from coming. She was worried about passing it on to me and then possibly having Miranda catch it too but I made sure we didn't make any physical contact and assured her I would be okay. Nevertheless, I think she was glad to see me leave this time. This was so typical of Mama, always thinking of others and never of herself.

When I got to the apartment, everything seemed to be in order and there was nothing in the mail to warrant my immediate attention. There were several messages on the answering machine, but none of them were of any consequence. I walked through the rooms and looked out over the park and thought about how lonely it was without my family there. I expected to feel relieved and relaxed to be completely on my own for two or three hours but the solitude was overwhelming. I considered calling Jazz to kill some time but remembered she was in Rome that weekend, so I called Aunt Jean. Uncle Frank answered the phone and I was surprised that he was home so early, "Cassie," he said, "How lovely to hear your voice. Where are you?"

"I'm at the apartment. I was just visiting Mama and came into the city to check on things."

"And is everything all right there?"

"Yes, everything's fine uncle. What are you doing home already?"

My uncle chortled, "I goofed off and now I'm just about to take Pepper out for a run. Your aunt's not here, by the way, she took a carrot cake she made over to Billy's and I don't think she'll be back for a while."

"That's okay, I can talk to her some other time. I only called to chat for a few minutes and then I should get back home," I lied, not wanting them to know I was staying over.

We talked some more and I brought my uncle up to date on Jeremy's condition, Miranda's return to school and Pilar's vacation. After about ten minutes, I rang off saying that I would call my aunt the next afternoon in the hope that she wouldn't try calling me in Westhampton. I still had quite a while before I was to meet Scott so I phoned to make an appointment to get my nails done and I was fortunate that they were able to accommodate me at such short notice. When I got back, I took a long relaxing bubble bath and then in a burst of inspiration decided to curl my hair. I had worn it in the same style for years, long with a slight wave, but I had always wanted curls, the more the better. As I stood with my curling iron, I thought about Jazz and how she had always hated her curly hair and now always wore it perfectly straight. I assumed that everybody wanted the opposite of what they were born with but a half hour later, when I surveyed myself in the mirror; I didn't like what I saw. It took me another half hour to straighten my hair again.

Next on my agenda, was to rifle through my closet for something to wear and I knew I had found the perfect dress when I spied a lavender silk sheath with a square neckline and cap sleeves, that I had purchased almost a year before, and had completely forgotten about. I remembered wearing the same shade once before and Scott commenting on the color and with my high-heeled black sandals, I knew I just couldn't go wrong.

Before I left the apartment, I called Pilar to be certain that everything was all right at home and she assured me that it was. I had not told her about the incident with Jeremy and I wondered if I had done the right thing when she told me that Miranda had spent an hour in the studio with her father working on a 'paint by numbers' picture. I felt reassured when she told me she had checked on them at least three times and then called them in for supper. She was just in the process of getting Miranda ready for bed and Jeremy was back in the studio again. I admit to feeling relieved but a little guilty as I exited the building and made my way to The Boathouse but the minute I saw Scott waiting in the bar area, I couldn't help smiling. He looked immaculate, although casual, in pressed jeans, a white button down shirt and navy blazer. "I think I'm overdressed," I said still smiling.

He shook his head, "You look marvelous," he responded kissing me lightly on the cheek, "but then you always do."

The maitre'd led us to a table with a view overlooking the lake and we dined on seared sea scallops, grilled filet of beef with creamed spinach and a wonderful passionfruit parfait. The delicious food and the bottle of merlot, which we consumed between us, put me in a very mellow mood and I felt more relaxed than I had felt in a long time. Scott was great company, witty, charming and very attentive and I didn't want the evening to end so, when he invited me back to his apartment, I only hesitated for a moment before I said yes.

When we arrived at his place on West 60th, it was exactly as Scott had described it to me earlier. It was tastefully decorated with a buttery leather couch, two deep armchairs, dark wooden tables, wall-to-wall bookcases and a large framed print of Van Gogh's 'Poppies' over the faux fireplace. While Scott was making coffee and searching for a bottle of Frangelico in the kitchen, I browsed through the bookshelves and smiled when I saw some of the titles. When he came back into the room announcing that coffee was almost ready, I was holding three books in my hands, "Now I know what you were talking about," I said.

He grinned, "What have you got there?"

I slowly turned the books over so that I could read the spines, "Well let's see, I have 'Lady Chatterley's Lover', 'Sons and Lovers' and 'Tropic of Capricorn'. Is this what you read in your leisure time?"

Scott laughed, "Hell no, too tame for me. I like something a little raunchier than that."

I put the books down on the table and walked towards him, "Oh you do, do you?" I teased.

He put both hands up as if to stop me, "Whoa, coffee. Don't forget the coffee."

I got even closer and grasped both of his hands, "Which do you want, coffee or me?"

"Oh, Cassie," he whispered, "you know the answer to that but are you sure you want to do this?"

"I'm sure," I whispered back. "Take me to bed please, Scott."

# CHAPTER 55

That night with Scott made me feel like a desirable woman again and brought back all the memories of our teenage romance in Asbury Park, but we weren't teenagers anymore. I realized just how naïve we had been back then and just how far we had come. Scott was now a skilled love maker, experienced in knowing exactly how to excite a woman and we couldn't get enough of each other. By morning we were exhilarated but exhausted. I didn't want to leave and so after we finished  breakfast on the small terrace, we crawled back into bed again.

Waking up just before noon, I panicked and immediately called home to tell Pilar that I had a little more shopping to do and would be home for dinner well before six o'clock.  First, I needed to go back to the apartment and change my clothes before I did any shopping and Scott offered to drive me provided that I had lunch with him. I made him wait in the car while I raced up and changed into the outfit I had worn on the drive from Westhampton and then threw everything else in my overnight bag and raced back down. We found a small café a few blocks away and spent almost an hour just gazing into each other's eyes, or at least it seemed that way. I had no regrets about what had happened between us and I hated to say goodbye. Scott begged me to come back the following weekend, at least for a few hours, but I couldn't make the commitment.  He even suggested that he could come to Westhampton and meet me somewhere but that wasn't possible. The chance of us being seen together was almost a certainty. In the end, I promised I would call him the very next day and that I'd be back in the city as soon as possible.

I only managed to last a week without seeing him again, this time for just a few hours in a shabby hotel room just off of I-95. I couldn't help myself, he made me feel alive and for that short span of time, all the stress in my life just fell away. I knew then that I had started something that I couldn't finish and Scott would have to be the one to end it. Eventually, the deception began to eat away at me. I was lying to Mama, to Pilar and my family in Asbury Park and the only person I had been honest with was Jazz. I had finally managed to meet up with her one Saturday, after spending the afternoon with Scott, and I told her exactly what had been going on. I don't know whether she was just caught up in the romantic aspect of it all but she didn't discourage me, in fact quite the opposite. She even offered to be my alibi whenever I needed one. After two months of sneaking away to see Scott whenever I could manage it, I felt compelled to tell Aunt Jean but I couldn't do it over the phone. Miranda was now on summer break from school so I decided to take her to Asbury Park and stay for at least a week. I think Pilar was happy to see me go, as I had been a little edgy lately, and Miranda was overjoyed to visit with my aunt and uncle and particularly happy to spend time with Pepper. The first full day was hectic, with Billy and Amanda dropping in and insisting that we come and see where they lived at the community home. They both seemed so happy in an environment where there were several other young people with special needs and I realized just how much I missed Billy's huge smile and his endearing ways. In fact, I missed all of my adopted family.

On the evening of the second day, with Miranda in bed and Uncle Frank out bowling with his team, I knew I had the perfect opportunity to talk to Aunt Jean. We were sitting on the back porch sipping on an ice-cold chardonnay when I finally approached the subject. I decided there was only one way to tell her and that was straight out, "I'm seeing Scott," I said without looking in her direction.

Aunt Jean only hesitated for a moment, "I thought you might be," she answered.

I turned to her trying to read the expression on her face, "You did? What made you think that?"

"Well, I knew he was back from San Francisco, of course, and I knew you had spoken to him but you never mentioned him again."

"Why did you never ask me about him?"

Aunt Jean turned and looked me straight in the eyes, "Because I suspected this might happen and I didn't want to give you the opportunity to lie to me."

I hung my head, "I feel so badly lying to you but I was so scared that you might think the worst of me. I am so sorry."

My aunt pulled her chair closer to me and took my hand, "Look at me. Cassie," she said. "Have you ever known me to be judgmental? I've seen first hand what you've been going through with Jeremy and bringing up a child like Miranda is difficult. We've talked about that before and it isn't hard for me to relate to because of Billy. I'm sure I know how Scott fills the void in your life. I haven't forgotten that he was your first love and you have a special bond. Not only that, he's attractive, he's smart and he's unattached. You're a young woman and you need to feel desirable so, if you think I'm going to condemn you, or discourage you from seeing him, then you're wrong."

I have to admit, I was dumbfounded for the moment and then finally managed to speak, "I hardly know what to say. I know you've always been fair and open minded but I didn't expect this reaction."

Then Aunt Jean amazed me even more when she said, "I'm here for you, Cassie. Always have been, you know that, in fact I have a suggestion. As you're already here, why don't you just leave Miranda with me this coming weekend and take off with Scott for a couple of days. You can pick her up on the way back and then go on home."

"I can't believe you're offering to do that for me but what will Uncle Frank say?"

Aunt Jean just clucked her tongue, " You just leave your uncle to me," she replied. "I'll just tell him you're with Jazz or something. He won't know any different."

I shook my head, "But then you'll be lying to him and I don't want to be responsible for that."

Now Aunt Jean just laughed, "You think I've never lied to your uncle? I'll tell you a little secret."

"Oh, oh, I don't think I want to hear this," I said.

"It's okay, it's nothing that earth shattering and it happened a long time ago. About a year after Billy was born I really needed a rest so I took a vacation with a friend I knew from high school. We went on a Caribbean cruise and we had a ball. There were so many young people on the ship and we started to hang around with a group of students from South University in Tampa. One night I ended up in bed with Ari. He was from Greece; tall, dark with classic features and very, very sexy."

I couldn't help cutting in, "So you had a one night stand, I wouldn't expect any woman to admit that to her husband."

Aunt Jean wagged her finger at me, "It didn't end there, Cassie. We spent the rest of the trip practically joined at the hip. It was so romantic being in that environment. We stopped off at Costa Maya and Cozumel and it was wonderful. I was in a completely different world but I knew I had to come back and face a lifetime of caring for Billy. When the cruise ended, we wrote to each other every week for about three months. Thank goodness I was here every day to pick up the mail while your uncle was at work. Then Ari told me he was flying to New York before he started back at university and I couldn't resist seeing him one more time. I had no illusions about the affair, it was a summer romance with a young man several years my junior and I was flattered. I spent a weekend with him at a hotel close to where your apartment is now; I can't remember the name of it. Then I told him it was over and I just couldn't see him any more. I think he knew it was coming and he accepted it rather graciously and promised that he would never forget me. I doubt that he really meant that, Cassie, but I've always remembered him and I've never regretted it. Yes, I lied to your uncle and I'm glad that I did because he's a wonderful man and I would never go out of my way to deliberately hurt him. It was just a time in my life when I was confused and scared to face the future. Ari gave me the confidence I needed to go on."

"That's quite a story," I said. "I feel a lot better now about what I'm doing but unlike you, I can't see what's in store for the future."

Aunt Jean got up and started to make her way indoors, "Just take it one day at a time, Cassie. That's all you can do. Now how about some more wine?"

Later that night, I called Scott and was relieved to find him at home. When I told him about Aunt Jean's suggestion he was astounded but overjoyed, "Tell your aunt, I think she's the tops," he said. "I'll scout out some places to go and I'll call you back by tomorrow night. We're going to have a fabulous time, Cassie."

By noon the next day, Scott had already made arrangements for the weekend. He had booked us in to the Catskill Lodge and suggested that I drive up to his place early on Friday and then we would make the two and a half hour trip up to the northern Catskills. He started to describe the lodge to me and I could hardly wait until Friday, it all sounded so wonderful and so far removed from my day-to-day life.

When Friday finally came and we arrived at the lodge, I was intrigued by the architecture. It was built in the Queen Anne style with verandahs and a turret and when we were shown to our room I was even more enchanted. The bed dominated the room with its oak headboard, fat floral comforter and several matching pillows bordered with lace. The drapes, in matching lace, added to the femininity of the room and I loved it. I hadn't realized that Scott had deliberately asked for this room because he knew how much I would appreciate it. He had never been to the lodge before but had done his research and I was touched by his thoughtfulness. I sank down on the side of the bed and looked around the room, "It's so cozy. I'm never going to want to leave," I said.

Scott sat down beside me and put his arm around my shoulders, "Well, that could be arranged, but do I get to stay too?"

I laughed, feeling a little uncomfortable, "You'd soon get tired of this place and you know it,"

Scott ran his fingers up through my hair, "Not with you here, I wouldn't."

We had only just arrived and the conversation was becoming rather serious. I decided to make light of it and jumped up off of the bed, "We should unpack and go exploring rather than sitting here. I also happen to be starving, it's been hours since I had breakfast."

Scott looked at me rather skeptically then got up too, "Okay, you're right. Let's unpack and then we'll go into Windham and find somewhere to eat."

Less than an hour later we were sitting in a French country restaurant sampling their delicious roasted tomato soup and Maryland crab cakes and I began to relax. "What shall we do this afternoon?" I asked, gazing around me at the people at other tables, most of whom were dressed as though they were ready for an all day hike.

Scott grinned as though he knew what I was thinking, "Well, we could go hiking but I think we should leave that for tomorrow. Why don't we go on the wine tasting tour?"

It didn't take me too long to think about his suggestion, "That sounds wonderful, is it far?"

"No, it's very close by and I think you'll really enjoy it. Have you ever been on a wine tasting tour?"

"Actually no, but I've always wanted to go."

"I've been just once before, in the Napa Valley in California, it's just a little north of San Francisco."

My mind immediately flew back to the time I had spent in San Francisco with Scott all those years ago, "I had a great time when I visited you, do you remember?"

Scott reached across the table and took my hand, "How could I forget," he said.

I withdrew my hand and toyed with my coffee spoon, "You'll be going back there soon and I'll probably never see you again."

Scott sighed, "I'm not sure when I'll be through here but even though I have to go back because that's where my job is, it doesn't mean I won't see you again. We have something special between us, Cassie, and I don't want to let that go, but your life is so complicated right now. I have no idea what the future will bring."

I shook my head, "I don't know what's going to happen in the future either so let's not talk about it. Let's just enjoy ourselves, that's what we came here for."

The afternoon at the winery was a brand new experience for me and quite an education. After we left there we took a drive around the area then watched the anglers fishing for large mouth bass and pickerel in one of the warm water lakes.

Scott suggested we have a cocktail back at the lodge before changing clothes and finding a place for dinner. I was all for that as I really needed to wash up and I was getting hungry again. But the best-laid plans, of mice and men, don't always happen.

# CHAPTER 56

I had intended to call home that evening before Scott and I left for dinner and I never expected to find several messages waiting for me when we got back to the lodge, all from Aunt Jean. My heart was racing as I telephoned her from the lobby of the lodge, I couldn't even wait to get up to the room. "What is it, Auntie?" I asked frantically, "What's happened?"

My aunt didn't pull any punches, "I think you should get home right away, Cassie. Pilar called here not too long after you drove off. Jeremy wasn't there when she got up this morning and she has no idea where he is. I've spoken to her twice since then but he hasn't shown up. Your neighbors have been out looking for him while she stayed behind, in case he came back, but they haven't had any luck. I told her she should call the police."

Scott was standing beside me and I grabbed his arm for support as I cried out, "Oh, my God, where can he be? Why didn't I call home before I came here?"

Aunt Jean tried to calm me down, "I'm sure he'll turn up, honey, but I think you should get home. You can leave Miranda here with me for the time being and I'll arrange to bring her to you once Jeremy's back."

"No, Auntie, I need to pick her up and take her with me."

"But it's too far out of your way, Cassie. It will just take you that much longer to get there."

"I can't help it, I can't go without her," I said, my voice wavering.

Scott gently took the telephone out of my hands, "Mrs. Marsh, it's Scott here. I do have a suggestion if it's not too much trouble."

I moved from one foot to other while he listened to Aunt Jean's response then continued, "Cassie's car is parked at my place on West 60th. Is there any possible way you can meet us there with Miranda?"

Scott listened intently, nodding his head, then proceeded to give my aunt his address and advised her to try and meet up with us at eight o'clock. I was so thankful for his being there at that moment, I was too upset to make any rational decisions and while he raced upstairs ahead of me to start packing, I called Pilar. She answered the phone on the first ring and sounded relieved to hear my voice. Jeremy was still missing and the police were out searching along with the neighbors. I told her I'd be there as soon as I could but that it probably wouldn't be before ten o'clock. "Oh, Miss Cassie," she cried, "I'm so worried, it's going to get dark in a little while and then he won't know his way home."

I felt as desperate as Pilar but I didn't want her to know that, "The police will find him before that, Pilar. Now I have to run and I'll see you soon."

We drove back to Scott's place in record time even though the traffic, as we came into Manhattan, was heavy because of rush hour. Aunt Jean and Miranda were already waiting for us in the lobby of Scott's building and we only spent a few minutes together before I piled Miranda into my car and I was ready to take off again. "I think I should follow you," Scott suggested.

I shook my head vehemently, "No, that's not a good idea. Pilar doesn't know who you are and it would just create a lot of confusion."

Scott looked a little hurt but he accepted my decision and made me promise to call him as soon as I had more news. I drove away leaving him standing next to Aunt Jean looking rather dejected but my thoughts were on Jeremy now. Where could he be?

I know I was exceeding the speed limit as I headed for home and when I glanced over at Miranda, I could see that she was nervous. It was impossible to tell her what was going on. There was no way that I was able to sign to her while I was driving or face her so that she could read my lips. I did consider, just for a moment, pulling over onto the shoulder so that I could tell her what was happening but I thought she might be even more alarmed.

When we got to the house Pilar came running out to meet us, "Any news?" I called out as she came towards us.

"No, Miss Cassie," she said ringing her hands, "they're still looking but it's so dark now. How will they ever find him?"

"Here take Miranda and put her to bed. Don't tell her, her father is missing. Make up a story; tell her Teddy's missing. Oh, I don't know. Pilar, tell her anything you can think of," I said frantically pushing Miranda into her arms.

Pilar looked at me anxiously, "Where are you going?"

"I'm going to find Jeremy," I cried, running into the house and into the kitchen to look for the flashlight.

When I raced out onto the beach I could see dozens of flashlights in every direction and I had no idea where to start. I finally caught up with a group of people who I had never met before and I must have looked demented as I rushed into their midst, "I'm Jeremy's wife, how long have you been searching?"

Before anyone had a chance to answer me, I felt a hand on my shoulder and turned to see Greg, "Cassie, we think you should just go home and wait. There's nothing you can do out here. There are dozens of people looking for him and the police have been asking a lot of questions about where Jeremy likes to spend his time. I believe they just came from the house after talking to Pilar for the second time tonight."

I gave Greg a hug and then raced back to the house again, calling for Pilar as I charged through the door. "Pilar, where are you? What did you tell the police?"

Pilar appeared at the top of the stairs, "I just put Miranda to bed, Miss Cassie. I'll come down now."

I waited impatiently while she descended the stairs, "What did you tell the police?" I asked again.

"They asked me lots of questions and I tried to answer as best as I could," she replied rather defensively.

"It's all right, Pilar," I tried to assure her, "I'm sure you were helpful but exactly what did you tell them?"

" I told them he liked to be in the studio and sometimes he would walk along the beach and he would always go in the same direction. I told them that sometimes I would worry because he would be gone for a long time but he always came back and he never left the house until after breakfast."

"Okay, what else? Can you remember anything else?"

"Yes, I told them about the boat, Miss Cassie,"

"Boat, what boat? What are you talking about?"

Pilar looked near to tears, "Mr. Jeremy's boat."

It suddenly dawned on me what she was trying to say, "You mean the yacht, Dreamcatcher? But that's at the marina in Hampton Bays, he couldn't have gotten that far."

Pilar nodded, "Yes the yacht, I couldn't remember the name and where it was but the police said it would be easy to check out."

"How long ago was that?"

"About an hour. Oh, sweet Jesus, I hope he didn't go on the boat, Miss Cassie," she said finally breaking down in tears and leaning against the wall for support.

I was just about to comfort her when I heard a noise behind me and turned to see two men in police uniform standing in the open doorway. "Mrs Kent?" one of then asked.

My throat closed up and I could hardly speak, "Have you found him?" I managed to whisper.

Both men stepped forward, "No ma'am but I'm afraid the yacht is missing and we've had to notify the coastguard. Unfortunately it's too dark to do a proper search until morning and the weather isn't helping. There's a thunderstorm in the forecast."

For some reason, which I can't explain, I became completely calm at that moment, "Please come in, you must both be tired. Pilar will make you coffee."

The older of the two officers shook his head, "That's very kind of you ma'am but we need to talk to the people who are out there still looking for your husband. I think it's pretty clear that he's taken the yacht."

"But how could he possibly have made it all the way to Hamptons Bays and then taken the yacht out in his condition? You must be aware that he is seriously ill and is barely functioning on a normal level."

"Yes ma'am, we know about Mr. Kent's illness but we've seen stranger things happen. I have to be honest though, he's been gone since early morning and we don't know how long he's been out at sea. Under the circumstances, his chances of riding out a storm aren't good. We'll be doing everything we can to locate him but I think you should prepare for the worst."

I heard Pilar gasp and slide down the wall behind me. One of the officers started towards her but I stopped him, "It's all right, I'll take care of her. Thank you for coming here and for all that you're doing to try and find my husband."

I closed the door gently as they left, then made my way back to Pilar who was slumped on the floor sobbing. Slowly I helped lift her to her feet and led her into the living room where she sank into the nearest chair. "You sit here and I'll get you a cup of tea, " I said.

I called Aunt Jean to tell her what had happened and promised to call her the next morning, then I called Scott to fill him in too but I was tired and quite frankly I just wanted to be alone.

Pilar and I sat in the living room all night, just waiting. Occasionally we would drift off to sleep for a few moments, only to wake up again and realize we were still in the middle of a nightmare. At about four o'clock in the morning, we could see lightning streaking across the sky and then hear the thunder, as it appeared to rumble directly overhead. I knew that, if Jeremy was on the Dreamcatcher, he couldn't possibly survive. By six o'clock we were sitting in the kitchen drinking coffee, but unable to eat anything, just waiting for the phone to ring or that knock on the door. I had never noticed the ticking of the clock before, but on that day it was loud enough to make me aware of every second that went by. The storm had passed and by eight o'clock the sun was shining, the sky was a brilliant shade of blue and yet we still had no word of Jeremy. I was just about to call the police department when there was a knock on the door. It wasn't the police, as I expected, but a member of the coastguard holding his distinctive white cap. He nodded, "Good morning, ma'am. May I come in?"

I stood aside as he walked into the entryway and then I led him into the living room. "Please sit down," I said calmly. "Would you like some coffee?"

"No thank you," he replied, "I'm afraid the news isn't good ma'am but we still haven't given up all hope of finding your husband. We were out searching as soon as it was light and we found the yacht but there was no sign of anyone on board, or any evidence that anyone had been on board."

"But didn't anyone at the marina see him take Dreamcatcher out?"

"Apparently not, there's only one individual on duty during the night but he claims not to have seen anything. Tell me, Mrs. Kent, is your husband a good swimmer?"

I shook my head, "Not any more, he couldn't even tie his shoelaces. I can't imagine how he could even get to the marina let alone maneuver a yacht the size of Dreamcatcher."

"I ask ma'am because the yacht was found only a quarter of a mile from Smith Point. That's not too far for someone who's a strong swimmer."

"No, there's no way Jeremy could swim that far and even if he did where would he be now. Are you still looking for him?"

The coastguard stood up, "We won't stop until we find him. We're still searching the waters all the way from Hampton Bays to Smith Point in case he went overboard somewhere in that area and the police are still concentrating on a ground search."

After he left, I went to tell Pilar the latest news. She had finally taken to her room and was lying on her bed, staring at the ceiling, with Teddy in her arms. She listened quietly while I told her what I knew and I saw the tears start to form in the corners of her eyes, "Just rest, Pilar," I said, "I'm going to get Miranda up and try and act like it's a normal day. I'll just tell her you're not feeling well. I don't want her to know anything about her father until we learn what has happened."

I got Miranda up and dressed and then made her favorite breakfast of scrambled eggs and waffles covered in maple syrup. Right after she had eaten she went to the window and pointed towards the studio, obviously wanting to see her father, but I led her to the front porch and pointed down the beach indicating that he had gone for a walk. That's when I saw Greg and Sally coming towards the house trailing Lacey behind them on a leash. As soon as they were close enough, I put my finger to my lips as a signal not to say a word in front of Miranda. It was awkward exchanging pleasantries knowing that Jeremy was out there somewhere and not knowing if he was dead or alive. It was only when Greg let Lacey off the leash and she ran into the waves, with Miranda chasing behind her, that I had the opportunity to tell them what had happened. I was still on the porch when I heard the phone ringing, so I asked Sally to watch out for Miranda while I raced back in to answer it.

It was Aunt Jean, anxious to know if I had heard anything. I brought her up to date as quickly as I could because I needed to keep the line clear in case the police or coastguard tried to contact me. No sooner had I hung up the phone, when it rang again, and this time it was Scott, "Cassie," he said, " without hesitating, "I'm sure you're aware of what's happened but I think you should know that CNN is reporting the story of Jeremy's disappearance. I expect it will only be a matter of time before your mother hears about it."

"Oh God no," I cried, "what are they saying?"

"Well, the latest news flash said they'd found his yacht but he wasn't on it. A reporter just interviewed a member of the coastguard. They suspect he took the yacht from the marina in Hampton Bays and he most likely fell overboard but they're still searching for him. I'm so sorry, Cassie."

"Did they say anything about him being ill?"

"Yes, I'm afraid so. They even aired a short bio about him and there were a number of photos. There was even one of your wedding day and two or three of both of you with Miranda."

I felt like I was going to faint and had to sit down, "And did they mention Miranda's hearing problem?"

Scott hesitated, "They said she attended the Cleary School for the Deaf on Long Island and there was something else, Cassie."

I could hardly breathe as I asked, "What else, Scott."

"Please try to stay calm, Cassie. They talked about your mother."

"No, No! Soon she'll hear all about this, maybe even see it on TV herself. How am I going to explain all the lies I've told her? What am I going to do Scott?"

"There's nothing you can do until you hear what's happened to Jeremy. Hopefully he'll show up and then you can go and see your mother and explain that you were just trying to protect her from worrying about you. In any event, she's not going to turn her back on you. She loves you and she'll understand."

I let out a huge sigh, "Thanks for letting me know, Scott, I just hope you're right about Mama. I have to go now in case anyone's trying to get hold of me. I'll try and call later if I have more news."

After I hung up the phone, I just sat there wondering how on earth I would face Mama. If only I had told her about Jeremy's sickness and Miranda's profound hearing loss. Now that the truth had been exposed, I realized just how stupid I had been.

# CHAPTER 57

It was noon when I got the news that would change my life again, forever. I had never been a religious person but that morning I had actually got down on my knees and prayed. I guess God didn't hear me because Jeremy's body was found washed up near Smith Point and they had no idea how long he had been in the water. He was being taken to the Medical Examiner's Office in New York and an inquest would be held as to the exact cause of death. The police officers that came to the house to give me the news were extraordinarily kind. They offered to stay while I called a family member to come and be with me but I explained that Pilar was there and I had my daughter with me too. They had no idea that Pilar would be a complete wreck once I told her Jeremy would not be coming back or that my daughter was too young to be of any real comfort.

I decided to wait before telling Pilar as I was already feeling thoroughly drained and wasn't sure if I could deal with her if she became too distraught or hysterical. Instead, I called Aunt Jean who was nervously waiting by the phone after following the story on local television. They hadn't yet reported on Jeremy's death, but she was prepared for the worst and said she was leaving immediately with Uncle Frank so that they could be with me. An hour later, Pilar, was still in her room, Miranda was sitting quietly at the kitchen table, still struggling with her jig saw puzzle, and I was pacing the front porch trying to comprehend what had been going on in Jeremy's head. Why did he take the yacht out? Was it an accident or was he trying to commit suicide? And if it was suicide, did he leave any clues? Was he even capable of any really rational thought?

I glanced across at the studio and felt compelled to go in. I had not been inside for several months. Jeremy refused to even let Pilar clean up in there unless he was present and the only other person allowed in, was Miranda. When I walked through the door, I was amazed to find so many paintings propped up against the walls. There were some marvelous scenic watercolors of the beach, the ocean and even our house but I couldn't see anything out of place. I wasn't really sure what I was looking for, maybe a note or some indication that Jeremy intended to end his life, but I felt sure I wouldn't find anything. I was just about to leave when I noticed an easel that was close to the far wall. There was a canvas resting on it but facing away from me. I paused for a moment thinking it was probably just another seascape but my curiosity got the better of me and as I got closer, I grew more apprehensive as to what I might find. Slowly I picked up the easel, turned it around, and then set it back down gently on the floor. That was when I felt all of the blood rushing to my head. There was no doubt that the girl in the painting was Miranda and she was running along the beach. Her arms were stretched out in front of her and just beyond her reach was a magnificent pink butterfly. I didn't even have to read the words scratched out at the bottom of the picture but they were there, 'Follow the Butterfly'. I was so overwhelmed my knees just collapsed and I sank down to the ground. Jeremy had remembered the poem my mother used to sing to Lexie and me. I knew that he was leaving us a message. It was almost unfathomable and I started to rock back and forth sobbing uncontrollably. Then just when I thought my heart would break, I felt a tiny hand on my shoulder and heard a sound that I will never forget as long as I live, a voice I had never heard before uttering just one word, "Mama!"

I turned to see Miranda's sweet face and gathered her into my arms, "Oh my God, you can talk, oh my God," and then I just started to laugh and I couldn't stop laughing.

By early afternoon, Uncle Frank was attempting, diplomatically, to deal with several reporters in front of the house and two or three who showed up on the beach behind the property. I had asked him to be courteous to them as I was well aware that they were just looking for a story, after all I had been there myself at one time. Meanwhile, Aunt Jean had relieved me of the burden of dealing with Pilar and had gone quietly to her room to give her the news. I expected to hear her scream or cry out but one could almost hear a pin drop in the house. Aunt Jean said that she just rolled over and buried her face in the pillow then drew the comforter over her head. My aunt wasn't sure what to do, so she tiptoed quietly from the room.

The phone rang incessantly during the next few hours but I didn't want to take any calls. I spent most of my time sitting with Miranda, still marveling over the breakthrough she had made. I didn't want to push her and Aunt Jean agreed that the professionals at Cleary would probably know exactly how to encourage her to speak, now that we knew she was capable. It was difficult explaining to her that her father was not coming back. I had always liked to think there was a heaven so I told her that's where he had gone. She looked very sad, but there were no tears, and moments later she was engrossed in drawing a picture with her crayola markers. I was completely captivated watching her adorable face, concentrating with such intensity on what she was doing, that when I finally looked down I could hardly believe what I saw. She had drawn the figure of a man, with a remarkable resemblance to Jeremy, sitting on a cloud and surrounded by angels. I had to turn away for a moment as I felt the tears beginning to form. I realized that she had understood what I had told her and I was so proud of her at that moment. I stayed with her while she continued to draw and every now and then Aunt Jean would come in to make sure we were all right and to tell me about various people who had telephoned. I had already called

Jeremy's parents myself and was glad that I had managed to catch them before they heard it on the news or from somebody else. Mark seemed to hold it together but Vivienne was devastated and could hardly talk. I promised I would call them as soon as Jeremy's body was released and I was able to make funeral arrangements. That call was hard enough and I really didn't want to deal with either Jazz or Scott, so Aunt Jean told them both that I would call them back when I was feeling up to it. However, there was one call that I couldn't ignore. It was almost dinnertime, although nobody really felt like eating, when Uncle Frank came into the kitchen and quietly said, "It's your mother, Cassie."

I looked at Aunt Jean in despair but she just nodded her head and so I walked slowly through to the living room. I hesitated before picking up the telephone, trying to gather my thoughts, and then all I could manage was a whispered, "Hello, Mama."

I heard my mother clearing her throat and when she spoke I could tell that she had been crying, "Cassie, oh my darling, I hardly know what to say except that I'm so sorry, I wish I could be there with you. Why oh why didn't you tell me Jeremy was so sick and what about your precious little Miranda? I can't believe you've been through so much, for so long, and never ever told me."

"Mama," I cut in, "I'm all right, I really am. I just didn't want to worry you. I know I lied to you and made you think I was having a fabulous life but it really hasn't been that bad."

"You're still not being honest with me, Cassie. I'm your mother, I'm the one who should be protecting you, not the other way round."

I sighed, "I know I should have told you but one lie just led to another. I'm relieved, in a way, that you finally found out, I guess you saw it on TV."

"Yes, I was absolutely shocked and I couldn't wait to call you. What can I do to help, honey?"

"Just be there for me to talk to when I need you, Mama. Right now Aunt Jean and Uncle Frank are here and they're taking good care of us."

"What about Pilar, isn't she there too?"

"Pilar's holed up in her room and I don't want to disturb her. It's especially hard on her because she's taken care of Jeremy for so long. I'm not sure if she'll stay with us now that he's gone."

"And what about Miranda, does she understand what's happened to her father?"

"Yes, in fact she drew a wonderful picture of him surrounded by angels and speaking of pictures, I have to tell you all about Jeremy's last painting but that will have to wait until I see you."

"What will you do now, honey. Will you go back to New York?"

"Probably, I'm not sure yet. I'm going to sit down with Aunt Jean tonight and we'll try and figure out what's best. I can't really imagine staying here after what happened, there would be too many memories."

We talked for a few minutes longer and then I heard some rustling on the other end of the phone and a faint murmur. I waited until Mama came back on the line, "I'm afraid I have to go, Cassie. I know you have a lot to deal with right now so I don't expect to see you for a while. I'll call back in a couple of days but I'll be thinking about you all the time. I love you so much."

"I love you more, Mama, bye bye" I said and gently put down the phone.


Uncle Frank and Aunt Jean stayed with me for the next five days until we finally got word that Jeremy's body was being released. The official cause of death had been determined as an accidental drowning although an excessive amount of paroxetine was found in his system. I had always worried about Jeremy having access to any of the drugs that he took, especially the antidepressants because of their tendency to result in suicidal thoughts. Pilar and I had always kept them in a safe place and were careful about giving him the exact dosage, but he had obviously found them. I silently cursed myself for not being cautious enough.

I had already decided to return to New York and had even packed up most of our belongings. I wasn't sure what I was going to do about the house or about Miranda's schooling but I just couldn't stay there. Both Aunt Jean and Uncle Frank agreed that it was the best thing to do and when I told Jazz about my plans, she had to admit, she was pleased for selfish reasons. She loved her life with Jules and all the places she got to see but she had no real friends and she missed me. As for Scott, I imagine that he knew it would hardly be appropriate, under the circumstances, to show his true feelings about my return to the city but I could sense his excitement. In my own heart, I was a little excited too but first I had to get my life in order.

# CHAPTER 58

I had arranged to have the funeral at St. Bartholomews, the same church where Jeremy and I had been married. Following the funeral, respecting Jeremy's wishes, he was to be cremated and his ashes taken out to sea and scattered. It was ironic, that the very place that had claimed his life would be the place where his last remains would finally end up.

Pilar had returned with us to the apartment but she was a ghost of her former self. She had hardly eaten since she finally emerged from her room after receiving the news from Aunt Jean and had been of little help with Miranda, or the packing for our return to New York. I hadn't yet approached her on what she had planned for the future but when I did, I wanted to assure her that she was welcome to stay with us. Teddy was never far from her side; she seemed to cling to him for comfort and I was getting worried about her. It was only when Vivienne and Mark arrived that I saw the first glimpse of the old Pilar. Vivienne seemed to have come to terms with her son's death and only hours after she had settled into the guest room, she was in the kitchen encouraging Pilar to cook her favorite seafood paella.

Jeremy's brother, Ethan, his wife Jane and their three grown children arrived later that same day and after a brief visit to the apartment, they checked into the Hotel Belleclaire. I was actually relieved that they only stayed for a short time. I was tired and rather overwhelmed with the thought of the funeral, being only a day away. Not only that, there was to be a gathering afterwards at the Park Central for up to two hundred people. When it was first suggested to me by Jeremy's friend, Paul, who had helped me to understand the devastating effects of Pick's disease, that there were so many people who would want to pay their respects, I didn't want any part of it. It took Aunt Jean to remind me how well known he was in literary circles and his books were still being sold around the world. I then decided to show everyone just how talented Jeremy had been, not just for his writing, but also for his paintings. Uncle Frank and I drove back to Westhampton, packed up all of the wonderful seascapes and arranged for the hotel to put them on the display for all of his friends and family to see, and the painting of Miranda was to be centerpiece of the exhibit.

The funeral was scheduled to take place at twelve o'clock but I was up at the crack of dawn, unable to sleep. At seven o'clock, Vivienne found me standing, nursing a cup of coffee, and looking out over Central Park. The sun was already shining and it looked like it was going to be a beautiful day. I turned as I heard Vivienne's steps, "Good morning," she said putting her hand gently on my shoulder and looking past me through the window. "It's a wonderful view, Cassie," she said, "in fact I almost wish I lived here myself. I miss living in a city and sometimes I wish we could move back to Portland but Mark is happy where we are."

I nodded, "It's a great place to live, there's so much to do but Jeremy preferred being near the ocean. I guess he took after his father."

We talked about Jeremy for almost an hour and it was comforting. I had done my share of grieving long ago, when he had first been diagnosed and I knew he was in a better place. Now I was prepared to really let him go and knew I had the strength to get through the day, no matter how difficult it might be.

Sitting in the front pew at St Bartholomews with Miranda beside me seemed surreal. My mind kept wandering back to the day we had both stood together repeating our vows, "Till death do us part", we had said. Now, directly in front of me, sat a casket covered in white roses and lily of the valley and my husband's body lay inside. I suddenly felt Miranda fidgeting and I knew she was getting restless. I quietly signed to her that it would all be over soon and she slumped down in her seat with a sullen look on her face. I had refused to put her in dark somber clothes. She was wearing her father's favorite dress, white silk with a pleated bodice and embroidered with tiny pink rosebuds. I really didn't care what anyone else thought; in fact I hadn't really thought about any of the people who might be attending the funeral. Despite my objections, Vivienne had convinced me to do the appropriate thing and dress all in black, so grudgingly I had worn a plain black sheath with the customary row of pearls and a rather large black straw hat adorned with a single white camelia. The camelia was supposed to express some small evidence of the nonconformist in me. Maybe it's just as well that I took Vivienne's advice because, half way through the service, I saw that nearly every pew was occupied and it looked like a sea of black.

Ethan gave a wonderful eulogy about growing up with his brother in Portland and when Mark got up to say a few words I could hear Vivienne, sitting on the other side of Miranda, quietly sobbing. I glanced over intending to reach out and grasp her hand but to my astonishment Miranda was leaning against her shoulder and gently rubbing her arm. At that moment, I thought I would break down myself, but I managed to hold it together.

In order to avoid crowds of people following the service, I had requested that Jeremy's casket was to be left in the front of the altar; to be taken to the crematorium after we had all left the church. It had been a difficult decision to make because it felt like there would be no closure but both Paul and Uncle Frank had thought it was the best thing to do. Jeremy's family and I, along with Miranda, rose from our seats and took a few steps forward to say goodbye. As we did so, I noticed Pilar standing nearby. I beckoned to her to join us and we surrounded the casket, deep in our own thoughts, then we silently left the shadowy confines of the church and stepped out into brilliant sunlight and the blinding flash of several cameras. I tried to shield Miranda as she clung to my side. She seemed frightened and I knew she couldn't understand what was happening.

There were no cameras when we arrived at Park Central and found Jeremy's paintings had been set up in the reception room, just as I had requested. His family were lost for words when they saw them, they had no idea how much his talent for art had progressed over the last few years. Vivienne looked at me with tears in her eyes, "I think he got better and better as his condition got worse," she said. "How can anyone explain that?"

I put my arm around her shoulders, "I don't think anyone can explain it. Maybe it was the only way he had left of expressing himself."

She was about the respond when we heard a commotion and I realized that several people were arriving and I needed to greet them. I wasn't sure who would be there but I expected people I had never met, like Jeremy's pals from university and everyone involved in the publishing of his books. In the church, I had been in a kind of fog and all the faces had been a blur, but now as they entered the room, I recognized friends and family and suddenly the somberness of the day seemed to evaporate. Aunt Jean and Uncle Frank led the way accompanied by Billy and Amanda. Billy gave me a hug and then with his disarming smile reached for Amanda's hand, "I know it's not a good day for you, Cassie," he said, "but I wanted you to know that we got engaged."

I suddenly felt my spirits lift, "Oh, my goodness, you couldn't have told me at a better time, Billy. I'm so happy for you. Have you set a date yet?"

Billy looked at Amanda shyly, "I think it has to be soon."

I hesitated for a moment and then I stammered, "You don't mean…..?"

Aunt Jean stepped forward grinning from ear to ear, "Yes, I'm going to be a grandmother. Can you believe it? "

I pulled both Billy and a startled Amanda into my arms, "That's fabulous, I'm so happy for you."

Just then, I felt a tug on my elbow; it was Miranda wanting to know what was going on. When I told her she threw her arms around Billy's legs, giggled and then struggling to speak, she finally uttered the word, "Baba".

Billy looked astounded while Uncle Frank and Aunt Jean beamed with pride, "She just started to speak, Billy," I explained. "It happened on the day that Jeremy died."

Billy patted Miranda's head, "That's wonderful. You're a very clever girl, Miranda." But he didn't realize that she still couldn't hear him.

Jazz and Jules arriving interrupted us. Jazz looked amazing, as always, in an aubergine sheathe and matching five inch heels with her hair piled high on her head and oversized silver earrings. They made such an attractive couple. Jules really complimented her with his model good looks and his preference for the latest trendy clothes. Today he was wearing a dark Armani suit with a crisp white shirt and silver tie. With his dark complexion and brilliant smile, he looked like he had just stepped out of the pages of GQ. We had barely had time to exchange greetings when I noticed Paul come in with Jeremy's lawyer, Ben Greenberg. I left Jazz and Jules to go and welcome them, "I wasn't aware you two knew each other," I said.

Paul looked at Ben and smiled, "Actually I'm Ben's doctor too. We used to all play golf together at one time."

I frowned, "I don't ever remember Jeremy playing golf."

Ben grinned, "That's before he met you, Cassie. He didn't have time for us old fogies after that."

"Well, I'm so glad you came today. He would be pleased to know that you were both here."

Paul lowered his voice, "I know the circumstances of Jeremy's death were hardly ideal, but believe me, it's better this way. Had he died the way most people do with this disease, it would have been a lot harder."

"Thank you, Paul. I needed to hear that. Let's talk some more later, perhaps you can stay for a while after the crowd has gone."

Paul nodded, "Yes, I'd like that. Now come on Ben let's not monopolize Cassie's time. Anyway I'm starved and if I'm not wrong, I smell food."

I pointed to the far end of the room, " There's a buffet table set up, help yourself and get a drink from the bar. Oh, and take a look at Jeremy's paintings, I think you'll be surprised."

Paul and Ben were just starting to walk away when Ben stopped and placed a hand on my arm, "How's your mother doing, Cassie," he asked.

"Five more years, Ben, and she'll be released. I can't wait for the day she walks out of those prison gates."

"I'm glad for you, and for her. I'm sorry we couldn't do more to help."

"It's water under the bridge now, Ben."

He started to walk away again and then looked back over his shoulder, "By the way, Cassie, I'll call you to set up an appointment about settling Jeremy's estate."

I think I must have looked a little shocked for a moment because I hadn't seriously thought about my financial position now that Jeremy was gone, "Oh, okay. I'm staying in New York now so you can reach me at any time."

I was beginning to wonder where Pilar was as I hadn't seen her for a while and soon found out that she had gone for a quiet cup of coffee with Vivienne and Mark. I couldn't really blame them for leaving the reception; the whole day so far had been quite an ordeal. Then I realized that I hadn't seen Scott and I was puzzled about his absence. I slipped out of the room and called him on the phone in the lobby but there was no response and I decided not to leave a message.

I turned to go back to my family and noticed a tall, thin man standing talking to my Westhampton neighbors, Greg and Sally. I walked over to greet them and when I looked up at the man, I was completely bowled over. There was that same Abraham Lincoln face but with the hair even grayer. It was Lester Graham, my old boss from the Asbury Press. I immediately reached up and hugged him, "Mr. Graham, how wonderful to see you," I cried.

He hugged me back and then took both of my hands in his, "I am so sorry, Cassie. Everyone back at the paper who worked with you sends their condolences."

"Thank you. I appreciate you coming today. Do you know my neighbors here?" I asked laying a hand on Sally's arm.

Greg shook his head, "We just met at the church. In fact, we were sitting next to each other. It was a lovely service."

"Well, while you're here please have something to eat and I hope to chat with you a little more later," I said, looking helplessly around me at the number of people circulating around the room.

"Not to worry," Greg responded, "we'll touch base again later on."

I waved at the three of them as they wandered off and then checked to see where Miranda was. I was relieved to see that she was sitting with Aunt Jean and Uncle Frank, at one of the tables that had been set up, and appeared to be enjoying a rather large piece of chocolate cake. It was right after that, when I observed a woman with blond hair, wearing a black Chanel style suit and black pumps, staring at the painting of Miranda. I walked over and stood beside her, "It's very good, isn't it?"

She turned to look at me and I could see that she was very attractive with amazing hazel eyes, that seemed to be smiling even though the rest of her face looked sad, "Yes, it's very good. You must be, Cassie," she said extending her hand towards me.

I accepted the handshake while I searched my mind trying to remember who this person was, but without success. It was obvious that she knew what I was thinking, "You don't know me," she said, " I'm Jeremy's first wife, Courtney."

I know I looked shocked, I had not anticipated her being there, in fact I hadn't thought about her in a long time. I heard my voice falter as I said, "It was very kind of you to come."

She smiled, a smile that lit up her face, "I never really stopped loving him you know," she said. "Oh, I wasn't in love with him any more but he was a good man and I'll always think of him with great affection."

"Yes, he was a good man," I responded. "I'm going to miss him."

Courtney tilted her head to one side as though she was studying me, "I think you were good for him, Cassie. I hope you don't mind me calling you that. Jeremy and I just didn't have a lot in common."

I wasn't sure what to say except, "Well, he always spoke very highly of you."

She grinned, "That's nice to hear, even if it isn't true. Anyway, I just came to pay my respects and now I must be off."

I shook her hand again, thanked her for the second time for being there and then watched her exit the room with a dozen pair of male eyes following her.

Two hours later, the crowd had begun to thin out and Miranda had fallen asleep with her head in Aunt Jean's lap. I was just beginning to wish everyone would go home when I saw my aunt looking rather startled and when she waved at me and then pointed towards the doorway, I turned around having no idea what I would find. The two people standing in the doorway took my breath away, a slight, incredibly lovely blond in a flowing white dress and a slim man, with a boyish face, looking rather uncomfortable in a brown suit. It was Lexie, and the man beside her had to be Todd. I felt myself being propelled forward as though someone was pushing me and I watched as Lexie hesitated and then held out her arms towards me. It was a glorious moment and one I had prayed for, for so long. "It's really you," I cried, "I can't believe you're here."

"We wanted to be here for you, Cassie," she whispered. "You've been through so much and I am so sorry."

"Can you stay?" I asked hopefully. "We have so much to catch up on."

"Yes, of course we'll stay. Let me introduce you to Todd. Todd, this is my big sister, Cassie."

After that I didn't want to leave Lexie's side, afraid she would disappear again and I finally convinced her and Todd to come back to the apartment and stay the night. All they had to do was call Todd's folks and persuade them to spend an extra day looking after baby Caroline. Aunt Jean and Uncle Frank were thrilled that Lexie had suddenly appeared back in my life and welcomed her with open arms. I think Lexie was a little apprehensive after the way she behaved the last time she saw them, but there was no evidence that they even remembered the incident.

# CHAPTER 59

I was grateful when, at four o'clock, Uncle Frank addressed the remaining people in the room. He thanked them all for gathering to celebrate Jeremy's life and then diplomatically reminded them that we only had thirty minutes left before we had to vacate the room. Soon after that, many of the guests left including Paul, Ben and Mr. Graham, who I was reluctant to say goodbye to and promised to keep in touch with. I asked Jazz and Jules to come back to the apartment but the wife of Trend Cosmetic's president had invited them to a birthday celebration in Forest Hills.

We were almost ready to leave when Vivienne and Mark came wandering back in with Pilar. I had started to become concerned about them; they had been gone so long. Vivienne assured me that everything was fine but she needed to discuss something with me later. I was curious but didn't have much time to think about it, as I was too busy saying goodbye to my family. I was sorry to see Billy and Amanda leave because I didn't expect to see them for a while but Aunt Jean and Uncle Frank promised they would keep me up to date on Amanda's pregnancy and the upcoming wedding. I knew they would be there to support me, as soon as I decided when I would be going back to Westhampton to scatter Jeremy's ashes. For a moment the conversation brought me back to the reason why we were all there. For a time I had almost forgotten, I was so caught up with seeing friends and family and especially Lexie. That was when I looked over and saw her holding Miranda's hand and walking slowly around the room looking at Jeremy's paintings. She was twenty-six years old now and had matured into a stunning young woman. I could hardly believe that she had suddenly come back into my life and I was grateful. Now, if only she would come back into Mama's life too.

When we got to the apartment, it was a little crowded as Vivienne and Mark were staying over for a couple more days. They suggested they should check into the Bellclaire Hotel where Ethan and his family were, but I wouldn't hear of it. I settled Lexie and Todd in one of the guest rooms and then went to talk to Pilar about dinner. I should have realized that Vivienne would have beaten me to it and I smiled when I saw the two of them in the kitchen already marinating steaks and preparing, what looked like, a rather elaborate spinach salad. Mark was sitting at the table reading the New York Times and nodded at me, "Why don't you sit down and have a rest, Cassie," he said.

"I will," I replied, "but not before I help out a bit around here."

Vivienne turned and waved a hand at me, "We have everything under control my dear. Why don't you spend some time with your sister and we'll let you know when dinner is ready."

"Right now, she and Todd are having a little rest. Apparently she was up most of the night with the baby. Anyway, you said there was something you wanted to discuss with me later. Maybe now would be a good time."

I noticed Pilar glance over at me and then at Vivienne. She looked anxious but Vivienne just touched her shoulder very lightly and then sat down at the table next to Mark. "Why don't you sit down, Cassie?"she said.

I felt a little alarmed, "What's going on?"

"Well, Pilar had asked me to speak for her. She's very grateful that you would be more than happy to keep her on but she thinks she will find it too painful. She has so many memories of Jeremy here and she thinks it would be better if she made a change. I hope you won't think it presumptuous of me, Cassie, but after I realized she was serious about leaving, I offered her a position with us in Laguna Beach. When she realized that meant she would be close to her sister and could bring Teddy with her, she just couldn't refuse"

I looked up at Pilar who was standing with her hands clasped up to her chest, "Is this what you really want, Pilar?' I asked.

She nodded and whispered, "Yes, Miss Cassie, I'm so sorry."

I could see that she was anxiously waiting to see what I would do and was surprised when I got up and hugged her, "I'm going to miss you, but it's a wonderful opportunity for you to be near Rosita and you must be so happy that you can take Teddy."

I could feel Pilar physically relax as I released her. She took both of my hands in hers and said, "You have been so good to me, Miss Cassie, and I don't know how to thank you. I don't like to leave you like this but I hope you understand, Mrs. Kent was so kind in offering me a job."

"You don't have to explain," I assured her, "and I can't blame you for wanting to move to California. Now you won't have to put up with our New York winters."

Even as I was talking, my mind flew to Scott and San Francisco. Is that where my future was? Where was he? Why hadn't he called?

It was almost nine o'clock before I got a chance to talk to Lexie alone. Miranda was fast asleep and Pilar and Vivienne had already retired for the night. Mark and Todd, having really hit it off, had gone for a walk around Times Square and for a beer or two at the Abbey Tavern on 3rd Avenue. I made some coffee and settled down in a wing chair across from Lexie on the sofa. She had changed into a mint green caftan that really brought out the color of her eyes and her hair fell in waves just below her shoulders. There was no doubt that she was Mama's daughter, the resemblance was almost uncanny.

I wanted to hear about her years in Somalia and I was appalled when Lexie told me about the conditions there and the masses of people starving to death. When Lexie pulled a packet of photos from her purse and beckoned me to sit down beside her, I cringed when I saw pictures of so many children with their swollen bellies. I was so horrified that I felt on the verge of tears and then suddenly she turned them face down on the coffee table and passed me a photo of a beautiful chubby baby with the brightest blue eyes and blond curls. "This is Caroline," she said.

I looked down at the picture in amazement. This was my niece. "She's absolutely lovely," I remarked marveling at how perfect she was, " I can't wait to see her."

"You'll have to come to Tom's River and visit with us. We have a house there. It's rather small but very quaint and Miranda would love it. She's an adorable child, Cassie, I'm sorry I missed seeing her before now."

I paused, sensing that this might be the time to talk about Mama but Lexie didn't give me the chance to broach the subject myself. "I'd like to see Mama," she said in a whisper, looking down at the photo in her hand.

I held my breath, "Do you really mean it, Lexie? You really want to see her?"

She looked at me and I could see tears in her eyes, "Yes, I really mean it. I see things so differently now that I'm a mother myself and Todd helped to change my thinking too."

"What do you mean? " I asked.

"Well he actually went back and dug up all the information about the trial and convinced me that Mama was probably just protecting me. He felt that Grandma acted the same way with Papa, after all he was her only son. She just wanted to protect him too, so she brainwashed me into thinking it was all Mama's fault. I know I would move heaven and earth to keep Caroline safe even to the point of taking someone else's life. I was stubborn and immature and I regret with all my heart that I wouldn't listen to you. I thank God now that Mama had you to support her, because without you she would have had no one."

"I understand, Lexie. You were really young at the time and it's no wonder that you believed what Grandma told you. She could never imagine that Papa was the monster everyone said he was. When I think about it, I can't really blame her. If only she had treated me differently, I think I could have forgiven her."

Lexie grinned, "Well you were a bit of a rebel, always running away.

I grinned back, "Yes, I guess I was and I'm sorry I've been angry at you. You're my sister and I really do love you. I just hope that you can mend your relationship with Mama."

"How is she? I'm longing to see her but I'm nervous too."

"She's doing well and she looks wonderful. You needn't be nervous either because she has never said a bad word against you. She's only ever wanted you to be happy."

"I realize how selfless she must have been and she must have been a great comfort to you when you were dealing with Jeremy's illness."

I got up and walked over to the window, "Mama only just found out about it and she had no idea about Miranda's hearing loss either, before Jeremy died. It was all over the news so it was quite a shock to her."

I didn't hear Lexie get up and walk over to me but I felt her hand on my shoulder, "Now who was selfless, you didn't want her to worry did you."

I turned and threw my hands up in the air, "I don't know, but I think it was a mistake. She wasn't happy that I kept it all to myself."

"You take after her, you know. I wish I did."

I took her hand and led her back to the sofa, "How can you dismiss everything you've done to help those poor people in Somalia. You put yourself in harm's way and you only left when you were forced to. I think you and Todd are remarkable."

Lexie started to put all of the photos back in her purse, "Well, he's remarkable, that's for sure. I'm so lucky, Cassie and I'm so glad he talked me into coming to see you. We were already talking about getting in touch with you when we saw the news of Jeremy's death. After that we couldn't wait to get here but I had nobody to look after Caroline until I got Todd's parents to come and stay at the house."

"Well, you're here now and that's all that matters. Now all I have to do is get Mama to put you on the visitors list and then when you're ready I can meet you in Clinton and we can go together."

We talked for a long time after that. We only stopped when Mark and Todd arrived back, in a very happy mood, considering they insisted they had only had two beers. I made them coffee and we chatted for a while and then suddenly I found myself alone. I was tired but not in the mood for bed. I kept thinking about the funeral service and the gathering afterwards and my mind just wouldn't shut off. I decided to warm up some milk when the phone ringing interrupted the silence. I wondered who would be calling so late and was surprised when I heard Scott's voice. I had completely forgotten about him in the last few hours.

"Hello, Cassie," he said very softly, "I hope I'm not disturbing you."

"No, it's fine. Everyone's gone to bed so I'm on my own. Where were you, Scott? I called you earlier today but there was no answer."

"Actually I was in the church but I didn't want to make things difficult for you so I decided not to come to the hotel."

I felt a little annoyed, "But I could have introduced you to everyone as an old friend. Only Aunt Jean knows I've been seeing you and she hasn't even told Uncle Frank."

"And what about Jazz? I saw her there too. I just didn't want to risk it, Cassie. Please forgive me, I just didn't want to make any waves."

"It doesn't matter now," I responded rather spitefully, "I've had more important things on my mind."

There was a pause and I realized I'd been a little insensitive, "I hope that doesn't mean that you had any problems today," he said. " I'm sure it must have been stressful but I know a lot of people were there to pay their respects and I expected you to find some comfort in seeing them."

"Lexie's here," I said without elaborating.

"Oh, that's great, or at least I hope it is. What happened?"

I was dying to tell him all about my conversation with Lexie but it was so late and I really needed to try and get some rest. I arranged to meet him for lunch the next day at Lansky's Deli on Columbus Avenue. I knew Lexie and Todd were leaving early in the morning but Vivienne and Mark would be staying over one more night and Pilar was still with us, so I knew they'd be there to look after Miranda.

It was awkward saying goodnight to Scott. I was still feeling a little miffed at him and I know he could sense it. I wondered how

I would feel when I saw him and I spent half the night tossing and turning unable to get him out of my mind.

I finally drifted off to sleep in the early hours and woke up at dawn to the faint sound of noises coming from the kitchen. I got up and put on a robe then padded out to see who was there and found Lexie making coffee. I should have known that she would be up at the crack of dawn after being accustomed to having a young baby in the house. She glanced over at me as I came through the door, "Good morning, Cassie," she said, "I didn't expect to see you up so early. I hope I didn't wake you."

"No, I replied," stretching and rubbing the back of my neck. "You didn't wake me. I just didn't sleep very well and I'm actually glad it's morning. How about you?"

Lexie smiled, "That's the best sleep I've had since we brought Caroline home from the hospital. I didn't realize how much work babies were."

I was glad we had more time to spend together before anyone else woke up. We talked about so many things but I still didn't tell her about Scott. When she finally left with Todd at nine o'clock I was sad to see them go but I told her that as soon as Mama called me, I'd make sure she was put on the visitor's list and we should be able to visit within the next two weeks. Just thinking about telling Mama, I felt almost giddy with excitement but I tried to play it down so that Lexie wouldn't be nervous.

After they left I told Pilar that Jeremy's lawyer had called and I needed to see him. She was more than happy to look after Miranda and she and Vivienne started making plans to take her to the Central Park Zoo. When I told her where she was going she started to giggle and then began to jump around the room imitating a monkey. We laughed so hard at her antics that our stomachs ached. I wish Lexie could have seen her.

I felt guilty not telling the truth about meeting Scott but then I was a master at deception. I even had a perfect excuse to put on a dress rather than wearing something casual. I pulled on a very fine gray jersey dress, with a cowl neck and cap sleeves from my closet and dressed it up with matching suede heels and some pear drop earrings in turquoise and silver. When I left the apartment, Mark whistled as I walked towards the elevator, "Wow, you're looking pretty smart, Cassie," he called out.

I turned and waved but didn't answer. I just hoped I looked like I was going to an appointment rather than to meet the man I had been having an affair with.

When I got to Lansky's, Scott was already there. My heart gave that little flip-flop when I saw him. He was dressed in a camel colored linen jacket with a cream tee shirt and darker brown slacks and I thought he could have given Jules a run for his money. He rose from the table as I walked towards him and then took both of my hands in his, "Hello, Cassie," he said very softly, "thank you for coming."

"Did you think I wouldn't?" I asked, looking a little puzzled.

He pulled out my chair and we both sat down before he answered, "I wasn't really sure," he answered. "I thought you might still be annoyed at me for not coming to the gathering."

"I have to admit I was upset, but there were a lot of people there to support me. It's over now, so let's just forget it and enjoy our lunch."

We ordered some wine and then both settled on the house specialty, a reuben sandwich with a bowl of their famous pickles. I felt relaxed for the first time for days and didn't really want to talk about the funeral or anything associated with Jeremy's death. I did want to talk about Lexie though, because even as a teenager I had often talked to Scott about her. He seemed almost as excited as I was when I told him she had agreed to see Mama. He knew how important it was to me.

We had finished eating and were sitting back drinking coffee when Scott asked me what I intended to do now. I hadn't really thought about it too much but, now that Pilar was leaving, I knew I had to make some important decisions especially about Miranda's education.

"I'm not really sure yet," I said, "I do know that I won't be going back to the house in Westhampton, it holds too many memories for me. I suppose I'll eventually sell it and stay here in New York but there's a lot to think about. Tomorrow, before Vivienne and Mark leave we have to pick up Jeremy's ashes. Thankfully their flight isn't until late so they've also agreed to stay with Miranda while I visit Mama. I know she was upset about the way she found out about Jeremy's death and how long he'd been ill. It's bad enough that I kept that from her, but not telling her about Miranda was even worse, I realize that now."

Scott leaned forward in his chair, "You were only trying to protect her, Cassie. I'm sure she'll understand. In any case, once you tell her Lexie's back, she'll be so excited, she'll forget to be angry with you."

I smiled at the thought of telling Mama about Lexie, "Yes, I guess you're right. I can hardly wait for the day that she sees Lexie walk through that door."

"What are you planning to do with Jeremy's ashes?"

"Well, I know he wanted them scattered at sea, so I've already talked to Uncle Frank about taking Dreamcatcher out. It's still moored at Smith Point so we have to bring it back to Hampton Bays Marina and then decide when to have the ceremony."

Scott frowned, "Won't that take some time?"

I nodded, "Yes, but Vivienne and Mark have agreed to come back to New York whenever I feel the time is right. I'm not sure whether Ethan and his family will be able to make it but I hope so. After that, I'm selling the yacht; I'm not going to need it. I thought of giving it to Uncle Frank but I don't think I can bear to see it again after we've finally laid Jeremy to rest."

"And what about Miranda? Will you send her back to her old school here?"

I sighed heavily, "I don't think so. I'm going to contact Tasha Ozerov, she's the tutor I had for her before she went to pre-school. St Frances provided in-home therapy for pre-school and kindergarten children but the last time I spoke to her she was doing freelance therapy. Miranda really liked her and, if she's available, it would give me some time to make plans for the future."

Scott looked serious, "I suppose you intend to live in New York permanently," he remarked.

I was feeling a little frustrated with all of the questions, mostly because I didn't have all the answers, "I don't know, I guess so," I responded impatiently. "I need time to think and actually I don't know what I'm doing here. My husband just died and I'm sitting here with you as though nothing's happened. What kind of person am I?"

Scott grabbed my arm, "Stop it, Cassie. You've watched the man you married become a completely different person. He wasn't a husband to you any more so stop feeling guilty. You did your best and now you need to take time for yourself."

"But I feel that's what I've been doing, " I said on the verge of tears. "I wasn't there for him really. I didn't even know how to be."

Scott beckoned for the check and started to get up, "I think you need a rest, Cassie. You're exhausted and you have a lot to think about."

I searched my purse for a tissue, dabbed my eyes, and then got up, "You're right, I need to go home and I'm sorry if I spoiled lunch."

Scott put his arm around me, "There'll be other lunches, Cassie. You just take care of yourself and I'll call you in a day or two."

Out on the sidewalk, Scott kissed me gently on the lips and then hailed a cab. As the cab pulled away, I looked back but couldn't see him. I had a strange feeling that I would never see him again.

# CHAPTER 60

Vivienne and I picked up Jeremy's ashes early the next morning. It felt strange holding the elaborate silver urn, knowing that what was left of my husband's remains was inside. Vivienne was driving and looked over at me every now and again but didn't speak. When we got back to the apartment she took the urn from me and I got into the drivers seat for the drive to Clinton. "Are you sure you're all right?" Vivienne asked clutching the urn to her chest.

"I'm fine thank you," I replied, "I probably won't get back until mid afternoon but we'll have plenty of time to talk before your flight."

Vivienne leaned through the door and rubbed my shoulder, "Okay dear, don't worry about Miranda and drive carefully."

I waved at her as I drove off and began to mull over what I would say to Mama. I just hoped she wasn't angry with me.

I was delayed for almost an hour by an accident on the Garden State Parkway and by the time I got to the prison, I was feeling a little frazzled. I think Mama sensed my mood the minute she saw me approaching her table. "Hi honey," she said, "you look a bit upset. Did you have a problem getting here?"

I sat down and sighed, "It was nothing, Mama, just a bit of a hold up on the parkway."

Mama smiled, "Well, you're here now and you can relax for a little while. I didn't really expect you to come today. I can't imagine what you've been going through and before you try and explain again why you didn't tell me about Jeremy and Miranda, you don't have to. I've thought about it a lot and I understand. I probably would have done the same thing myself if I'd been in your shoes. There's no sense in regretting anything that has happened in the past. All I want to know now is, how are you coping? Tell me all about the service; how many people were there?"

I paused for a moment trying to take in the fact that there were to be no recriminations, but then why should I be surprised. This woman, my mother, who sat across the table from me still looking beautiful in my eyes, was the same caring person I always knew she was. For the next half hour, I told her everything I had learned about Jeremy's death, even though she had probably gathered every detail from the media, and about the service at St. Bartholomews. I told her about all the people that had shown up, Mr. Graham, Jeremy's lawyer, his doctor, his accountant and even his ex wife. Then I told her about the paintings and especially the one of Miranda with the inscription. I could see her eyes well up, "Oh, honey," she said. "Do you think Jeremy was really trying to tell you something?"

"I like to think he was, Mama but he was distant for so long, I can't imagine him remembering the poem but maybe somehow he did."

"What about Miranda? How is she coping with all this?"

"She seems fine but it's hard to know what she's thinking because she has trouble expressing herself. Although, on the day that her father died, she spoke for the first time."

I heard Mama gasp, "Oh, my goodness. What did she say."

"Mama. That was it, just Mama. She's spoken the odd word since but nothing significant. I'm going to try and get Tasha back to tutor her privately."

"That's the Russian lady from the school that tutored her before isn't it?"

"Yes, she's freelancing now so I'm hoping she's available."

Mama pushed her hair back from her face, "What are you going to do now, Cassie?"

I grinned and she looked at me obviously puzzled, "What's so amusing?"

"I have something to tell you. In fact, I don't know how I've been sitting here for so long without just blurting it out."

Mama looked alarmed now, so I looked around furtively to see if the guard was watching then reached across and grabbed her hand, "Lexie came to the service," I said.

I felt Mama jerk and put her other hand to her throat, "My Lexie, she actually came to the service?"

"Yes, and she brought her husband with her. They couldn't bring the baby but I saw a picture of her and she's adorable. They even came back to the apartment and stayed the night before heading back to Tom's River early yesterday."

"Oh, that's wonderful news, Cassie. So I gather you two have made up?"

"Yes," I answered still grinning, "and she's coming to see you as soon as you put her on your visitor's list."

Mama started to cry and it was all I could do not to get up and embrace her. "It's okay, Mama, she understands everything now. Becoming a mother has changed her and she realizes that Grandma brainwashed her into thinking that Papa was completely blameless for what happened. Anyway she wasn't sure if you would want to see her."

Mama wiped the tears way, "I hope you told her that I prayed for her every night."

I chuckled, "Well, I didn't quite tell her that, Mama, but I did tell her that you were longing to see her and you were thrilled when you heard about Caroline."

I had made Mama so happy that on the drive home, I felt like a weight had been lifted from my shoulders. I had no idea what the future was going to bring but I was ready to face whatever challenge came my way.

When I got back to the apartment, I found Vivienne sitting with Miranda at the kitchen table looking through a photo album. Vivienne smiled at me as I came through the door, "How did it go with your mother, Cassie?" she asked.

"It was perfect," I replied, "she understood why I kept everything from her and I really made her day when I told her Lexie was back and wanted to see her."

"How wonderful that your sister is back in your lives, I'm so happy for all of you. She seems like a charming young woman and so attractive."

I started to respond but Miranda had gotten impatient and was tugging on Vivienne's sleeve. I sat down next to her and tapped her on the shoulder so that she would look at me. "What are you looking at?" I asked.

She glanced down at a photograph of Jeremy looking handsome in white shorts and a blue polo shirt on the deck of Dreamcatcher, "Dada", she said.

I saw the tears start to well up in Vivienne's eyes and reached over and touched her hand, "It's going to be okay. We'll all be able to smile when we think of him one day very soon. He was a wonderful man and you must have been so proud of him."

Vivienne squeezed my hand, "Thank you, my dear. I'm going to miss him but we have his precious child, and you. I hope we will always be close no matter what happens in the future."

"No question of that. I couldn't have wished for better in-laws. I wish you weren't leaving today but I know you'll be back within weeks. Has Pilar arranged her flight, by the way?"

"I think she wants to stay until we scatter Jeremy's ashes, rather than traveling back and forth. Is that going to be okay with you?"

"Of course, she may stay as long as she likes. I'll be sorry to see her go but I think she'll be happy with you and I know she's excited about being close to Rosita and her family"

While we had been talking, Miranda had slipped out from between us, still clutching the album, and we found her sitting cross-legged on the carpet in the living room with Teddy beside her. She was pointing to each picture and making unintelligible sounds, as though she was trying to get his attention. Mark was in the living room, reclining comfortably in one of the wing chairs, reading the New York Times. He looked up as we came in then looked over at

Miranda, "What a cute picture," he said. "I think she's going to do a lot better once you get that tutor for her, Cassie."

"Yes, well I just hope she's available, in fact I should call her right now."

I learned, right after Tasha answered her phone that she had just got back from visiting her relatives in Moscow and had only just heard about Jeremy's death. She had already been hired, under contract, to coach a deaf child located just a few blocks away but she still had her afternoons free and was interested in my proposal. When I asked her if she thought I was doing the right thing by not integrating Miranda back into an environment with other children, she suggested that it would be beneficial to give her one-on-one tutoring for the next twelve months, especially in view of the fact that she was beginning to attempt to utter words. "I'm sure the loss of her father must be quite traumatic for her and she'll probably feel a lot more secure being at home for a time," she said.

She arranged to meet with me the next afternoon so that we could go over the details and then we talked a little about Jeremy and about her trip to meet her folks. When I got off the phone, I felt relieved that I had resolved the issue of Miranda's schooling for at least the next year.

"How did that go?" Vivienne asked. "Is the young lady available to help with Miranda?"

"Yes, she is. She'll be here tomorrow so that we can discuss the details but it looks like she'll be tutoring from Monday to Friday in the afternoons."

"And what about you, my dear? What are you going to do in your spare time?"

I sighed heavily, "I'm not sure yet. We still have to decide about Jeremy's remains and I know at some point I'll have to go and see Ben Greenberg about Jeremy's estate. Here I am talking about getting rid of the Westhampton house and the yacht and I don't even know if they're mine to sell."

Mark frowned, "You mean, you have no idea what's in Jeremy's will?"

I shook my head, "Actually, I don't. I never thought about it and we never discussed finances.

Jeremy took care of all the major expenses and when he got sick, his accountant took over. He set up a bank account for me right after we got married and transferred funds every month so that I could pay for food, clothes, and gas for the car and anything else I needed. He was very generous and didn't want me worrying about, what he called, trivial matters. He didn't even question the fact that I had quite a healthy bank account of my own. All the time I worked for the newspaper, I was living at home so I managed to save a great deal. I can always fall back on that and go back to work if I have to."

Vivienne looked at me in disbelief, "Nonsense," she said. "I'm sure Jeremy left everything to you including any royalties from his novels. In any case, Cassie, you were his wife so you are entitled to benefit from his estate and Miranda would have to be provided for."

"I suppose you're right," I remarked feeling a little uncomfortable. "I don't really like talking about Jeremy's money. It doesn't feel right somehow."

"Nevertheless, you can be sure you'll be well taken care of," Mark said getting up from the chair and walking towards the kitchen. "Now enough of all this chatter, it's making me thirsty. I'm going to see what Pilar is up to. Maybe if I'm nice to her she'll make me a cup of tea and give me a nice big slice of that coffee cake she made."

Vivienne looked at me and rolled her eyes, "Can you imagine what he's going to be like when Pilar is living with us?" she said.

Right after dinner, I drove Vivienne and Mark to the airport and I was genuinely sorry to see them leave. "Call me as soon as you decide when you want us to come back," Vivienne said hugging me tightly as we heard the announcement for their flight over the public address system. I stood in the departure lounge and watched them disappear from sight and then I stood by the windows and waited while the huge Boeing 747 taxied onto the runway and then took off. I felt very much alone at that moment.

On the way home, I thought about Scott and decided to call him that night. I was hoping that he would pick up the phone because

I didn't want to leave a message. I was lucky because he answered almost immediately, "Hi, Cassie," he said softly.

I was surprised, "How did you know it was me?" I asked.

"I have caller ID, " he answered.

There was an awkward silence, "Oh, I see. I know you probably didn't expect to hear from me so soon after our lunch but I just saw Vivienne and Mark off at the airport and was feeling a little blue."

"I can't deal with blue right now, Cassie," Scott remarked with an edge to his voice.

"I'm sorry, did I catch you at a bad time?"

"No but we do need to talk."

"Okay, when's good time?" I asked feeling a little impatient.

"Well, I guess there's no really good time. It's just that I've been thinking a lot about the two of us, and maybe you don't want to hear this, but I can't see our relationship going anywhere."

I didn't expect that response and I could feel a tightness in my chest, "What are you trying to say?" I asked, not really wanting to hear the answer.

"Let's face it, Cassie, I think it's pretty obvious that you'll probably stay in New York. You have to think about Miranda and then there's your mother in fact there'll always be the problem of your mother."

The apprehension I had felt just seconds ago turned to anger, "Mama is not a problem. She never has been and she never will be. How dare you speak to me like that."

Scott cut in, "It's the truth and you know it. How can there be a future for us when you won't even consider leaving here. The same thing happened years ago, I loved you then but I couldn't wait for you forever and I can't wait for you now."

"So don't wait," I snapped back, "go back to San Francisco and have a good life."

I slammed down the phone and I was shaking like a leaf but I felt a weight lift off my shoulders. Jeremy was dead and had never known about my affair but I had still felt guilty over my betrayal and now it was over. I actually slept right through the night.

# CHAPTER 61

Early the next morning I explained to Miranda that Tasha would be coming back to tutor her rather than sending her back to school and, to my surprise, she reacted rather badly. She refused to eat her breakfast and grabbing Teddy roughly from his favorite chair; she stormed into her room and slammed the door. Pilar look at me and shrugged her shoulders, "She no like it, Miss Cassie."

"That's too bad," I said feeling a little impatient. "I'm sure once she sees Tasha she'll change her mind, they always got on well together before."

Pilar made no further comment and turned back to the counter where she was rolling out the pastry for a rhubarb and raspberry pie she was making.

After lunch, which I insisted Miranda eat, even though it wasn't much of a chore considering it was a hamburger smothered in onions and relish, and one of her favorites, she went back to her room and once again, slammed the door. When Tasha stepped out of the elevator, looking just as I remembered her, the same cloud of blond hair, light blue eyes and that wonderful smile, she hugged me, "Hello, Cassie," she said with her delightful accent. "It's so lovely to see you again."

"And you too," I responded returning her embrace. "Come on into the living room and we can talk. Miranda's holed up in her room having a sulk so we'll let her stew there for a while."

Tasha looked past me down the hallway, "I don't think she's in her room any more," she said and then she side stepped me and held out both arms.

Miranda, who was half hidden by the doorframe, obviously trying to hide, hesitated for a moment and then came running at full tilt and threw herself into Tasha's arms.

I stood with my hands on my hips, hardly believing what I was seeing, "Well, that takes the cake," I said. "She's been sulking all day because she wasn't going back to school and now it looks like she couldn't be happier."

It was the beginning of a new awakening for Miranda. Tasha drew her out in so many ways and within a month she was speaking short sentences. Often her words weren't easy to understand but she tried so hard and she made us both proud. Tasha would spend three hours with her every weekday and sometimes they would go out on, what Tasha called excursions, either to the zoo or the museum or anywhere that would stimulate Miranda and get her interested in the outside world. I was so thankful to have her there and during that first month I decided it was time to organize the ceremony for the scattering of Jeremy's ashes.

I called Uncle Frank and he had no hesitation in helping me arrange for the transfer of Dreamcatcher from where it was moored in Smith Point, back to the marina in Hampton Bays. I had special invitations made up with Jeremy's photograph, as he had appeared on all of the back covers of his novels, and sent them to a small group of people outside of his own family, Jazz and Jules, Ben Greenberg, Paul Radcliffe and of course, my own family, including Lexie and Todd. I heard back from Lexie almost immediately, upset that they were unable to make it to the ceremony because Todd's parents were on vacation and they had nobody to look after Caroline. I was disappointed but I had just discovered that Lexie had been added to the list of Mama's approved visitors and she was ready to meet me in Clinton at any time, as long as Todd was available to baby-sit. She assured me she would be thinking of me as we stood on the bow of Dreamcatcher saying a sad goodbye to Jeremy.

The week after I sent out the invitations I spoke to Mama and asked her if she was ready to see Lexie the following Thursday. She seemed nervous but assured me that she had been waiting for this moment for twenty years and she couldn't wait another moment. When I called Lexie to see if she was available, she sounded nervous too but like Mama, she couldn't wait any longer. I got the feeling that she was feeling very guilty about abandoning Mama for so long and I had to reassure her that it wasn't her fault; if anyone was to blame it was Grandma.

I arranged to meet Lexie in a coffee shop in Clinton before we went to the prison. I knew it would be a traumatic time for her and she had never been inside a prison before. I sensed her anxiety and told her that compared to what she had gone through in Somalia, entering those prison gates was really not that bad. We had an hour before we were due to see Mama, so we had a light lunch and Lexie showed me photos of their house in Tom's River and more pictures of Caroline. I was hoping the guard on duty today was one of the more agreeable ones and would allow her to show them to Mama. Eventually it was time to leave, so Lexie followed me in her car and after we parked in the prison lot, I gently held her hand and walked her up to the main gate. I was used to the process of being checked through but I think it unnerved Lexie a bit and I felt her grip my hand a little tighter as she looked around at the iron bars everywhere and the sickly institutional color of the walls. Thankfully, we only had to sit in the waiting room for five minutes, then we were being ushered into the visiting area. I saw Mama immediately, anxiously watching the people coming through the door, and as soon as she saw me she glanced at the person beside me and her hand flew to her throat. Lexie must have seen her at the same time because she suddenly broke away from me but I had to stop her so I grabbed her arm and pulled her back, "Remember Lexie, no touching is allowed."

When we reached Mama's table I was still holding onto Lexie's arm, "Look who's here, Mama," I said.

Both Lexie and Mama looked like they were in a trance and I had to force Lexie to sit down. Mama spoke first, "Hello, honey," she said almost in a whisper, "I can't believe you're here. You look exactly the way I imagined. You've grown into a beautiful young woman."

I saw tears start to form in Lexie's eyes, "Oh, Mama," she said, her voice shaking with emotion, "how can you ever forgive me."

Mama shook her head, "There's nothing to forgive. You're here now and that's all that matters. I wish with all my heart that I could hold you in my arms but I can't. I just need to tell you how proud I am of you. Cassie has told me all about your work in Somalia. Thank God you managed to escape unharmed and now you're a mother. My little Lexie actually has a daughter of her own. I am so happy for you."

All the time Mama was talking I could see Lexie staring at her "You look the same as I remember you. Cassie told me you hadn't changed but I didn't believe her."

Mama chuckled, "Well, the hair's not quite as blonde as it was and I see a few wrinkles when I look in the mirror."

"You look marvelous," I said. "All in all we're not a bad looking family, although I did get a little help along the way."

I looked over to see which guard was on duty and noticed it was Benny. He had always been pretty lenient so I took my chances, "Why don't you show Mama your photos, Lexie." I suggested.

Benny didn't try to stop her when Lexie handed the photos, one by one, across the table to Mama and I watched her face light up when she saw the first picture of Caroline. "Oh, what an adorable looking baby," she said, then she looked at me and continued, "I can hardly wait for the day when I can see both of my granddaughters."

I reached over and stroked her hand, "That day will come, don't worry, Mama."

We stayed until visiting hours were over and Lexie and I went our separate ways. As I watched her drive off, I knew that we had turned a corner that day and no matter what happened now; we would never be apart again.

Two weeks later, I was back at the Westhampton house waiting to greet the small group of people who had accepted my invitation to attend the ceremony for Jeremy. Both Uncle Frank and I had

driven down early that morning and he was on board Dreamcatcher
making sure that she was shipshape. Aunt Jean arrived a little later
with Billy and Amanda to help Pilar and me with the refreshments.
I had decided to leave Miranda in New York as I thought it might
be too traumatic for her and Tasha had kindly offered to stay with
her.

I was glad that my loved ones were with me because I could
hardly bear to be in that house anymore. Sadly, Vivienne and Mark
had not been able to make it as Mark had come down with a kidney
stone and was in a great deal of pain. Everywhere I looked I could
see Jeremy and I could hardly wait for the day to be over. By noon
everyone had arrived and we made our way to the Hampton Bays
marina. We seemed like a somber group, even Jazz was exceptionally
quiet and looked very funereal, dressed all in black from head to toe.
Uncle Frank greeted us as we came on board and I marveled at the
fact that he had left the house in jeans and a tee shirt and was now
wearing a suit and tie. I was so thankful that he was there with me
and had even offered to say a few words, knowing how difficult it
was for me to talk about Jeremy myself.

When we left the marina, there were ominous clouds looming
overhead but after we were about a mile from shore, the sun suddenly
came out and I thought it would be the perfect time to begin the
ceremony. We all stood crowded into the bow of Dreamcatcher,
with me clutching the silver urn to my chest and Pilar sobbing
quietly beside me as Uncle Frank read a poem that he had written
specially for the occasion. When he finished, he looked at me and
nodded and I slowly released Jeremy's ashes into the ocean. Then
Aunt Jean handed me an armful of red roses and one by one I tossed
them overboard as I heard the murmur of people saying goodbye
around me. With the last rose, I said my own silent goodbye and
buried my face in Aunt Jean's shoulder unable to face anyone for a
few moments.

Back at the house, Pilar took over, insisting on making coffee
and serving everyone with refreshments. I think it was her way of
coping; she just had to keep busy. Meanwhile, I was happy to be
with people that had known Jeremy and could now talk about him

and even smile, recalling some of the experiences they had shared with him.

As dinnertime approached, people started to leave and I felt sad saying goodbye to the ones that I probably would never see again, especially my neighbors in Westhampton, Sally and Greg. I had already told them that I would be selling the house and as Ben left, he reminded me that he would be in touch with me within the next week or two so that we could proceed with tying up Jeremy's estate.

Jazz and Jules stayed behind for a while so that we could spend more time together and when they left, Pilar and I followed them back to the city. I couldn't wait to get home and leave all the sad memories behind me.

During the next few days everything seemed to settle down. Tasha appeared every afternoon to tutor Miranda and in the morning I would usually take her to the park. She liked to go to the playground area where she could interact with other children even though they had trouble understanding her. I tried to relate to the other mothers but I felt out of place and I didn't want to talk about the fact that my husband had just died. I tried not to think about Scott but every now and then, he would pop into my mind and I would get angry all over again. I knew it was time to go back to doing something constructive with my life but I needed to know where I stood financially before I could move ahead.

I had almost forgotten that Pilar was going to be leaving us, so I was surprised when she told me that she had been talking to Vivienne and had decided go at the end of the month. That was only just under two weeks away and I wanted to do something special for her. I asked her if she had purchased her airline ticket yet and she told me she hadn't so I offered to put her in first class and she would be able to take Teddy with her in a cat carrier. She seemed overcome with gratitude as, unbeknown to me, she had been stewing over Teddy, imagining him in cargo completely traumatized by the whole experience. She kissed my hand over and over, "Thank you, thank you, Miss Cassie," she said, "I worry so much about him."

"Well, now you don't have to worry any more," I assured her. "We are going to really miss you, Pilar, in fact I don't know how I'm going to cope without you."

Pilar looked downcast so I took a step towards her, "Give me a hug," I said. "It's not going to be goodbye forever. Miranda and I will come and visit Jeremy's parents real soon, then maybe you can take me to meet Rosita."

Pilar's face lit up, "You'll like Rosita, Miss Cassie, she's always in a happy mood. My Mama always said that she was born with an angel on her shoulder."

The day I drove Pilar to the airport, I tried to keep upbeat but it wasn't easy. The one person, who had a real connection to Jeremy, was leaving and deep down I felt a tremendous sense of loss. Miranda, meanwhile, was devastated saying goodbye to Teddy and insisted on sitting in the back seat holding him in her lap and refusing to put him in the carrier until we got to the airport. Pilar was just as nervous before the flight as she had been on her last trip to California and I had encouraged her to take some Gravol to calm her down a little. I expected Miranda to be very upset when it was time for Pilar to leave the departure lounge but I had no idea that she would cling to Pilar's skirt and howl so loudly that she attracted the attention of all of the other passengers. Eventually I had to pull her away and all the way home she sobbed uncontrollably as though her little heart would break. I knew I had to do something to distract her so I swung into a Ben and Jerry's, ordered her favorite Chunky Monkey ice cream and then suggested we go to the New York Aquarium. I was hoping that after that day there would be no more upsets in my life for some time to come, but that isn't exactly the way it turned out.

# CHAPTER 62

Pilar telephoned as soon as she arrived at Vivienne's house and I breathed a sigh of relief after hearing that she had actually enjoyed the flight. Teddy, apparently, slept most of the way and soon settled down with some tasty treats when he woke up, just a short time before landing. He had already decided that he preferred the queen size bed in the master suite to any other bed in the house and it looked like Mark was going to have a hard time removing him. Teddy could get very feisty if he didn't get his own way. I spoke to Vivienne briefly and she thought it was all very amusing and when I finally went to bed myself I couldn't help chuckling.

Two days later, I got a call from Aunt Jean and she sounded very upset, in fact she was crying. "What on earth's happened?" I asked.

"It's Amanda, she lost the baby."

"Oh, my goodness, I'm so sorry Auntie. Is Amanda all right?"

"Yes, she's fine now but Billy is a mess. He won't stop crying and your uncle and I don't know what to do with him. Will you come, Cassie, please? I know I shouldn't be asking you but he always listened to you, maybe you can calm him down."

I didn't have to think about it for too long, I had always had a special place in my heart for Billy and thought of him as my brother, "Of course I'll come. Where is Billy, is he with you?"

"Yes, Amanda's in the hospital, she lost a lot of blood so they want to keep her for a while. Billy didn't want to go back home so he came here and he's going to stay, at least for tonight."

"Okay, Tasha's here right now with Miranda but I prefer to bring her with me. Will it be all right if we stay over too?"

"Absolutely, thanks so much, honey. I guess I'll see you in a couple of hours."

"Yes Auntie, I just have to throw a few things in a bag and we'll be on our way."

Billy was an absolute wreck by the time we got there. Before we left home I had explained to Miranda, as best I could, what had happened but I'm not sure she fully understood. She got upset when she saw Billy lying distraught on the living room sofa with tears running down his cheeks and immediately crawled up beside him and started to stroke his hair, "S'okay, Billy," she muttered, "s'okay."

Billy looked at her, his eyes widening in astonishment, and then glanced up at me, "She's really talking," he said.

Before I had a chance to respond, Miranda thumped him hard on his shoulder, "I talk," she said angrily, "not stupid."

Billy began to laugh and then he couldn't stop while Aunt Jean stood in the doorway shaking her head, "Well, I didn't expect it to be Miranda who would bring him out of his funk."

After that Billy seemed to brighten up a little but he was obviously concerned about the future. He and Amanda had been warned that there was the possibility of a miscarriage and if Amanda had carried to term, there was also a chance that the baby would have Down's Syndrome. I knew he had been struggling with their decision to become parents, but once a baby was on the way, he was delighted at the prospect of becoming a father. Now, that there was no baby, he was having second thoughts. Uncle Frank knew more than anyone about the role of a father with a Down's Syndrome child and he was reluctant to discourage Billy without appearing to regret having ever had Billy himself. As it turned out, later that afternoon, when we visited Amanda in the hospital, she told Billy that she refused to get pregnant again and if he didn't like it then she suggested he marry someone else. I saw the hurt on his face but he was determined not to let her see him cry, "Okay," he said shrugging his shoulders, "but I still want to marry you."

Aunt Jean looked at me helplessly. She knew, at that moment, that she would never be a grandmother.

We stayed in Asbury Park overnight and I drove Billy back home early the next morning. I suggested that once Amanda felt better, they come and visit me in New York and maybe we could go to the theatre. Billy was enthusiastic and when we dropped him off, he almost seemed like his old self, with that adorable grin on his face that always made everyone around him smile.

I was hoping now to enjoy a little peace and quiet but after a week when I did little else outside of the apartment, other than visit Mama, I was beginning to get bored. I felt like I was in limbo because I still wasn't sure of my financial position and then just when I was feeling really low, I got a call from Ben asking if I was available to meet with him at his office. I had always imagined that the reading of a will would involve Jeremy's family so when I asked if they should be contacted, he advised me that it wouldn't be necessary. I thought I would dress appropriately for the occasion, and then felt rather silly when I arrived in the reception area of Adams, Bernhardt and Greenberg looking rather like a potential job applicant in a light gray suit and black pumps. Meanwhile, Ben's secretary looked like she had come from a garden party in a calf length flowery dress with ruffles and strappy red sandals. She ushered me into Ben's office, and then quietly slipped away as Ben came around from his desk and gave me a hug. "You're looking well, Cassie," he remarked. "How have you been and how's Miranda?"

"We're both well," I answered as I sat down. "I decided not to send Miranda back to school, so she has a private tutor now and she's made some remarkable progress."

"That's wonderful to hear, but what about you. What have you been up to?"

"Truthfully, I've been a little unsettled. I'd like to make plans for our future but I need to know where I stand financially".

Ben showed no hint of what was to come as he returned to his chair and then opened a rather bulky folder in front of him, "Well, I don't think you have too much to worry about on that score," he said. "I can assure you that Jeremy was in very sound mind when he had his will drawn up and I'd like to suggest that we forgo all the legalese. I can tell you exactly what you are entitled to and then give you a copy so that you can read it over in detail later, if you wish."

"I'd appreciate that Ben, I'm not very good at understanding these things."

That was when Ben looked across at me and smiled, "Okay, well basically Jeremy left you everything he owned, the New York apartment, the Westhampton house and their contents, the Jaguar, the yacht, all of his stock holdings which have a current value in the neighborhood of thirty million dollars plus any forthcoming royalties from his novels. In addition, he had a life insurance policy worth two million dollars."

I sat for a moment trying to take it all in, I was absolutely dumbfounded, "What about his family and Miranda. Surely, I'm not the sole inheritor?"

"Well, he thought that his family was wealthy enough. As you know, his father was in the antique business and was very successful. As far as Miranda is concerned, he did set up a trust fund for her. It's current value is one million dollars but she won't have access to it until she's twenty-five. By then, of course, it will be worth a whole lot more. The only other beneficiary is Pilar, he left her fifty thousand dollars but these amounts are insignificant compared to the value of Jeremy's estate. Incidentally, you don't actually inherit the royalties from his novels; technically you inherit the copyright, which will entitle you to any royalties. You're a very rich woman, Cassie."

I realized I was holding my breath, I could hardly believe what I was hearing, "This is unbelievable, I knew Jeremy was a wealthy man but I didn't know just how wealthy and I certainly didn't expect him to leave almost everything to me. I'm happy he remembered Pilar, she will be overwhelmed when she hears."

"Yes, I expect she will be and now, as soon as we tie up some loose ends, you can start moving forward, Cassie. Have you decided what you're going to do?"

I nodded, "I've definitely decided to sell the Westhampton house and the yacht. I haven't made up my mind about the apartment yet but I'll probably sell it too."

"Oh, and where will you go then?"

"I'm not sure, " I replied, but I already had the germ of an idea in my head and I couldn't wait to get home to call Aunt Jean.

I said goodbye to Ben, thanking him for being such a good friend to Jeremy, and left his office feeling rather overwhelmed.

Uncle Frank answered the phone when I called and he was relieved to learn that I never had to worry again about Miranda or myself, as far as finances were concerned, but he wasn't surprised at Jeremy's generosity and thoughtfulness. "Obviously he loved you a great deal, honey," he said, " and he knew his parents didn't need the money, although truthfully it would have been nice if he'd left his brother a few dollars. I assume they got along."

"Yes, they did and as a matter of fact I was thinking about Ethan on the drive home. I'd like to give him and his family something but I don't know what's appropriate and it might be upsetting to him that it comes from me and not from Jeremy."

"Well, there's nothing you can do about that now, Cassie, but why don't you speak to Ben Greenberg, he can probably advise you on the best approach."

I was thankful for my uncle's advice, "That's a great idea, I'll call him tomorrow and see what he suggests."

After chatting for a few more minutes Aunt Jean picked up the extension in the kitchen, "Hello dear, did you want to talk to me about something?" she asked.

"Yes Auntie, but Uncle stay on the line will you, I need to run something by you."

"Go ahead, I'm listening, Cassie," my uncle responded.

"Well, now that I won't be having any money worries, Uncle will tell you all about that after I get off the phone Auntie, I don't want to bore him, I've thought about what I want to do now."

Uncle Frank cut in, "What do you have planned, we're anxious to hear?"

"Well, I've thought about it a bit and want to see what you both think. I can't make any real plans for quite a while because I have so much to take care of, like selling the Westhampton house and Dreamcatcher and then later, this apartment."

Aunt Jean cut in this time, "You mean you're thinking of moving? Where, out of New York, that's quite a big step?"

At this point, I thought I'd just blurt it out, "I'm thinking of moving back to Asbury Park."

I heard Aunt Jean gasp and then Uncle Frank said, "Why would you want to come back here, Cassie?"

"Because the people I love most in the world are there. It's lonely here in the city, I don't even know any of the people that live in this building, in fact the only people I know are Jazz and Jules and they are so busy all the time, I hardly ever get to see them. I expect it will probably take almost a year to sort everything out and by then Miranda will have improved a lot and I can enroll her in school there. I want to buy a house right near the ocean with at least three bedrooms and a huge back yard and then I'm thinking of going back to work."

"Oh, Cassie, it would be wonderful to have you close by," Aunt Jean said, "but if you don't need the money, why would you need to work?"

"I don't need to work, Auntie, I just need to do something constructive. Maybe Mr. Graham can find me something to do back at the paper."

I heard Uncle Frank mumble something under his breath and then he asked, "Is that the only reason you want to come back here, Cassie?"

I paused before I answered, Uncle Frank knew me too well, "No, it isn't. I want a place where Mama can be comfortable when she comes out of prison, she deserves that after all she's been through."

Uncle Frank was his usual discerning self, "It's an admirable thought, honey, but I think you have to mull this over for a while. Having your mother living in your house may not be an ideal situation. What if you meet someone and decide to get married again, not every man wants his mother-in-law living with him."

Suddenly I felt very defensive, "I'm not likely to get married again and if I do, he'd have to accept me on my terms."

"That's a little unrealistic, honey," Aunt Jean said as gently as she could.

"Maybe, maybe not," I replied abruptly, "but that's the way it has to be."

"Maybe your mother might have her own plans," Uncle Frank said, attempting to redirect the conversation.

"I hardly think she would have any idea of what to do or where to go. She's been locked up for almost twenty-one years and so many things have changed. She's going to have a hard time adjusting and I need to make her feel at home wherever she goes. What better place than with Miranda and me?"

"I know your heart's in the right place, honey, and you may be right. I'm just asking that you think about it a little more," Uncle Frank suggested.

"I will, I promise," I replied but a few minutes later when I got off the phone I knew I had already made my decision. Now all I had to do was tell Mama.

# CHAPTER 63

After thinking it over, I decided not to tell Mama about my plans to move back to Asbury Park. I wanted to wait until I found the ideal house and then I would surprise her. She was overwhelmed with happiness for me when she discovered how generous Jeremy had been, and couldn't wait to hear what I had planned for the future but I merely told her that I hadn't really decided what to do but I was staying in New York for the time being.

The day after my visit to Ben's office, I called Pilar to give her the news and she just wouldn't stop crying. Finally Vivienne came on the phone and told me that she was in shock and needed a little time to recover. At that point, I felt I had to ask Vivienne if she was disappointed about Jeremy's will and she assured me that she couldn't be more pleased. I realized it was a good time to mention Ethan and she agreed, it would have been a nice gesture if he had inherited even a small amount of money but she didn't agree with me giving over part of my inheritance to him. "I think you have to go along with Jeremy's wishes, Cassie," she said. "He basically wanted you to have everything. Mark and I certainly have no problem with it and Ethan shouldn't have any problem either."

I was reluctant to let the matter drop but I appreciated her telling me how she felt and after considering it for a few more days and even talking to Jazz about my concern, I decided to let it go.

I had no idea it would take almost another year before I would have access to any of Jeremy's estate but I soon came to realize, after several meetings with Ben, just how much red tape was involved. Finally in June 1994 I was able to put the Westhampton house on the market and within a matter of a month I had a buyer. After that, it was a simple matter to dispose of Dreamcatcher, I had already had several offers right after Jeremy's death but for some reason I had trouble letting it go. I had no use for the contents of the house so I donated them to a local charity and Aunt Jean was in seventh heaven when I insisted she take the Jaguar to replace her ten-year-old Toyota. Now all I had to think about was selling the apartment and finding a new home in Asbury Park, as well as enrolling Miranda in school before the next term, beginning in September. It was a tall order but Aunt Jean assured me that if there were any snags along the way, we could always stay with her and Uncle Frank. Knowing that I had a contingency plan, I didn't feel quite as much sense of urgency but I was very much aware that Miranda's needs came first. She had progressed enormously under Tasha's tutoring and I was reluctant to terminate the arrangement but I had no choice. I couldn't ask Tasha to move to Asbury Park and I really felt that Miranda needed to be integrated back into an environment where she could interact with other children.

The Katzenbach School for the deaf was in Trenton, just over an hour away along route I95. It wasn't feasible to send Miranda there especially in the winter when we would have to negotiate ice and snow. I decided to investigate the programs offered by Asbury Middle School where I had been a student. I couldn't believe my luck when I discovered they paid special attention to children with disabilities and that there was a whole Child Study Team in place to determine the most appropriate educational program. The Child Study Team consisted of a psychologist, a learning disabilities consultant, a social worker and a speech/language specialist. It looked to be ideal and I immediately made the necessary arrangements to insure that Miranda would start school right after Labor Day.

Lexie and I had visited Mama together on several occasions during the past months and then in July, just as I was preparing to put the apartment up for sale, she invited me to her home in Tom's River for the weekend. Miranda was excited when we piled into the car early on a Saturday morning and drove out of Manhattan. Tom's River was only forty minutes south of Asbury Park but I had never been there before. I was looking forward to spending some time with Lexie and to seeing Caroline for the first time. When we arrived at the house I was surprised to find that it was a little smaller than expected and much more rustic, but it had a huge back yard dominated by towering white pines. When Todd greeted us at the door, he welcomed us both with a hug and whispered, "Lexie just put Caroline down, she was fussing most of the night so we didn't get much sleep. Hopefully she'll settle down for a while now."

When I finally got to see Caroline in her crib I had to admit she was one of prettiest babies I had ever seen. Even with her eyes closed, she had such a sweet look to her and her hair was so fair it was almost white. Miranda wanted to touch her but we couldn't risk waking her up so we tiptoed out of the nursery and onto the patio where Todd was waiting with a pitcher of fresh lemonade.

Minutes later, Miranda discovered that there was a rabbit hutch at the far end of the yard and inside, an enormous white rabbit, appropriately named Harvey. I should have known that Lexie would have had an animal of some kind but was surprised it wasn't a dog or cat. "I'm afraid I'm allergic," said Todd apologetically, "but fortunately rabbit fur doesn't seem to bother me."

During that weekend, I got to know Todd quite well. I found him to be a very intelligent, thoughtful individual and he doted on Lexie and Caroline. Watching them being so affectionate with each other, I felt envious and then I felt guilty. I just hoped that maybe one day I could find love again.

On the drive back home, I thought a lot about Lexie's situation and I really wanted to do something to make her life more comfortable. I had more money than I knew what to do with and I wanted to share my good fortune but something was holding me back. I tried to concentrate on my immediate concern, selling the apartment and finding a house in Asbury Park and by the time we reached Manhattan I had decided to speak to a realtor the very next day. The apartment sold within two days of being put on the market, which was no surprise to anyone but me. We had a closing date of mid August and I suddenly felt in a bit of a panic because now I definitely had to find a house and there was a lot of packing to do. Jazz informed me, in no uncertain terms, that as I was now very, very rich I could afford to let the movers pack up everything and just sit back and watch. It was hard for me to accept what she was saying, it seemed so extravagant, but I eventually agreed that it made a lot of sense, after all why shouldn't I take advantage of my situation.

By the middle of August I still hadn't found the house that I was looking for so I had all of the furniture from the apartment put into storage and moved in with Aunt Jean and Uncle Frank. I was actually relieved to have a break and relax in the company of the people most dear to me and Miranda and I were welcomed with open arms. Uncle Frank even decided to take some time off from work so that he could spend more time with us. While Aunt Jean and I often enjoyed just sitting quietly reading in the garden, he would take Miranda and Pepper for a drive or for a stroll along the boardwalk. On two occasions we spent the day at the beach and took a dip in the ocean. Miranda seemed to thrive in the water, but I was always worried that she couldn't hear the waves rushing up behind her, so Uncle Frank always stayed within a yard of her the minute she set foot in the ocean.

I knew I should have been trying to locate a new home for us but I realized this was probably the last time we would be staying with my family, for more than a day or two, and I wanted to be sure that Miranda enjoyed herself before starting school. One week into our stay, a tragic event sent us all into a depression. Pepper was fourteen years old and had slowed down considerably over the past few months. We knew she had very little time left but didn't expect the suddenness of her death. One morning, Uncle Frank got up early as always, to take Pepper out but she was nowhere to be seen. He found her behind the living room sofa where she had peacefully passed away during the night. My uncle was absolutely devastated and seeing him cry, for the first time in my life, made my heart break. Miranda had no idea what had happened and was upset and confused when she saw the state of my uncle and the tears in both my own and Aunt Jean's eyes. She looked at me with a puzzled expression on her face and very gently I had to explain to her what had happened. She insisted on seeing Pepper and when I wouldn't allow it, she stamped her feet in frustration causing Uncle Frank to put his hand on my arm and say, "Let her see her, Cassie, it will be all right."

We watched as he held her hand and led her to the chair where Pepper was lying wrapped in a blanket. She slowly knelt down and then lifting Pepper's head she slipped her arm around her neck and held her against her chest murmuring, "Bye, bye, Pepper."

Uncle Frank was so overcome with emotion he walked out into the garden and I could hear him sobbing again. I looked at Aunt Jean helplessly and she put her arm around me and said, "I know exactly what to do."

Two days later, joined by Billy and Amanda, we scattered Pepper's ashes. Uncle Frank rented a small boat and we sailed out for about a mile before handing the tiny urn over to Miranda. She understood what she had to do and when she scooped out some of the ashes and threw them onto the waves we were all astounded when we heard her whisper, "Say hello to Dada."

That same afternoon, at Aunt Jean's insistence, we drove to the Monmouth County SPCA. There were so many dogs, some strays and some abandoned, sheltered there that it was difficult to pick out one special one. Aunt Jean had already announced that it was to be Uncle Frank's choice and when he finally noticed a golden retriever puppy, who reminded him of his beloved Sheba, it was love at first sight. There was a moment's hesitation when he discovered that the new puppy was male but the minute he held him in his arms, there was no question that he was coming home with us. An elderly lady had brought him to the shelter. She had purchased him at a pet store and then found she couldn't afford to keep him. At that time he was only eight weeks old and had been at the shelter for almost three weeks. His owner had named him Morris, but Uncle Frank wasn't happy with that, so he renamed him, Barney. That night we had great fun watching Barney running around the house and digging up areas of the garden, while Aunt Jean looked on in dismay shaking her head. "What have I done?" she kept repeating.

# CHAPTER 64

Following Labor Day weekend, Miranda started attending classes at Asbury Middle School. Aunt Jean drove her there each morning and picked her up in the afternoon so that I could devote all my time to house hunting. This was a completely new experience for me and being naturally frugal I had to keep reminding myself that money was no object. If I saw a house I really liked, no matter what the cost, I could afford to buy it. Finally after viewing at least a dozen properties, I found the house of my dreams. It was located just north of Asbury Park city in the Interlaken area and with a view of Deal Lake from the back garden. The sweeping lawn surrounded by willows, stretched right down to the water and had it's own dock. The house itself was large; over seven thousand square feet, with five bedrooms and six bathrooms, fireplaces in both the living and dining room, rose granite kitchen counters, beautiful French doors and windows and a games room in the basement with a wet bar. From the outside, the house had an elegant look to it. The white stonework was capped with a gray-shingled roof and an enormous porch with double doors that had two columns on each side and a pitched roof on top displaying a single round stained glass window. The driveway leading up to the house was circular and flanked by trees and at the back, to the left of the garden, was an in-ground pool and pool house. I knew the moment we drove up that this was the one and after I had walked through the rooms and looked out of the windows on the second floor, to the lake beyond, there was no doubt in my mind. "I'll take it, " I said to the real estate agent without even asking the price.

"It's just over two million dollars, Mrs. Kent," she informed me looking a little doubtful.

I suddenly felt very rich and a little devilish, "I'll pay cash," I said grinning from ear to ear, and I couldn't wait to tell Mama.

When I got back to Aunt Jean's, I was bubbling over with excitement but nobody was home. I took Barney out of his cage, where Aunt Jean always kept him confined while they were out, and decided to go for a walk to kill some time. Naturally, Barney was happy to be released and decided that he was taking me for a walk rather than the other way around but we didn't get far before I saw Aunt Jean, driving her prized Jaguar, turning the corner onto our street. After that, my poor Aunt Jean must have been sick of hearing about the house, I just couldn't stop rambling on about it and then when Uncle Frank got home, I got excited all over again. Despite my enthusiasm, I did have some concern about the double garage and the pool house. They were both looking a little run down and needed, at the very least, a new coat of paint. I knew that Uncle Frank had hired someone to replace their roof one summer and asked if I could get the name so that I could get some minor renovations done. Uncle Frank searched his desk drawer and came up with a business card for Brady Renovations located in Neptune, just a few miles west. "Give Jake Brady a call," he said. "You'll find he does a good job and he's reasonable."

"Not bad looking either," Aunt Jean piped up.

Uncle Frank gave her a sour look, "I didn't notice."

Aunt Jean rolled her eyes at me, "That's because you're not a woman," she said.

After that I was a little apprehensive about meeting Jake Brady.

A few days later, I drove my family over to see the house and to meet Jake Brady there. I had called him and spoken to him briefly about what I thought needed to be done and he had agreed to meet with me and give me an estimate. My impression of him on the telephone was one of a professional individual, all business, but he had a wonderful voice that reminded me of a radio announcer on station Z100 in New York.

We got to the house a little early, so that I could walk Aunt Jean and Uncle Frank through and get their opinion. We attempted to leave Barney in the car but he whined so pitifully when my uncle shut the door that we decided to take him with us. It didn't take long for Miranda to pick out the bedroom she wanted, which was the smallest of the five, but it gave her a wonderful view of the lake. Meanwhile, I stood with Aunt Jean in the adjacent bedroom, which shared the same view, and said, "This will be Mama's room."

My aunt smiled and put her arm around me, "It's wonderful, Cassie, she'll love it. Have you thought how you're going to decorate it?"

I looked around at the plain white walls and dark hardwood floors. "Mama's favorite color is green so I think maybe avocado with cream accents. I think it would all blend in with the view of the grass and the trees and I could get some wonderful gauzy drapes."

"It sounds perfect but what about all the other rooms? Are you going to renovate the whole house?"

"Maybe over time but for now, except for this room, I'm pretty satisfied with what the previous owners have done. Miranda's room is a pretty shade of yellow and the rest of the house is neutral, so for now all my furniture will fit in nicely. I will need to furnish this room and the extra bedroom but, other than that, drapes to fit all of the windows are about all I need."

Aunt Jean frowned at me, "I expected you to start completely fresh and buy all new furniture."

I shook my head, "No, I may be able to afford it but everything from the apartment is top quality and I'm not going to get rid of it. The dining room table alone must be worth a fortune, it's solid mahogany and the chairs are all original Chippendale. Jeremy had wonderful taste and I'd like to be surrounded by the things that he loved even though I couldn't bear to keep the Westhampton house."

Aunt Jean was just about to respond when we heard a man's voice calling from downstairs "Is anyone up there?"

I started for the door and called back, "Yes, we're coming down."

I motioned for Aunt Jean to precede me down the staircase and I peeped over her shoulder to take a look at the visitor, whom I assumed must be Jake Brady, but he was nowhere to be seen. When my aunt got to the bottom step I noticed her glance towards the kitchen and there he was leaning nonchalantly against the doorframe, "Good morning, Jake," she said extending her hand to greet him.

He stepped forward and gripped her hand, "Good morning, Mrs. Marsh. It's good to see you again."

Aunt Jean turned and motioned me forward, "Cassie, this is Jake Brady. Jake, I'd like you to meet Mrs. Kent."

I stared into a pair of the most amazing blue eyes and immediately thought of Robert Redford. I had recently seen the movie "The Way We Were" on television and I couldn't help drawing a comparison. It seemed like forever before either one of us spoke and then I heard that voice again that I had heard on the telephone, "Good morning, Mrs. Kent. I hope you don't mind me just walking in like this but the front door was open."

By then I had regained my composure, "Not a problem, and please call me Cassie. If you'd like to follow me out to the back, I'll show you the pool house."

Aunt Jean stayed behind as I headed for the back door but as soon as I stepped outside with Jake following behind, Barney came rushing towards me with Miranda right on his tail. I put up my hands trying to signal her to stop and she came crashing into me. "Bird, bird," she cried out, obviously distraught.

I turned around to see Jake picking Barney up and gently extracting the tiniest bird from his mouth. "Oh my goodness," I said, "is it dead?"

Jake put Barney down and examined the poor creature lying traumatized in the palm of his hand, "No, but it's had a shock and even if we could find the nest, we can't put it back, the mother bird would kill it."

Just then Uncle Frank arrived on the scene and I watched as they exchanged a few words while Miranda and I stood there anxiously, holding hands. This really gave me the opportunity to take a good look at Jake. He was obviously in good shape, either from working out or from the type of work he did. I figured he was just less than six feet and probably in his mid thirties but the most striking thing about him was his hair, which was almost as light as my own, except that his was natural. I had always been attracted to tall, dark haired men with dark eyes and Jeremy had been the perfect example but there had been something about those blue eyes, when I first met Jake, that had captured my attention. My mind was conjuring up all sorts of scenarios involving him and myself when Uncle Frank jogged me out of my reverie, "I'm going to take it over to the wildlife center. They'll know how to take care of it."

Miranda looked up at me and smiled, "Bird okay now, Mommy," she said.

Aunt Jean had been standing behind us, holding onto Barney, and watching the little drama play out, "Good looking and kind to animals too," she remarked.

I just looked at her and grinned, "Sometimes Auntie, you are a hopeless romantic."

After showing Jake the garage and the pool house, he found that some of wood on the garage door needed to be replaced and he agreed to return at the end of September, just before our moving in date, to do the repairs and the painting. I told him I would send him an extra key so that he could have access to the grounds and by the time he left, I thought I might have imagined the chemistry I felt when I first met him. One thing I knew for sure, I wanted to see him again.

We moved into the house on the last day of September and I was disappointed to see that the work on the garage and the pool house had already been done. I assumed that all I could expect from Jake Brady now, would be a bill in the mail but after the movers left, I suddenly remembered Mama's room and I was no painter. I waited for a couple of days so that we could really get settled in and then

I called him asking if he could come back when he wasn't busy to paint one of the bedrooms. "Have you picked out the paint?" he asked.

I felt a little stupid, "Actually no, I know what color I want though."

"And what color is that?" he said with what sounded like amusement in his voice.

"Avocado green,"

I heard him start to laugh, "Cassie," he said, "I need to know the kind of paint you want as well as the exact color. That means, do you want matte or eggshell and do you have a number for this avocado color?"

In the most plaintive voice I could conjure up, I replied, "Could you please bring a catalogue."

I heard him sigh, "You mean a paint swatch book."

"Yes, that's what I meant to say," I lied.

"I'll be there tomorrow afternoon, that's providing you're going to be home."

I suddenly felt a little adrenalin rush; he was actually going to be there the next day.

The next morning, being a Tuesday, I woke up early as always and drove Miranda to school. She had settled in very well and was enrolled in a program specially designed to suit her particular needs. Tasha had been kind enough to accompany me on my visit with the Child Study Team so they were aware of the kind of tuition she had already received. I stopped on the way back and picked up some bagels, lox and cream cheese and suddenly realized I was running a little late. Jake told me he would be at the house at around ten and I still felt that I needed to change out of my jeans and put on something more presentable. It didn't make much sense really, after all I'd been wearing jeans the last time he saw me and he had been dressed in a tee shirt and chinos, but I guess I wanted to make an impression. It took me less than five minutes to change into a pair of cocoa colored slacks, a cream cowl neck cashmere sweater and a pair of low heeled sandals. All I had to do was dab on a little more make-up, brush my hair and find my favorite topaz earrings but then I heard a car pulling into the driveway and I started to panic. I just managed to apply more lipstick when the front door bell rang and I had no choice but to run downstairs and let Jake in. When I opened the door, that's when it hit me again, that moment of electricity between us where neither one of us spoke for a second or two. He was carrying a heavy looking binder under one arm and wearing the same chinos as before but with a different tee shirt emblazoned with the logo of the Boston Celtics. "Good morning, Cassie," he said, "I hope I'm not too early."

"No, I was just pottering around not doing anything in particular," I lied.

"Well, you're looking mighty fine for someone who was just pottering around," he remarked with a sly grin.

I decided to change the subject. "Come on into the kitchen. By the way, I didn't realize you were from Boston."

He looked puzzled and then looked down at his tee shirt, "Oh, I'm not from Boston," he said, "I'm not even a basketball fan. I was actually born and raised in Trenton."

I motioned him into the kitchen, "Would you like some coffee," I asked.

"Yes, thank you. I take mine black, no cream or sugar."

I started to make some fresh coffee while he sat down at the kitchen table, "So, how come you ended up in Neptune?" I asked.

"I'm just not the big city type," he said, "and so after I started my own contracting business, I decided to move to a small town. Neptune suits me just fine and it's close to the water."

I sat down on the opposite side of the table waiting for the coffee to percolate, "Does your family still live in Trenton?" I asked wanting to know a lot more about Jake Brady.

"My parents are both dead. My mother died from breast cancer when I was twelve and my father was killed in a car crash the first year I was in university."

My hand went to my chest, "Oh, I'm so sorry. What about brothers and sisters?"

Jake sighed, "There aren't any I'm afraid. I was an only child."

I glanced down at his left hand and wondered why I had never even thought to do so before, but there was no ring. I struggled about whether to ask him if he had a family of his own but I just couldn't do it. "How about a bagel," I asked, "fresh from the bakery this morning and I have some wonderful cream cheese?"

Jake declined my offer and this was followed by an awkward silence so I got up to pour the coffee and then heard, what sounded like, Jake sliding the binder across the table, "Here's the swatch book," he said, "there are dozens of shades of green to choose from and I'd suggest that you look at them in the room you want painted because the light can make quite a difference.

I passed him a mug and then responded "Then we need to go upstairs to the bedroom," and as soon as I said it, I felt myself starting to blush.

He just took the mug and grinned, "We can do that as soon as I've swallowed this down."

That remark caused me to blush even more but thank goodness the sound of the telephone ringing saved me and I was able to excuse myself. It was Aunt Jean checking to make sure everything was okay and as soon as I told her Jake was there she chuckled and said, "Then I won't hold you up, I'll let you two get back to whatever you were doing."

I managed to compose myself by the time I got back to the kitchen where Jake was just putting his empty mug in the sink. He looked over as I walked through the door, "Ready?" he asked.

He was very patient while I picked my way through dozens of swatches searching for exactly the color I wanted and eventually I settled on a shade that, as far as I was concerned, most closely resembled avocado. All that I had left to do was pick a shade of cream, which was much simpler, decide whether I wanted matte or eggshell and set up a time for Jake to come back to do the work. I was disappointed when he told me that he would be busy for the next three weeks, but Mama certainly wouldn't need the room before that so I set a day for the end of October.

After Jake left, I hoped that he would find an excuse to call me but after two weeks I dismissed it from my mind and concentrated on finding someone to replace Pilar. I had decided that I wanted to return to work and there was no way I could look after such a large house and take care of Miranda as well. I placed an ad in the Asbury Park Press and the following week I interviewed six applicants. The first three seemed very young, with little experience, and I had a feeling they were just filling in time before they went back to school or found something more fulfilling. The fourth and fifth applicants were both men in their forties who had been let go from their jobs and were desperately looking for work. I felt sorry for them but again, they had little experience and I wouldn't be comfortable employing a man. I was beginning to wonder if I would ever find anyone when Mildred Mitchell showed up on my doorstep and I knew I'd hit pay dirt. Mildred was in her early fifties, about the same age as Pilar, but that's where the similarity ended. She was as fair as Pilar was dark, having the wonderful peaches and cream complexion so typical of the English and she was very slight, unlike Pilar who had always had a problem with her weight. She had been working for a family in the area for the past three years but they had recently moved back to Minneapolis and she had no desire to go with them. Before that she had been employed all her working life as a nanny to a family in London and she had impeccable references. She had left England to marry an American she met while on vacation in France and they had only stayed together for a brief period before splitting up. Rather than run back home, she decided to stay and had never regretted it. I was fascinated with the way she spoke and when I told her about Miranda and the fact that she had a profound hearing problem, she said she absolutely adored children and had looked after a Down's syndrome child at one time. Naturally that got me talking about Billy and at the end of the interview, I hired her on the spot. That's when she insisted I call her Millie.

# CHAPTER 65

Millie moved into the spare bedroom, which had already been made habitable with most of the furniture from our guest room in New York. It was next to Miranda's room and also looked out onto the back garden and the lake. It had a separate area, large enough to accommodate a lounger, a small entertainment unit and even a writing desk and most convenient of all, it had it's own ensuite bathroom. I had purchased a new Laura Ashley comforter and matching curtains and when Millie walked through the door for the first time, she just sighed with contentment, "Oh, Mrs. Kent," she said. "This is lovely, I know I'm going to be very comfortable here."

That same morning, when Millie had arrived driving a rather broken down blue Volvo and hauling her meager belongings, I introduced her to Miranda. I watched as Millie sank to her knees and looking directly into Miranda's eyes, announced in her very clear English accent, "Hello, my name is Millie. I'm very pleased to meet you and I hope we can be friends."

Miranda took her time looking Millie over and then she haltingly replied, "Me Miranda, I'm six and I go to school. Are you going to live here now?"

Millie put her hand gently on Miranda's shoulder, "Yes, I am dear and I'm going to help your Mommy look after you and this lovely house."

Miranda shrugged off Millie's hand and said, "Okay, you can have the room next to me." Millie stood up and responded, "That's very nice of you. That mean's we'll be neighbors."

Miranda looked up at me with a frown, "What's neighbors, Mommy?" she asked.

My answer seemed to satisfy her and she ran off into the kitchen where she had been helping me make peanut butter cookies. "She has trouble with a lot of words," I explained to Millie, "and her grammar leaves a lot to be desired."

Millie smiled, "Don't worry Mrs. Kent, we'll soon have her talking almost perfectly."

"That would be wonderful. Now let's get your things upstairs and settle you in."

The day before Jake was due to start painting Mama's room, Millie came to me looking a little upset. I was worried for a moment because so far, everything had been working out perfectly. Miranda had really taken to Millie and they spent a lot of time together. It was obvious that she was used to taking care of children and enjoyed doing it, in fact I was beginning to think that my daughter preferred Millie's company to my own, but I felt no resentment. Miranda really needed someone who could understand her and help to expand her horizons. "What's wrong, Millie?" I asked. "Is something bothering you?"

"Oh no, Mrs. Kent, "she replied, "everything is just fine but I did want to ask you something."

"Is it something you need? All you have to do is tell me and I'll see if I can help."

"It's not me, it's Miranda. She's been telling me about the housekeeper who was here before me. I think she said her name was Pilar."

"Yes, that's right, she was actually my husband's housekeeper for years, even before I met him. After he died, she didn't want to stay so she went to work for his parents in California."

Millie nodded, "I see, well apparently she had a cat."

"Yes, Teddy, she took him with her when she left."

"Well, that's the problem your daughter really misses him and she wanted me to ask you if she could have a cat of her own."

"Oh dear," I sighed. "I didn't realize she missed Teddy so much."

"I'm sure you've had enough on your mind and Miranda didn't want to bother you."

I felt a little teary eyed, "I can't believe it, she's only six years old and she's worrying about bothering me. I wish she had come to me herself but I'm grateful Millie that she can talk to you. She's been a lot happier since you've been here."

"She's a wonderful child, Mrs. Kent, and she loves you very much. She told me so."

"Thank you Millie. I know, why don't we surprise her and take her to the Monmouth County SPCA on Saturday. That's where my uncle got his dog Barney and I'm sure they must have dozens of cats that need a home."

Millie's face lit up, "That would be wonderful, she'll be so happy."

Just then I saw Miranda coming along the hallway so I put my finger to my lips, "Remember it's a surprise," I whispered.

I was driving back from taking Miranda to school the next morning, when Jake showed up at the house. I hadn't expected him until later, so I was surprised when Millie told me he was already upstairs and had started priming the walls in Mama's room. I felt awkward about going up to see him and decided to wait until around ten o'clock and then take him a cup of coffee. I had one foot on the bottom step and a mug, almost filled to the brim, in my hand when Millie stopped me, "I'll take that up," she suggested.

I paused feeling a little conspicuous, "Oh, that's okay, Millie, I want to see how it's coming along anyway."

She watched me as I slowly ascended the stairs and I couldn't help noticing the slight grin. I wondered what she was thinking as I walked along the hall and turned into Mama's room. Jake was kneeling on the floor applying tape to the skirting and looked up when he heard me, "Good morning," I said, "I thought you might like some coffee."

He got up and walked towards me and I felt that little pitter patter in my chest, "Good morning. That's very kind of you, I actually brought a thermos with me but I'm sure your coffee will taste a lot better."

I handed him the mug and looked around at the walls, which were now white with primer, "You've done a lot of work already."

Jake nodded, " Shouldn't take too long to do the painting, in fact I'll probably be finished by supper time."

Before I even stopped to think, the words came tumbling out of my mouth, "Why don't you stay then and have supper with us?"

Jake looked down at his overalls, covered in paint, "Thanks for the invitation, but I don't think I'm dressed for that."

I felt myself flush with embarrassment; I wasn't usually so impulsive. "Maybe some other time?" I asked.

"How about Saturday, but I insist on taking you to dinner?" Jake shot back.

I was startled for a moment, I never expected him to ask me out. After a pause, I managed to answer him, "I'd like that very much."

"Good," he remarked. "I'll call you on Friday after I've made a reservation."

His eyes never left mine as I slowly backed out of the room, "Okay, well I guess I'd better let you get on with the painting."

I never saw him again until about five o'clock when he announced that he had finished the room and suggested that I take a look at it. I loved the color and couldn't wait to furnish it. "Thank you," I said. "It looks wonderful."

He left almost immediately after that but not before reminding me that we had a date on Saturday. I think I almost skipped back into the kitchen, I was feeling like a giddy schoolgirl. Millie glanced over at me from the counter where she was peeling potatoes, "You look like you had a good day, Mrs. Kent," she said.

"As a matter of fact, I had a wonderful day," I replied.

On Saturday morning, Millie reminded me that we were going to pick out a cat for Miranda. I had almost forgotten in my excitement about my date with Jake. He had called me the night before to tell me that he had made a reservation at Jack Baker's Wharfside restaurant in Point Pleasant. We only spoke briefly but it wasn't awkward, in fact it was almost like talking to an old friend. I was still thinking about him as we drove over to the Monmouth County SPCA until Miranda tapped me on the shoulder and said, "Where are we going, Mommy?"

"It's a surprise," I answered, we'll be there soon.

"Nooooooo," she moaned tugging at Millie's sleeve, "I want to know now."

"Patience, honey," Millie said. "We promise it will be worth the wait."

When we eventually reached our destination, Miranda was none the wiser. It was only when we walked through the main door and she saw all the posters of dogs, cats, rabbits and gerbils that her eyes lit up, "Are we getting a cat, Mommy?" she cried hopping up and down on one foot.

"Yes, and you can pick out the one you want."

An hour later we were back home with the new addition to our family, a two-year-old gray Persian named Smudge. He had looked so lonely sitting in the back of his cage that Miranda couldn't resist him and when she was allowed to pick him up and he licked her face, she was smitten. Millie and I couldn't stop smiling all the way home and when Miranda was out of sight, I gave Millie a hug, "Thank you," I whispered, "you've made one little girl very happy today."

I suggested that I meet Jake at the restaurant, as I didn't want him picking me up at the house. I wasn't ready to let Millie know too much about my personal life. I casually mentioned that I was going out to dinner with a friend and by the way I was dressed, it didn't look like I was going on some romantic date. I had deliberately put on some charcoal jeans and a white fisherman knit sweater, convincing myself that I was appropriately dressed for the Wharfside. When I got to the restaurant, a little after seven o'clock, I was relieved to see that Jake was already there and was also wearing jeans with a blue polo neck sweater. He greeted me by putting his hand on my arm and helping me into my seat and only when we were both sitting did he say, "It's good to see you again. How was the drive over?"

We continued with small talk until after the waiter had finished filling our glasses from the bottle of Sauvignon Blanc that Jake had ordered, and then he asked that we be allowed a few moments before making any selection from the menu. I had the feeling that he wanted to say something important so I sat back and waited, expecting him to tell me he was married or something equally disturbing. Finally he smiled and said, "I guess I should tell you that I know exactly who you are. When I was at your aunt's house, I noticed a wedding photo. I recognized your husband. I was a great fan of his; in fact, I've read every book he ever wrote. It was impossible to ignore all the news coverage when he died, Cassie, and that's when I learned that your mother had been incarcerated for over twenty years. Your aunt told me that she and your uncle were really your foster parents and you had a sister who lived in Tom's River. So you see, I know a lot about you and I know you've had a difficult life. I just want you to know how sorry I am about your husband and I admire your courage for the way you've been able to handle everything."

I sat for a minute not sure how to respond, then rather abruptly said, "Well, I'm glad I don't have to tell you my life story."

Jake looked hurt and I realized he didn't deserve that, "I'm sorry," I said leaning towards him, "that wasn't fair. I should be grateful that you know all about Jeremy and my mother. It's painful talking about Jeremy though; he was a good man and a good father to Miranda, up until the time he got really sick."

"I can't imagine going through what you went through," Jake said.

"You've had your share of bad luck too, losing both of your parents. It's just a shame that you don't have any siblings." I hesitated for a moment then decided to ask the question that had been on my mind for some time, "Have you ever been married, Jake?"

Jake smiled, "Yes, for about two minutes. I was nineteen and she was eighteen. I met her at a party and thought she was the prettiest girl I'd ever seen. I was smitten and three months later, we got hitched. I quickly found out that she was a shrew and spent money like water. I couldn't take it, so after four months, I walked out."

"So you don't have any children then?"

Jake laughed, "Not that I'm aware of. Seriously though, I would have liked to have had children but I think I'm getting a little too old for that now."

I searched his face for any obvious signs of aging and except for a trace of lines around the eyes, there were none, "You aren't that old, if I had to guess I'd say you were about thirty-eight."

"That's flattering, but I'm actually forty-two. I figure if I had a kid in the next two years, by the time he's ready to play baseball I'd be fifty and needing a cane."

I knew he was kidding and I had to laugh, "Are you sure you won't need a wheelchair by then," I teased.

Just then we noticed the waiter hovering near our table so Jake suggested he order for both of us and beckoned him over, "I recommend the tuna" he said looking across at me as he closed the menu.

After a wonderful appetizer of Clams Casino and an entrée of pan seared tuna steak, I sat back with a sigh, "That was lovely," I said, "I've never been here before."

"I'm glad you enjoyed it. We'll have to come here again. Meantime, how about dessert?"

"Couldn't eat another bite," I replied, "but coffee would be nice."

# CHAPTER 66

On my third date with Jake, he invited me to his home in Neptune for dinner. Up to that point, he had only kissed me lightly on the lips as we said goodnight and I was nervous anticipating what might happen, when we were finally completely alone. I arrived at the address he gave me on Riverside Avenue just across from Memorial Park and found myself outside a modest single story home with steps leading up to an arched doorway. As I stepped out of the car, Jake came out to greet me wearing an apron indicating that he was the world's greatest cook and I had to smile. The interior of the house was minimally furnished with few personal touches but the kitchen was a complete surprise; ultra-modern with stainless steel appliances, a natural stone floor and a huge center island topped with black marble. Jake had completed the renovations single-handedly and he was obviously proud of the result. I soon discovered that the message on his apron wasn't far off the mark. After a pre-dinner drink of a very dry martini, Jake served up a simple arugula salad with cherry tomatoes and pine nuts and then a linguini scampi dish that was absolutely wonderful. "Where on earth did you learn to cook like this?" I asked.

"Just did a lot of experimenting on my own," he replied while pouring me another glass of wine. "I got a little tired of take out and frozen dinners so I bought a couple of cook books and found that I had a bit of a flare for it."

"I wish I could cook like this," I said rather despondently.

"I'm sure you have a lot of other talents," Jake countered with a grin.

I looked over the rim of my glass and batted my eyelashes, "Are you flirting with me?"

Jake shook his head, "No, we haven't had dessert yet."

I don't know what came over me at that moment, but I was suddenly on my feet and grasping Jake's hand across the table, "Later," I said pulling him towards me.

Minutes later we were in the bedroom peeling off each other's clothes and I felt totally liberated. When I had been with Scott, Jeremy had always been at the back of my mind but now I was a free woman and Jake made me feel beautiful. We made love three times in the space of about three hours and I didn't want to leave that night but I was expected back home and needed to be there in the morning, when Miranda woke up. It was almost two o'clock when I finally drove away but I wasn't nervous making my way in the dark, I was too pumped up, too excited and nowhere near ready for sleep.

Millie must have heard me come in but she didn't mention it the next day, however Miranda seemed to sense that I was feeling really upbeat so she took advantage of my mood and persuaded me to take her to Aunt Jean's house. I knew her real motive was to see Barney and I didn't want to disappoint her so we set off in the early afternoon and stayed for supper. All the time I was there I was dying to tell my aunt about my evening with Jake, leaving out the intimate parts of course, but I never really got the opportunity. It was only two weeks later after I had spent more time with him that I finally told Aunt Jean, Uncle Frank and Mama that I had been seeing him and it was much more than a casual friendship. They were all pleased for me, especially Mama who said she had been praying every night that I would meet someone new.

A month later, with Christmas now approaching, I decided that I would start looking for a job in the New Year and the first place I would apply, would be the Asbury Press. In the meantime, I started to prepare for the holidays and Jake, Miranda and I spent almost a whole day just decorating the house. By the middle of December, we had already had our first heavy snowfall and the house looked wonderful, lit up with hundreds of fairy lights. Miranda was in her element and loved being outside, building snowmen and having snowball fights with Jake. One morning I caught her trying to sneak Smudge into the back garden and had to remind her that Smudge was an indoor cat. She sulked for a few minutes and then she was off, happily putting the finishing touches on Alfie, her latest creation, a four foot chimpanzee made out of snow.

We spent Christmas Day at Aunt Jean's and the house was full. Lexie had come up from Tom's River with Todd and Caroline, Billy and Amanda were there too and then there was Jake. My aunt had also invited Millie, thinking she had nowhere else to go, but Millie graciously declined saying that she was visiting a friend, who had no family left, and would otherwise be alone. It was a wonderful day; the table was groaning under a huge twenty-four pound turkey, yams, roast potatoes, brussel sprouts and a traditional plum pudding, which Uncle Frank nearly destroyed when he poured brandy over it and then set it on fire. I remember looking around the table at all the smiling faces and thinking how fortunate I was, but at the back of my mind I was wondering what Mama was doing. I missed her so much.

New Year's Eve, Jake and I attended a local dinner and dance in Neptune and I stayed overnight. I think Millie had come to accept the fact that Jake and I were now a couple and she certainly didn't expect me to drive home in the wee small hours. We had actually settled into a really comfortable relationship and I treasured the time we spent together. When we weren't together I thought of him constantly and I couldn't help wondering where our relationship would end up.

A week into January I telephoned Lester Graham and asked if he had time to see me. He was delighted to hear from me and agreed that we should meet the very next day. It was strange walking through the newsroom that morning. I only recognized one or two people but everyone seemed to know exactly who I was and several of them stopped me and introduced themselves. Mr. Graham greeted me with a hug and wanted to hear everything that had happened in my life since he had last seen me right after Jeremy's death. Needless to say, he was surprised to hear that I had abandoned my apartment in New York and moved back to Asbury Park. We talked for quite a while before I found myself telling him about Jake and finally asking if it would be possible to return to the paper to work.

He paused for quite a while before he answered me and I knew I wasn't going to like what he had to say. Apparently, the paper was going through a rather rough time and he had already had to cut down on staff; obviously there was no place for me there. He was curious to know why I needed to work when Jeremy had left me so well provided for and I explained that I felt I needed something constructive to do, in order to fulfill my life. He paused again, got up and started pacing the room and then finally asked me a rather personal question, "Please don't be offended," he said, "but I assume you have pretty unlimited funds."

I felt flustered for a moment before I replied, "Yes, but I don't need all that money. That isn't the issue, I need to do something for me, something that makes me feel good about myself."

Mr. Graham pulled up a chair and sat down opposite me then reached for both of my hands, "Do you remember Rosemary Wallace?" he asked.

"Of course," I replied, "what about her?"

"Well, if you remember her, you must remember what she stood for. Think about it, Cassie, you could build a home, maybe a whole chain of homes, strictly for abused women. You could do it for your mother as well as for yourself."

I felt such a mixture of emotions after he stopped speaking, excitement, guilt and stupidity for not having thought of it myself, "Oh, my God," I said squeezing his hands. "It's brilliant, what a fabulous idea. I have all this money that I don't know what to do with but now I can help so many women. How can I ever thank you for coming up with this, it will give me a whole new purpose and Mama would be so proud."

Mr. Graham was smiling, "Good, I'm glad you like the idea. Maybe you should take a trip over to Rose's Retreat and talk to

Rose's granddaughters. I'm sure they'll be happy to help you get started."

My head was in a whirl and I started to babble, "I'll need a lot of help. I'll have to figure out where to build and I'll probably need permits. Jake can help with that. Then I'll have to come up with a name. Oh, there's so much to do, I don't even know where to begin."

"You'll figure it out," Mr. Graham said gently, "but I suggest you just start with one home first, don't try to be too ambitious. As for a name, why don't you simply call it Ella's?"

The next day I had a courier deliver a check for a half-million dollars made out to the Asbury Park Press. The last thing in the world I wanted to see was the newspaper shut down.

Aunt Jean and Uncle Frank thought the idea of building shelters for abused women was brilliant but they agreed with Lester Graham that I should start out reasonably small until I knew exactly what I was doing. Meanwhile Jazz thought I was biting off more than I could chew and would have preferred that I spent my time just traveling the world and enjoying myself. I was so excited about telling Mama at first, but then I imagined she might agree with Jazz, so I decided not to say anything until I had the first shelter up and running, even if it took a year or two. As for Jake, I knew he would support me, but when I suggested he enter into a partnership with me and take care of the building aspect; he refused. I was a little taken aback at his attitude until he explained that he didn't deserve to be a partner as I was financing the project and he would rather work for me under contract. He also suggested that rather than building the first shelter, it would be more economical to find a suitable house for sale and make the necessary renovations. I realized then that he had no interest in my money and wondered if it was a result of male pride and whether that would affect our future together. There was no doubt in my mind that I wanted to cement our relationship. I had fallen in love with him and, although he was a man of few words, I knew he loved me too.

I decided the first thing I needed to do, was visit Rosemary's granddaughters. I wondered if they would remember me but I needn't have worried, they welcomed me with open arms. They were thrilled that I was going to follow in their footsteps and wanted to help me as much as they could, so I spent hours with them learning about running a shelter and all the red tape that goes with it. Two months later I felt ready to start looking for a house but first I had a wedding to go to. Billy and Amanda were finally getting married. Billy had announced it at Christmas and Aunt Jean, along with Amanda's mother had been preparing for the wedding ever since.

At the beginning of March, on a blustery day but with the sun shining brightly, I watched while Billy stood at the altar in Trinity Church and vowed to cherish Amanda for as long as they lived. The bride looked lovely in a flowing chiffon gown and I had never seen Billy look more handsome. I was so proud of him. Aunt Jean choked back tears throughout the ceremony and afterwards, during the reception at the English Manor in Ocean Township, she was glowing as she danced with Billy while Uncle Frank danced with Amanda. Jake fit right in with my folks and looked particularly handsome in a dark navy suit that complimented my own light blue outfit. Meanwhile, Miranda had a grand time sampling nearly everything on the buffet table which was laden with mountains of sesame chicken, scallops in bacon, Maryland crab cakes, barbeque pork and all manner of desserts. She was wearing a lovely apricot dress of the finest muslin but, by the time she was unable to take another bite, her dress was covered in stains. I should have been angry or a little annoyed but she seemed so happy that all I could do was smile.

A few days after the wedding, I contacted two real state agents, one in Belmar and one in Long Branch. I didn't want to open another shelter too close to Rose's Retreat, so I decided to go a little further afield but still stay near the Jersey shore. Within a day I was deluged with listings of various houses but one really caught my attention. It was a five thousand square foot Victorian with seven bedrooms and four baths on Cedar Avenue in Long Branch. I asked Aunt Jean if she would go and see it with me and we fell in love with it on sight. It had a separate suite with it's own kitchen and bathroom that would be perfect for a resident manager and was situated on a beautifully landscaped area, just steps from the beach. The agent was a little surprised when she closed the deal within an hour of our setting foot through the front door. I still needed to get a permit to operate any kind of business out of the house but as a non-profit organization, I already knew that approval was just a formality and we were on our way to open our first 'Ella's Haven'.

Just before we closed on the sale of the house, Jake took a tour with me and made several suggestions for improving the property. We had to take into consideration that not only women, but also their children might be living there for several months at a time and some of these children might even be infants. We wanted to make the rooms as comfortable as possible and we needed to make sure that the walls were soundproofed. There was a lot more work to be done than I had ever imagined and I was glad that I had Jake around to advise me.

Almost a year later, we opened our first safe house for abused women. It had been a busy time with so much to do. Not only did we have to deal with the renovations but also, there was a mountain of paper work and the hiring of staff. This meant interviewing individuals for counseling, and housekeepers and cooks. Sometimes, I got depressed and felt I had no idea what I was doing but Jake and Aunt Jean kept pushing me ahead. On opening day, the Asbury Park Press was there to help us celebrate. At the same time, Lester Graham was about to retire so we decided to turn it into a huge party and the house was crowded with family, friends and reporters including one from the local radio station in Belmar. I no longer worried that anyone would dredge up the fact that I was the widow of Jeremy Kent, the famous author or that my mother was serving time in prison. I realized that it would probably get us the publicity we needed to put Ella's Haven in the public eye, encouraging women out of harms way and into the safety of this amazing refuge that we had built.

The very next day, there was a two-page spread in the paper with a wonderful article written by Lester Graham himself. As expected, my life story took up a lot of space but it was tastefully done and reading it, for the first time, I felt proud. I still hadn't told Mama what I'd been planning and now that the house was in operation, I couldn't wait to see her. That afternoon, I drove to Clinton and after begging to be allowed to take the newspaper into the visitor's room, I spread it out on the table in front of her. She glanced at the headline, 'Ella's Haven Opens in Neptune' and then across at me frowning, "What's this all about, Cassie," she asked.

"Read all about it, Mama," I replied with a grin, "I think you'll be pleased."

I sat and watched her face as she read the whole article and stared at the photos but I couldn't tell what she was thinking. Finally she sat back and slowly shook her head, "I can't believe it. It's incredible, Cassie. I'm so proud of you and all that you've accomplished. I worried about you so much after Jeremy died and wondered what you would do with your life but I never dreamed you'd do something like this."

I reached across the table and grasped Mama's hand, not caring if I was violating the rules; "I did it for you, Mama. I did it because I wanted the world to know that I supported you all these years and all the women who fight back against abusive men. I'm going to build more shelters; I'm already looking at some property in Point Pleasant and Lexie's looking for property where she lives in Tom's River. It's exciting, Mama, and I want you to be a part of it."

"It sounds amazing, but how can I be a part of it? I have over two more years to serve and then I'm not sure what I'm going to do. I'll be fifty-nine years old, almost an old woman."

"That's not old any more, you're still young and attractive and two years isn't so far off. You'll come and live with Miranda and me and then you can help run the shelters. I can't think of a better person to champion the cause and put all of the Ella's Havens on the map."

"Oh, Cassie, what would I have done without you all these years. No matter what problems you've been going through yourself you've always been there for me. Isn't it time I was there for you? That's what I really want when I leave here, I want to help you with your precious daughter and make your life easier."

I shook my head knowing it was useless trying to tell Mama that she was the one who deserved looking after. Like I always said, she was the most selfless person I had ever known, "We'll help each other," I whispered.

# CHAPTER 67

At Christmas the following year, just before opening our second shelter, Jake and I got married in a civil ceremony. It was a simple affair, celebrated afterwards at the Watermark restaurant with only Jazz and Jules and my family in attendance. When Jake had proposed, I hadn't hesitated for a single moment, he had been my rock from almost the first moment that I met him and he adored Miranda. After Jake moved into our house she even started to call him Poppa. I was a little disturbed by this at first, but one day I noticed the two of them looking through an album of old photos. Miranda pointed to a picture of Jeremy walking on the beach, "That was my Daddy," she said, "I miss him." I knew then that she hadn't forgotten her father.

Miranda had never been told about Mama's situation. She knew she had another grandmother, besides Vivienne, but she thought she lived a long way away, much too far from Asbury Park to ever visit. Even when Mama and I spoke on the telephone, she couldn't hear what we were saying so it was easy to make up a story but Miranda was nine-years-old, the same age as I was when Mama was taken away from me, and I knew it was time to tell her the truth. She seemed intrigued and wanted to know every detail. Jake suggested that I just let her read all of the newspaper articles that I had stored away, including those that Aunt Jean had saved for me before I was old enough to take care of myself. She must have read those articles three or four times before she asked me when her grandmother would be coming home and I got teary eyed when I told her, "In eight more months, she'll be here with us, Miranda, and I know you are going to love her as much as I do."

On a brilliant sunny day in September 1998, Lexie and I stood hand in hand outside the prison waiting for Mama to come through the gates. We both expected to see a reporter or two lying in wait but I gather Mama's story was old news to the local media. A week before her release, I made sure that she had something decent to wear to come home in and suddenly there she was being led out by one of the guards. As he smiled at her and actually shook her hand, Lexie and I just stayed where we were, transfixed by the sight of our mother outside of the prison walls. She looked so waiflike in blue jeans and a cotton sweater with her hair in a ponytail but when she turned and saw us then broke into a smile, she was radiant. That's when we ran to her and held her in our arms, laughing and crying at the same time. I don't know how long we stayed like that but we just didn't want to let go. It was Mama who finally said, "Can we go now please, darlings? I never want to see this place again."

On the drive home Lexie and I couldn't stop chattering and Mama couldn't stop looking out of the window. I knew that she was going to have trouble adjusting to all the changes over the last twenty five years and I wanted to help her as much as possible. As we got closer to the house, she looked a little nervous and when we pulled up in the driveway, her mouth dropped open, "This is your house, Cassie?" she asked.

"Yes, Mama and it's your house too now," I answered as I jumped out and ran around to open her door.

She got out very slowly and then noticed the small figure standing on the front step, "Miranda?" she said in a gentle voice, at the same time holding out both arms.

Miranda didn't hesitate, she ran forward and threw herself at Mama and that's when Lexie and I both lost it. It was Jake that broke the spell when he appeared from around the side of the house and came towards us. Holding out his hand, he said, "You must be Ella, welcome home."

Mama gently released Miranda and gave Jake a hug then she turned to me and said, "What a beautiful family you have, Cassie."

After that Miranda wouldn't leave Mama's side and grasped her hand as we led her into the house and walked her through the ground floor rooms so that she could get her bearings. "Can we show Grandma the garden?" Miranda asked, "And Smudge, she has to see Smudge."

"Yes, after I take her upstairs to her own room, honey," I answered.

"Oh okay," Miranda said a little grudgingly as she let go of Mama's hand.

Lexie stayed downstairs with Jake and Miranda while I led Mama up to the second floor. I think they both sensed that I wanted to spend a few moments alone with her. She gasped as we entered her room with its avocado walls, matching carpet and cannonball bed covered in a plump cream comforter and matching lace trimmed pillows, "Oh it's gorgeous, honey. I'll never want to go to sleep."

I chuckled and slowly took her by the shoulders so that she was facing the wall opposite the bed. For a moment she was stunned and then she groped for my hand, "Is this Jeremy's last painting?" she asked.

I nodded, "I knew you would love it, Mama, that's why I put it here."

Mama started to cry but they were tears of joy, "You taught him the lullaby I used to sing to you and your sister. Somehow he must have remembered it and was sending you a message."

Then she drew me into her arms and whispered, "Follow the butterfly."